CANCELLED

TYRANT

KING OF THE
BOSPORUS

CHRISTIAN CAMERON

An Orion paperback

First published in Great Britain in 2011
by Orion Books
This paperback edition published in 2011
by Orion Books, an imprint of The Orion Publishing Group Ltd
Orion House, 5 Upper St Martin's Lane
London WC2H 9EA

An Hachette UK company

3 5 7 9 10 8 6 4 2

A CIP catalogue record for this book
is available from the British Library.

ISBN 978-1-4091-0275-5

Typeset by Deltatype Ltd, Birkenhead, Merseyside

Printed and bound by
CPI Group (UK) Ltd, Croydon, CRO 4YY

The Orion Publishing Group's policy is to use papers that
are natural, renewable and recyclable products and made
from wood grown in sustainable forests. The logging and
manufacturing processes are expected to conform to the
environmental regulations of the country of origin.

www.orionbooks.co.uk

Fire all around him, and then he was walking, hands guiding him, more pain as someone handled his arm and he screamed and fell and the pain almost – *almost* – knocked him out. Satyrus gasped, gulped air and voices told him to drink, and he drank a thin, milky liquid – bitter and somehow *bright*.

Then he was cold, and then hot, and then the colour of the fire exploded around him, so that colour defined everything – war and love and missing friends, Amastris's kisses, Philokles' love, all had a colour – and he was swept away on a surge of these subtle shades, lifted and carried, and the pain roared its lavender disappointment and went far away.

Christian Cameron is a writer and military historian. He is a veteran of the United States Navy where he served as both an aviator and an intelligence officer in the first Gulf War, Somalia, and elsewhere. He lives in Toronto with his wife and daughter, writing his next novel, while studying classics. To find out more, visit www.hippeis.com

By Christian Cameron

The Tyrant Series

Tyrant
Tyrant: Storm of Arrows
Tyrant: Funeral Games
Tyrant: King of the Bosporus
Tyrant: Destroyer of Cities
Tyrant: Force of Kings

The Killer of Men Series

Killer of Men
Marathon
Poseidon's Spear
The Great King

The Chivalry Series

The Ill-Made Knight
The Long Sword

Other Novels

Washington and Caesar
God of War

Ebook Exclusives

Tom Swan and the Head of St George Parts One–Six

For my daughter, Beatrice

GLOSSARY

Airyanãm (Avestan) Noble, heroic.

Aspis (Classical Greek) A large round shield, deeply dished, commonly carried by Greek (but not Macedonian) *hoplites*.

Baqca (Siberian) Shaman, mage, dream-shaper.

Chiton (Classical Greek) A garment like a tunic, made from a single piece of fabric folded in half and pinned down the side, then pinned again at the neck and shoulders and belted above the hips. A man's *chiton* might be worn long or short. Worn very short, or made of a small piece of cloth, it was sometimes called a 'chitoniskos'. Our guess is that most *chitons* were made from a piece of cloth roughly 60 x 90 inches, and then belted or roped to fit, long or short. Pins, pleating, and belting could be simple or elaborate. Most of these garments would, in Greece, have been made of wool. In the East, linen might have been preferred.

Chlamys (Classical Greek) A garment like a cloak, made from a single piece of fabric woven tightly and perhaps even boiled. The *chlamys* was usually pinned at the neck and worn as a cloak, but could also be thrown over the shoulder and pinned under the right or left arm and worn as a garment. Free men are sometimes shown naked with a *chlamys*, but rarely shown in a *chiton* without a *chlamys* – the *chlamys*, not the *chiton*, was the essential garment, or so it appears. Men and women both wear the *chlamys*, although differently. Again, a 60 x 90-inch piece of cloth seems to drape correctly and have the right lines and length.

Daimon (Classical Greek) Spirit.

Ephebe (Classical Greek) A new *hoplite*; a young man just training to join the forces of his city.

Epilektoi (Classical Greek) The chosen men of the city or of the *phalanx*; elite soldiers.

Eudaimia (Classical Greek) Well-being. Literally, 'well-spirited'. See *daimon*, above.

Gamelia (Classical Greek) A Greek holiday.

Gorytos (Classical Greek and possibly Scythian) The open-topped quiver carried by the Scythians, often highly decorated.

Himation (Classical Greek) A heavy garment consisting of a single piece of cloth at least 120 inches long by 60 inches wide, draped over the body and one shoulder, worn by both men and women.

Hipparch (Classical Greek) The commander of the cavalry.

Hippeis (Classical Greek) Militarily, the cavalry of a Greek army. Generally, the cavalry class, synonymous with 'knights'. Usually the richest men in a city.

Hoplite (Classical Greek) A Greek soldier, the heavy infantry who carry an *aspis* (the big round shield) and fight in the *phalanx*. They represent the middle class of free men in most cities, and while sometimes they seem like medieval knights in their outlook, they are also like town militia, and made up of craftsmen and small farmers. In the early Classical period, a man with as little as twelve acres under cultivation could be expected to own the *aspis* and serve as a *hoplite*.

Hoplomachos (Classical Greek) A man who taught fighting in armour.

Hyperetes (Classical Greek) The *Hipparch's* trumpeter, servant, or supporter. Perhaps a sort of NCO.

Kithara (Classical Greek) A musical instrument like a lyre.

Kline (Classical Greek) A couch or bed on which Hellenic men and women took meals and perhaps slept, as well.

Kopis (Classical Greek) A bent bladed knife or sword, rather like a modern Ghurka kukri. They appear commonly in Greek art, and even some small eating knives were apparently made to this pattern.

Machaira (Classical Greek) The heavy Greek cavalry sword, longer and stronger than the short infantry sword. Meant to give a longer reach on horseback, and not useful in the *phalanx*. The word could also be used for any knife.

Parasang (Classical Greek from Persian) About thirty *stades*. See below.

Phalanx (Classical Greek) The infantry formation used by Greek *hoplites* in warfare, eight to ten deep and as wide as circumstance allowed. Greek commanders experimented with deeper and shallower formations, but the *phalanx* was solid and very difficult to break, presenting the enemy with a veritable wall of spear points and shields, whether the Macedonian style with pikes or the Greek style with spears. Also, *phalanx* can refer to the body of fighting men. A Macedonian *phalanx* was deeper, with longer spears called *sarissas* that we assume to be like the pikes used in more recent times. Members of a *phalanx*, especially a Macedonian *phalanx*, are sometimes called *Phalangites*.

Phylarch (Classical Greek) The commander of one file of *hoplites*. Could be as many as sixteen men.

Porne (Classical Greek) A prostitute.

Pous (Classical Greek) About one foot.

Prodromoi (Classical Greek) Scouts; those who run before or run first.

Psiloi (Classical Greek) Light infantry skirmishers, usually men with bows and slings, or perhaps javelins, or even thrown rocks. In Greek city-state warfare, the *psiloi* were supplied by the poorest free men, those who could not afford the financial burden of *hoplite* armour and daily training in the gymnasium.

Sastar (Avestan) Tyrannical. A tyrant.

Stade (Classical Greek) About 1/8 of a mile. The distance run in a 'stadium'. One hundred and seventy-eight metres. Sometimes written as *Stadia* or *Stades* by me. Thirty *Stadia* make a *Parasang*.

Taxeis (Classical Greek) The sections of a Macedonian *phalanx*. Can refer to any group, but often used as a 'company' or a 'battalion'. My *taxeis* has between 500 and 2,000 men, depending on losses and detachments. Roughly synonymous with *phalanx* above, although a *phalanx* may be composed of a dozen *taxeis* in a great battle.

Xiphos (Classical Greek) A straight-bladed infantry sword, usually carried by *hoplites* or *psiloi*. Classical Greek art, especially red-figure ware, shows many *hoplites* wearing them, but only a handful have been recovered and there's much debate about the shape and use. They seem very like a Roman gladius.

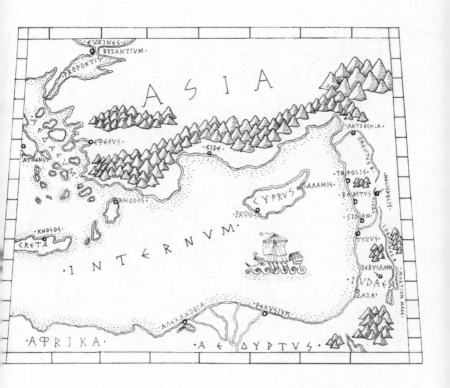

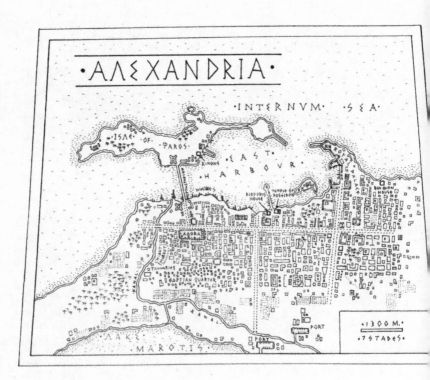

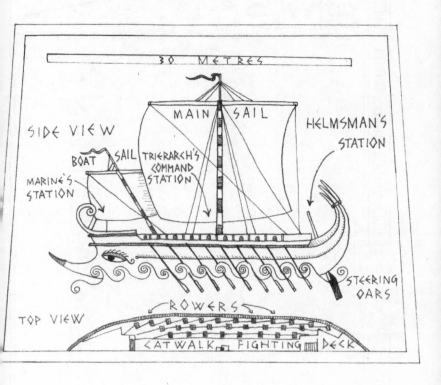

30 METRES

SIDE VIEW

MAIN SAIL

HELMSMAN'S STATION

BOAT SAIL TRIERARCH'S COMMAND STATION

MARINE'S STATION

STEERING OARS

TOP VIEW

ROWERS

CATWALK FIGHTING DECK

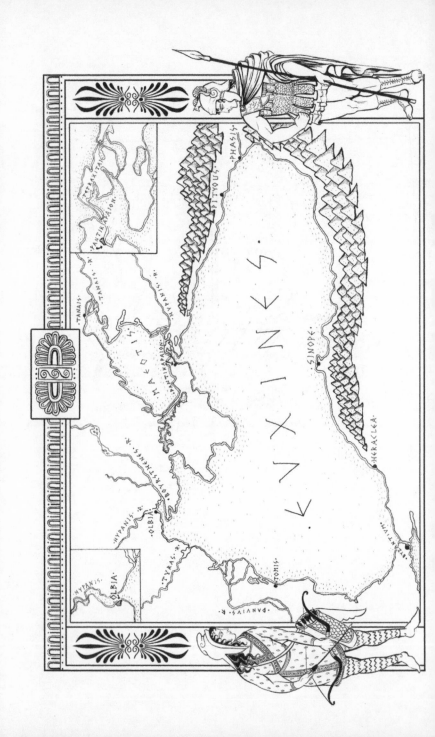

Eumeles sat at a plain table on a stool made of forged iron, his long back as straight as the legs on his stool and his stylus moving quickly over a clean tablet. He pursed his lips when he inscribed a sloppy sigma in the red wax, and he rubbed it out fastidiously and went back to writing his list of requirements.

Most of his requirements had to do with money.

'The farmers are not used to a direct tax,' Idomenes, his secretary, said.

Eumeles glared at him. 'They'd best get used to it. This fleet is costing me everything in the treasury.'

Idomenes was afraid of his master, but he set his hip as if he was wrestling. 'Many won't pay.'

'Put soldiers to collecting,' Eumeles said.

'Men will call you a tyrant.'

'Men already call me a tyrant. I *am* a tyrant. I need that money. See that it is collected. These small farmers need some of the independence crushed out of them. We would grow more grain if we pushed out the Maeotae and used big estates – like Aegypt.'

Idomenes shrugged. 'Traditionally, *my lord*, we have taxed the grain as it went on the ships.'

'I did that, as you well know. That money was spent immediately. I need more.' Eumeles looked up from his tablet. 'I've really had enough of this. Simply obey.'

Idomenes shrugged. 'As you wish, lord. But there will be trouble.' The secretary opened the bag at his hip and withdrew a pair of scrolls tied with cord and sealed with wax. 'The reports from Alexandria. Do you want them today?'

Eumeles pursed his lips again. 'Read them and give me a precis. Neither of our people there ever seems to report anything I can *use*. I sometimes wonder if Stratokles didn't recruit mere gossips.'

Idomenes cracked the wax, unwound the cord and rolled his eyes. 'Cheap papyrus!' he commented angrily, as the scroll fragmented under his fingers into long, narrow strips.

Eumeles grunted. He went back to his lists – headed by his need to hire competent helmsmen to man his new fleet. He needed a fleet to complete the conquest of the Euxine – a set of conquests that would soon leave the easy pickings behind and start on the naval powers, like Heraklea and Sinope, across the sea. And the west coast, which would bring him into conflict with Lysimachos. He feared the wily Macedonian, but Eumeles was himself part of a larger alliance, with Antigonus One-Eye and his son Demetrios. His new fleet had been built with subsidies from One-Eye. And the man expected results.

'Ooi!' Idomenes shouted, leaping to his feet. 'The woman actually has something of value. Goodness – the gods smile on us! Listen: "After the feast of Apollo, Leon the merchant summoned his captains and announced to them that he planned to use his fleet to topple Eumeles, with the approval of the lord of Aegypt. He further announced that he would finance a *taxeis* of Macedonians and a squadron of mercenary warships." Blah, blah – she names every man at the meeting. Goodness, my lord, she's quite the worthy agent. There's a note in the margin – "Diodorus ..." That name means something? "... has the Exiles ... with Seleucus"?'

Eumeles nodded. He found his fists were clenched. 'Diodorus is the most dangerous of the lot. Damn it! I thought Stratokles was going to rid me of these impudent brats and their wealthy supporters. It's like a plague of head lice defeating Achilles. Hardly worthy opponents. So – they're coming?'

Idomenes checked the scroll, running his fingers down the papyrus. 'Ares, Lord of War – they may already have sailed!'

'Why haven't we read this scroll before?' Eumeles asked.

'I see – no – they'll sail next week. He's buying a squadron of mercenary captains – Ptolemy's offcasts.' Idomenes smiled.

'Ptolemy will never win this war if he keeps shedding his soldiers as soon as he wins a victory,' Eumeles commented. 'He's the richest contender. Why doesn't he keep his fleet together?'

Idomenes considered telling his master the truth – that Ptolemy was rich because he *didn't* overspend on military waste. But he kept reading. 'This is their scout. They're coming before the autumn rains – to raise the coastal cities against you and sink your fleet. The army will come in the spring.'

Eumeles got to his feet and smiled. He was very tall and too thin, almost cadaverous, and his smile was cold. 'A scout? How nice. Kineas the *strategos* used to say that if you wanted something done well, you had to do it yourself. Send for Telemon.'

Telemon was one of the tyrant's senior captains. Idomenes passed the time reading aloud the list of ships from the marginal notes and their captains. 'Satyrus will command *Black Falcon*.'

'Some professional helmsman will command. He's just a boy. Well, may he enjoy the adventure, for he won't survive it,' Eumeles said. He called a slave and ordered that his armour be packed for sea.

Telemon swaggered in, announced by another slave. He was a tall man with ruddy cheeks and fair hair.

'You took your time,' Eumeles said.

Telemon shrugged. When he spoke, his voice was curiously high-pitched, like a temple singer – or a god in a machine. 'I'm here,' he said.

'Cancel the expedition to Heraklea,' Eumeles said. 'Get the fleet ready to sail south.'

'We're ready now,' Telemon intoned. His voice implied that his master wasn't very bright.

'Good.' Eumeles ignored other men's tones, or had never understood them. Idomenes wondered if his master's ignorance of other men's feelings towards him was the secret of his power. He didn't seem to care that he was ugly, ungainly, single-minded, unsocial and unloved. He cared only for the exercise of power. 'They'll come up the west coast. We'll await them west of Olbia, so that they don't raise the malcontents in that city.' The tyrant turned to Idomenes. 'Contact our people in Olbia and tell them that it is time to be rid of our opponents there.'

'The assembly?' Idomenes asked.

'Simple murder, I think. Get rid of that old lack-wit Lykeles. People associate him too much with Kineas. As if Kineas was such a great king. Pshaw. The fool. Anyway, rid us of Lykeles, Petrocolus and his son, Cliomenedes. Especially the son.'

Idomenes looked at his master as if he'd lost his mind. 'Our hand will show,' he said. 'That city is already close to open war with us.'

'That city can be treated as a conquered province,' Eumeles said. 'Kill the opposition. The assembly will fear us.'

'Kill them and some new leader might arise,' Idomenes said firmly. 'What if a knife miscarries? Then we have one of them screaming for your head.'

'When Satyrus's head leaves his body, all the fight will go out of the cities. And we own the Sakje – Olbia needs their grain. Stop fighting shadows and *obey me*.' Eumeles gave his cold smile. 'What you really mean is that I'm about to go beyond the law – even the law of tyrants. And you don't like it. Tough. You are welcome to board a ship and sail back to Halicarnassus whenever you wish.'

Once again, Idomenes was amazed at how his master cared nothing for the feelings of other men, and yet could read them like scrolls.

'And you got me out of my slave's open legs for a reason?' Telemon sang.

'Spare me,' Eumeles said. He didn't even like to listen to bawdy songs, his secretary reflected. 'Await my pleasure.'

Telemon turned on his heel.

'Isn't it enough for you that my enemy is about to put his head on the block?' Eumeles called, 'And that after he goes down, I will release you and your wolves to burn the seaboard?'

Telemon stopped. He turned back. 'Yes,' he said. 'Yes, that is news indeed, lord.' He grinned. 'What ship will your enemy be in?'

Idomenes was always happy to have information to share. '*Black Falcon*, Navarch,' he said.

'*Black Falcon*,' Telemon sang. 'Stratokles' ship. I'll know him,' he said.

PART I

THE SMELL OF DEATH

1

NORTH EUXINE SEA, AUTUMN, 311 BC

Satyrus leaned against the rail of the *Black Falcon* and watched his uncle, Leon the Numidian, arguing with his helmsman, just a boat's length away. Satyrus waited, looking for a signal, a wave, an invitation – anything to suggest that his uncle had a plan.

Next to him, on his own deck, Abraham Ben Zion shook his head. 'Where did a pissant tyrant like Eumeles get so many ships?'

Satyrus didn't turn his head. He was still waiting for the signal. 'I don't know,' he said. His dreams of being king of the Bosporus this autumn were fading rapidly, rowed into froth by the sixty or seventy triremes that Eumeles of Pantecapaeum, his mother's murderer, had somehow mustered.

Leon had stopped talking to his helmsman. He came to his rail and put his hands to his mouth. 'Lay alongside me!' he called.

Satyrus turned and nodded to his own helmsman, Diokles, a burly man whose curling dark hair showed more Phoenician than Greek. 'Alongside the *Lotus*,' Satyrus said.

Diokles nodded. 'Alongside it is, sir.'

Satyrus owned only one ship, and that by the laws of war. The year before, he had taken the *Black Falcon* in a sea fight off the coast of the Levant in a rising storm. *Falcon* was lighter and smaller and far less robust than Leon's *Golden Lotus* or the other four *triemioliai* of Leon's squadron – all his own ships, for Leon the Numidian was one of the richest men in Alexandria, one of the richest cities on the curve of the world.

Falcon was a small, old-style trireme, built light and fast the Athenian way. He had good points and bad points, but Satyrus loved him fiercely – all the more as he suspected he was about to lose the ship.

Falcon turned to port and 'folded his wings', all the oars coming inboard together to the call of Neiron, the oar master amidships, so that he slowed into a long curve. Diokles' broad face was a study in concentration, a hard frown creasing the corners of his mouth as he leaned on his oars.

Lotus closed on the reciprocal course. The two ships had been side by side, each leading a column of ten warships eastward along the north coast of the Euxine. They didn't have far to close, and the rowers on both ships pulled their oars in well before their blades might foul, and the helmsmen steered small, guiding the hulls together as they coasted along.

Leon stepped up on the rail, holding one of the white-linen shrouds that held the mast. He leaned out, and just before the sides of the ships touched, he leaped – easily crossing the distance between ships, his left foot on the *Falcon*'s rail, his right foot stepping down on to the deck of Satyrus's ship just forward of where the bulwark rose in the sharp curve of the stem.

'We'll have to fight through them,' Leon said, as soon as he was aboard. He nodded to the statue of Poseidon on the mast. 'No other choice, I'm afraid – unless you want to beach and burn the ships. And I don't think we'll survive that.'

'Twenty ships should have been enough,' Satyrus said.

'Somebody gave Eumeles plenty of warning,' Leon said. 'Listen up, lad. I'm going to put my ships in line and you'll form line behind me. My ships will bite into his line and you punch straight through. Don't stop to fight. Just keep going.'

Leon's plan was practical – if the goal was to save Satyrus's life. Eumeles would execute him without a thought – or worse.

'Don't be a fool, boy!' Leon said. 'If I fall, you avenge me another time.' His dark skin glowed with vitality, and it didn't seem possible that Leon could speak so blithely of his own death. 'If Eumeles captures me, he'll ransom me. I'm worth too much to kill. You – you'd be dead by nightfall. Don't be a fool. Do as I order.'

Abraham nodded soberly. 'He is correct, Satyrus. You can try again next year. Dead, we have all lost our wagers, eh?'

Satyrus bowed his head. 'Very well. We will form the second line and go straight through.'

Leon put his arms around his adoptive nephew, and they hugged, their armour grinding and preventing the embrace from carrying any real warmth. 'See you in Alexandria,' he said.

'In Olbia!' Satyrus said, his voice full of tears.

*

The Alexandrians formed their two lines as they advanced. They had practised formations all the way out from Rhodos, three weeks of sailing and rowing, and their rowers were in top shape. Leon's ships in the first line were as good as Rhodians – highly trained, with professional helmsmen and standing officers who had been at sea their whole lives – indeed, many of them *were* Rhodians, because Leon paid the best wages in the east.

Satyrus had the mercenaries. They weren't bad – again, they were professional seamen. Few of them had the quality of ships that Leon had, although Daedalus of Halicarnassus had a mighty *penteres*, a 'five-er' that stood a man's height further out of the water than a trireme and mounted a pair of heavy scorpions. The *Glory of Demeter* was in the centre of the second line.

None of Leon's captains needed special orders. They could all see the direction of the wind and the might of the opposing armament. The choices were narrow and they were professionals.

Satyrus was on the right of the line, and the next ship over was a former Alexandrian naval vessel, hastily built and hastily sold after last year's campaign, called *Fennel Stalk*, with his flamboyant friend Dionysius in command. 'Bit off more than we can chew, eh?' he called across the water.

'Break through, get your sail up and head for home,' Satyrus called back.

The enemy fleet was just a couple of stades ahead, the eyes painted above the beaks of their rams clear in the golden light. Despite everything, the fact that Leon's ships were coming straight at them seemed to have thrown them into confusion.

'Ten more ships,' Satyrus said.

Diokles nodded, but Abraham shook his head. 'What?'

'He means that they look so bad that if we had ten more ships we could take them – or make a fight of it.' Diokles spat over the side, apparently unconcerned by the odds.

Satyrus ran down the centre catwalk. 'Kalos! Deck master, there! Any man who has a helmet needs to get it on. Oar master, relieve the benches in shifts.' If they actually broke the enemy line, their whole length would be vulnerable to enemy archers. He went back and put a hand on the steering oars. 'That means you, Diokles. Armour up.'

'You have the helm,' Diokles said.

'I have the helm,' Satyrus replied, and the dark-haired man ran off down the deck.

The Alexandrians were closing under a steady stroke, saving energy. The enemy columns – all six of them – were still deploying. The two centre columns had fallen afoul of each other and were delaying the formation, but the consequence was that as the centre fell behind, the flanks reached well out on either side – the worst thing that could happen to the smaller fleet, whether by intention or by accident.

'Leon's signalling,' Abraham called. He had his helmet on, and his voice had a strange resonance.

Satyrus had his own helmet in his hand, but he swung up on a shroud to watch the bright bronze shield flash aboard *Golden Lotus*.

'Arrowhead,' he said. But the flashes went on, and on.

'By the hidden name!' Abraham muttered.

Diokles came back, buckling his scale breastplate. 'Of course, wearing this fucker, I drown if I go over the side.' He looked up. 'Poseidon's watery dick, that's a long signal.'

Satyrus saw that it was in repeat and jumped down from the rail. 'Arrowhead – we're to be the point of the second line. He's not going to engage the centre – he's going to go for the southern edge of the line. At least, I *think* that's what he means. Prepare to turn to starboard!' Satyrus called the last in a command voice.

Diokles got his last buckle done. He tugged the scale shirt down on his hips so that the *pteruges* sat right, and then put his hands on the steering oars. 'Got him!' he said.

Satyrus shook his head. 'After the turn,' he said. 'Find me my greaves, will you?'

Diokles ducked his head and started to root through the leather bags stuffed under the helmsman's bench.

Satyrus watched the shield. There. The command ship gave a single flash and all down the line, ships turned to starboard, so that the two lines of ten ships heading east were once again two columns of ten ships heading due south.

The shield flashed again, repeating the next order. In the column next to them, Theron's *Labours of Herakles* was slow to turn and almost fouled the *Glory of Demeter*. The two ships brushed past each other, oar-tips entangled, but momentum saved them and Theron's rowers had the stroke back.

Abraham shook his head. 'I can't watch!' he said. 'This is not like fighting elephants!' Abraham had proved his courage at Gaza the year before, capturing Demetrios the Golden's elephants and winning a place on the list of Alexandria's heroes.

The shield flashed on, now repeating the order. Then the flashes stopped.

'Any time,' Diokles said.

'Take the helm,' Satyrus said.

'I have it,' Diokles said, suiting action to word.

'You have it!' Satyrus said, and ran for the command spot amidships. 'Watch for the signal! Neiron, the next signal will require us to slow.'

'Aye aye!' Neiron, the oar master, was Cardian – a prisoner of war who'd chosen to remain with his captors. He seldom wore hat or helmet, and had the habit of rubbing the back of his head. He did so now.

The bronze shield gave a single flash.

'Got it!' Neiron called. 'All banks! Cease rowing!'

Behind them, *Fennel Stalk* made a quarter-turn out of line to the north and the ship behind *Fennel* made a quarter-turn south, so that in a few heartbeats they were ranging almost alongside, just a few oar-lengths behind. The next two ships came up on their flanks, so that Satyrus's second line was shaped like a wedge.

Whatever the odds, it was well carried out, and despite some spacing issues created by the size of the *Glory of Demeter*, they were formed in a wedge before the enemy could react. Ahead, Leon's better-trained column had angled in to cover them and then formed a wedge themselves, so that *Golden Lotus* was the centre of the first line and *Black Falcon* was the centre of the second wedge, all rowing east against the flank of the enemy line.

The enemy ships were caught broadside-on, strung out over a stade of quiet sea in the morning light. Moments before, they had been the horns of a giant envelopment, hunters of the doomed prey. Suddenly they were the target, and the opposite horn was

II

six stades away – hopelessly far to take part in the sort of *diekplous* head-to-head engagement that the Alexandrians were forcing.

Diokles grinned. 'That was something worth seeing,' he announced.

A stade to go, and the enemy ships were turning to face them. The enemy centre, now more than two stades off to the east, was still tangled.

Another signal from the *Lotus* and the first line picked up speed. *Fennel* took up the stroke in the second line, advancing at battle speed until his helmsman realized his error. The second line was there to take advantage of the chaos caused by the first. They continued to move at cruising speed, and *Fennel* coasted back to his spot.

'Don't board unless we're sinking,' Satyrus said to Abraham. 'Understand?'

Abraham gave his sarcastic smile. 'All too well, brother.'

They embraced briefly, and then Abraham buckled the cheek-pieces on his high-ridged Thracian helmet and ran down the catwalk to the marines that he commanded.

Satyrus had time to gulp a few lungfuls of air and to feel the flutter in his chest and the cringing in his bowels – the fear that never seemed to change for him when danger came. He spat over the side and prayed to Herakles, his ancestor and patron, for courage.

Half a stade ahead, *Golden Lotus* seemed to dance, a swift quarter-turn and then back to his course, his oars suddenly in. *Lotus* was the point of the wedge, the first ship to hit the enemy line, and he was ramming an enemy trireme head to head, the most dangerous manoeuvre in war at sea and the most likely to cripple the attacking ship.

There was a sound not unlike that of two phalanxes crashing into each other – or like a lightning storm ripping through the woods on the slopes of a mountain – and the engagement was over, the *Lotus* already getting his oars out and coasting free, the enemy ship half-turned to starboard and showing his flank to the *Falcon* because the *Lotus* had ripped his starboard oar gallery and mangled his oarsmen on that side.

'Ramming speed,' Satyrus said.

Diokles made a face in the stern. The oar master called the new speed and the ship leaped forward.

'What?' Satyrus asked.

'We're supposed to break free, not kill ships,' Diokles said.

'I'm not afraid to fight,' Satyrus said.

Diokles shrugged and said nothing.

'Ready for impact!' Abraham bellowed from the bow.

'Oars in!' Neiron called.

Satyrus braced himself against the stern and Diokles crossed his arms over the steering oars.

As they crashed together, the ram went in, and there was resistance – and then something gave. Men on the deck crew were thrown flat, despite their best efforts, and Satyrus only just kept his feet.

'Reverse oars! Cross your benches!' Neiron called.

Satyrus ran forward. The enemy ship, caught almost broadside-on, was turning turtle, his shallow side crushed amidships, so that he was filling with water. But the upper strakes of his well-built hull were caught on the *Falcon*'s ram.

'Back water!' Satyrus called. 'We're caught!'

The oarsmen had to get under their oars and sit on the opposite bench to put their full strength into backing water. It took precious time.

Falcon's bow began to sink. The strain on the bow timbers was immense, and there were popping noises all along the hull.

Neiron stood on his deck by the mast, watching the oarsmen and rubbing his head. 'Don't rush 'em, sir,' he said. 'We need three good pulls, not a new mess as they panic.' He flashed Satyrus a smile and then raised his voice. 'Ready there?'

A deep roar answered him.

'Backstroke! Give way, all!' he called, and the oars bit into the water. One stroke and there was a grinding from the bow – a second stroke and every man standing was thrown flat as the ram slipped out of the stricken enemy and the bow rose sharply. The rowers lost the stroke and oars clashed.

Satyrus fell heavily and Neiron fell on top of him, and it took them long heartbeats to get back to their feet. Neiron began to yell at the rowers, getting them on beat again.

Satyrus ran for the bow, looking everywhere. To the east, *Fennel* had swept down the side of a heavy trireme, destroying his starboard oars just as the ship in the first line had done to his port oar bank, so that the ship lay on the water like an insect with all its legs plucked.

To the west, a Cardian mercenary vessel had sailed right through the enemy's first line and continued into their half-formed second line, where he was preparing a *diekplous* oar-rake of his own.

Dead ahead, *Lotus* had rammed a second adversary and left him wallowing, oars crushed and the upper oar box literally bleeding red blood where the ram had crushed wood and bodies together.

Farther east and west, however, the enemy was rallying. They had so many ships that the local disaster didn't materially affect the odds. The enemy centre was still not organized, but a dozen ships, better rowed or more aggressive, were leaving the centre and racing to relieve the beleaguered flank.

Satyrus took this in and ran back amidships. 'Switch your oars,' he said to the oar master.

'Switch benches for normal rowing!' the oar master called.

Satyrus pointed at the second cripple left by the *Lotus*. 'I want to put that ship down – but don't hit it so hard!' Then he ran aft to Diokles. 'Straight into the blue trireme!' he called.

Diokles narrowed his eyes. 'Not what your uncle ordered,' he said.

'Just do it!' Satyrus said. An arrow hit him in the shoulder, skidded across the scales of his corslet's left shoulder, dug a furrow across the back of his neck and sank into the planking that was supposed to protect the helmsman. 'Ares!' he cursed. He put his hand to his neck and it came away covered in blood.

Satyrus turned to see where the arrow had come from. A dark-hulled trireme was coming up on his port side, from behind, and the enemy ship's archers were trying to clear his helm.

'Where in Hades did he come from?' Satyrus asked. 'Hard to port!'

Diokles swung the oars hard. Satyrus turned forward. 'Port-side oars, all banks, drag your oars!'

The oar master echoed his command and the *Falcon* turned

like his namesake, his stern pulled clear of the oncoming ram. The oar-raked carcass of *Glory of Demeter*'s first victim had hidden the enemy ship, and now he shot by *Falcon*'s stern at ramming speed, already turning to find new prey. Forward, Abraham's marines shot a shower of arrows into the enemy ship's command deck and then he was gone.

Falcon's evasive manoeuvre had carried him out of his place in the formation and now he was heading almost due north, into the oncoming rams of the enemy's relief column.

'*Glory of Demeter* is through the line,' Diokles said. 'Getting his sail up. Just where we ought to be, sir.'

Satyrus's neck hurt as if he'd been stepped on by a horse. He put a hand to it again and was shocked to see how much blood there was. 'Diokles, we need to go hard to starboard – see the dark green-hulled ship with the golden statue in the bow?'

'I see him,' Diokles answered.

'Right at him – at ramming speed. But just short of him, we turn – and pass under his stern. If he turns towards us—'

'I have it!' Diokles yelled, waving him away.

Satyrus ran for the oar master. 'Ramming speed. Turn to starboard – see the big green? Straight at him – ramming speed. And when I say, a little more. We'll pass under his stern and never touch him.'

Neiron had an arrow in his side. 'Fucking point is in my skin,' he said, face already grey-white with shock. The arrow had punched straight through his tawed-leather cuirass. 'Aye! Starboard bank – drag your oars! Port banks, full speed! Now!' His voice lost none of its power. Then he sank against the mast. 'Pull it out, sir?'

Satyrus glanced forward – the next few heartbeats would be vital.

'As soon as we're past the green,' he said.

'Aye,' Neiron said grimly. His feet slipped out from under him and he sat heavily, with his back against the mast. 'You'd better call the stroke,' he said.

Satyrus stepped over him. 'Pull!' he called. An arrow hit his helmet hard enough that he smelled copper and his ears rang. 'Pull!' he called again. The bow was almost on line – time to stop the turn. 'Cease rowing!' he called. 'All oars! Ramming speed! Now!'

He felt the surge of power under his feet. 'Pull!' he called.

He felt the change in weight as Diokles made a steering adjustment. The big green ship was turning to meet them. He towered over them – a quadrireme at least, perhaps the biggest ship in the enemy fleet.

'Pull!' Satyrus wanted to get past the green so his bulk would shield them from the rest of the enemy squadrons. He looked down at his oar master, who was losing consciousness, his face as pale and grey as the sea on a cloudy summer day. There was blood coming out from under his cuirass. Another arrow struck deep in the mast, its barbed head a finger deep in the oak.

'Pull!'

Sakje bows.

He glanced south as he took a breath to call the stroke and almost lost his timing. There was Theron's *Herakles* at ramming speed, bow-on to the same target – going ram to ram with a ship of twice his burthen. 'Pull!' he called.

Diokles saw Theron too. 'He'll foul us!' the Phoenician roared. 'Sheer off, Corinthian!'

'All you have, now!' Satyrus roared at the rowers. *Falcon* moved under his feet. 'Pull!' The great loom of the oars moved, the oars, the length of a Macedonian sarissa, all pulling together like the legs of a water-bug or the wings of a bird. 'Pull!'

Diokles made a sharp adjustment and Satyrus struggled to keep his feet. 'Pull!' he roared. *Herakles* was not turning – he was in his final attack run, moving as fast as a running horse.

'Pull!'

The green enemy turned to put his bow on to the *Herakles* – a terrible decision, possibly a misheard order, so that at the last the great ship showed his naked and vulnerable flank to the *Falcon's* ram.

'Pull!'

Herakles, faster because he'd had a longer start, rammed her just aft of the bow – a single thunderclap – and his bow was forced around.

'Pull!'

Diokles slapped his steering oars with precision, aiming for the gap at the edge of possibility where the stern of the enemy ship would *not* be in a few heartbeats.

'Pull!'

The green ship shuddered and his stern came *at them*, swinging sideways through the water with all the transmitted energy of *Herakles*' attack.

'Pull!' Satyrus roared.

'Brace!' Abraham yelled from over the ram – and they struck, the ram catching the enemy stern just below the helmsman with a hollow *boom*, and then Satyrus was on his face on the deck.

'Switch your benches!' Satyrus managed from his prone position. 'Do you hear me, there? Switch benches!' he called, trying to rise. There was a sailor on top of him, a deckhand – a dead deckhand. Satyrus got him off, rolled over – his neck awash in pain, his eyes hazed red. The big green ship was *above* them, and arrows were *pouring* into the waist of the *Falcon*. 'Switch your benches!' Satyrus called again. He felt as if he was very far away. Just below his feet, men were getting under their oars.

An arrow hit him in the top of the shoulder. It hurt, and its force knocked him back a step. 'Backstroke!' he shouted, his voice sounding thin and very far away. 'Now!'

The ship gave a shudder like a wounded animal.

'Ram's stuck!' Abraham called. ''Ware boarding!'

Sure enough, there were men coming down the side of the green – leaping aboard *Falcon*. Satyrus was three steps from his *aspis*, the huge round shield of the Greek soldiers and marines. It stood in the rack at the edge of the command platform.

Satyrus had an odd moment of hesitation – he almost didn't move. It seemed *too far*. He just wanted to fall on the deck and bleed.

A javelin, slightly miscast, struck him shaft first and skittered off along the deck.

There was a pair of enemy marines on the command platform. He noticed this with professional interest. *How had they come there?*

He turned his back on them and grabbed for his aspis. It came to him in stages that were prolonged by the nakedness of his

17

posture to their weapons – his hand on the bronze-shod edge, his right hand lifting it clear of the rack, his left arm pushing into the *porpax*, his shoulder taking the curved weight as he turned—

Thrunk – as the lead marine crashed shield to shield and the harmonic bronze sounded.

Satyrus set his feet and reached out with his empty right hand to grab the rim of his opponent's shield. One-handed, he ripped the shield round a half-circle to the right, breaking the man's shield arm, and then he slammed the enemy's shield rim into his nose. The man went down and Satyrus leaped at his partner, drawing his father's heavy *kopis* from under his own shield arm even as he put his head down and rushed his new opponent. Movement from the stern. Satyrus struck his enemy shield to shield and cut hard around the lower edge of the aspis. His blade went deep into the man's thigh and he was over the side. Satyrus whirled, but the man coming from the stern was an armed deck-crewman with a spear – one of his own.

'Pull!' he called. The oars bit the water – the stroke was lost and had to be restored.

As the oars came up, he saw more men coming from the bow. Was Abraham dead? 'Pull!' he called as the top of the stroke was reached. 'Neiron! I need you to call the stroke. Pull!'

Neiron was sitting against the mast, his eyes unfocused.

There were three more enemy marines, and they were cautious. On the leader's command, they all threw their javelins together, and Satyrus took them on his shield and charged, shouting 'Pull!' as his war cry. He got his shield into the middle one, took a light cut on his greaves from the one to his front right and punched the hilt of the Aegyptian sword into the man's face over his shield rim – all feint for the backhand cut that Greeks called the 'Harmodius blow'. Satyrus stepped forward with his sword foot, changing his weight with the feint and pushing his shield into the other two, and then cut *back* at the man who had wounded him, the weight of his blow sheering through the man's helmet.

Satyrus ripped the Aegyptian weapon free of the man's head and the blade snapped – and Satyrus fell back a step. *My father's sword!* he thought.

The deck-crewman behind him saved his life, plunging his

spear past Satyrus's shoulder into the centre man's face. The blow skidded off the man's chin and through his cheek and he went down, fouling his file-partner, whose feet had been grabbed by an alert oarsman on the oar deck below. He fell into the rowers and died at their hands.

'Pull!' Neiron called.

With a shriek like a wounded woman, *Falcon* pulled free of the green vessel, trapping the enemy marines on his decks. Many elected to jump – men in light armour could swim long enough to be rescued – but the officers in heavy bronze were trapped. Satyrus watched sailors pull one down and throw him to his death in the water. Abraham accepted the surrender of another – Abraham was the only man Satyrus had ever seen accept surrender in a sea fight.

'Oh, Ares!' Satyrus said. He could just walk.

'Pull!' Neiron called, and the *Falcon* was a ship's length clear of their enemy.

'Switch your benches!' Satyrus called. He looked aft. Diokles had an arrow through his thigh and was using the oars to keep himself erect.

Their ram had, in fact, ripped the stern right off the green ship, and he was settling fast, his rowers in chaos. But the enemy was trying to take Theron's ship over the bow as a stolen life-raft. Satyrus could see Theron with his marines fighting in the bow. He was the biggest man in the fight.

North and west, the whole enemy fleet was bearing down on their fight. The rest of their squadrons were gone. Just a stade away, a pair of golden-yellow triremes had bow waves – full ramming speed.

'Diokles!' Satyrus yelled, pointing at the new enemy.

Diokles was already leaning on his oars, using the momentum of the backed oars to turn the bow south.

Satyrus saw it as if a god had stepped up next to him and put the whole idea in his mind – he saw the fight and what he had to do.

As the bow swung south, he saw more and more enemy sailors and marines flooding aboard *Herakles*.

'Lay me alongside *Herakles*,' Satyrus said.

Diokles bit his lip and said nothing.

Satyrus accepted his unspoken criticism and ran forward, collecting deck-crewmen with weapons as he went.

'Abraham!' he called.

Neiron called the first stroke of the new motion. His voice was weak, but he had to hold on. Satyrus was running out of options, and he was *not* going to abandon Theron.

Abraham was kneeling by a dying marine. The man was bleeding out and Abraham was holding his hand.

Satyrus waited until the man's eyes fluttered closed. Then he seized the dead man's javelin and his sword. 'We're going aboard *Herakles*,' he said.

Abraham shook his head. 'You're insane,' he said quietly.

'I'm not letting Theron die when I can save him,' Satyrus bit back.

'What about the rest of us?' Abraham asked. '*Punch straight through!* Isn't that what we're supposed to do?'

Satyrus shook his head to clear it. It seemed so obvious to him. 'We put the green ship between us and those two,' he said, pointing at the nearest new enemies, now just half a stade away. 'We rescue Theron and we're gone.'

Abraham shrugged. He had blood leaking out of an eye – or perhaps just out of his helmet. 'Whatever you say, *prince*.'

The rest of the marines looked tired but hardly done in. Most of them had fought at Gaza.

'On to the deck of the *Herakles*,' Satyrus said. 'Clear it and we're gone. A gold rose of Rhodos to every man who follows me on to that deck.'

Even as Satyrus spoke, Diokles had the speed to turn them back east, so that the oarsmen pulled in their oars and *Falcon* coasted alongside his stricken brother.

Satyrus leaped on to the rail. 'Clear the deck,' he called, his voice breaking, but then he was over the rail of the *Herakles* and his javelin took an enemy marine in the side of the head, knocking him unconscious inside his helmet. Satyrus went straight into the next man, shield up, so that the rim of his own aspis crashed into the man's armoured jaw and he smelled the sweat on his enemy as the man tried to turn and got a spear in his teeth from a sailor. Satyrus bore him down and pushed on into the flank of the enemy boarding force, into the unarmoured sailors who didn't have shields and died like sacrificial animals under his borrowed blade. And when they broke, he kept killing them, cutting them down as they fled into the bow, killing them even as they jumped over the side, as if by killing these men who served his enemy he could regain his lost kingdom.

Theron was by the mast, his back against it. He was covered in blood and wounded several times – his left thigh was lacerated with shallow wounds so that blood ran down his legs like lava from a new volcano. He held up a hand, the same way he would when he'd been fighting the *pankration* on the sands of the palaestra in Alexandria and he took a fall. He managed a smile. 'Still in the fight, eh?' he said.

Satyrus took his hand and hauled him to his feet. He looked fore and aft along the deck. The marines from the heavy green quadrireme were rallying in the bows of their own ship, and a shower of arrows swept the decks of *Herakles*.

'We could board him,' Satyrus said.

'If you want to die gloriously, that would be your path,' Abraham said by his elbow. He was wrapping his shield arm in linen stripped from a corpse. 'Look!'

The two golden-hulled triremes from Pantecapaeum were almost aboard them, rowing hard – but their speed had fallen off, because they'd started their sprint too early and their crews were under-trained. In the press of ships, they couldn't see what was friend and what was foe. Behind them were a dozen more triremes.

'We could take him,' Satyrus said.

'You are possessed by a bad spirit,' Abraham said. 'Do not succumb to these blandishments.' He leaned in. 'You must live, or all this is for nothing. *Get your head out of your arse and think like a commander.*'

Satyrus felt the heat in his own face – felt rage boiling up in his limbs. But he also saw the faces of the men around him. He saw Theron's nod of agreement. The marines' studied blankness.

'Very well,' he said, more harshly than he wanted. He looked across to the *Falcon*. 'Abraham, keep us from getting boarded again. When I have *Herakles* clear of that green bastard, take command and row clear. Understand? Theron – someone get Theron looked after. No, better – sling him across to *Falcon*.'

His head was clear – tired, but clear. It was like waking from a fever. Now he could *see*, and what he saw was the last few moments of a disaster. As soon as the pair of golden triremes figured out which side was which, he'd be dead.

He leaped for his own ship and landed with a clash of bronze on the deck. 'Diokles!' he roared.

'Aye!' his helmsman called. The arrow was gone from his thigh and a loop of wool was tied in its place.

'Port-side oars! Pole off! Pole off the *Herakles*!' Satyrus ran to Neiron, who was lying at the foot of his mast, mouthing orders to Thron, one of the Aegyptian boys who served the sailors. The boy shrilled the orders down into the rowing decks.

'Still with me?' Satyrus asked Neiron, who raised an eyebrow.

'Must be nice ... young.' He croaked. 'Poseidon, I hurt. Hermes who watches the sailormen, watch over me. Arggh!' he shouted, and his back arched.

Along the deck, a handful of deck-crewmen pulled Theron aboard and dropped him unceremoniously to the deck so that they could return to using pikes to pole off the *Herakles*. Satyrus loosed the ties on Neiron's cuirass and then, without warning, pulled the arrowhead from the wound. It had gone in only the depth of a finger end, or even less – enough to bleed like a spring, but not necessarily mortal.

Satyrus stood in his place. 'Port side, push!' he shouted. Rowers used the blades of their oars to push against the hull of the *Herakles*. 'Push!'

'We're away!' Diokles called from the stern. The gap between the two ships was growing. *Falcon* was light – fifty strong men could pole him off very quickly.

Quick glance aft – the golden hulls were changing direction, the early sun catching the bronze of their rams and turning them to fire. He wasn't going to make it.

He wasn't going to stop trying, either.

'Switch your benches!' he roared, the full stretch of his voice, as if a restraint had burst in his chest and now he could use all of his lungs.

A thin cheer from the green quadrireme. The enemy crews were shouting for rescue – shouting to the golden ships.

His archer-captain shot into the enemy, and an enemy archer fell – a man in robes. A Sakje. Satyrus cursed that Eumeles had suborned *his own people*. There were many things that he and Leon had taken for granted.

The greens cheered again and the golden triremes turned harder, now certain of their prey.

'Oars out! Backstroke! Give way, all!' Satyrus called as soon as the majority of his rowers had switched their benches. He considered everything he had learned of war – that men responded so much better when they understood what was needed. His teachers had insisted on it.

He leaned down into the oar deck. 'Listen, friends. Three strokes back and switch your benches – two strokes forward – switch again. Got it? It will come fast and furious after that. Ready?'

Hardly a cheer – but a growl of response.

'Pull!' he called.

'Athena and strong arms!' a veteran cried.

'Athena and strong arms!' the whole oar deck shouted, all together, and the ship shot back his own length.

'Athena and strong arms!' they repeated, and again *Falcon* moved, gliding free.

'Switch your benches!' Satyrus called, but many men were already moving with the top of the stroke, switching benches with a fluidity he hadn't seen before.

He ran along the deck to Diokles. He wanted to stop and pant. *No time.*

The nearest golden hull was just three ship's lengths away.

'Into the starboard bow of the green!' Satyrus shouted. 'We have to ram the green clear of *Herakles*.'

Diokles turned and looked at the onrushing golden ship in the lead.

'Yes!' Satyrus shouted. He read Diokles' thoughts just as the helmsman read his. With luck – Tyche – the lead golden hull would foul his partner.

There were a dozen more triremes behind that pair, strung out over two stades of water.

The rowers had switched benches. 'Pull!' he bellowed into the oar deck.

The hull changed direction. The oars came up together, rolled over the top of their path.

'Pull!' he roared. The hull groaned and *Falcon* leaped forward – already turning under steering oars alone.

'Pull!' he called as the oars crested their movement. He waited for the splintering crash as the lead golden ship rammed their stern, but he didn't look. His eyes were fixed on his oarsmen.

'Pull!'

'BRACE!' yelled a sailor in the bow.

Falcon hit the enemy quadrireme just where his marine box towered over his ram – just where men were rallying for another rush at the *Herakles*. It was a glancing blow, delivered from too close, but the results were spectacular. Something in the enemy bow gave with a sharp crack – some timber strained to breaking by the *Herakles* snapped. The marines' tower tilted sharply and the whole green hull began to roll over, filling rapidly with water.

'Switch your benches!' Satyrus called. Now was the moment. But the *Herakles* was saved – he was rocking in the water like a fishing boat after pulling a shark aboard, his trapped ram released from the stricken green.

The lead golden trireme shaved past their stern, having missed his ram by the length of a rowing boat. He was still turning and his oarsmen paid for his careless steering as they began to get tangled in the wreckage of the green as the stricken ship turtled.

Just to the port side, beyond *Herakles*, the second golden hull swooped in to beak the *Herakles* amidships – the second ship had been more careful, biding his time, waiting for the two damaged Alexandrian ships to commit to a reverse course.

The oarsmen were reversed, their faces to the bow. 'Back water! Pull!' Satyrus called. Had to try.

Had to try.

Diokles shook his head and braced himself against the side. When the golden ship struck the *Herakles*, his hull might be pushed right into them.

Abraham was shouting at his rowers, trying to get them to pull together. They had been locked in a boarding action for too long and many men had left their benches to fight. *Herakles* was dead in the water.

Why was *Herakles* cheering? Satyrus stood on his toes, then jumped up on the rail, grabbing for a stay.

Leon's *Golden Lotus* swept past the sinking stern of the green like an avenging sea monster and took the second golden hull right in the stern quarter, his bow ripping the enemy ship like a shark ripping a dolphin, spilling men into the water and goring his side so that he sank still rowing forward, gone in ten heartbeats, and *Lotus* swept on.

Herakles got his rowers together. With time to breathe, Abraham rowed clear of the sinking green and turned for the open water to the east. He had only two-thirds of his oars in action, but they were together.

Falcon handled badly – light as a feather, down by the stern, tending to fall off every heading. The rowers were pulling well, and he handled like a pig.

Satyrus was staring over the stern, where *Lotus* had rammed a second ship.

His ram was stuck.

Even as he watched, an enemy ship got his ram into *Lotus*, and the great ship shuddered the way a lion does when he takes the first spear in a hunt.

Satyrus ran to the stern, as if he could run over the rail and the intervening sea to his uncle's rescue.

'Nothing we can do,' Diokles said.

'Ares – Poseidon. We can do this. With *Herakles*, we'll—'

Diokles shook his head. 'Can't you feel it, lad? Our ram's gone. Ripped clean off when we hit the green.'

Satyrus felt as if he'd been punched in the gut. Leon was *so close*.

'He did it for you,' Diokles said. 'Let's save the ships we have and run.'

'Herakles, Lord of Heroes,' Satyrus choked on his own prayer. *Run, boy.*

A second ram went into *Lotus*. And while he contemplated suicide in the form of rushing his ship to Leon's rescue, the gap widened to two stades, then three. Then five. Now there were a dozen enemy ships around *Lotus*.

'Run,' he said, hanging his head.

'Aye,' Diokles said. 'Now get yourself into the bow and set the men to plugging the gaps in the strakes, or we're all dead men.'

2

ALEXANDRIA, AEGYPT, 311 BC

O f all the places in the world for a woman to give birth, there weren't many that could better Alexandria.

Melitta lay on the special *kline* that the doctors had brought her and chewed idly on the leather strap she had for labour pains. She was covered in sweat, and her bloated body was fighting with all of its not-inconsiderable strength to push the baby out, and she still had the capacity to think about her brother, out on the wine-dark sea, conquering their kingdom while she lay on a bed conquering her pregnancy. That's how she had come to think of it – a conquest. Nothing in her life – not war, not abduction, not the threat of assassination – had prepared her for the discomfort, the enforced idleness and the *boredom* of pregnancy.

'Here they come again,' she muttered. Her room was full of doctors and midwives – too many people, she thought. Sappho had ignored Nihmu's advice – that Nihmu and Sappho should deliver the baby themselves.

Wave of pain. She bit down on the leather strap, convulsed with the thing – palpable, like lying in water, except that this was inside and outside her.

'Not long now,' the man nearest the bed said. Nearchus – Leon's personal physician.

Nihmu had one of her hands. 'Breathe!' she said in her Sakje-accented Greek. 'He is right,' she said with a smile that Melitta could just see through the tangle of her hair. 'You are almost done.'

'Very lucky, for such a young girl,' another voice said.

Wave.

As she surfaced from the latest wave, she realized that they were right, and everything that the priestesses of Hathor and the priestesses of Hera said was true – the waves came closer and faster and lasted longer. She could no longer hold an image of her brother's expedition in her head. There was no reality beyond the—

Wave.

27

This time, she became aware that something around her was wrong. Nihmu's hand was gone and there were men shouting – and blood – blood like red water flowing over her. She reached out – shouted. She could feel the next wave building already, could feel her whole groin convulsing, could feel that lovely alien presence coming – it was happening *now*.

If that's my blood, I'm in trouble! she thought. Something or someone landed right on her legs, and she gave a choked scream and the next wave came—

She fought to escape it, to *see* ... brushed the sweaty hair out of her eyes and screamed. Shouting ... the ring of bronze and iron ... the scent of blood. She tried to focus ... something ... fighting?

'Get him!' roared a voice by the door, and then another ... clang of bronze ... 'Guards!' ... 'See to my lady!'—

Wave!

'Still there, love?' Nihmu said by her ear. People were pressed against her so tightly she couldn't breathe, and there was weight on her legs that she didn't like, and shouting – men's voices.

'Breathe, honey bee.' Nihmu was there. 'Get her off her legs,' she said.

The weight came off her legs even as she felt herself opening, opening—

Wave! This one didn't stop. She rode it like a ship on the sea, and suddenly—

'I see the head!' Nihmu shouted. 'Clear the room!'

'Yes, lady!' Hama answered. Even in waves of pain and the confusion of whatever had just happened, Melitta knew Hama's Celtic Greek. What on earth was he doing in her *birth room*?

'Push!' Nihmu and Nearchus spoke together, sounding eerily like a god.

She didn't really need to push any more than she already was. Her hips rose a fraction and suddenly it all came together. She tasted blood in her mouth and the muscles in her stomach and pelvis found a different purchase, almost like the first time she had mounted a horse under her own power – the triumph of the heartbeat in which all her weight shifted and she *knew* she would make it up Bion's back – a flood of release, a wet triumph.

And a cry. 'Now see to Sappho!' Nihmu said.

'A boy!' Sappho said, and her voice sounded weak.

Melitta seemed to surface, as if she'd been swimming in murky water. The room looked as if someone had tossed buckets of blood at it – the smooth plastered walls were strangely splashed, and the floor was wet.

'Hathor!' Melitta said. She saw her son – the blood – her son. 'Artemis!' she said. 'Ah, my beauty,' she said and reached her arms for him.

There was blood everywhere. Sappho was lying on the floor, her head on Nearchus's lap. Nihmu stood between her legs with the baby in her arms. Even as Melitta watched, Nihmu caught the cord in her teeth and cut it with a silver knife – a Sakje tradition. The baby wailed.

The child's grandfather – Coenus, a Megaran gentleman and now a mercenary, whose son, the newborn's father, was eight months in his grave – appeared at Nihmu's shoulder. He had a sword in his hand that dripped blood on his hand.

'Gods!' he said, his eyes wide. 'He's splendid! Well done, little mother!' And to Nihmu, 'I have two files of men hunting him – them. What in Hades happened?'

Melitta sank back on the kline. 'May I hold my son?' she asked.

Nihmu placed the baby on her breast but her eyes were still on Coenus, because he looked grey. 'What happened?' he asked again. He was looking at the floor.

'One of the doctors tried to kill Melitta,' Nihmu said. 'Sappho stopped him.'

'That's insane!' Coenus said. 'The blood!'

'Mine,' Sappho murmured. 'And his!' She pointed at the Jewish physician who their friend Ben Zion had provided. He was lying on top of his own guts, already dead. 'He tackled the man – gods, he died for us, and he didn't even know us!' Sappho was bleeding slowly from her upper thigh – a wound that Nearchus held together with one hand while he scrambled to make a tourniquet with the other.

'Help me!' he shot at Coenus.

Coenus knelt by Sappho and vanished from Melitta's view.

'Put your hand here and grab – *harder!* Don't be afraid of

a woman's thigh – she's going to *die* if I don't get this closed.' Nearchus was suddenly a battlefield commander, his voice hard.

'The curtain ties,' Nihmu said. 'Or her girdle.'

Nearchus had the ties off the seaward window in three heartbeats, and in two more he had the rope around her thigh.

'Hold that there. No, like this. Now I have to find it and sew it. Hippocrates, stand with me. Hermes, by my shoulder.' Murmuring prayers, Nearchus snatched a set of tools from his bag between Melitta's feet.

Melitta couldn't watch – she had her infant on her breast and she couldn't muster the strength to rise.

Nihmu crouched by her head and took her hand. 'Let me see him, honey bee. See? Perfect. Not a flaw. Take my hand. He's just stitching her thigh – oh, Lord of Horses, that's a big cut. I'm sorry, honey bee, I'm ... she's—'

Melitta raised her head to see Sappho's foot stomp the floor weakly.

'Hold on, lady! I've got the vessel!' Nearchus sounded triumphant. 'Hippocrates, this stuff is hard to sew.'

'Do it, man!' Coenus grunted.

'One more turn! One more. Got it – let off that rope – slowly – one turn. Another turn. Aphrodite stand by this woman. Artemis, stand away – you need not take my mistress yet. ...' Nearchus's voice trailed on – endearments, comments.

'Now what?' Coenus asked.

'Now we wait,' Nearchus muttered.

A day later, and Sappho was alive. Melitta was alive – in fact, she felt better already. She sat up, nursed her son and watched slaves and house servants clean the birth room with religious intensity. The servant women came and looked at her baby and complimented her, cooing at it and suggesting names.

Melitta had expected to be bitter – she was missing the great adventure, the reconquest of the Tanais. Even now, her brother was probably master of Pantecapaeum.

She found that she was perfectly happy to be a mother with a healthy baby, and two days later, when Sappho, pale as death from blood loss, allowed her eyes to flutter open and was pronounced likely to live, Melitta was happier still.

It took her several days – feeding her son all the time, watching the slave girls change him and being visited at regular intervals by an absurdly uncomfortable Coenus – before she got the whole story: the mad doctor who drew a knife and was stopped only by Sappho's reckless courage in putting her hand under the knife and then her body across Melitta's; the Jewish doctor who tackled the assassin, dying for his efforts but getting the man clear.

'Sophokles,' she said, shaking her head.

Coenus, sitting stiffly at the foot of her bed, nodded. 'So I assume. Which means he's still in Alexandria.'

'And we let him in!' Melitta said. 'As a doctor?'

Coenus shook his head. 'None of the other doctors knew him. He might have come in with slaves, with servants – we weren't taking any precautions.'

'Well,' Melitta said, with all of her returning strength. 'Well, it'll be all right. You'll see.'

Coenus shifted uncomfortably. 'Have you thought of a name, my dear?'

Melitta shrugged. 'No,' she said. 'Among the Sakje, we name a child on the thirtieth day after its birth. When we know it will live.'

Coenus nodded. 'This boy – he'll be my heir. He means a great deal to me, Melitta. When Xeno died—' Coenus didn't choke a tear, he was too strong and too much the aristocrat for that, but his pause was eloquent. 'This child – I mean to stand by him. Despite the fact that you were not formally wed, I – I hope that—'

'Foolish uncle!' Melitta shook her head. 'You will be his father in many ways, Uncle Coenus. And of course I see your interest. Men! Heirs! A daughter would be your heir with twice the surety!' She gave him an impish grin and he returned a frown.

'A daughter would not have carried my name,' he said.

Melitta laughed. 'Oh, Uncle Coenus, Greeks are all fools. What would you like me to call this lovely boy?'

Coenus leaned close, inhaling the fragrance of his grandson. 'Kineas,' he said.

*

The summer sailing season drew on, the wind from the north freshening every room in Leon's great oceanside house. In the courtyard, figs began to ripen. The yearly convoy from Massalia in far-off Gaul came in on time and heavily laden, and Leon's fortunes soared.

Sappho healed slowly, rebuilding her blood with sweets and the small beer that the Aegyptians drank. She sat on a kline in the private courtyard – a colonnaded space between Leon's house and Diodorus's, where the women gathered unless it rained. Slaves brought wine and dates and other sweets while she held court, dispensing wisdom and even justice to her household.

Nihmu, a Sakje woman from the sea of grass, had four quivers of arrows and she stood at one end of the courtyard shooting bronze-barbed shafts into a target hidden in the shadow of the colonnade. Unlike Sappho, who ran her husband's affairs, Nihmu had virtually no interest in the trade that drove her husband. But she never spoke of what she missed.

Melitta sat in the grass, envying Nihmu her archery and yet fully engaged in talking nonsense to her son as she walked him around the grass, hands under his tiny armpits so that his feet just barely brushed the ground.

'Who's going to be a great athlete, eh? With long, long legs?' she asked as he managed a grab at her breasts. 'And grabby, grabby arms?'

He spat a little, and reached out for her. He was just a few days short of two months old, and she named him Kineas – in the Temple of Hathor and in the Temple of Poseidon. And now she spent her days playing with him in the garden.

'You could let Kallista play with him,' Sappho said, raising her eyes from a scroll. 'He's not a toy, or a chore. Shoot your bow!'

Melitta sighed. Motherhood – fatherless motherhood – had not changed her status in the household. She was the veteran of battle, a grown woman, a mother – and Sappho still spoke to her as if she needed a lesson in every aspect of life.

'Kallista is not his mother,' Melitta said.

Sappho shrugged, her eyes never leaving her scroll. 'She'll be a mother in a matter of days,' she said. 'But – as you wish, dear.'

'What are you reading, Auntie?' Melitta asked.

'Aristotle. This is Philokles' copy – I'm going to see that it goes to the library. I'm cataloguing all his scrolls. He had hundreds.' Sappho looked up.

'What's it about?' Melitta asked.

'Well,' Sappho said. She sat back on her couch. 'It says that it is a study of nature, but so far, it seems more like a survey of other men's ideas.'

'Philokles didn't think much of Aristotle,' Melitta said.

Sappho raised a beautifully manicured eyebrow. 'You have read Aristotle?'

Melitta shrugged. 'Some. His work on gods – on religion. Philokles copied it all out for me to read.'

Sappho leaned forward as if noticing her niece for the first time. 'Really?' she asked.

Melitta was stung by her surprise. 'I studied every day with Philokles from the time I was six!' she said. 'I've read Aristotle, Plato, all the speeches of Isocrates, all the sayings of Heraklitus, all the books of Pythagoras. All! Even that useless twit Pericles.'

Sappho smiled. 'I know, dear.'

'You act as if I'm too stupid for conversation!' Melitta said.

'You act as if you never plan to read a scroll again,' Sappho said.

'I have a baby!' Melitta shot back.

'Often the result of ill-considered sex.' Sappho smiled. 'Needn't determine the rest of your life.'

'Ill-considered?' Melitta stood up, gathering Kineas in her arms. She took a breath for a tirade.

'The *hetaira* Phiale,' announced Kallias, the steward. He bowed, and Phiale – not, strictly speaking, a beauty, and yet the most attractive woman in Alexandria – entered, flinging off a dust-coloured shawl into the arms of her attendant slave, a hard-faced woman named Alcaea.

'Oh, despoina!' Phiale said. She came and knelt by Sappho.

Sappho's face closed up. Her eyebrows seemed to harden in place, and her mouth became a hard line. 'Oh, Phiale! Is it so bad? Or are you just being dramatic?'

Phiale shook her head. The tears in her eyes suggested that her abject posture was unfeigned. 'No, despoina. No drama. There is a report in the palace – a report from Rhodos.'

Sappho took both of the hetaira's hands between her own. 'Tell me quickly. Is it Diodorus?'

Phiale shook her head. 'No – no. Diodorus is well. It is the expedition to the Euxine.'

Melitta felt as if her blood had stopped flowing. 'What?' she asked, her anger forgotten.

Nihmu's arrow flew through the air with a sound like a bird – *thwit!*

'It was a trap,' Phiale said. 'That's what they are saying at the palace. A trap.'

'You are not the person I would choose to deliver bad news,' Sappho said through her mask of a face. 'Say it, Phiale!'

Phiale buried her head in Sappho's lap, and Sappho began to stroke her hair. 'Satyrus?' she asked.

Phiale bobbed her head up and down. 'They say his ship sank – from damage. That no one – could save him. He – had Theron and Abraham aboard.'

Melitta sobbed. She almost fell. Suddenly, Nihmu's calloused hands were under her elbows, and Kallista appeared, heavily pregnant, and took Kineas, who burst into tears and squalls.

'And my husband?' Nihmu asked.

'Eumeles has captured him,' Phiale said. 'But he lives, and will be ransomed.'

'Only when he is humiliated and broken,' Nihmu said.

The sound of weeping filled the garden. Phiale was weeping, and Kallista, and Melitta – Kallias wept, and both of their slave women. Alcaea watched with her usual indifference to the sufferings of others. Her demeanour suggested that suffering was the norm and the rest of them had best get used to it, as she had.

Nihmu was also dry-eyed, and Sappho pinched her lips and shook her head. 'We are not beaten yet,' Sappho said.

Melitta watched as Sappho and Nihmu locked eyes. Something passed between them, and both of them turned, as if they were one being, to look, not at her, but at her child.

3

The west coast of the Euxine consisted of mudflats, deep bays, endless estuaries and sea marshes stretching away to the sea of grass.

They were still ten stades from the coast. They had fled out into the deep water, the 'great green' where coastal sailors never went, bailing the *Falcon* and fothering his bow to prevent the in-rush of water from the damage left by the loss of the ram – three great holes under the waterline, each the size of a fist, where the heavy bronze retaining bolts had ripped through the planking.

Satyrus was utterly exhausted – past the point of careful decision-making, past the point of hope and fear. He merely acted. He was in the bow, naked except for his boots, strapping a tow-stuffed aspis to the outside of the hull over the holes. The stress on the bow had ripped every patch free and started the water again, and the oarsmen were rowing with the lowest rowing deck half full of water and worse to come.

Satyrus pinned the shield over the holes – it covered all three – while two Urartian deck-crewmen drew the ropes over and through it tight. Satyrus was fighting the sea and his own fatigue, and even as he pushed, a wave caught something on the shield and all the ropes slipped. His arm hurt – the salt water licked at the deep cut there and the pain was intense.

Water began to rush in once more.

'Fuck it,' Satyrus said. He didn't think he had the energy to start again, so instead, he pushed the shield back into the ropes by the simple expedient of falling on the upper rim – and then past it into the water. He grabbed hold of the naked bow timbers as the water hit him, wrenching his shoulder, and got his head above water. Now the force of the ship's passage pinned him against the shield, and the shield was held in place.

'Pull, you bastards!' Satyrus managed.

Ba'alaz, the bigger of the two, hauled his rope back until it sang. Kariaz, the smaller, belayed it against a cross-member that had supported the weight of the ram and then hauled on the other line until Ba'alaz got to him and added his weight.

'She's home, master!' Ba'alaz said.

Satyrus was already sinking under the bow.

'Stand up and fight, boy!'

Theron stood over him on the sand of the palaestra, his hands still in the fighting stance of the pankration.

'Are you down? If you are one of mine, get up! Get up and fight!'

Theron was even larger here – and the sands stretched to an infinite horizon. Theron towered over him, his lion-skin chlamys whipping in the winds – the smell of wet cat.

'Get up and fight!'

Satyrus struggled to get a foot under his own weight – to rise on an arm. All the weight of the world seemed to press him down. He got an arm out from under his body and he pushed against the sand. The force pinning him to the ground was like the hand of the gods. He pushed.

Suddenly, the weight on his back released ...

Only the will of the gods kept Satyrus alive – his foot caught in the mess of old rope and canvas that marked their first attempts to fother the bow, and he was held there, drowning, until Theron reached into the water and pulled him up by sheer strength. It took Diokles hundreds of heartbeats to revive him – or so they told him after his choking breaths had turned to steady breathing.

'You were there,' Satyrus said to Theron, catching his hand.

'So I was,' Theron agreed. He wiped his nose. One of the wounds on his thigh had opened, and watery blood ran down his leg, deeply marked where he had stripped off his greaves.

'No – I saw it. Was I dead?' Satyrus asked.

He could see on their faces that they thought his wits were wandering, so he didn't say more. 'Any sign of the other ships?' he asked.

Diokles shook his head. He'd been at the steering oar for ten hours. 'None,' he said. 'We ran west. They ran east.' He shrugged.

Theron slumped heavily. 'Zeus Soter, lad. If you'd left me, you'd be halfway to Rhodos now.'

Satyrus managed a smile. 'Sounds bleak, doesn't it? We're much better off as we are.'

Diokles stared ahead woodenly.

Satyrus made his shoulders rise off the deck. To one of the boys, he said, 'Get my satchel.' To Diokles, he said, 'We're not dead yet.'

'Close,' Diokles said.

Satyrus put raw wool on Theron's thigh, twisting the ends as Philokles had taught him, washing the wound as Sophokles – a traitor, a poisoner, an assassin, but an excellent doctor – had instructed him years before in Heraklea.

Heraklea, where Amastris would be tonight. Would she see the sunset? He looked out to the west, where the sun was setting as they edged into the low-lying swamps. There was nothing on this coast – nothing but the channels of a hundred forgotten watercourses and the swamps their passage left.

He could just see the land under the setting sun, and just north of the brightest part of the sun's red disc, he saw the notch of a sail. He pointed.

'Poseidon's watery dick,' Diokles said. 'Zeus Casios who conquers all the waters. Thetis of the glistening breasts.'

Satyrus could just about manage to stand erect. 'Could be Dionysius,' he said hopefully.

Diokles shook his head, spat over the side. 'That golden bastard who shaved our stern.' He looked forward. 'That rig of yours strong enough that we could rig the boatsail after dark?'

Satyrus was watching. The oarsmen were tired – so tired that the ship had little more than steerage way despite all banks rowing. 'He doesn't see us,' he said.

'We're on the dark horizon and all our masts are struck down,' Diokles said. 'But it means that we can't get in with the land. We could sink in the night, and you know it. We need to get this hulk ashore.'

'There's nothing on this shore but mud and bugs,' Satyrus said.

'A man can wade through mud, and bugs don't usually kill you,' Diokles said. 'With the ram gone, there's nothing holding that bow together but four copper bolts – hear me, *sir*? We will

37

not make Tomis, or wherever you think we can get. If the wind comes up and there are cross-waves, we're gone.'

Satyrus wanted to rant that this wasn't his fault and Diokles was being unfair, but he lacked the energy. 'So?'

'So we need to land,' Diokles said. He looked at Theron.

Theron shrugged. 'You put me in command of a ship,' he said. 'I won't take one again! I grew up with the sea and still I know nothing of him. But Diokles seems to have the right of it, lad. When the wind rises towards morning, we'll open like a flower. Philokles would ask you to think of the oarsmen.'

Satyrus nodded. Despite everything, his eyelids sank, as if he was going to fall asleep, cold and wet, huddled by the rail of a sinking ship.

'As soon as dark falls,' he said, 'we raise the boatsail mast. If that holds, we raise the mainmast. We turn north and put his bow into the mud. Get every oarsmen up on deck with his sea bag and every weapon we have aboard. Serve out the dead marines' gear and all the stuff we got off the enemy. If we can run him far enough ashore, we save the drinking water.'

Diokles nodded. His lip curled in a fraction of a smile. 'I was afraid you'd decide to try and board the bastard and take him.'

Satyrus stretched warily. The idea of getting back into his armour made his body hurt all over again. 'I thought about it,' he said, by way of humour.

'That's what I'm afraid of,' Diokles said.

Full dark, and half a moon – a clear, cool night with enough starlight to read a scroll. As soon as the *Falcon* got his boatsail up, his motion changed. Diokles got the deckhands to bring their bags on deck and then sent all of them aft except the work party for the mainmast. Satyrus stood in the bows, his hands on the lines fothering the shield. *His* shield.

Not that he could do much if the patch gave way, except curse, and drown.

He turned and watched the mainmast rise. A spar that big could sink them if it fell from its cradle of lines and hit the deck, but he lacked the energy to worry about such a thing. Instead, he watched the pink western horizon. The enemy vessel – if it was an enemy – was invisible, hull down and sail down. He might even have landed for the night, although few sailors would risk the mudflats on this stretch of coast.

The thought made him give a tired smile, because he was about to beach his precious *Falcon* on those very mudflats. And he'd never get *Falcon* back. His grip on the cross-brace tightened.

Before the last line on the mainmast was pulled taut, the pink was gone from the sky, and the great path of stars rolled overhead from horizon to horizon. Only a few oarsmen had the energy to look up, but those that did exclaimed – a comet, bright as the moon, was rising above the eastern sky.

She'll see that in Heraklea, Satyrus thought.

By the second watch of the night, all the oarsmen were packed in the stern, lifting the bow almost clear of the water. As long as the wind held, they'd be in with the land before dawn.

'Do I see a glow to the west?' Theron croaked. He wasn't moving much, the wounds having stiffened and his muscles strained.

Diokles nodded. 'He put ashore. You know what that tells me?'

Satyrus grunted.

'Tells me they know you're aboard this ship and there's money in it. No one would be on this coast unless there was some reward.' The man shrugged. 'With the bow out of the water like this, we're safe. I'll keep heading west until I feel the wind start to change.'

Satyrus grunted his assent.

The next thing he knew, he was waking up. The sky was lighter – the false dawn – and he was damp from the morning mist. 'Diokles?' he asked.

Diokles grunted.

'Let me have the helm,' Satyrus said, forcing himself to stand. His knee joints burned like fire.

'Breeze is dying. We passed their fire two hours ago. We can't be more than a stade offshore, but this cursed fog—' Diokles kept his voice low.

'What's our heading?' Satyrus couldn't see a thing.

'West and north,' Diokles said. 'Listen!'

Satyrus listened. He could hear birds, and the gentle surf of the Euxine. 'Thanks for keeping the oars all night,' Satyrus said. 'I feel – like a fool. I'm the navarch.'

Diokles shook his head. 'Men say things in heat,' he said. 'I'm not so proud of the way I spoke to you yesterday.'

Satyrus put his hands on the helmsman's. 'I've got the helm,' he said. 'I'm not so proud of – anything.' He ducked under the oar-yoke. 'I've got him.'

'You have the helm.' Diokles stood for a moment. 'Get us ashore, eh?'

Satyrus tried to work the kink out of his neck. 'This is the last time I'll handle *Falcon*,' he said. 'He feels odd.'

'He's dying,' Diokles said, curling up by the helmsman's bench. 'But he's a good lad. He'll get us ashore.'

Satyrus found it as hard to track time in the mist as it was to see his course. Twice he caught sight of stars overhead, and once he heard surf, clear as a conversation in the theatre, just off his right shoulder – a quarter of an arc *away* from where it ought to be.

Turn the ship? Steady on this heading? He peered overhead, watching the growing light and the white haze for an answer. He should have been in with the coast by now – should have felt the touch of mud under his keel.

He looked down at Diokles and Theron, now tangled together, deeply asleep. He didn't want to wake them.

He felt very young. He felt the way he had when he was twelve years old, standing his first real watch with the Macedonian veterans, Draco and Amyntas, in the mountains of Asia. Afraid of every noise, and doubly afraid to seem a fool.

A seagull screeched off the bow.

He listened so hard he felt he might strain his ears – and heard nothing. The surf noise was gone.

'Poseidon, god of the sea, stand at my shoulder. Herakles, god of heroes, be my guide.' He muttered prayers.

All around him, exhausted men lay huddled together, snoring.

The ship sailed on, and the sky grew lighter.

By now he was in danger of discovery, his raised sails probably sticking up above the fog, an easy target for wakeful sentries anywhere on the coast.

Nothing to be done now.

The sky lightened further still. The fog was thick, but he could see the grey-blue of the morning sky directly overhead. He forced his back to relax and realized that he'd been waiting for the crunch of sand under the bow. *Where is the land?* he asked himself every fifty heartbeats, and still *Falcon* sailed on.

When the fog began to glow pink off the port bow, a sense of his location went through him like the voice of a god – he was sailing north of west. He leaned over the rail by the steering oars and spat in the water.

They were moving well – he was sailing north of west at the pace of a trotting horse. He should have been ashore before first light. He shook his head, fought off panic and tapped Diokles with his bare foot.

'Ho!' Diokles snorted. 'What?'

'I need you,' Satyrus said quietly. The urgency in his voice carried, and the Tyrian rubbed his eyes, pulled his chlamys tight about his shoulders and settled on the steering bench.

'We're still afloat,' he said.

Satyrus nodded. 'We're sailing north of west and we've never even brushed a shoal. It's an hour after first light.'

Diokles spat in the water, just as Satyrus had. Then he went forward, cursing, and returned with the 'porpoise', a lead weight attached to a rope. 'I'm sending the porpoise for a swim,' he said, and ran off forward into the fog.

Satyrus listened for the splash of the porpoise. All around him, men were waking. The fog was burning off – above him, the boatsail shone clear. He had minutes to get the *Falcon* ashore before he'd be spotted – if he hadn't been spotted already.

Diokles came trotting back with a gang of deckhands at his tail. 'Sandy bottom and shoaling slowly – but there's five tall men's worth of water under your keel.' He shook his head. 'Where the fuck are we? How can we be sailing north of west? We should be sailing on grass by now!'

Theron was awake just forward, his eyes rimmed in red. 'Artemis, I'm too old for this,' he said.

'Keep throwing the porpoise, helmsman,' Satyrus said.

'Aye, lord.' Diokles gave a wry smile. 'Like that, is it?'

More quietly, Satyrus asked him, 'What do you think?'

Diokles stepped very close. 'The bow's leaking water. I think we have until the sun is high in the sky, and then he'll open like a whore's arse in the Piraeus. Best put him ashore before then.'

Satyrus shook his head. 'I tried. I missed the shore. I don't know *how* I missed it.'

Theron shook his head. 'Don't look at me, lad. I should never have offered to captain one of these. My expertise ends on the sands.'

Before rumours of their predicament could run the length of the deck, the sun and the rising fog showed them trees and scrub – due east, a great shore running parallel to their course.

Men gasped at the absurdity of it.

All around the stern, men asked how this could be.

Diokles rubbed his beard. 'I wish we had a real Euxine pilot,' he said. He pointed to one of his deckhands. 'Rufus thinks we've sailed into the netherworld. I'm going to smack him if he spreads that notion.'

Theron, now on his feet and rubbing out his muscles with the slow care of an athlete, pointed his chin at a group of men coming up the deck. 'Best listen to yon,' he said.

An oarsman stepped up at the head of the delegation and briefly Satyrus feared mutiny – the kind of rebellion hopeless men might make, but the leader bowed his head respectfully. 'Tisaeus, late of Athens, master. Second bank, fourth oar. I think I know where we are.'

'Speak up, then!' Satyrus said, trying to keep the squeak out of his voice.

'I think,' the man hesitated, apparently afraid to commit now that he had the ear of authority. Behind him stood a dozen oarmates who had obviously pushed him to speak. They prodded him gently.

He looked at the deck. 'Nikonion, master. You've passed through the shoals off Nikonion and we're in that monster deep bay. I used to sail on a pentekonter that coasted here for grain. Locals call it the Bay of Trout.'

Diokles slapped the man heavily on the shoulder. 'That's a

silver owl for you, mister!' He turned to Satyrus. 'He must be right. We're embayed.'

'Poseidon! Thetis's damp and glittering breasts!' Satyrus felt as if the weight of the ship was coming off his shoulders. If they were embayed, then there was no chance that the Pantecapaeans had seen them in the morning light. 'We must have made the gods' own time yesterday.'

Diokles looked up. 'Twenty parasangs, more or less.' He nodded. 'Maybe losing his ram made him faster.'

'Doesn't matter now,' Satyrus said. 'We need to get him ashore as close to intact as possible. A farm with a slip would save us all.

Before the sun was a red ball balanced on the rim of the world, the bow began to give way and water came in faster, so that *Falcon* became difficult to handle.

'Let's get him ashore,' Diokles said.

Satyrus wanted to save as much cargo as possible. 'Listen, helmsman,' he said. 'We're thirty long parasangs from a friendly town – we're in enemy country. Even if we can walk through the delta to Tomis, we'll need every scrap of food in this hull – and our weapons and armour. I need to beach *Falcon* right.'

'And you want to save him, don't you?' Diokles said. He nodded.

'Marker on the beach!' the lookout shouted. 'Marker and some sort of stream entrance – might be a channel.'

Satyrus and Diokles shared a glance. Even the entrance of a small stream cutting through the sand would make a channel – allow them to beach the hull where it could be saved.

Satyrus raced forward, leaped up the standing shrouds and made the *Falcon* roll as he leaned out.

'There you go, sir!' the lookout said. Satyrus followed his outthrust arm and saw a cairn of rocks in the rising sun, and just past it, a stream that glowed like a river of fire coming off the high bluffs beyond, and a trace of smoke on the wind.

Satyrus nodded. 'Good eye,' he said, and slid down the stay to the deck, burning his hands and the inside of his thighs in his haste.

'Keep calling the course,' he shouted up to the lookout.

'Aye!' the lookout called.

Diokles had the oar.

'Put us ashore,' Satyrus said. 'I'll con from the bow.'

'If that stream has a sandbar, we'll never get across it,' Diokles said.

'Let's get the sail off him and then we'll make our throw with Tyche.' Satyrus gave the orders, and the boatsail came down with reckless efficiency. Every man aboard was aware of how close they were to disaster, even with the shore in sight.

'Make your course due east,' Satyrus said, as the deck crew were folding the boatsail, their heads turning constantly as they watched the bow's opening seams and the looming beach.

'Into the sun, aye,' Diokles said. 'Helios, be our guide, bright warrior.'

'Bow-on to the creek!' the lookout shouted.

'Shoaling fast!' came the voice of the man with the porpoise in the bow. 'I can see the bottom!'

'Sandbar,' Diokles managed before the jolt.

The sandbar hit them like a strong man landing a glancing blow on a shield – it rocked them but they kept their feet, and they heard the bar whisper along the length of the hull, the ship's momentum driving him over, probably digging a furrow in the old mud as they drove on, the bow now flooding too fast to be saved.

'He's going,' Diokles said through clenched teeth.

'No, he'll last the race,' Satyrus said. 'Every man aft! Now!' Satyrus had been waiting until the stern gave the anticipated dip of coming off that sandbar, and he felt it, like a rider feels the weight change in a horse about to jump. 'Aft! For your lives!'

The deck crew pounded aft and the rest of the crew followed, somewhere between discipline and panic, and the bow rose out of the water – not by much, but up he came, the ugly scars of the lost ram and the heavy beam ends showing wet, like the bones from an amputation.

Diokles grinned at him. 'That was slick. You're a quick learner and no mistake,' he said.

Bow up, stern down, they glided another ship's length into the mouth of the creek, and then another, and then with a sigh, the keel grated, slid and stuck. The cessation of movement was so gradual that not a man lost his footing.

'Zeus Soter!' Satyrus shouted, and every oarsman and sailor gave the cry.

The deck crew scrambled ashore with ropes and they got the oarsmen off, straight over the side and on to the beach where the stream cut it, men kneeling to kiss the ground and making prayers to the gods as they touched, other men making sure of their equipment.

It took them half an hour to get everyone on the beach, to set up a hasty encampment. Theron took a pair of marines and set off up the beach to see if the smell of smoke would reveal a farmhouse.

Satyrus watched the *Falcon* settle in four feet of water with mixed feelings. On the one hand, he was savable – he could have him clear of the water in two days' work. But the feeling of failure – of defeat – from the day before continued to linger, alongside the pressure of the knowledge that enemy warships would be hunting him in the dawn.

'Get the oarsmen armed and build us a wall – stakes, anything,' Satyrus said to Diokles.

Diokles shook his head. 'With all respect, lord, there's not ten trees in fifty stades. That there's the sea of grass, or so I've been told. You grew up there, eh?'

Satyrus nodded miserably. 'Too true, my friend. But digging trenches in the beach seems foolish.'

'Here's Theron and a farmer,' Diokles said.

The farmer, an old man with a straight back, met Satyrus's eye without flinching. 'Alexander,' he said, offering his hand to clasp. 'Gentleman here says you are the son of Kineas of Athens. You have the look.'

Satyrus had to smile. 'You knew my father?'

'Only two days,' the farmer said with a nod. 'That was enough to know him well. Are you the same stock? Or are you some reiver come to pillage my house?'

Satyrus stood straight. 'I am my father's son,' he said. 'We fought Eumeles of Pantecapaeum yesterday and had the worst of it. My ship lost his ram. I need to refit the *Falcon* and not fall afoul of Eumeles' jackals.'

Alexander the farmer rubbed his bearded chin. 'See that cairn?' he said.

Satyrus nodded. 'I see it.'

Alexander nodded back. 'That's one of your father's men, died in a skirmish here – must have been twenty years ago.'

Satyrus shook his head in wonder. 'I know who you are! You sold my father grain! That's the grave of Graccus!'

'Graccus, aye, that's the name.' Alexander nodded. 'If you will come and swear on his grave and in your father's name to do me no harm – why, then, I'll open my barns to your men.'

'And if not?' Diokles asked.

Alexander smiled. 'Always best to know both sides of a bargain, eh? If not, I light my signal fire, and my friends come off the sea of grass to see why I need help.'

Satyrus laughed. 'Assagatje!' he said. Suddenly the day was lighter.

Diokles shook his head but Theron came forward. 'His mother's people. Cruel Hands Assagatje.'

Satyrus took Alexander by the hand. 'Let's go and swear on the grave of my father's friend,' he said.

4

ALEXANDRIA, 311 BC

Men – at least, the kind of men who kept their women in cloisters and forbade them education and company – might have been surprised by the speed with which Sappho, Nihmu and Melitta planned the overthrow of Eumeles.

Phiale's news was less than an hour old before they had the outlines of their plan made.

'The old gods of Chaos are waiting in the wings,' Sappho said, her lips smeared with ink. She was writing lists. 'We leave a great deal to chance.'

Nihmu was packing, quickly and quietly, slipping in and out of the room to stack bags against a wall. She paused, comparing two bows and choosing one. 'There is always something for chance,' she said.

Sappho chewed on her pen. 'Where will you land?' she asked.

Nihmu stopped as if this hadn't occurred to her before. 'Where we can get horses immediately,' she said.

Melitta was struggling with the idea that she was going to leave her precious baby with a wet-nurse and sail away. The indecision was like agony – the thrill of the adventure she had craved for so long, balanced exactly against the pain of leaving the small body that had grown to fill her life in just two months. 'We could land at the Temple of Herakles,' she said. 'Remember, Coenus?'

Coenus nodded. 'She's right, by all the gods, and the more fool I for forgetting. The old priestess – gods send she still holds sway, but I suspect she's gone across the river by now – she hates Eumeles. Gorgippia, for sure. We can buy a dozen horses and be gone into the Maeotae country before Eumeles has any word of us.'

Sappho wrote a note. 'I wish we had time to distract him with something on the west coast of the Euxine before you go,' she said. 'You truly think that the three of you can raise all the east?'

Nihmu nodded. 'Yes,' she said. 'Listen – it is simple. We find Ataelus, who is still up-country. We find him and we spread word to all the people.'

Sappho nodded, the nod of someone not quite convinced. 'Ataelus has been fighting the Sauromatae for ten years,' she said. 'What makes you think that in one summer he can raise all the Assagatje?'

Nihmu shrugged. 'When I was a prophet, I said that Marthax would hold sway on the plains until the eagles flew,' she said. 'Now is the time. Satyrus tried to go like a Greek – with a fleet to open the way for an army. Melitta will do this like a Sakje. She will raise the people, and the people will give her the sea of grass.' Nihmu leaned over and kissed the baby. 'But she must go in person. The Sakje will follow a person, not a name. If Melitta stays here, I cannot do it. Ataelus cannot. But you can, honey bee.'

Coenus bit his lip. 'You'll still need an army,' he said. 'Eumeles has four thousand foot and more peltasts and Thrake than he ought. He can hold a set of walls for ever, and much as I respect the Sakje, they can't take a city. And a city can support a fleet, and that fleet will still need to be beaten before we can land our army.'

Nihmu nodded. 'That is all Greek thinking,' she said. 'It is good. I am not so foolish that I spurn it. But I am Sakje. Melitta and I will go and put the grass under our hooves, and Eumeles will feel the thunder.' She smiled. 'When Melitta is queen of all the Assagatje, then it will be time to send for a fleet and an army.'

Sappho nodded. 'I agree. I am writing to Diodorus to tell him to stay in the field – with Leon gone, we'll need the income.' Diodorus had the *hippeis* of Tanais – a mercenary cavalry unit that men called the Exiles, and he also had a taxeis of Macedonian foot raised from the prisoners taken after the Battle of Gaza, where Ptolemy had smashed Demetrios the Golden's army.

Melitta leaned over Sappho's letter. 'Once we have the support of the Sakje,' she said, 'we can have any port we want. Perhaps the Sakje can't take Pantecapaeum, but Olbia will declare for us as soon as we have a force in the field.' Seeing Coenus's face, she shook her head. 'That's what Satyrus and Diodorus both said!'

'Clearly, Olbia did *not* rise,' Coenus said. 'And there are rumours of – murders. Of friends of ours, killed in public.'

'They had too few ships,' Sappho said. 'Leon was afraid of it before he sailed, but he was hurried. This has to be done while Antigonus is hurt, while his son licks his wounds, or Eumeles will have Macedonians manning his walls and we'll never take him.'

Coenus shook his head. 'Leon sent a boy to do a man's job,' he said. 'Either he took too many ships for a reconnaissance, or too few for an invasion.'

Melitta found them both frustrating. 'Uncle Leon did the best with what he had!' she said. 'Listen to *me*. Whatever the truth of Olbia may be, the Sakje can take any of the smaller ports. Once we have the sea of grass, Eumeles' days are numbered – he can scarcely lead an army on to the plains to relieve a port!'

Coenus put a hand on her shoulder. 'Beware the lesson of Sparta,' he said. 'As long as Eumeles holds the sea, he can send reinforcements to any town he likes. Leon knew this.'

Nihmu had never stopped readying her things. Now she stood up. 'Despite all that,' she said, 'when he hears our hooves in his chill dreams, he will know fear. And then he will make mistakes.'

Melitta hugged Nihmu. 'From your lips to the ears of the gods,' she said.

Coenus shrugged. 'Better than sitting here.' He looked at Nihmu. 'How do we rescue Leon? If we pressure Eumeles hard, he'll threaten the lad – or kill him.'

'When Eumeles hears our hooves, his blood will run like ice,' she said again. 'Scared men make errors. There will be a moment.'

'Are you a seeress again, Nihmu?' Coenus asked.

'I am a woman who has made war,' Nihmu replied.

The pentekonter looked as if it would sink at its moorings, but Leon's chief factor insisted that it was seaworthy, and he'd filled the hull with the very best of Leon's rowers and crewed the deck with half a dozen officers from the successful Massalia fleet, so that the awful little boat had the air of a Rhodian naval vessel.

Most of the sailors were openly concerned at carrying women, especially women who had brought weapons aboard, but the officers knew she was their master's wife, a figure of legend, and all of them knew Coenus – one of Alexandria's most feared and revered warriors.

Cardias was the helmsman, a Rhodian sailor who had directed

the entire squadron on the Massalia run and saw no demotion in commanding a fifty-oared scow on a cruise up the coast of Asia.

On the beach beneath her own bedroom window, Melitta hugged her aunt Sappho goodbye and held her son for a long time, all too conscious that she might never see either of them again, and conscious too, that for all her claims of being a Sakje, her youth – much of her life – was tied to the sweaty streets of Alexandria. She had intended to walk once more in the night market, but she hadn't had the time.

Idomeneus, the man who had commanded her unit of archers last year at Gaza, came up and put an arm around her waist. 'Little mother,' he said in his Cretan accent.

'You bastard,' she smiled. 'What are you doing here?'

Idomeneus jutted his chin at Coenus. 'He hired me to run the archers on this ship.' He smiled. 'I wanted to come – and the wages were incredible.' He whistled. '*Are* there any archers on this fishing boat?'

Coenus came up. They had a fire on the beach and men were coming from all directions. The rendezvous had been made carefully, to prevent news of the sailing. 'Eight,' he said. 'And you're one of them. Cretans – what can I say?' Coenus clasped hands with the Cretan. 'Thanks for making it here.'

Idomeneus smiled. 'I would come far for this one,' he said. 'I was sorry to hear of your son. He was brave.'

Coenus didn't even show a strain in the firelight. 'He was,' Coenus agreed. 'May his son be as good as his father.' Coenus looked at the baby in Melitta's arms. 'My heart misgives me, honey bee. I think you should stay.'

Melitta drew herself up and carefully handed her son to Sappho, who handed him to Kallista. 'The tribes will not rise for you, Coenus,' she said.

Nihmu nodded agreement.

Idomeneus raised an eyebrow. 'So? We go on a mission, I suppose.'

Coenus nodded.

Idomeneus laughed. 'You don't have to tell me. Cretans grow up with these games.' He shrugged.

'At sea,' Coenus said. To Melitta, he said, 'Say your goodbyes.'

Nihmu hugged Sappho. 'We will win,' she said simply.

Sappho nodded. 'I know.'

Pounding footsteps on the sand, and Phiale came up, running in cork-soled sandals, attended by Alcaea. 'Melitta!' she called.

'Phiale!' Melitta answered, hugging the other woman. 'What are you doing here?'

'I caught a rumour that you were slipping away!' Phiale said. 'Where are you going?'

'Massalia,' Melitta said. 'To be safe.'

'Oh!' Phiale said. 'I suppose it is a secret. I'm sorry to be so thoughtless! But I worry so much about – about all of you!'

Kallista was still light on her feet despite her advanced pregnancy, and she interposed herself between Melitta and Phiale. 'Let me get you a cup of wine, since you've joined our beach party,' she said brightly.

Something sparked behind Melitta's eyes. She turned to Sappho. 'Don't let her leave for a day or two,' she said quietly.

Recognition glittered in Sappho's fire-lit face. 'Of course!' she said. 'How blind of me not to have seen it. Curse her.'

Melitta clasped her aunt more closely. 'We don't *know*. But why else is she here?' Then she choked on a sob. 'Take care of him for me!' she said, unwilling at the last to leave her son.

Before she left, she went and held him again, though she'd promised herself that she would not. While she held him, Hama emerged from the darkness behind Phiale. He had a whispered exchange with Sappho and vanished into the mansion.

'She won't leave us for a while,' Sappho said with satisfaction. 'With a little luck, she can shit her treason out.' She showed her niece a papyrus packet of orange powder.

'Awful if we're wrong,' Melitta said.

'Too bad,' Sappho said, her eyes hard. 'Goodbye, honey bee.'

And then they were aboard with a smell of verdigris and old fish, and the rowers picked up the beat, and they were away into the first colour of dawn.

They made Rhodos in six days, having come up the south coast of Cyprus. Melitta had been to Rhodos with her brother, but the City of Roses remained a place of mystery and intrigue to her.

The helmsman went to report at the Temple of Poseidon and Coenus accompanied him. The two men returned, scratching their beards.

'The pirates are worse,' Coenus announced to the table of officers in a comfortable wine shop on the waterfront. 'So bad that Rhodos can no longer suppress them, and her trade is being choked. The worst of the bastards are around the town of Byzantium – in the Propontis.'

'Where we are going,' Melitta added. 'Why do Greeks call everything the Propontis? Assagatje have real names – the Strait of Fast Water, the Strait of Horses.'

Cardias shrugged. 'The Thracian Bosporus divides the lands of the Thracians in Asia and Europe – and is the entrance to the Euxine. That's the Great Propontis. The Cimmerian Bosporus divides—'

'Lands that the Cimmerians don't hold any more and the Bay of Salmon!' she said impatiently.

'That's right.' Cardias shook his head and looked at his master's wife. 'Mistress, I'm against this. Such a small ship? They'll bottle us up in the narrows and we'll be fishbait – and you'll decorate a brothel.'

Nihmu shrugged. 'No. That will not happen.'

Coenus shook his head. 'Lady, I've seen you in action, and you are deadly sure with a bow – and so were your winged words. But you yourself said that you lost your gift of prophecy with your marriage.'

Nihmu shrugged. 'No pirate will touch this vessel,' she pronounced. 'I have seen it.'

'Poseidon's member – your pardon, ladies. Very well. Listen, the Rhodians have a convoy for the Euxine in ten days. Can we wait and sail with it?' Cardias was pleading.

'Of course!' Nihmu said. 'You think that because I am sure I am also foolish?'

Coenus shook his head. 'I remember you like this,' he said, 'but I haven't missed it.'

The convoy was ready in just eight days, and they were away, up the coast of Asia. They touched at Chios and Mytilene and then they were rowing north, right into the wind to make the mouth of the Hellespont before dark. The whole convoy passed Troy in the last light of the sun, Melitta and Coenus saying the verses to one another as the rowers carried them past the tomb of Achilles. They made the fishing town at Sigeion after dark, and suffered through the perils of camping on an open beach, lighting fires from fire pots in the dark and collecting wood from the driftwood piles at the high-water mark by touch and feel.

Melitta sank into her sheepskins thankfully and dreamed that she had lost her son and that spirits brought her his swaddling clothes, covered in blood, and she awoke screaming with Nihmu's arms around her.

In the morning she arose, feeling as if she'd been beaten with a stick, to watch the men load all their kit back aboard the pentekonter. The Rhodian convoy was slow to form in a contrary breeze, and the pair of triemioliai provided by the Rhodian navy as guards tacked back and forth like worried dogs with a herd of recalcitrant sheep, but before the sun was high they were rowing again to the curses of the oarsmen for the contrary wind and the bad luck.

Early afternoon and they were in the Propontis, the little sea in the midst of the Hellespont, and Parium was clear on their bow as they crept up the north coast. They made Rhaidestos with a freshening breeze that quieted some of the grumbling of the crew, and ate crabs on the beach and drank a terrible local wine sold off two-wheeled wagons by local farmers.

'We're in luck,' Coenus said, looking at Nihmu. 'The local pirates – the whole fleet – are on the opposite coast, making a grab at one of the cities, if you can believe it. They are strong – fifty warships, or so the farmers assure me.' He drank wine and made a face. 'Gods – who would want to be a colonist?'

'So Auntie Nihmu was right,' Melitta said.

'I'll sacrifice a new lamb to Poseidon when we're through the strait,' Coenus said. 'But yes – I think she's right.'

5

GRACCUS'S STELE, EUXINE SEA, 311 BC

'What we need is wood,' Satyrus said.

It had taken a day to build a camp on the bluff behind the stone farmhouse, out of sight of the shore and well watered by the creek. Another day had been filled in cutting the boatsail mast free, floating the *Falcon*, jury-rigging a bow and pulling the hull up the creek to the new camp, so that he could receive the care he deserved, out of sight of cruising ships in the great bay.

By the third day, Satyrus was standing in Alexander's largest stone barn, eyeing the curved joists that held the main beams. 'What we need is wood,' he said again.

'I don't think that Alexander, however well disposed to us, would fancy our stripping his barns of their innards to rebuild the bow.' Theron was still tired, and still moved stiffly. Six men had died of their wounds, and Satyrus was beginning to wonder if he would ever run well again himself – his hip was not knitting well, and he had trouble sleeping because of the pain in his arm, but Theron was recovering his sense of humour, and Satyrus had begun to feel that he might yet survive this.

'Those beams and joists came from somewhere,' Satyrus insisted.

'We could just ask him,' Theron said.

So Satyrus did.

'Sakje brought them – dragged them overland from up-country on sledges,' Alexander said. 'I traded them for wine – forty amphorae, good stuff from Mytilene.'

Satyrus thought about that while he looked at the bow of his ship, now protruding from the water at a gentle angle, pulled up by the might of two hundred men and four oxen until the whole hull was clear of the creek. The wrecked bow stuck up over his head the height of a man. He walked back and forth. 'Even if we get timber,' he said to Diokles, 'we need a ram.'

'One thing at a time,' Diokles said. 'I say we rebuild the bow without a ram and sail him home – as fast as we can. A new ram in Alexandria is just a matter of money.' He looked at Satyrus and Satyrus was afraid he saw pity in the man. 'You think you can fit him for war and rescue your uncle – that ship sailed four days ago, lord. He's taken, or dead. It's us as needs to get free – and no ram bow will save us in these waters.'

Satyrus drank herb tea and walked back and forth, looking at his ship and at Diokles. After an hour, he nodded.

'Right,' he said. 'You're right. Wooden bow. We'll have to rebuild him – move the masts. Without the ram, he's a pig – we know that. Have to rebalance the whole hull.'

Diokles nodded slowly.

Theron came up, his dark chlamys thrown back because the weather was fine. 'I have some talent for mathematics,' Theron said. 'So does Satyrus. Let's design him while Alexander summons the Sakje, and perhaps we'll have wood by the time we're ready to build.'

The Sakje appeared within a day of the beacon being lit, as Alexander had predicted, thirty horsemen with two hundred horses who arrived at twilight. Alexander greeted them in his orchard, where all Satyrus could see was a flash of gold and a whirl of horseflesh that made his eyes fill with the *hominess* of it. Without meaning to, he ran out into the orchard, no longer the staid lord and navarch, but a boy coming home to his mother's people.

A tall man on a tall horse covered in red paint clasped hands with Alexander and they spoke rapidly, like old friends too long separated. Satyrus knew the man immediately from his boyhood hearth.

'Kairax!' he called. His mother's tanist in the west, now ruler in his own right of the western gate of the Assagatje confederacy. He had grey in his beard where it had been all dark, and furrows in his cheeks, but the hand tattoo of his clan was still bold and dark on his bicep, and his arms were still heavy with muscle.

Kairax turned at his shout and whooped. In a moment, Satyrus was enveloped in the Sakje's heavy arms, and it was all he could do to fight back tears. 'I didn't know it was you!' he said. His Sakje came out haltingly.

'Nor I you, little cousin! And not so little!' Kairax nodded approvingly. 'You are a man. And yet you came here by ship and not by horse? How is that?'

Satyrus spoke – for too long, he suspected – of the adventures of exile, and Kairax bowed his head when Satyrus spoke of the murder of his mother.

'Too long have we borne with this Eumeles,' Kairax said. 'Marthax always counsels patience – but he hated your mother, and he is old, and my young men grow restless.' He looked at Satyrus from under his bushy brows. 'What kind of cousin are you, that you came with ships before you asked your relatives for help? I think that perhaps you have spent too many summers on the sea of water, and not enough summers on the sea of grass.'

Satyrus bowed his head in acknowledgement. 'Elder Uncle, I stand corrected,' he said, the Sakje coming back to him like a memory of youth.

Kairax grinned. 'Bah – you're too big to get a beating,' he said. 'Alexander of the Stone House says that you need wood.'

'Big wood – big trees. Like the ones in his barn,' Satyrus said.

Kairax nodded. 'If I bring them, then what?'

Satyrus didn't know what to say.

'Listen, lad,' Kairax said. 'The Assagatje are like dry grass on a summer's day, and you could be the lightning in the sky. Come with me and light the grass.'

Satyrus was tempted – so tempted that he had to remember everything that his uncle Leon and his uncle Diodorus had said about sea power to refuse the offer. 'Eumeles must be beaten at sea,' he said. 'Until then, he can use his ships to fight the Sakje.'

Kairax laughed. 'Ships against the Sakje? I would like to see that!'

'Every town closed against you?' Satyrus said. 'Garrisons of men who could arrive and leave by sea and never come within bow-shot?' Satyrus remembered something. 'And some of the Sakje must be loyal to Eumeles, Kairax. There were Sakje archers on every ship – good ones, who shot well, like men who have given their word.'

Now it was Kairax's turn to hang his head. 'It is as you say,' he said. 'Marthax sends young men to serve Eumeles and they go willingly, for the treasure.'

Satyrus took his arm and squeezed it. 'I am back to stay,' he said. 'I intend to kill Eumeles and make a kingdom of the Euxine.'

Kairax shook his head. 'That is not a Sakje thing,' he said.

Satyrus nodded. 'No – a Greek thing. But it will make the Sakje and the farmers free. And it will rid you of Marthax and me of Eumeles.'

Kairax made a Sakje gesture with his nose, like a man smelling something interesting – a sign of approval, if you knew the ways of the people. 'It is a big dream,' he said.

'I need wood to make it happen. I need to repair this ship, slip away past Eumeles' fleet and find my friends.' He didn't add that he needed to find a fleet of his own. 'I'll come back with ships.'

Kairax was no longer alone. While the two of them had spoken, his trumpeter and several of his principal warriors had got the drift of their conversation, and now they gathered around.

'Srayanka's son!' they called. A tall young woman reached out and touched his cheek. 'For luck!' she said in Greek.

He was reminded of Ataelus, and again tears filled his eyes.

Twice, warships passed along the coast, but neither chose to land.

'They fear the Sakje,' Alexander said with satisfaction. 'Taxing sons of bitches. I pay my tenth to Kairax, and he is worth every penny. I don't pay an obol to that bastard in Pantecapaeum. His writ don't run here, and those sailors know it.'

'But they're still looking for us,' Satyrus said.

On the third day after Kairax came down from the hills, twenty Getae men and two women came with forty mules and twenty oak trees dragged between them. Satyrus paid gold – almost the last of his ready money – and before the sun set that night, his men were at work with the farmer's ample tools, cutting new timbers for the bow.

'Three days,' he told Diokles and Theron.

'And you're coming with us?' Theron asked. His glance slid over Satyrus to the Sakje girl, Lithra, who hadn't left Satyrus's side for two days – and nights.

57

Satyrus knew he was being mocked, but he shrugged. 'We need a fleet. I can't get that here.'

'She's not going to be happy,' Diokles said.

Satyrus shrugged again. 'She is not a Greek girl, who needs me to wed her. She's a spear-maiden of the Cruel Hands, and we've already had that little talk. Gentlemen, if you've completed your inquest into my personal life, we can get this ship built and be away.'

'He's just like his father,' Alexander said into the silence.

Despite a growing irritation with the older men around him, Satyrus couldn't find anything in 'he's just like his father' to earn anger, so he smiled at them and walked off to find Lithra.

'You are for leaving soon,' she said. They were curled together in the hay – the air had a bite in it – and something awkward was making him want to scratch, but post-coital dignity demanded that he lie as if unconcerned.

'Yes,' he said.

'I for understanding Greek better,' she said. 'So?'

'I'll be back,' he said. It sounded pitiful, even to him.

'I know!' she said. She rolled him over. She was a tall girl with small breasts and a waist so small, chest muscles so hard, that passing his hand over her stomach made him hard. Her body was wonderful, and despite the partial barrier of two not-quite-shared languages, he knew her well enough to find more to like than just her body. Already.

She reached down and ran a practised finger up the base of his penis. 'Greek girls do this?' she asked.

Satyrus thought of Amastris. There was a mixture of guilt and something else – something hard to describe – in thinking of Amastris with another woman's hands on his *hoplon*. 'No,' he said.

Lithra leaned over. 'For you losing if not coming back, Satrax. Lithra rides ten days and never tires, five arrows in the mark before turning, ten men killing in the hills.' She leaned down, her face lit by the late sunset. 'Come back. I for liking you.'

Satyrus loved it when she called him Satrax. He caught her hands, rolled her under him and their mock struggle filled the air with straw, the dust rising in a cloud like smoke in the setting sun until they were coughing and laughing, despite the pus on his arm wound and the now permanent ache in his thigh.

'I'll be back,' Satyrus said, wondering if he was lying or telling the truth.

She smiled and stayed in his blankets one more night, but in the morning she was mounted with her warriors, and they rode away. She waved once, and was gone over the first range of hills, and Satyrus couldn't decide which of his actions deserved the biggest share of the guilt he felt. Guilt from inside and shame from the taunting of his elders, until he shunned them to work on the bow himself, adzing the timbers with the best of the sailors and the farmer's grandsons, who had more experience of woodworking than any of the sailors.

He worked until he slept, and slept only to rise and work again, and on the fifth day the last plank was fitted into its mate, the long pieces carefully edged and fitted to each other with wafers of flexible poplar between them to keep them together, and the bow was rebuilt heavily in stacked oak beams. The mainmast was fixed back into the deck a little farther aft, and so was the boatsail mast, so that the *Falcon* had something of the look of a triemiolia, and they gave him a broader central deck, a cataphract that would add weight and make him stiffer under sail – or so they hoped. And protect the rowers, in a fight.

Theron had all the men not engaged in work out in the countryside all day, hunting or practising with their weapons, so that by the time the bow was ready to ship, they were, to quote Theron, the most dangerous crew of oarsmen in the Euxine. 'Some of them can even throw a javelin,' he said with a smile.

'You look better, master,' Satyrus said. 'Perhaps we could fight a fall or two.'

Theron shook his head. 'Your hip is still bad, and I can smell that arm from here. You need to get that looked at. It's still weeping pus. And I'm not willing to be the target of your anger,' he said.

'I'm not angry,' Satyrus said. But no sooner were the words out of his mouth than he knew that he was.

Diokles came up with a pair of spears over his shoulder. 'Well, if we have to, we could board,' he said. 'No one expects the oar benches to clear in the first moments of a fight.'

He was probably joking, but Satyrus nodded. 'We should practise,' he said. 'Tomorrow, while we take him out in the bay with the deck crew, you should see how fast we can get them off the benches.'

'By Ares, he's serious,' Theron said.

'He's a serious man,' Diokles said, 'when his dick's dry.'

Satyrus decided it would be bad for discipline if he said what was on his mind, so he forced a false smile and walked away to supervise the final fitting of the bow timbers and the new rails. He understood in his head that he'd done a bad thing by taking a lover – that he'd had something that the other men didn't have, which made him the target of a lot of teasing. He knew this in his head, but in his gut he was angry at them for being so *petty*.

In the first of the sun, they were afloat off the creek, the lower hull full of rocks from the beach to stand him up. He wasn't the *Falcon* – or rather, he was the *Falcon* some moments, and then, in a heartbeat, he was another ship altogether – stiffer, better under sail, harder to row and down by the stern, sloppy in a turn. The bow leaked. Satyrus spent much of the day crouched over the new bow timbers, feeling the water and worrying.

'You need to relax,' Diokles said. 'They'll swell.'

'You need to shut up and do your work by yourself,' Satyrus spat. 'You're a good helmsman – but I can replace you. I promoted you from the oar bench. My personal life is not part of your deck, and neither is my head. Walk away.'

Diokles turned on his heel and headed to the stern.

Satyrus cursed his temper and his foolish words – but he did not retract them.

They didn't exchange a word while they loaded, making every effort to bring his bow down in the water. They stood well apart while Satyrus was embracing Alexander and all his sons at the edge of the beach.

'Your father's friend – the hero. He's brought me nothing but luck. Glad I could help you.' Alexander had given them a farewell dinner, a big fish from the bay and wine for all hands that must have cost the man a small fortune.

'When I am king, you will never pay a day's tax,' Satyrus promised.

'That's right, I won't!' the farmer responded. 'Don't now, neither. Good luck, lad. You're the image of your dad – a little longer, I think, but a good man. Go and put the bronze to that bastard in Pantecapaeum for all the other farmers.'

The old man embraced Theron, who had spent time with his grandsons, and Diokles, who bore it stiffly, and then they were away, tearing up the bay on a fresh breeze.

'If the wind holds, there's no cruiser in the Euxine can take him on this reach,' Diokles said, to no one in particular. He nodded to Theron. 'Quit wrestling and become a shipwright.'

Theron gave a half-smile. 'I suppose something of my father rubbed off on me,' he said, watching Satyrus.

Satyrus knew that Diokles meant his little speech as a peace offering, but he couldn't bring himself to answer, or apologize, and that made him feel like a fool. His arm was becoming heavy and swollen and he felt light-headed.

If there was an enemy ship off the bay, they never saw him, flying along with the wind astern as soon as they turned south, so that the farm seemed a dream. Satyrus spent the morning watching his precious bow like a mother cat with her first kittens, but the leakage was no more than any dry ship gives in his first hours at sea, and by noon he was dry, as the wood swelled to close the gaps in the new construction. Satyrus wiped his hand against the fresh-cut timbers, smiled in satisfaction and walked up the new cataphract deck to the stern.

'Straight on for the Great Bosporus?' Diokles asked. It was the closest to direct communication that the two of them had tried in two days. 'We might make it if we sailed the deep green. Tomorrow night, with a good landfall and the will of the gods.'

'Tomis,' Satyrus said, and regretted his terse answer immediately. Diokles was trying to apologize. Satyrus had the ready wit to know that this flow of conversation wasn't really about their course. Was and wasn't. He tried the same in return. 'Tomis is in Lysimachos's satrapy. Should be friendly. Besides, we have friends there – my father's guest-friends and others. At this rate, we'll be there before nightfall. We'll weather the strait in daylight, day after tomorrow.'

'Tomis?' Diokles said. 'I could get a new ship there.'

'Don't be an ass, Diokles,' Satyrus said. He braced himself. 'I need you,' he said, with the same effort he'd use in a fight.

'Huh,' Diokles said, with the air of a man with more to say.

They'd coasted all day, never losing sight of the Ister delta and her thousands of islands and broad fan of silt, and then followed the coast as it turned due south, the land visibly civilized, with Greek farms as far as the eye could see and the loom of the Celaletae Hills in the west.

'Tomis breakwater!' the lookout called.

'High time,' Neiron said. He'd had an easy day, with the wind just right for sailing.

'Ships on the beach,' the lookout called.

Satyrus nodded to his officers. 'I'll go.'

None of them seemed inclined to argue. He pulled his *chiton* over his head and dropped it on the deck and raced aloft up the boatsail mast. The lookout was Thron, the youngest and lightest of the ship's boys.

'Look at that, sir!' he said, pointing at the sweep of the beach beyond the breakwater. Tomis boasted two galley beaches, one each side of a rocky headland. They could only see the northern beach.

There were three triremes on the beach and a fourth warship floated at a mooring in the broad curve of the bay. He was the *Golden Lotus*.

'Kalos! Get the sails off him! Now!' Satyrus called from the lookout.

'Aye, sir!' Kalos called back, and bare feet slapped the decks as the deck crew ran to their stations.

'Good eye, boy,' Satyrus said. He pointed at the deck. 'A silver owl for you when your watch is over.'

'For me?' Thron beamed.

Satyrus ignored his hero-worship and dropped to the deck.

Diokles was already turning them out to sea. 'What's up?' he asked.

'*Golden Lotus* is in the roadstead,' Satyrus said. He looked around. 'All officers!' he called.

Neiron was getting the rowers to their benches. He waved.

Kalos had the telltale sails down. An observer on the beach would have only bare poles to look for against the sunset now. He came aft, pausing to curse a deckhand who was sloppy in his folding of the precious sail.

Apollodorus, another survivor of Gaza, came forward from the bow. Unarmoured, he was magnificently muscled, though short. A very tough man, indeed. With Abraham gone, he was the phylarch of their marines.

Satyrus pointed at the harbour. 'Leon might have come here,' he said.

'Can't be Leon,' Theron said. 'He had ten ships around him when we escaped. He was taken.'

'We escaped,' Satyrus said.

'He didn't,' Theron insisted.

'No chance at all?' Satyrus asked, which quieted them. 'Tomis is a friendly port. If those are Eumeles' ships, he's an idiot, or his navarch is. And we have a hull packed with oarsmen trained to fight. But – if that's Leon, we'll look like fools and possibly kill some of our friends. We need to *know*.'

Kalos shrugged. 'Sail in, lay alongside and put our knives to their throats. If it's friends, we say we're sorry and let them buy us some wine.'

'That's why you're not a navarch,' Neiron said, rubbing the back of his head. 'I agree with the master. We need to know.'

Theron nodded slowly. 'I agree.'

Satyrus nodded. 'Good. I'll go.'

Theron shook his head. 'Don't be foolish, lad.'

Satyrus turned and looked at his former athletics coach. 'I am not a lad, and I am not foolish, Theron. We'll talk of this another time.' He spoke carefully, without anger as best he could manage. Time to stake out some new ground with all of them, he decided. 'I have guest-friendships here. I am young, and I can swim, and I'm mostly unwounded.'

'Let Diokles go, or one of the boys,' Theron said. He was clearly stung by his former student's rebuke. 'Your arm is *bad*.'

'I've had worse,' Satyrus said.

'Bullshit, boy.' Theron stepped forward.

'Watch yourself, sir. I am not your pupil here. I am your commander. And I *am not boy to you*. Understand?' He turned.

'Very well, *sir*.' Theron was angry. 'Send Diokles!'

'Diokles is my first officer, but he lacks the social distinctions that will protect me,' Satyrus said.

'Which is a nice way of saying that they could just pick me up and make me row, if they was hostile,' Diokles said.

'If they capture you, you won't live an hour,' Theron said.

'The price of glory,' Satyrus said. 'I'm going. Diokles, lay me ashore just north of the headland. Go up the coast, get a meal in the oarsmen and come back for me tomorrow night. Off and on until the moon rises. If you see three fires on the beach, come in and fetch me off. If there are just two fires, I'm taken and it's a trap. No fires – well, I'm not there. Clear?'

Theron shook his head. 'I'm against it.'

Theron was a gentleman and a famous athlete, and the rest of them were plain sailormen. None of them spoke up, either way. Satyrus looked at his former coach. 'Your reservations are noted,' Satyrus said, a phrase of Leon's that leaped to his mind and sounded much more adult than *fuck off.*

Theron's face darkened, but over his shoulder, Diokles grinned and then turned away to hide it.

The water was cold – winter was less than two feasts away and the Euxine was already more like the Styx than seemed quite right. Satyrus went over the side less than a stade from the shore, his leather bag and sword belt and all his clothing inside a pig's bladder, which he tried to keep over his head as he swam with a spear in his left hand. The distance was short, but the first shock took the breath from his lungs, and he was labouring by the time his feet brushed the gravel of the beach, his arm burning like fire from the salt and the exertion. He lay on the shingle, panting, for a minute before he got up, brushed the sea-wrack off his body and got dressed. Water had penetrated the bladder and his wool chiton was wet, and so was his chlamys – but they were good wool, and he was warmer by the time he pulled the sword belt over his head, set his bag on his shoulder, picked up his hunting spear and loped over the dune and on to the road.

There were farms on either hand, their vines along the road and their barley fields stretching away in autumnal desolation, interspersed with scraggly olive trees and heavy apple trees. Even as Satyrus watched the fields, he saw a slave propping a branch that was heavy with fruit.

Satyrus jogged along the road behind the dune until he came even with the slave. The man was quite old.

'Good evening!' Satyrus called out.

The slave turned, looked at him and went back to cutting a prop.

'How far to Tomis?' Satyrus asked.

The old man looked up, clearly annoyed. He pointed down the road. 'Not far enough,' he said.

Satyrus had to laugh at that. He set off again, running a couple of stades to where the road turned as it rounded a low headland and the farms fell away because the soil was so poor. Olive trees on terraces climbed beside the road, and just past the turn, a big rabbit perused a selection of wild fennel in the sunset. Satyrus put his spear through the animal and gutted it on the spot, and he ran on with a prayer to Artemis on his lips and the rabbit dangling from his *lonche*.

A few stades further on, he found an apple orchard full of men and women picking in the last light. Satyrus smiled at two women who were sharing a water bottle by the road, and they lowered their eyes and retreated towards the trees.

'How far into Tomis?' he called.

The younger maiden shook her head and kept backing up. The elder stopped well out of his reach and shrugged. 'Around the headland, you see her,' she said in Bastarnae-accented Greek.

A man came up from the apple trees, holding a spear. 'Greetings, stranger,' he called from a good distance.

Satyrus bowed. 'I am Satyrus,' he said.

'Talkes,' the man said. He was wary, but he eyed the rabbit greedily. 'You were hunting, sir?'

'I was lucky,' Satyrus said. 'I'm looking for friends. Where can I find Calchus the Athenian? Or Isokles, son of Isocrates?'

'You are in luck,' the man said. 'My pardon, sir. My mistress is Penelope, daughter of Isokles.'

'Does she reside on this farm?' Satyrus asked. He vaguely remembered that Isokles had a daughter. She'd be twice his age. Married – to Calchus's son Leander. Or so he seemed to recall.

'Not safe in town just now,' the man said quietly. 'If you hadn't come up so quiet, we'd have been gone ourselves – we're supposed to flee armed men. She'll be at the farmhouse. If you tell me your errand, I'll approach her.'

'I'd rather tell her myself,' Satyrus said.

Talkes shook his head. 'No, sir. These are hard times round here. No one is getting near my mistress 'less she says.' Talkes held a spear like a man who regarded the weapon as an old friend, the partner of many a day in the field. A dangerous man.

Satyrus nodded. 'Very well. Tell your mistress that I am Satyrus, and my father was Kineas, and I am a guest-friend of her father's, and I crave her hospitality.' Satyrus sighed for the foolishness of it – if any of these slaves talked, he could be taken very easily. 'Do you know who has those boats on the beach in town?'

'They're the king's. Not our satrap – not old Lysimachos. They belong to the new king. Eumeles.' Talkes shook his head. 'Killed some men from the militia yesterday morning in a fight on the beach. Killed mistress's father, too. Burned some farms. Thought you might be one of them. Still not sure, mind. Teax, get back to the house, now. Tell mistress about the stranger. I'll wait here.' The man looked at him, tilting his head. 'You are Satyrus, then? The one the soldiers are looking for?' Talkes turned. 'Run, girl!'

The woman so addressed – the younger one – vanished like a foal from a spring hunt, pulling her heavy wool chiton up her legs and running as fast as an athlete.

'I have some wine I could share,' Satyrus offered.

'Keep it,' Talkes said. 'The rest of you, back to work.' Talkes backed away and lowered his spear, and he stood in the shadow of an old apple tree, watching his labourers and Satyrus by turns.

Satyrus thought that he probably knew everything he needed to know. But curiosity held him. He drank a mouthful of his own wine and hunkered down on his haunches to wait.

'I'd have a swallow of that now, if you was to offer again, stranger.' Talkes took a hesitant step closer.

Satyrus nodded. He put the stopper back in his flask and set it on the ground. Then he picked up his spear, rabbit and all, and stepped well clear. 'Be my guest.'

Talkes sidled up to the canteen carefully, as if afraid it might be a dangerous animal. But he took a swallow and smiled.

'You're a gent, and no mistake,' he said. 'Mind you, you could still be one of the tyrant's men,' he added, and took another swallow. He grinned, and went back to watching his workers.

Satyrus had another swallow of his wine. 'How long have they been here?' he asked.

'Four days,' Talkes responded.

Three weeks and more since the sea battle. Plenty of time for Eumeles to refit a captured ship and sail it here – especially as fine a ship as *Golden Lotus*.

'Mistress says bring him to t'house,' Teax said from the near darkness. 'Say he guest-friend.'

The walk to the house was tense, at best, and Satyrus felt as if Talkes' spear was never far from his throat. They climbed the rest of the hill and went down the other side. The house was dark, but up close, Satyrus could see that the shutters were tight on every window.

'Spear and sword, young master,' Talkes said at the door.

Satyrus considered refusing, but it seemed pointless. He handed over his weapons and was ushered inside. 'My rabbit is a guest gift,' he said.

'I'll send her to cook, then,' the Bastarnae man said. 'Mistress is this way.'

The house wasn't big enough to be lost in, but Satyrus followed Talkes as if he was in Ptolemy's palace in Alexandria, and soon he was standing before a heavily draped woman in a chair, sitting with a drop spindle in her hand and three oil lamps. She smelled a little of roses, and a little of stale wine. Satyrus couldn't help but notice how bare the house was – all the furnishings he could see were home-made.

'You are really Kineas's son?' she asked without raising her head.

Satyrus nodded. 'I am,' he said.

The lady choked a sob. 'They killed my father two days ago,' she said. 'He would have loved to have seen you.' She raised her head and mastered herself. 'How may I serve you?' she asked.

'I would like to claim guest-friendship of your house,' Satyrus said.

'My house has fallen on hard times,' she answered. 'Rumour says you are a great captain in the army of the lord of Aegypt? How do you come to my door with a rabbit on your spear? Eumeles' captains are searching for you.'

Satyrus decided he would not lie to this gentle, grey-eyed woman, despite her faint smell of old wine. 'I tried to take my father's kingdom back from Eumeles of Pantecapaeum. I failed and nearly lost my life and my ship.'

She rose, placing her spindles – carved ivory, better than most of the other objects in the room – in an ash basket full of wool. 'They know all about you, Satyrus. You will not survive staying here. They killed my father for being your friend, and Calchus is next, if they catch him. If I keep you, they'll come here and kill us.' She shrugged. 'But I am an obedient daughter and I will not refuse you. Perhaps it would be better for me to end that way.'

'Hide me overnight, and I will avenge your father at nightfall,' Satyrus said. 'I will not be your death.'

She came out of an unlit corner with a cup in her hand. 'I am Penelope,' she said. 'Here is the cup of welcome. No one here will betray you. I welcome you for the sake of your father, the first man I ever looked on with a woman's eyes. He might have wed me.'

'He wed my mother, the queen of the Sakje,' Satyrus said. He drank from the cup. There was cheese in it, and barley, and it went down well. He could smell the rabbit cooking.

'It is better to have a queen as a rival than another woman, I suppose,' Penelope said. 'At any rate, your father never promised, and he never returned.'

'And did you marry?' Satyrus asked, after a pause.

'Do I look like a maiden?' she laughed, and her laugh was angry. 'I married Calchus's youngest son.' Her bitterness was obvious. 'No queen for a rival there!' she said, and snorted.

Satyrus lacked the experience to know how to pass the subject over. 'I'm sorry,' he said.

She raised her head and glared at him. 'Spare me your pity, boy.' Then she shook her head. 'How do you plan to avenge us? And what makes you think that more killing will make this better?'

Satyrus drank his wine to cover his confusion. Finally, he shrugged. 'I have a ship,' he said. 'I will clear them out of the town.'

She nodded. 'The satrap will be here any day, and then Eumeles will find himself in a war. Best stay clear of it, Satyrus son of Kineas.'

Satyrus shook his head. 'Who commands them?'

Penelope shook her head. 'I could find out, I suppose.' She smiled, then raised her eyes and gave an odd smile that seemed to catch only half her face. 'When you let yourself die, it is often hard to bring yourself back to life,' she said. And then, 'Never mind. Pay me no heed. I'm a bitter old woman, and might have been your mother.'

'You aren't old,' Satyrus said, gallantly. Indeed, under the heavy folds of her drapery, she was no less attractive than Auntie Sappho – and that was saying something.

'Hmm,' she said softly. 'I had forgotten the taste of flattery.'

'Dinner, mistress,' Talkes said from the doorway.

Dinner was simple. His rabbit vanished into a stew made of barley and some late-season tubers, with good, plain bread and a harsh local wine. The slaves – or servants, he couldn't tell – ate at the same table as their mistress, a big, dark table worn to a finish like the black glaze of the Athens potters.

He ate and ate. The stew grew on him; he'd been eating whatever his mess cooked up on various beaches for weeks. The wine was acidic, but hardy. The bread was excellent.

'My compliments to your cook,' Satyrus said.

The four Bastarnae girls all tittered among themselves.

'You will stay the night?' Penelope asked.

'Yes, despoina,' Satyrus answered.

'Do not, on any account, try to have sex with my girls. Teax is young enough, and silly enough, to warm your bed – but I can't afford to lose her or feed her baby. Understand, young sir?' Penelope's hard voice was a far cry from her apparent weakness earlier. Satyrus concluded she was a different woman in front of her staff. A commander.

'Yes, despoina,' Satyrus said.

Penelope raised an eyebrow. 'You are a most courteous guest, to obey the whims of an old woman.'

Satyrus went back to eating his soup. Talkes, the overseer, watched every move he made.

Satyrus was just reaching for a third helping of stew when there was a rattle at the gate of the yard.

'Open up in there.' The voice was sing-song, as if a clown or a mime was demanding entry.

Talkes looked at his mistress.

Penelope stood up and looked at Satyrus. 'I'll hide you,' she said. It was a simple statement of fact. She took his hand and led him up into the exedra. She opened a heavy wooden chest and pulled out a quilted wool mattress, which she shook out and placed on her bed. She had his sword, and she handed it to him.

'Get in,' she said.

'I could—' he began.

'You could get us all killed. Now get in.' She held the lid and he climbed in, clutching his sword between his hands. He just fitted, with his ankles pulled almost under his head. The position hurt, and it hurt even more a few minutes later, when the screams in the courtyard began.

The next hour was the longest, and worst, of Satyrus's life. His curse was that he could hear everything. He heard the men in the courtyard, the mime's voice mocking Penelope, the soldiers spreading out to search, the sounds of breaking crockery. He heard himself betrayed by the old slave up the road, and by the blood and offal he'd left cleaning the rabbit.

He heard the clown voice threaten Talkes, and he heard the same voice threaten to sell Penelope into slavery.

'Or I could give you what your father got, stupid woman. Where is he? *Where is he?*' The man sounded honestly angry.

'Do as you will,' Penelope said. 'When Lysimachos comes, you are a dead man.'

'All you dirt farmers sound the same sad song. Look, slut, your precious satrap is *not* coming. I'm lord here now. Eumeles is king of the Euxine and I'll be archon here. Want me to burn the house? Tell me where this man is.' The sing-song voice sounded unnatural, like a priest or an oracle.

'Nothing in the barns!' shouted another man, deeper voiced.

'Search the upstairs – the exedra. Slash every mattress and dump the loom. Everything!' clown-voice said.

'Two slave girls in the cellar. No men.' Another deep voice, this with the accent of the Getae.

'Let's see 'em!' came a shout, and then there were hoots, cat-calls. More broken crockery and the sound of screams, and two men were in the exedra with him, searching. He could hear them poking around, he could *smell* the results as they broke a perfume jar. And below, he could hear Teax being raped – catcalls, sobs.

'May all of you rot from inside! May pigs eat your eyes!' Penelope screamed.

'Shut up, bitch, or you'll be next.' A laugh, and more laughing.

'I want a piece of that,' said a voice near his box.

His knees burned like fire and his sense of his own cowardice rose like the fumes of wine to fill his head. *If I were worth a shit, I would rise from this box and kill my way through these men or die trying*, he thought. He clutched his borrowed sword, prepared to kill the man who opened the chest.

'Athena's curse on you, man with the voice of a woman!' Penelope's voice, strained with rage and terror, carried clearly. 'May your innards rot. May you never know the love of a woman. May jackals root in your innards while you still have eyes to see. May worms eat your eyes. May all your children die before you.'

Teax screamed again.

'Why are we up here? The fucker's long gone – if he was ever here.' The deeper voice kicked the box where Satyrus lay.

Penelope screamed.

'Burn it,' clown-voice said in the courtyard. 'Kill them all. Stupid fucking peasants.'

They lit the roof, but the beams never caught, and Satyrus

71

crept from his box and dragged himself, his legs unusable, down the stairs to the courtyard, heedless of the danger. But poor as they were at arson, they were skilled at killing. Penelope lay in a black pool of blood, so fresh that it glittered in the fitful light of the burning roof, and Teax lay naked. The look on her face – the horror, the terror, the loss of hope – burned itself into his brain. He closed her eyes, fouling his legs with her blood, and he threw his good wool chlamys over her.

Talkes was still alive. Someone had rammed a spear right through his guts, but he was alive when Satyrus found him.

'Killed!' Talkes said. 'All killed!' His eyes met Satyrus. 'You lived.'

Satyrus nodded. 'I did,' he said, feeling wretched.

Talkes nodded. 'I – want to live, too.' He nodded again, and died.

Satyrus thought of burying them all, or putting their bodies in the farmhouse and burning it. Both were gestures he couldn't afford. When his legs would function, he gathered his spear from the entryway and ran off across the orchards towards the coast. Inside his head, he was walling himself off from the image of Teax. He'd done it before, with the girl he'd killed by the Tanais River, with the feeling that he'd abandoned Philokles to die at Gaza. He knew just how to push that image down to concentrate his fear and his hate on one end.

Revenge.

6

PROPONTIS, EARLY WINTER, 311 BC

Two cold camps, because Sarpax, the navarch, didn't fancy showing fires. They rowed up the Propontis into the teeth of a strong autumn wind and passed Byzantium at first light, rowing hard, so that the oarsmen grumbled. They parted with their convoy there and continued north.

Melitta could only think of how much she missed her son. Her breasts were heavy with milk, and they alone served to keep Kineas on her mind all the time – milk so plentiful that it hurt her, and every time she considered donning her armour she flinched from the thought. The lightest brush of fabric on her nipples started the flow again, so that she lived in a perpetual state of embarrassment and her chitons were all stained with milk and the biting wind froze her nipples.

So much for the great adventure of her life. She missed her son, and she played no role at all in the ship, except to watch the horizon and worry.

And miss her son.

Nihmu was little help. She stood in the bow, watching the sea, smelling the air like a dog, scrutinizing every ship they passed as if Leon might be aboard.

It was Nihmu who spotted the patrol ship, just as the water changed colour and the high banks of the Propontis fell away on either side. She came back, her leather boots scuffing the deck.

'Trireme,' she said. 'Just on the horizon.'

Coenus went forward with the navarch and came back shaking his head. 'He's got the wind,' Coenus said. 'And he's coming for a closer look.'

Sarpax joined him. 'Ladies, into the tabernacle, if you please. Serve out weapons. Gentlemen,' he said, as the ship's officers gathered, 'we will act as if we're willing to be boarded until I give the word. The word is "attack". If I give the word, do your best to kill them. The truth is – once they're alongside us, we have more marines. Eh? But if ever they break away, we are all dead men.

73

Eh?' Sarpax's oiled moustache gleamed like the pearl he wore in his right ear.

'I can shoot,' Nihmu said. She grinned at Idomeneus. 'Better than him.'

'Me, too!' Melitta blurted.

'Take your bows to the tabernacle, then,' Sarpax said. 'No archery before I say. Quickly now! If they want a quick peek below decks, we all look as innocent as lambs.'

Melitta opened the hatch cover in the forward bulkhead of the tabernacle – the small, enclosed space just under the bow, the only closed space on a ship as small as a trade pentekonter. Through that narrow aperture, she saw the other ship closing on the opposite tack, her great square sail drawing with all the wind that had forced curses from the rowers for five days.

'Heave to!' the other ship called. 'What ship?'

'Who says?' Sarpax roared. '*Tunny*, fifteen days out of Rhodos.'

'Heave to!' the other commander called. 'I'm coming under your lee.'

The trireme got her mainsail down neatly enough, although they made a hash of closing the last few boat-lengths to come alongside.

'Throw me a grapple!' the other man called.

Melitta could hear Sarpax mutter something as he ordered a grapple thrown across. Then he ordered another.

'Who are *you*?' Sarpax roared.

'*Wasp*, of Pantecapaeum. In service to the king of the Bosporus. Now stand clear – I'm coming across!'

Melitta couldn't see a thing, but the pentekonter was so small that she could feel as six men crossed, the smaller boat rolling and shaking as each new weight came aboard.

'What cargo?' the commander asked.

'Wine for Tomis, copper ore for Gorgippia,' Sarpax replied.

'Twenty silver owls,' the other man demanded. 'Tax.'

'Tax on the open sea?' Sarpax sounded outraged.

'Tax for our suppression of piracy,' the other returned. 'Pay, or I'll sink you.'

Playing the injured merchant, Sarpax cursed. 'You're the only pirate I see here!'

The other man laughed. 'Pay up, little cock.' Melitta heard his feet moving. 'We're looking for a man – twenty to twenty-five years old, tall, dark-haired. Goes by the name of Satyrus. Seen him?'

Sarpax laughed. 'What, walking on the sea?'

The other man did not laugh. 'Satyrus of Alexandria. Know the name?'

'Of course I do. What of it?'

'Seen him?' the other man pressed.

His tone had changed. Melitta felt something stir in her chest, something as profound as the urges of her body. *They were looking for her brother. That meant they didn't have him!*

'Last year at Rhodos. Listen, Trierarch – I'm a poor man with my way to make. Here's your *tax*. Can we go?'

Melitta could hear his booted feet on the narrow plank that ran between the oar benches. 'Where's this cargo? Gods, this is a smelly scow you have here.'

'Wine's in the ballast. Copper pigs *are* the ballast.' Sarpax sounded too confident, as far as Melitta was concerned.

'What's in the bow, then?' the other man asked, and Melitta could hear his steps coming closer.

'Barley and cheese for the lads,' Sarpax said.

'And whatever you put aboard for your private trade, you sly-minded Tyrian. A little purple dye? Some ostrich eggs?' He laughed. 'Open it!'

Melitta put an arrow on her bow. By the light of the scuttle, she saw Nihmu do the same.

'I'd rather not,' Sarpax said. 'It won't be good for you, either.'

'Was that a threat, you dirty fucker? Get it open, right now, and I won't put my boot up your arse.' The other man put his hand on the hatch. Melitta could see it move.

'I'm just so worried about an – attack!' Sarpax said, and the door opened.

Melitta shot the boarder from the length of her forearm, and her shaft went in under his arm where he'd pushed on the hatch. Nihmu's slipped into his right eye.

Before she had her second arrow on the string, all the marines were dead or pushed over the side, and Idomeneus was up on the rail, shooting down into the *Wasp*'s cockpit, the command centre of the enemy ship. Unlike Auntie Nihmu, Melitta had been in a sea fight and she knew Idomeneus. She ran along the deck, avoided slipping in all the blood and stepped past the rowers – the benches were clearing as they all surged up, swords and javelins ready for action, over the rail. *Tunny* lay lower in the water than her opponent, but the difference wasn't enough to deter boarding.

'Just like old times!' Idomeneus said. He shot again.

Melitta couldn't pick a target – the enemy deck was full of men, and most of them were bare-backed oarsmen – her own.

'We're done here,' Idomeneus agreed. He looked at Nihmu, who drew to her ear and lofted a long shot at a man on the stern – an enemy archer. He fell into the sea.

'Nice shot!' Idomeneus said.

It was the last blow of the action. The enemy rowers were paid men – perhaps pressed, perhaps slaves – and they didn't rise from their benches. The *Tunny*'s men cleared the cockpit in no time.

Coenus came back aboard, his sword dry, but a big smile on his face. 'Master Sarpax, you are now owner of that trireme.'

Sarpax was standing on the rail next to Melitta. 'What the fuck do we do with him?' he asked. 'I'm a fucking Rhodian – I can't bear to kill the rowers and sink him.'

Melitta felt the milk starting. As the *daimon* of combat fled her body, she felt all the irritations flood back, but she still had room for a smile. 'I have an idea,' she said. Inside her head, she was rejoicing, because Satyrus was alive.

Two days later, a military trireme slipped on to the beach south of Gorgippia near the Temple of Herakles. It caused a certain consternation at the temple until Melitta jumped over the side and ran all the way up the beach and up the steps. The same old priestess greeted her with open arms. The cataracts in her eyes showed her to be quite blind, but she smiled and embraced Melitta tightly. 'The god told me you would come,' she said. 'Eumeles hunts your brother everywhere since the battle.'

Melitta laughed. 'Eumeles' days are numbered,' she said.

Down on the beach, Nihmu clambered over the side and walked up the shingle until she had dirt and leaves underfoot.

She waved her bow at Melitta and Melitta waved back. Then the Sakje woman fell on her knees and kissed the ground, and let forth a war cry that echoed off the ship and the walls of the temple.

'A Sakje!' the old woman said. 'Once, they used to come here. It has been many years.' She ran a hand over Melitta's face. 'You are a mother!' she said. 'Where is your child? A boy?'

Melitta smiled. 'Back in Alexandria,' she said. 'The milk still runs. But I had to save my brother.'

'Let us go in and see the will of the god,' the old seeress said. 'Your brother is in his care – one hero to another. But it is good you came.' She leaned on Melitta's shoulder and gestured to an attendant, a pretty young girl. 'Lissa can get a tisane for the milk in your breasts. What else do you need? I look forward to playing my part in repaying Eumeles. He has been a hard master to the people here.'

'Horses,' said Nihmu, who had quickly made her way up from the beach. She smiled as she said it. 'The smell here is the smell of home! I can smell the grass! Horses, reverend lady, and we will be gone.'

The old priestess sniffed. 'You took all my best horses last time,' she said. Then she shook her head. 'Oh, the demands of the young – and the gods. I'll have horses fetched.'

A day later, they were mounted, in Sakje clothes, their *gorytoi* by their sides, riding across the first blades of the sea of grass. Behind them, Coenus pulled in his stallion to wave at Sarpax, who paused in his stream of orders to unmoor the *Wasp* to wave back.

'I may never go to sea again,' Nihmu said with a laugh. 'Oh, I pray that Leon is well – but I am happy to be back on the grass!'

'Where to, Nihmu?' Coenus asked. They were at the top of a long ridge that ran east into the foothills of the Caucasus Mountains. North and east, the plains rolled away beneath their feet to the river, and again beyond the ferry. A cold wind blew from the north, rippling the grass and making them shiver.

Melitta pulled her fur cap down over her ears. 'North?'

Nihmu shook her head. 'North and east – to the high ground between the Tanais and the Rha.'

'That's where the bandits live!' Melitta said.

'That's where we will find Ataelus,' Nihmu said. 'He is the bandit now.'

7

NEAR TOMIS, EARLY WINTER, 311 BC

The countryside was empty – not a man moved, no one picked the ripe apples or trampled the grapes. Word of the atrocity at Penelope's farm must have spread quickly.

Satyrus moved warily from hayrick to byre. Twice he found other men hiding – both times he moved on with a nod. There was smoke on the air and he stayed away from the road after he saw a column of two dozen men in armour. His mind closed to thought, he slipped along the coast, south, until he crossed a rocky headland and was able to look down into the harbour. Three triremes on the beach and the *Lotus* anchored in twenty feet of water, moored fore and aft to the breakwater. He lay there for an hour, watching it all, and watching the soldiers in the town, his gut roiling. Then he began the trek back up the coast.

Near nightfall, he heard dogs. He climbed over a low headland near the cursed farm and down into the icy water, and then swam around the point and on down the beach as far as he could stand before muscle spasms and chills drove him ashore. When he landed, the baying of the dogs was far behind. He set to gathering driftwood. He got together a bundle, wrapped it in his girdle and carried it with him as he walked in the surf up the beach, going north in the last light as fast as he could manage. He ran when he was cold and walked when he was tired, thankful for the stew he'd had the night before – stew he'd eaten with people now dead because of him. Like Xenophon and Philokles and all the men who'd fallen at Gaza and the girl in the meadow—

'Stop it,' he said aloud.

Show your gods who you really are, Philokles said at his elbow.

Satyrus smiled, wondering how tired he was. Or fevered. There were red lines on his arm that scared him.

But he felt better immediately.

At full dark, Satyrus sat on the beach and set to building a fire. The dogs were two headlands behind him, their barking lost in the dark. *Black Falcon* would be close, unless he was going to miss his rendezvous altogether. Not worth thinking about that.

He got the fire lit with dry lichen and sparks from the pyrites in his kit and thanked Herakles that it had not rained. He couldn't have started a fire with wet wood. He lacked the practice.

After the first fire, the second was easy. He gathered wood and poured it on, gathered more and started his third fire, made sure that they were in an even line across the beach. Now he could hear the dogs again.

With his fires going, he sat on the dry sand and cleaned his sword and his lonche, polishing the blades carefully with the fine sand by firelight, his concentration so complete that he almost missed the looming bulk of the *Falcon* as he rounded the point.

He left the fires burning, dived into the surf and swam the half-stade to his ship.

Theron's strong arm helped him up the side. 'You look like shit,' he said.

'Due south for Tomis,' Satyrus barked to Diokles. He met Theron's eyes in the light of the ship's lamp.

'We're going for them in the dark?' Theron asked.

'They have quite a force,' Satyrus said. 'Eumeles' men.'

'We could sail past,' Theron said.

'No.' Satyrus was rooting under the helmsman's bench for his kit. 'No, we can't. People are dying for me here, Theron. I just learned a lesson – about being a king. About even trying to be a king. Again.'

'Those are the worst lessons, lad,' Theron agreed. 'I'm sorry—'

'Don't be. I've grown up a little since last night. Call me boy if it suits. Neiron! Arm the crew. All officers!' Satyrus threw his blood-soaked chiton over the side and pulled on a dry one from his pack, then pinned his heavy red chlamys at his neck.

Kallias came from amidships with Apollodorus.

'Gentlemen, this has to be fast and sure,' Satyrus said. 'The enemy has three ships on the beach and the *Lotus*. I want you, Diokles, to put us right between *Lotus* and the breakwater – right over his mooring ropes. We board him and kill anyone aboard. Kallias, tell off every man who's served aboard *Lotus* and enough rowers to move and fight. We'll strip *Falcon*. Diokles – as soon as we're away, take *Falcon* out into the roadstead.'

'And then?' Theron asked.

'And then we're in the hands of the gods,' Satyrus said. 'Are you with me?'

'You won't run off without us?' Theron asked. 'No pointless heroics?'

'I'd bathe in their blood if I could,' Satyrus said. 'But I want to win.'

Men shuffled on the deck. He made them nervous when he talked like that.

'We're with you,' Diokles said.

'Let's do the thing,' Kallias added. His fist hit his open palm with a meaty sound.

Falcon slipped out of the dark of midnight along the path that the moon seemed to light from the open sea to the breakwater. A sentry up on the mole, or perhaps on the deck of the *Golden Lotus*, called out. No one answered.

'Hey there!' he yelled the second time. Satyrus could see his white face in the moonlight. He was on the stern of the *Lotus*. 'Hey!' he said again.

Falcon's bow brushed down the length of Leon's flagship, conned to perfection with Diokles' hands steady on his steering oars and his boatsail already struck.

'Alarm!' the man on the stern called, several minutes too late.

'Boarders away!' Satyrus roared.

He leaped from his own rail on to the rail of the *Lotus* – a feat he'd done fifty times – and down into the waist.

The ship was empty except for a handful of sailors asleep under an awning below the mainmast and the sentry. Satyrus raced for the sentry, who was slow to make the decision as to whether he should run or fight. At the last moment, he got his spear up, but Satyrus took his spear on his own shield and crashed against him, shield to shield, his sword reaching around and cutting the other man's sinews even as they crushed together, and down he went. Satyrus stepped on his neck, crushing his windpipe, and thrust his sword into the man's eye.

The sailors under the awning were spared by their very help-lessness. Otherwise, *Lotus* was empty, and Kallias was already pushing men into their stations. The triemiolia's rig was different enough to cause chaos and similar enough that they were cleared for action before there was any reaction from the town, although dogs were barking on the beach and a voice was calling out from the shore.

'Rowers on your benches?' Kallias shouted. When he got a growl in answer, he blew a whistle. 'Oars out! Look alive there! Give way, all!'

Only two-thirds of the oars were manned, but they shot out and caught the water in two crisp motions, and Satyrus felt the living ship under his feet. He had the steering oars, and now he leaned heavily into the steering rig.

'Hard to starboard!' he called.

'Starboard oars! All banks! Back oars!' Kallias ordered.

Behind them, as they started their turn, *Falcon* began to pull away into the darkness, his oarsmen cheering thinly, only a quarter of the benches manned, but the rowers were scenting victory.

'Blood in the water and silver in our hands,' Satyrus muttered. He was daring himself to shout it aloud – Peleus's war cry, a piratical phrase that gave him goose pimples in the midst of action.

He raised his voice and shouted it. 'Blood in the water!' he cried, and the rowers cheered. 'And silver in our hands!' they chanted back at him, and they were moving faster, Kalos thumping the mainmast to keep the time.

Eumeles' troops were pouring out of the town, and some of them had lit fires on the beach – fires that served only to illuminate their helpless ships.

'Half-speed,' Satyrus called to Kalos, who slowed the rowers. They were moving well.

'Prepare to reverse your benches,' Satyrus called. He waved to Apollodorus. 'Get into the bow and ready to throw the grapples.'

'Aye,' Apollodorus called.

'Back water!' Satyrus yelled. Too fast. He had bitten off too much ...

The oars dug into the star-speckled water, churning it to a black froth, and the *Lotus* slowed. Satyrus pointed his ram just to starboard of the northernmost beached trireme and then steadied the steering oars while the rowers continued to back, cursing him – he could hear the mutters – but the ship slowed, slowed …

Thump. His bow brushed the enemy's stern, clearly backlit by the fires on the beach, and he caught the flicker of the grapples sailing through the clear, dark air.

'Reverse your benches!' Kalos roared over the sounds of combat from the bow. Enemy marines were trying desperately to fend off the *Lotus.*

'Grapples home!' from the bow.

'Give way, all!' Kalos called, and Satyrus had nothing to do but steer steady as the *Lotus* slipped away from the beach stern first. There was a jerk as the ropes on the grapples caught and tugged – the whole weight of the enemy ship on the oarsmen – but they knew they were rowing for the value of the prize and they pulled, short, powerful strokes at Kalos's command, and the enemy ship slid into the water and followed them as meekly as a lamb following a girl to market, coasting along behind them with his marines still struggling, now fighting for their lives. A stade off the beach they lost heart and tried to surrender, but Apollodorus had his orders, and he drove them into their own stern and then over the side, to drown.

Panting with exertion and speaking too quickly and too loudly, Apollodorus came to the cockpit with a shield and a helmet, the tangible signs of their victory. 'Ours, by the gods!' he said. 'I didn't lose a man – once they felt their keel grate on the sand, they panicked and we reaped them like ripe wheat.'

Satyrus smacked him on his backplate. 'Well done. But they've left the fires burning and we need every hull. Let's take another.'

Apollodorus nodded, put his hands on his knees and crouched, breathing hard. 'Let me get my breath!'

Satyrus nodded. 'Kalos!' he called.

His acting oar master ran aft. 'Aye?'

'I intend to empty *Falcon* and take every man.' Satyrus said. 'Push 'em all forward with arms to help the marines. You run the oars and have Diokles at the helm.'

'Done,' Kalos pointed at the looming mast of the *Falcon.* 'Mind your helm, sir!' he shouted, and Satyrus had to steer hard to avoid putting the stern of his uncle's flagship right on the bow of his own ship. So much to watch, all the time – he leaned on the oars and prayed while Kalos bellowed for the oars to come inboard.

But he got them alongside – backing was easier, in many ways – and they lashed the captured trireme to the *Falcon*.

'Let's get everyone aboard *Lotus*,' Satyrus called across to Theron, who waved a torch in reply. In the time it took to swear an oath, the skeleton crew of the *Falcon* was across, all armed with spears or javelins. They left the other two ships floating free, lashed together.

'They're *still* lighting new fires on the beach,' Diokles said. 'They've never fought at night, that's for sure.'

'The southernmost boat looks to be a little bigger,' Theron said. 'Maybe just a trick of the firelight.'

They were already inbound, Diokles at the helm, and the southernmost boat *did* look bigger.

'Someone's fighting on the beach,' Theron said. He went forward, still favouring his left hip but moving fast despite his full armour.

Satyrus went with him, having no immediate duty. He stepped up into the *Lotus*'s ram-box. It was packed with marines and sailors, and Satyrus stepped up on the rail and used the boatsail-mast shrouds to walk around the rail to the bow. Theron was right on his heels.

There were sounds of fighting from the beach – shouts and the clash of bronze and iron and a man bellowing in rage or fear – or both.

'I will burn this town and every arse-cunt in it!' sang that voice – the clown voice.

Satyrus realized that all his muscles had clenched together, and he made himself relax. 'The town has risen against the raiders,' he said.

'Easier pickings for us,' a marine said. 'They can't cover the beach and the boats at the same time.'

Satyrus shouted orders as he climbed around Theron and then ran along the rail, heedless of the fall to the water and instant death for a man in armour. 'Apollodorus – I'm going to put us ashore. Empty the boat – you take the marines, Theron, Kalos – take the sailors.'

'What?' Theron asked, but Satyrus had moved on. He jumped down to the deck and ran along the gangway, repeated his orders to Kalos and the deck crew, and then ran aft to Diokles.

'Past the southernmost boat – turn us around and beach us stern first. Everyone over the side – everyone.' Satyrus was bouncing on his toes, scared by his own decision but committed to it. The local men were dying on the beach, facing professional soldiers and paying the price, fighting in the dark. He was not going to leave them to it.

Diokles shook his head, his teeth gleaming in the distant firelight. 'You're mad, you know that? Didn't your friend Theron say something about not running off in mad heroics?' He drew himself up and shouted, 'Starboard rowers – reverse benches!' He grinned at Satyrus. 'I'm mad too. We'll have them all – or die trying.'

Satyrus wasn't even thinking of the potential prizes – only of the fact that Calchus, his father's guest-friend, was almost certainly fighting on the beach against the men who had killed Penelope – raped Teax. People he barely knew.

Perhaps he was mad.

'Ready about ship!' Diokles called. To Satyrus, he said, 'I have the ship. Go and organize your landing.'

Satyrus saluted him and ran forward, his greaves already chafing at his ankles, his shield banging against the shoulder-plate of his cuirass. 'As soon as the stern bites the sand,' he called, 'marines and deck crew over the side. Don't pull *Lotus* up the beach – just form as you practised with Theron – marines in the front, sailors in the next ranks, oarsmen behind. Understand?'

Theron was shaking his head, but he didn't say anything.

'Straight up the beach and into the enemy,' Satyrus said.

'We ought to be behind them,' Apollodorus agreed.

'Don't stop to throw a javelin or any of that crap,' Satyrus said. 'They're formed up – I saw it in the firelight. Get right into them. Stay together – don't kill each other in the dark.'

'Beach!' several men called. Satyrus saw that his time for planning was past – they were so close to the southernmost enemy trireme that their oars almost brushed his beak, and then Kalos shouted 'Oars in!' and they rammed the beach so hard that every man on deck fell flat.

'Over the side,' Satyrus yelled, getting to his feet. He jammed his helmet on his head and jumped into the water, found it deeper than he expected – almost to his chest – and started pushing ashore, the cold water like a reminder of mortality. 'Form up! Form up!' he yelled, over and over again, and Kalos was ahead of him on the strand, yelling the same, and Apollodorus had the marines in a gaggle, then the gaggle began to spread out and became a line.

'Sailors!' Satyrus yelled. Sailors – and oarsmen – were coming up, taking posts behind the thin line of armoured men. Half a stade down the beach, other men were shouting by the fires. Closer, an archer shot and the arrow plucked at the crest on Satyrus's helmet. Another arrow hit his ankle *hard* and he looked, expecting to see the shaft pinning his leg to the beach, but the arrow was gone, and his ankle bone hurt as if he'd been kicked by a horse.

No idea what had been happening here, except that there were bodies by the stern of the middle boat and no defenders. Battle madness raged with common sense.

'Diokles!' Satyrus called. 'Take twenty men and get these hulls afloat!'

A roar of approval from his own oarsmen – floating the enemy hulls insured against defeat, meant there would be no pursuit.

Apollodorus waved his spear. Theron was standing next to him, a tower of bronze in the firelight.

'Ready?' Satyrus called. His voice was going – too much shouting. 'On me – let's go!'

It wasn't really a phalanx – it was more like a mob with some shared direction, a hundred men trotting down the beach with a thin front edge of bronze and iron. The sailors were contemptuous of formations, and they opened out as they ran. Men fell over bodies, driftwood – a whole file struck an upturned fishing smack in the dark and was lost, a human eddy of confusion – but the mass swept down the beach, Satyrus running at their head, past the other ship, past the fires, up to the top of the beach and almost into the town.

And there they were – suddenly, there were men on the seaward edge of the agora, where most of the town's fishing boats had been pulled up clear of the storm line by careful men. In and among those hulls, the invaders were killing the townsmen and the farmers of the countryside around the town.

'Kill them all!' the sing-song voice said.

Satyrus saw him, standing on the upturned hull of a big fishing smack.

'*Falcons – charge!*' Satyrus forced his lungs to fill and bellow the orders, and his men growled and cheered and fell on the raiders.

Satyrus ran up and killed an unarmoured man with a spear-blow to the kidney, so that the man's blood burst forth and he fell, his eyes huge as he rolled on the wound like a man trying to put out a fire, and Satyrus was past him.

His next opponent wore armour, and the man was turning when Satyrus came up and jammed his spear, the point guided by the hands of the gods, into the armpit of the man's shield arm – a miraculous blow, but the man was down, crumpled, and Satyrus had to stop his charge because he was deep in the enemy ranks. They were turning, and Satyrus planted his feet.

'*Falcons!*' he roared. He thrust hard with his spear – it caught the top of a helmet and glanced off, but he snapped the man's head sharply and the man went down, unconscious, stunned or simply hurt. Satyrus didn't follow his fall – he whirled and stabbed in the other direction, and this man – an officer with a plume – caught the thrust on his shield and stabbed back, but Theron blocked the blow, stepped in and hammered away at the man with a sword, pounding the blade down again and again until the man fell.

Now there were men all around Satyrus shouting '*Falcon!*'. Satyrus pushed forward beside Theron. He thrust and thrust again, and blows came back, a rain of painful iron that banged on his shield and clanged against his bronze helmet, making his arm throb with pain under the shield. There was no blocking them – it was dark, and Satyrus couldn't see any more to parry – so he set his feet again and *pushed* with his shield. An enemy trapped his spear and it snapped between the shields. He pushed again, shouting mindlessly. There was an enormous blow to his head, and the taste of copper in his mouth. He sank to one knee, but he knew where that would lead. He *pushed* with his legs, got erect and lashed out with a flurry of blows from his butt-spike wielded as a club – roaring, shouting, his voice raw.

The enemy broke. It wasn't the slow erosion of will that Satyrus had experienced at Gaza, but a sudden cracking, as if an irrigation dam had burst on a farm, the warm spring rain pouring down the hillside and ruining a spring planting. The raiders broke in a few heartbeats, and they were running off into the dark.

The Falcons stopped. No one called an order – but all the men around Satyrus simply knelt in the blood-soaked dirt and panted like dogs.

'Who in Hades are you people?' a voice from the darkness growled. 'By Pluton, giver of good gifts – I think we owe you our freedom.'

Satyrus found that his right hand was still locked around his butt-spike. He let go and forced himself to his feet. His head was ringing and something was dripping down his beard. He licked it; it was blood.

'By Herakles,' Satyrus said, 'I think we may owe you our lives.' He walked towards the other man, just visible with a crowd behind him at the far edge of the agora. When Satyrus got clear of his own men, he called, 'I'm Satyrus, son of Kineas,' and kept walking forward.

'Ah! Guest-friend!' came the voice. An old man – too old to be wearing bronze – came forward from his own mob. His white beard stuck out of an old-style Attic helmet.

'Calchus?' Satyrus asked.

'By Zeus, protector of oaths, this is something to be remembered!' Calchus said, and Satyrus was swallowed in a metallic embrace. 'We heard you were in the countryside. It was too good to be true, but when the attack started in the harbour, I raised the hoplites – what's left of them.'

'We heard you,' Theron said.

'But they beat us,' Calchus said. 'Just the way they beat us the other day. Bah – we're not the men we were twenty years ago.'

Satyrus was bleeding from his nose; he couldn't get it to stop

88

and it distracted him. Suddenly his ankle hurt like blazes and his arm throbbed from stress on the old wound.

'We ran,' Calchus said. 'Good thing, too. Because they followed us into the town and you came up behind them. They turned on you—'

'Almost had us, too!' Theron said.

'And I rallied the boys for one more try. Ares, it was close!'

'Too close,' Satyrus said through the liquid in his nose. 'Mercenaries?'

Calchus grunted. 'War whores,' he said. 'Ahh – I feel like a man tonight!' He laughed.

'What of the men who ran?' Satyrus asked. He was looking at his own men now. There were gaps in the ranks.

Calchus pointed his chin at the mob behind him. 'See? Not just hoplites – every slave in town. Bastards have raped and killed their fill. Every housewife's on the roof with a handful of tiles – every boy with a sling is in the streets.'

'In that case, there'll be a lot of dead kids in the morning,' Theron said. He shrugged his great shoulders. 'They need our help, Satyrus. I assume that's why you landed us – to save the town?'

Satyrus grunted.

'You're a god-sent hero,' Calchus said. 'Athena Nike, you even *look* like your father.'

It was hard to feel like a hero with blood running out of his nose and his arm on fire, much less face the idea that he should go into those dark and narrow streets and fight again.

But he could hear the screams already – women and children and men, too.

'All right,' Satyrus said. 'Marines only. Deck crew, get all the armour and shields lying around and follow us. Where's Kalos?'

'Right here,' the man said, his satyr-face showing from under a battered Boeotian helmet.

'Take all the oarsmen and help Diokles get the ships off the beach,' Satyrus managed. His brain seemed to be moving along without his body.

Kalos nodded heavily. 'Can I take a nap first?'

'Those men fleeing might decide to make a fight for their boats,' Theron put in.

'All right, all right.' Kalos shook his head. 'Anyone have a wineskin?' he called out to his men, who were already stripping the dead.

'Apollodorus?' Satyrus called.

'Took an arrow back by the boats,' Theron said. 'The longer we wait—'

Satyrus had to force himself to move. 'Let's do the thing,' he croaked, and shambled off towards the town. Seeing a spear, he leaned down and picked it up – a marine's lonche without a butt-spike.

Good enough.

There was a house on fire a few streets inland, and the fire was catching. Calchus was bellowing orders to his own people, and the hoplites came and joined Satyrus's marines – just a dozen or so men in armour.

'Where are all your men?' Theron asked.

'Face down in the sand,' said a voice that rang with fatigue and anger. 'No quarter for these fuckers.'

They moved cautiously into a broad street lined with ware-houses and a pair of wine shops.

'I'm Kletes,' one of the local hoplites said. 'I know this part of town. Follow me.'

Just like that, Kletes was in charge, and under his direction they spread out to cover two parallel streets and swept inland. Twice they found bodies – once an invader, already stripped naked, the next time two young slave boys with spear wounds front and back. Then they heard fighting a street away – close to the source of the burning.

'Straight at 'em!' Kletes called, and Satyrus obeyed as naturally as Theron or any of the others. They jogged up the streets and into a crossroads – too small to be a square, but a small opening. A dozen invaders were locked with a crowd of locals – fishermen and their wives. A roof tile struck Satyrus's helmet, and his head roared again and he lost a step. The others crashed into the thin line of the invaders – desperate men now, with nowhere to run.

Satyrus was out of the fight, and so he saw the trap. 'Ware!' he yelled. 'Our flanks!' Some canny bastard had used his own men as bait, holding half a dozen troopers in reserve in the shadow of a big house.

Satyrus was alone against the rush. He shook his head to clear it and then, without much thought, cocked his arm back and *threw* the lonche overarm at the leading enemy, backlit by the house on fire.

The throw was true and the man never tried to block or duck – a spear thrown in the dark is hard to see. He went down with a clatter – *Ares, the raiders are well equipped*, Satyrus thought as he ripped his sword from the scabbard under his arm and charged three steps into the second man, knocking the bastard flat on the earth. Satyrus pounded his right foot into the man's throat even as he put his shoulder and shield into the third man, the routines of pankration adapting to fighting with weapons by the light of a house-fire. The third man's spear came past his shoulder, slicing bare skin on his lower bicep, but Satyrus got his sword in close, cut at the man's hands and then *around* his helmet, smashing into the back of his head – once, twice and the man was down.

The other three hesitated.

'He's just one man!' that hated voice sang. 'All together!'

Satyrus stepped back – they weren't eager to come to grips with him – and spat. It wasn't a gesture of contempt – his mouth was full of blood. He looked over his shield at the three of them, and they kept their distance, more than a spear's length away.

'Why don't you come and try me yourself?' Satyrus heard himself say. Inside his helmet, he flashed a painful smile. It was the kind of line he dreamed of saying. A god had put it in his mouth. He felt his back straighten, he stood straighter and the bronze didn't weigh his limbs.

None of the three men came forward. Behind Satyrus, he heard the roar of men fighting and dying and the screams of women, and he thought of Teax. 'Harder than killing women in the countryside, isn't it, you bastard?' he shouted.

'Fuck you, kid,' the voice said. The middle warrior pushed forward. 'Let's get him and run for it,' the voice added. 'No fair fights in the dark, kid.'

Satyrus waited one beat, crouched and then leaped to the right, engaging the man at the end of the enemy group. He landed, put his shield up over his head, leaned low and cut *under* the man's shield, but his sword rang on the man's greave. Nonetheless, the man stumbled back, and Satyrus pressed him, got his shield up and took a heavy blow on it from his left, then tripped over something on the ground – *clang*, and he was down in the dirt, his shield face up, arms spread wide.

'Nice try,' the voice said, and Satyrus saw the man stomp on his shield – unbelievable pain in his already wounded arm, a white flare of pain. Satyrus screamed.

Neither Satyrus nor his opponents saw Theron coming, but the athlete knocked clown-voice flat, turned on his partner and dispatched him with two quick spear-thrusts to the face.

Quick as a cat, clown-voice was back on his feet, his spear licking at Theron in the orange light. The fire was starting to spread.

Satyrus got the shield off his damaged arm, and screamed again. He couldn't help it. But he had endured years of pain – of fighting in the palaestra, broken bones and contusions galore – and he somehow stuffed the arm into his sword belt, unable to breathe with the pain, and for the third time that evening he rose to his feet like Atlas shouldering the weight of the heavens. He felt for the dagger that was strapped to the inside of his shield, got his good right hand around it, blood still flowing over his face, and slammed the knife into clown-voice's kidneys while the man had his whole being focused on Theron. The triangular blade punched right through the bronze and sank a hand's depth with the power of Satyrus's blow. Clown-voice stumbled, turned his head and got Theron's spear through the bridge of his nose.

Satyrus sank to his haunches and then fell over, twisting to keep his broken arm off the ground and landing heavily.

'How bad are you, boy?' Theron asked.

Satyrus screamed. 'Arm – broken!' he said, and then crouched on the blood-soaked earth, wishing that he could faint but not quite able to do it. Instead, he vomited.

He lost track of the actions around him, not quite unconscious and not quite able to register anything, floating on a tide of pain like a beached ship refloated on the highest tide. Theron said some things to him, and he found himself explaining that in

92

Olympic pankration, he would never have double-teamed an opponent – he was explaining this to an offical wearing a long white robe and a chaplet of olive leaves, who looked at him with weary distaste.

'We were fighting in the dark,' he said. 'Not the Olympics! The man refused single combat!'

The old man shook his head, and then Theron said something about the ship.

'What ship?' Satyrus asked.

'We have poppy juice,' Calchus said clearly. 'I'll get him some.'

Fire all around him, and then he was walking, hands guiding him, more pain as someone handled his arm and he screamed and fell and the pain almost – *almost* – knocked him out. Satyrus gasped, gulped air and voices told him to drink, and he drank a thin, milky liquid – bitter and somehow *bright*.

Then he was cold, and then hot, and then the colour of the fire exploded around him, so that colour defined everything – war and love and missing friends, Amastris's kisses, Philokles' love, all had a colour – and he was swept away on a surge of these subtle shades, lifted and carried, and the pain roared its lavender disappointment and went far away.

8

Against Coenus's judgment, she didn't hide her identity.

The first night, they stopped at a byre, a small stone cottage with fields that stretched away from the track. The people were Maeotae, dark-haired, cheerful, with a yard full of freckled girls in good wool smocks, and two young boys who were sword-fighting with sticks.

Dinner was mutton, served with barley soup on fine Athenian plates. And good Greek wine.

The farmer was Gardan, and his wife was Methene. They eyed the travellers with some suspicion, and spoke quietly at their own end of the great table that dominated the house's one big room.

After dinner – delicious, and doubly so for the cold rain that blew against the door – Gardan moved to their end of the table, the end closest to the hearth, for he was a hospitable man. 'What news, then?' he asked. He was speaking to Coenus.

'We come from Alexandria,' Melitta said.

The farmer gave her a startled look, as if he hadn't expected her to speak. But he smiled. 'As far as that?' he said, but he wasn't very interested.

Coenus sipped his wine. 'Do you care for news from the Inner Sea?' he asked.

The farmer shook his head. 'Not really,' he said. 'Nothing to do with folks hereabouts.' He glanced at their bows, stowed snugly in a hutch by the door. 'Not so many Sakje folk on the roads any more,' he said. And let that sit.

'That's what they said at the Temple of Herakles,' Melitta said.

'Temple has no love for the tyrant,' the farmer said. He looked from under shaggy brows, and the comment was muttered out into the air, as if he could disclaim it, if he needed to.

'Who is this tyrant?' Nihmu asked.

Melitta was disturbed to realize that Nihmu's leg was pressed close to Coenus's under the table.

'Eumeles of Pantecapaeum. He claims all these lands, but

mostly, it's Upazan of the Sauromatae who sends his raiders to collect what they call "tax".' The farmer shrugged.

'He's no proper tyrant,' Methene said. 'We used to have law.'

'Tish, woman. Not the place.' The farmer gave his wife a mild look and turned back to his guests.

'You will have law again,' Melitta said.

The farmer nodded, as if this was a commonplace, but his wife looked at Melitta and then put her weaving back on the loom. 'Husband,' she said, standing, 'she's a Twin.'

Coenus stood up. 'We don't want trouble.'

Gardan went to his wife. Only when he stood between her and the strangers did he turn. Their children clustered around them, aware that something dangerous had just been said.

'Is that true?' Gardan asked.

'Yes,' Melitta said, ignoring Coenus. 'I am Srayanka's daughter, Melitta of Tanais.'

'By the Ploughman,' Gardan said.

'I knew you in the yard,' Methene said. She shrugged. 'But my eyes is old, and I thought again.' She looked at the three of them, all on their feet. 'You have nothing to worry about in this house,' she said. 'We've sheltered Temerix and his foreign lady many times, and their band, too.'

'Temerix?' Coenus said. 'Temerix the smith?'

Gardan relaxed a little. 'The same,' he said.

'I thought he was dead,' Coenus said.

'Not last summer, anyway,' Gardan said. 'You really a Twin, lady? You three going to raise the Sakje?'

'Yes,' Melitta said.

'Only we ain't seen a Sakje in four years,' he said. 'Word is that the Sauromatae have wiped them off the plains. Leastwise, round here.'

Melitta looked at Coenus, and then at Nihmu.

'If you make war on the tyrant ...' Gardan said, and paused. 'He's a hard master, and no friend to the farmers,' Gardan said. He raised his cup. 'But we do well enough. Lady, if you plan to make a war in the Tanais, be sure. Be fucking sure. Because the farm folk will rise for your name alone.' He nodded, emphasizing his words. 'Name alone. I will myself. But if you fail – by the Ploughman, he'll make us slaves on our own farms. What he wants, the bastard. Sorry, wife.'

But Methene nodded. 'Truth, guests. If you have some wild plan to raise us to make war – pass us by.'

Melitta went to bed in a pallet of river rushes on the floor, having refused to move the farmer and his wife off their bed. She had much to think on.

The issue of her identity arose again at the ferry over the Hypanis River the next day, where it flowed across the soggy autumn fields near the great cairn at Lahrys. Melitta could remember her first crossing here, with Upazan's horsemen behind her.

Coenus looked at it. 'This is what – the Hypanis?' he asked.

She nodded.

Coenus shook his head. 'Why do the Assagatje give the same name to every river? Tanais – or Hypanis. There's one by Olbia.'

She shrugged. 'And this is the Hypanis of the east. Don't be so Greek.' She looked around. 'Philokles cut their rope. I hope they don't remember!'

But they did remember. The ferryman knew her as soon as he saw her, and shook his fist at Coenus. 'There's new law here!' he yelled. 'Rope-cutters! Worse than thieves!'

Melitta pushed her horse forward. 'I am Melitta,' she said. 'Queen of the Eastern Assagatje.' It made her choke a little just to say it. 'This is my river – my ford. You pay your taxes to my people.'

'Not any more, barbarian!' the ferryman shouted, pushing his boat off into the stream. 'This is all the land of the king of the Bosporus. No barbarian rides here but the king's man – Upazan!' But the man was clearly afraid.

Coenus restrained her – she was about to ride into the river.

'Forget him,' Coenus said. 'I wish you'd let us ride on. He'll tell all the world.'

'Good,' Nihmu said. She smiled a strange, faraway smile. 'Eumeles will spend the winter gnawing on the ends of these rumours.'

Coenus pointed at the swollen river. 'Eumeles' rage won't help us cross the Hypanis.'

Nihmu shrugged. 'Let's stay on the south bank until she's a little stream in the foothills of the mountains,' she said. 'I was a little girl here, before the Great War. I know the paths.'

Coenus pulled his cloak tighter. Then he dismounted, opened his bedroll and donned a second cloak. 'It must be old age,' he said. 'But I'm cold just thinking about the foothills of the Caucasus.' He smiled at both of them. 'I'd like to find Temerix.'

Nihmu nodded. 'I, too. But he could be anywhere in these hills.'

They rode east for two days, through fields shorn of their wheat and then across scraggly fields of barley that gave way to smaller plots and bigger patches of woods between narrow villages where highland peasants raised oats and sheep. After the second night, Nihmu refused to sleep in another peasant hut – the last one had held more insects than food. But the people knew Temerix, and they were hardy folk – a bow and an axe in every hut. They disdained the valley farmers and their slavish obedience to the tyrant, but none knew where to find Temerix.

'He comes and goes, like,' said an old Maeotae, braver than the rest.

'Bah, dirt people,' Nihmu said with all the contempt of the sky people.

'You've lived in a house for ten years,' Coenus said.

'A house with a breeze and a bath,' Nihmu said, 'and still I've wished every night for stars. Alexandria – oh, the haze in the sky. Tonight, I will feast my eyes on the whole of the sky god's road!'

Coenus hunched in his cloak. 'Tonight, I'll freeze,' he said. The two women wore trousers and heavy coats. Coenus, the most aristocratic Hellene Melitta had ever known, was wearing a chiton and a chlamys and no trousers at all. High Thracian boots were his only concession to riding.

'You should wear trousers,' Nihmu said. Not for the first time.

'When Zeus Soter comes down from Olympus and shows me how to put them on,' Coenus answered.

'Blasphemy!' Melitta said, because an argument with her child's grandfather passed the time.

Coenus shook his head. 'It would be blasphemy if I claimed not to believe in Zeus,' he said. 'It would be *hubris* if I refused to obey his bidding to wear trousers. As it is, I'm secure in the knowledge that should I run across a Megaran ephor in this gods-forsaken wilderness of peasants, wolves and winter, I will still look like a civilized man.'

Melitta had to laugh, because Coenus, despite his manners and his accent, was the best of hunting companions, a man with a hard-won knowledge of the plants and animals of the wilderness, a man who rode from dawn until dusk without complaint. Coenus was a good rider, even by Sakje standards.

He just wouldn't wear trousers.

'My mother used to say that my father wore trousers,' Melitta said.

'Your father was in love with your mother,' Coenus said. 'Love makes people do strange things.' He shrugged, as if acknowledging that he was doing a strange thing that moment.

'You would be more comfortable,' Nihmu said.

Coenus laughed and rubbed at a bare thigh, red with cold. 'That's just it,' he said. 'I *wouldn't* be more comfortable.'

They continued to ride east.

The next day, they saw a herd of deer in the distance and they killed one, riding wide of the herd and then pushing it back on Nihmu's bow, the Sakje way. Coenus shook his head at the waste – he wanted to ride in among the deer with his javelins, but it was not to be. They needed meat, not sport.

Nihmu's arrows did the job, and Coenus butchered the young buck and they all rode on, bloody, with fresh meat in net bags on all the mounts. That night they feasted on venison and then had to stand watches to protect the rest of the meat from wolves. In the morning they rose early, built up the fire and ate again. The villages and farms of the high ground were gone. They were in the empty space, where of old the Sakje had ridden.

'I feel more like a Sakje every day,' Nihmu said.

Coenus said nothing. He was sitting on his haunches, looking into the fire. Melitta noticed how often his eyes fell on Nihmu, and how often the Sakje woman's eyes rested on Coenus.

'We'll need to hunt again in three days,' he said. 'And the horses will need something better than this grass if we're going all the way to the Tanais high ground.'

Nihmu put a hand on his cheek – a very personal gesture, for her, and one that made Melitta's spine stiffen. 'Hush – you worry too much, Greek man.'

They laughed at each other for a moment, and Melitta was distinctly uncomfortable.

They rode east again all day, and by the evening the Hypanis looked small enough to cross – the more so as they'd soaked themselves crossing a pair of tributaries that day. There was a tiny settlement – three stone huts and a cairn. The peasants at the ford said that the cairn and kurgan – a big one, hundreds of years old – were called Tblissa.

'I was here as a girl,' Nihmu said. They made a fire at the foot of the kurgan, and used a fire pit that had cinders as deep as Coenus bothered to dig. 'Tip-lis was a chieftain of the old times, when the people rode into Persia and made war on the Medes and the Great King. He guards this ford.'

Melitta was falling asleep, lulled by the sound of their horses eating grain purchased for ready cash from the peasants at the ford.

'We should lay out our blanket rolls,' Nihmu said.

Melitta sat up. 'I'll do it,' she said.

Neither of the other two denied her, so she placed herself in the middle.

They didn't quibble or look askance at the arrangement, and she felt guilty for her suspicions. She was warmer than she wanted to be, almost crushed with the weight of sleepers on either hand, and then she was asleep.

In the morning, they splashed through the ford, their baggage riding high to keep clear of the water, and then they were across. Coenus built a big fire and they dried everything that was damp and changed. It was too cold now to ride in wet leather or even wet wool.

Even the horses came up to the fire.

'Still some weeks until winter,' Nihmu said, and Coenus grunted. Nihmu was warming herself by the fire, naked, and Coenus was smiling at her, and Melitta wanted to growl at them. *Were they flirting, or serious?*

'Winter will come soon enough,' Coenus said. He held his

hands out to the fire. 'Sooner to some of us than others,' he added. He was fifteen years older than Nihmu and thirty years older than Melitta.

An hour later they were away, climbing out of the vale of the Hypanis and heading north, into winter.

Later that day there was snow – not enough to bury them, but enough to worry them. They kept going through it and made camp in the deep woods at the top of the biggest ridge they'd encountered so far – a quarter of the day to climb it. Now they were out of the peopled country, on the high plains where only the Sakje travelled, and Nihmu admitted to a certain dismay. There wasn't a fire sign or a track to be seen.

'Wait a few days,' Coenus said.

'The Dog Horses should have had a camp in that valley,' Nihmu said. But she shrugged and ate three-day-old venison.

That night, Melitta found that Coenus had built a shelter of brush and branches – very low, but snug and warm. He was quite proud of it, in a male way, but she had to admit that it *was* well contrived. He raked the fire into a heap of coals near the mouth of the shelter and they all got in. Melitta found that he'd built the shelter around their blanket rolls and that Nihmu was in the middle.

It seemed pointless to protest. Melitta was determined to think no more about it. Later, she thought that perhaps she would stay awake and see what happened. But the next thing she knew, it was the grey light of morning, and she could hear the fire crackling away outside as Coenus fed the shelter into the fire. Melitta got up, rolled the blankets and tied them in neat bundles, the habits of her youth returning quite naturally, and looked around for Nihmu.

'Swimming,' Coenus said. He shrugged. 'I know – insane. But she insisted.'

Below them, Nihmu shrieked like a woman in childbirth, and Melitta could see her splashing water in the stream. When she came up to them, her skin was bright red, but she had filled the water bottles and their one kettle. Coenus put it on the fire and they had hot herb tea with a little wine in it before they set off.

That day, they rode north and east on high ridges. It didn't snow again, and the sun came out, fresh and warm, and the horses were playful.

That night, they laughed at the fire, and sang Sakje songs to Coenus, who shook his head and told them they were both barbarians. Melitta discovered that she didn't really care if two of her favourite adults were choosing to behave badly.

'None of my concern,' she said to the darkness.

They sang more, and Coenus repaid them with parts of the *Iliad*, sung in a curious high voice that soothed and scared at the same time.

'That part has a curious meaning,' Coenus said when he was done telling of Thetis bringing new armour to her son by the sea.

'Hush,' Nihmu said, putting two fingers across his lips. 'How often were you told as a child that retelling spoils the story?'

Coenus grinned like a boy. 'Too true, my lady.' He sprang to his feet. 'I'll tell it to the wolves instead,' he said, and walked off into the darkness.

Melitta thought that her child's grandfather was behaving like a much younger man.

Seconds later he was back. His return took Melitta by surprise – she had just snuggled closer to Nihmu to share the other woman's warmth. Coenus sprang past them and cast the deerskin from their kill straight on to the fire. It was untanned and still wet, if a little frozen, and they smelled burning hair and roasting meat.

'Right below us,' Coenus hissed. 'Bottom of the valley. Twenty riders, all Sauromatae.'

'You saw them?' Nihmu asked, incredulous. It was quite dark.

'Heard them,' Coenus said. 'Get the horses.'

'I can just talk to them,' Nihmu said. 'The easterners would never trouble a Sakje party.'

'Never is a long time,' Coenus said. 'The sea of grass is changed, and not for the better.'

Coenus pulled the deerskin off the fire and they packed in the last of the firelight. Melitta's heart pounded. While she packed her cloaks and blankets on her horse's rump, she actually saw the fire glimmering below her in the valley.

'They must have seen ours,' Melitta said.

Coenus shook his head, a blur of motion in the dark. 'No – I put the camp in a hollow. I'm used to this sort of thing.'

Melitta was annoyed with herself on a number of different levels – for allowing Coenus to make camp in *her* country, for not knowing as much about stealth as the Greek man.

They heard a horse noise just over the rim of the hill.

'They're coming for us after all!' Coenus hissed. 'Leave the rest and ride!'

He was on the back of his horse and moving, and there was a hissing in the air. Melitta got her leg over her horse's haunch and wished for her dear Bion, who would have been been ten strides away by now. But she settled her seat and grabbed her bow, ready strung, from her gorytos. Even as she rode her mount in among the trees, she had an arrow on the string. Some skills are never forgotten.

Now she could hear shouts behind her – Sauromatae voices, their eastern accents and odd words carrying clearly on the cold air.

'They were right here!' a young man shouted. 'Look! Coals and ashes!'

'I shot one!' another shouted.

Melitta put her heels to her mount, dropped her bow back into its cover and her arrow into the quiver behind the bow case. There was nothing to shoot and riding through trees in the dark was hard enough.

She kept going downhill, sure that this, at least, would carry her *away* from her pursuers. When she arrived at the base of the next valley, after a disorienting ride whose distance could only be measured in fear, she jumped her horse over the thin, black stream and rode along the open meadow, looking up the hill behind her to the south.

She couldn't see horse or riders, but there were shapes moving on the hillside, and shouts.

She had lost Nihmu and Coenus and all the packhorses. She was alone in the dark, and there were ten or more riders pursuing her.

She allowed her horse to find its own way along the meadow

to the base of the next ridge while she considered her options. She wasn't afraid – or rather, fear underlay her analysis, but didn't push it.

They had multiple horses; she had but one, and that one was average at best. That meant that a single error – a foot in a hole, a bad cut – and she would be taken. She knew a thousand tales of the people about pursuits like this – sometimes the hero ran, and sometimes he pursued. Such tales were often about the merit of horses.

There was already snow on top of each ridge, but none in the valleys. Plenty of light on the snow – none at all in the woods.

She went up the next ridge, clucking at her animal to make him go faster, taking the chance of laming him to gain the wood line and its relative concealment. She chewed on the end of her hair, and then, decision made, she rolled off her horse and led him in among the trees. Somewhere in her hasty dismount she lost arrows from her quiver and cursed, but she moved fast, tethered her gelding just over the crest of the next ridge and came back across the top with an arrow on her bow and two javelins from her saddle case tight in her cold fingers.

It felt better to be the hunter than the prey. She lay down in a hollow of grass near the ridge's summit, the frost heavy and white on her dark blue soldier's cloak. Then she waited.

She'd spent a fair amount of time waiting in her life – waiting for assassins, waiting for labour pains. She had the patience of the survivor. She lay still, colder and colder, her heart running faster or slower as the sounds of her pursuers came to her on the frosty air. The stars were different here, but childhood memory said that it was the middle of the second watch.

She bit her lips to avoid nodding off. The whole idea of ambushing her pursuers seemed foolish now – they had seemed so close behind her, but now they seemed cautious. She thought of rising to her feet, collecting her horse and fleeing again – but then there was a noise, quite close.

That option was gone.

'One of them came this way!' a young voice shouted. 'I have found an arrow!'

'Hush!' an older voice said.

They were close. Without turning her head, she could see a shadow – and a rising cloud of steam from a beast's breath. The easterners were *quiet.*

'I'll blow my horn!' the younger one said, in a mock whisper.

'You'll do no such thing!' his companion hissed.

Melitta's heart was pounding, and her mind, wandering free in the last seconds before action, focused on the notion that she used to feel less fear. *How does fear creep in?* she asked herself. Then she took a deep breath and rolled to her left – feet planted, hips on line, the bow drifting up, the tension of the string and her arm and the draw, all one. She didn't actually see her target or even, consciously, loose the arrow, but she was reaching with icy fingers for a second arrow – draw through the fingers, nock—

Screams.

Loose – drop the bow, left hand back to put it exactly into the gorytos, even as her right took a javelin. She was running forward. One was down, gut-shot and screaming, and the other was lying pinned under his horse, where her arrow had gone through his leg and into the horse's guts and the beast was flailing in the snow. She didn't bother with a throw, but pushed her slim javelin into his unprotected neck. The snow under him went black as the blood spurted and she ran on, straight at them. There *were* two more, and her legs were already tired, the tension in her hips left from childbirth and still not worked away, so that she was afraid to stop for fear she wouldn't run well again. She swept down the hill and found a third man – his bow out. He shot, and she threw her javelin, and she was still running. She was above him on the steep ridge. Without time to plan, she jumped and hit him squarely, toppling him from his horse and getting a vicious stab in her face – flare of pain – her *akinakes* across his throat, and she rolled off him and grabbed at his horse's reins.

The beast didn't move – the gods were with her, and she got herself into the high-backed Sauromatae saddle and was going, up the trail towards her own horse. Her new mount shied at the smell of blood and she clenched her knees and thumped her toes against his barrel and he was past the dead man and the wounded boy, still whimpering, and over the crest – she didn't even dismount to get her horse, just dropped her remaining javelin into its scabbard, collected her horse's reins and was away down the hill. As soon as she was back among trees, she made herself slow, made her horses walk. No snow this far down in the woods – nothing to give her away.

Behind her, she could hear the fourth man calling for his friends – terrified.

She was across the next stream and starting to worry about the wound on her face, which kept bleeding, so that the blood ran down her neck, colder and colder as it soaked the neck of her cloak. Then she was climbing again. She turned just short of the snow line and rode north and east, as best she could estimate in the moonless dark.

She saw motion on the last ridge and shouts reached her, and later, a horn call, but she was still moving fast, wishing she had not taken a wound and wishing, too, that she'd taken the other two horses.

Her new horse was a fine beast, with a deep chest and a wide rump, and she only changed horses to give him a rest. He had scars on his chest and a set of ritual scars on his hindquarters in the barbed shape of a gryphon. So she called him Gryphon, happy in the knowledge that he was a warhorse of some age and thus a proven mount.

She lay up for an hour in a circle of tall spruce trees high on a ridge, where the snow was deep enough to hide the flames of a small fire. She needed the fire to melt water and refill her canteen and her water skin.

Her whole face throbbed.

She had lost her guide and her mentor. She had no food except the snack in her wallet, a honey cake wrapped in leaves and a big slice of cheese, both of which she consumed immediately, her cheek burning with pain as she chewed. She melted water in her helmet and filled her water skin and her canteen.

Only then did it occur to her to search the big wallet on Gryphon.

It was decorated in the Sauromatae way, made from two caribou skins sewn back to back, fur in, with decorations in dyed hair all over the outside.

I killed someone important, she thought. She poured a little water from her helmet into her horn cup and had a sip. Even just warm enough to steam, it was marvellous. She looked at the embroidery, a full winter of work for someone sitting in a lodge or a yurt on the sea of grass, and shook her head at the ways of fortune – *Tyche*, as the Greeks said. This man had been a warrior – a good one, with a fine horse and good kit. Probably veteran of a hundred raids – smart enough to be well back of his scouts. But his one arrow had missed her, and she'd killed him – as much by luck as skill. If she'd come over the hill a few horse-lengths either way, and given him time ...

She sighed, wanting only to sleep. She reached her hands inside the warm softness of the embroidered wallet – so like Greek saddlebags, but made on the plains – and found that the wallet held two sets of treasures. She actually laughed aloud at the joy of it. There was a heavy fur hat, which she immediately put on her head, and a magnificent pair of embroidered mittens, made of caribou, lined in some fur that was soft and instantly warm on her fingers, and she almost cried.

But she couldn't stop. With her water bottles full and some food in her belly and mittens on her hands, she rode to the top of her ridge and looked north and south. Coenus and Nihmu, if they lived, would try to go back for her.

If they lived. And if Melitta went back the way she had come, she was more likely to fall in with her pursuers. She still had no food – she was exhausted.

'They'll just have to get on without me,' Melitta said aloud, and turned her horse's head across the ridge, heading north and east, to the Tanais high ground of her girlhood.

Three ridges further, and no sign of pursuit. She was afraid to sleep – afraid to stop at all – but her own horse was flagging. She got them into a creek bottom, with running water, overhanging trees and no snow over the grass. She hobbled *and* picketed her mounts. Then, cursing herself for a barbarian, she opened up the dead man's beautiful wallet with her knife, slitting ten nights' worth of sewing to open it out as a sleeping pad, put her cloak roll under her, and lay down.

She lay open-eyed for longer than she could believe. Her horses made more noise than she could have imagined – whickering back and forth, crunching near-frozen greenery, belching, farting, drinking.

She awoke to cold and dark. Her head and shoulders had come loose from her pile of blankets, and she was cold right through. She got up, wished she had some food and drank her canteen dry. Then she refilled it from the icy stream, working cautiously to avoid wetting any part of her, and collected her kit, making the sloppiest of knots to tie her bed roll. She could *feel* the pursuit. She'd killed a man of consequence. They would track her.

She got the bed roll on to the back of her horse with an effort of will, surprised and dismayed at the loss of strength from just two days without food or much rest. The wound on her face felt odd, and she was light-headed, and all her dreams had been full of colour.

She wondered at the possibility that she might die out here, alone. It made her laugh. The sheer *unlikelihood* of her survival cheered her – long odds had an appeal of their own.

An unshod horse hoof struck a rock, somewhere upstream, clear as the noise of a temple gong.

This time, she didn't hesitate. Her choices were clear – even stark. She was up on Gryphon in a heartbeat, and she didn't even untether her other horse. She rode downstream, moving from one stand of trees to the next in the new moonlight, her bow strung and in her hand, an arrow nocked and three more clutched along her bow.

'All or nothing,' she said aloud. There were three of them again, riding single file on the far bank. They were bickering. Words and pieces of words came to her on the still air – the older man wanted to stop for the night.

The stream hid the sounds of her horse's hooves, and when she was just a few dozen horse-lengths from them she half-rose and let her mount go, galloping across the moonlit river meadow. One hole, and she was dead.

She swept alongside them, just the thin rivulet of the stream and its steep banks between her bow and their soft skin, and she shot the last man first. No following the flight of the arrow in the dark. She drew and shot again, and again, and again, and then her last arrow was gone.

One man was whispering, perhaps grumbling to his gods, but he was face up in the long grass, and all three horses were standing in the new moonlight, as if waiting for their new owner to come and take them.

She left the horses and rode on, cantering through the dark along the stream in the weak moonlight, confident in her mount and still terrified, still amazed at her own boldness and the totality of its result. She rode almost two stades downstream, but she was alone in the valley.

Then she rode back. Two of her victims were still alive – the elder she had shot three times and he still tried to shoot her as she rode up, but his left arm couldn't support his bow and he fell to his knees.

She rode up, a javelin pointed at his face, a white circle in the moonlight.

'Who are you?' he asked.

She couldn't think of anything to say – exhaustion robbed her of speech – so she killed him.

The other wounded man watched her with open, glittering eyes as she searched their bodies and their kit – a good hide tent on a packhorse and a bronze kettle. She collected the horses and rode back.

'I have to kill you,' she said to the young man, after some thought. But even as she spoke to him, she realized that she couldn't kill him. She had, quite simply, had *enough*.

He nodded, though, and turned his face away.

When she had mounted, she shook her head, wondering if the borders of the waking world and the sleeping world had drifted, because she felt as if she could *see* the dead men following at her horse's tail – quite a few dead men, for a girl her age. The shock robbed her of speech for a moment and made her neck hairs quiver. She rode back to the boy with the arrow in his chest. The ghosts were terrifying apparitions – as if they were being tormented by some mad god.

'I've changed my mind,' she said to the wounded boy. 'If you live, you live.' She put a heavy wool blanket of Greek weaving over him, and then another.

He grunted.

She watched him for a moment, and knew her sudden burst of mercy was for nothing. He coughed blood, cursed her and died. She *watched* as his shade dragged itself from his corpse like some slithering maggot leaving the skin of a dead thing and joined the grim troupe at her tail.

'Artemis, stand with me,' she said, and slitted her eyes to avoid seeing the apparitions. Then, ever practical, she stripped the blankets back off him, rolled them tight and rode back to her camp, mind blank. There, she made a big fire for the first time in three nights, killed the smallest horse and gorged herself on half-cooked horsemeat before falling into a dream-haunted sleep that made her moan and toss. Twice she awoke, to relieve herself and to shiver in fear at the killing and the blood and what she had so easily become. Both times, she went back to sleep, and the third time she awoke it was day, and the ghosts were gone, and no new pursuers were on her trail.

She bathed in the icy stream and washed the blood off her hands and the pus off her cheek. The water was as much of a shock as the ghosts, and she wondered how bad her fever was. Then she warmed herself by the fire and put on the fresh, dry wool shirt of one of the dead men.

Her cheek smelled bad. She couldn't get away from it – she smelled like death. Perhaps the man's arrowpoint had been poisoned. Perhaps she was already dead – that might be why she could see the dead so clearly.

She didn't remember packing up her camp or riding – only that sunset came and found her still mounted, moving directly away from it, following the shadows of the trees as they pointed north and east.

But suddenly, as if by magic, she was sitting on a bluff, look-ing down at an immense sheet of water – ten stades across. She laughed, because she knew this place – indeed, the last rays of the sun shone on the distant Temple of Artemis on the far bank, impossibly remote from her and yet painfully close. Coenus had built the temple of white marble with the spoils of his campaigns.

She was on the Tanais, in country she knew. She just couldn't make her mind work.

She rode east all night, on the firm high ground above the river. She rode, not so much because she feared pursuit as because she feared to get off her horse.

Finally, in the first faint grey light of not-dawn, she dismounted and squatted to piss, her back against a birch tree, her reins in her hand like some hero in a Sakje tale, and she understood, as if it was the most profound thing of her life, that she *was* living in a Sakje tale – as if Coenus and her father had *lived* in the *Iliad*. She saw it as clearly as she saw the salmon running in the winter river at her feet.

To no one in particular, or perhaps to the gods – perhaps to the dozens of ghosts who screamed in silent torment at the edge of her vision, she spoke. 'If I live,' she said, 'this feat of arms – this endless butchery of men and horse – will live for ever among the people.' She shrugged. Then she smiled and her face hurt. 'I smell of death,' she said suddenly, to the ghosts.

They never answered her, but they followed, and as the sun climbed the sky she saw that they came closer and closer, and she cursed them. 'Coenus must have killed a hundred men!' she said. 'Haunt *him*!'

And later, as she crossed a feeder stream running white and cold down the hillside above her, she addressed Nihmu. 'Why are you lying with him?' she asked, but received no answer.

She's not here, silly, she reminded herself, unsure whether that was good or bad.

That night, she made no fire and she lacked the strength to cook the horsemeat or even to unpack the animals. She pulled her riding horse down to the ground with her, drew the dead man's furs over her head against the horse and slept fitfully. She was awakened when her horse, annoyed, pushed itself to its feet, dumping her on the ground and letting in the icy air.

She tried to lie still – perhaps even to accept death. Death was very, very close; she could smell his carrion breath. The moon had set and it was utterly black. Her heart roared and pounded, and she waited for him to take her.

Her horse farted.

She laughed, and forced herself to her feet. With the patience of the survivor, she rolled the furs in a bundle and got them tied with thongs, and then slung them over her riding horse. She was unsurprised to find that all the horses were still gathered around her. She picked up the lead rein and mounted Gryphon, then rode away into the utter dark.

She slept while riding, the horses finding their own way, and awoke to pale grey light and the sound of her own horse whinnying and another horse answering from her right. She froze. Half asleep, half in the world of dreams, she raised her head and saw a figure from her childhood sitting on a shaggy pony – Samahe, 'The Black-Haired One'.

'Oh, Auntie,' she said, and then shook her head. 'Silly me.'

But the image of Samahe didn't waver. Instead, she pushed her mount forward and emerged from the grey light, a bow bent in her hand and the arrow pointed right at Melitta's breasts. 'Who are you?' her aunt asked.

'Oh,' Melitta said. 'Am I dead?'

The arrowhead lowered a fraction. The Sakje woman whistled shrilly between her teeth.

Then Melitta had time to be afraid, because suddenly she was surrounded in the dawn, the first pink light showing her a dozen riders, both men and women, all around her, their breath rising on the frozen air and their horses making the noises of real horses in the world of the sun.

'Sauromatae girl,' said a man at her shoulder. 'I have something nice and round for her!' he said, and gave a cruel laugh.

But the woman shook her head. 'I think I know her. Girl! What's your name?'

Melitta shook her head. 'I smell of death,' she said.

'That's true,' said another Sakje, a bearded man in a red jacket at her elbow. 'She's got five Sauromatae horses and her quiver is empty. How d'you get that cut on your face, girl?'

'Killing,' Melitta said.

'Her Sakje is pure enough,' the older woman said.

'Samahe?' Melitta asked. She was hesitant, because this could still be a dream.

The men and women around her fell back in wonder.

'You *know* me?' Samahe asked, her voice eager.

'Of course I know you. You are the wife of Ataelus, and I am the daughter of Srayanka. We are cousins.' All this seemed as natural as breathing. 'Am I dead, or do you yet live?'

As soon as she said 'Srayanka', the woman pushed her horse forward and threw her arms, bow and all, around her. And the horsemen began to shout, a long, thin scream – *Aiyaiyaiyaiyai!*

'Oh, my little honey bee. What – what has happened?' Samahe ran a finger down her face and shook her head.

'I killed some men, and I thought perhaps that I died.' Melitta took a breath. 'I smell like death.'

And with those words, she fell straight from Samahe's arms to the ground, and the world fled away.

PART II

LIVING WITH LIONS

9

PROPONTIS, WINTER, 311 BC

Poppy juice and bone-setting got Satyrus through the days in Tomis alive, although the arm never ceased to trouble him. A gale blew against the breakwater and all hands worked to save the captured ships. Then winter closed in a sheet of rain, and then another. His arm was setting badly, but Calchus's physician put more and more water and milk into the poppy juice, gradually weaning him from the colours and the poetry. The man was an expert, and Satyrus missed only the happiness of the dreams.

His appetite returned in a rush, and they had been ten nights in Calchus's big house when he found himself reclining at a dinner, eating mashed lobsters and drinking too much and almost unable to follow the conversation in his urge to eat everything that the slaves brought him.

'By all the gods, it takes me back to see you lying there, lad,' Calchus said. He raised a cup and swigged some wine. 'Eat up! More where that came from.'

Theron ate massively as well, and Calchus watched him consume lobster with an ill-grace. 'You eat like an Olympic athlete,' Calchus said.

'I was an Olympic athlete,' Theron answered.

Silence fell, as the other guests looked at each other and smirked.

Satyrus almost choked on his food. Calchus was his guest-friend, his father's friend, and his benefactor, his host – and yet, a hard man to like. His childhood visits to Tanais had always been full of ceremony and self-importance, and Satyrus could remember the face his mother would make when she heard that the man was coming. And yet, in his sixties, he'd risen from his bed to lead the men of the town against the raiders – not once, but three times, taking wounds on each occasion. He was not a straw man – but a brash one. Just the kind to have Theron in his house ten days and never trouble to learn that the man was an Olympian.

Calchus shrugged and drank more wine. 'Satyrus, I have another problem for you,' he said. 'Those pirates locked up all their rowers in our slave pens – mercenaries and hirelings and slaves. Thanks all the gods they weren't free men like yours, and armed, or we'd all be dead!'

Satyrus tried to roll over. Without the poppy, the break in his arm ached all the time. The old infected wound was polluting it, and Satyrus missed Alexandria, where the doctors knew about such things. He had other wounds, but they weren't so bad. But it wasn't polite to lie flat at a party, and his left hip had a bad cut, so there was just one position that suited him.

'I was going to order them all killed,' Calchus said. 'But it occurred to me that you might take them – you could make them row your ships as far as Rhodos, at least. And then let them go – or sell them. Or keep them – they're hirelings.'

Theron nodded. 'Better than killing four hundred innocent men,' he said.

'Innocent? Athletics doesn't teach much in the way of ethics, I suppose,' Calchus said.

'Not much beyond fair play,' Theron said.

'They came here to rape and burn,' Calchus said, mostly to the audience of his own clients on their couches across the room. 'Their lives are forfeit.'

Theron raised an eyebrow at Satyrus. Satyrus nodded. 'We'll take them. When our wounded are recovered, we'll take them away.'

'That's a load off my mind,' Calchus said. He shrugged. 'I'm a hard man – but four hundred? Where would we bury them all? The pirates were bad enough.'

Two hundred pirates – two hundred armoured men – all killed in a night of butchery, and their bodies lay unburied for too long, so that the charnel-house sweetness crept into everything, even through the poppy juice.

Satyrus couldn't be gone too soon, once he was free of the poppy.

The town and the crew of the *Falcon* shared the armour and weapons of the dead men, and the *Falcon*'s crew – a little thin on the decks of the *Golden Lotus* – was probably the best-armoured crew in the Mediterranean, although it was all stored below in leather bags under each man's bench.

The professional rowers from the enemy ships were mustered and sent to row in their original ships, but with every man stripped and a handful of heavily armed Falcons on every deck. Satyrus, Diokles, Theron and Kalos made difficult choices, promoting men to important positions just to get the captured ships off the beach.

One of them was Kleitos. He'd failed once as an oar master – too young, and too afraid of his sudden promotion. This time, on a rain-swept beach on the Euxine, he pushed forward and asked for the job.

'Let me try again,' he said to Satyrus. He stood square. 'You was right to put me back down – but I can do it. I thought and thought about it.'

Theron didn't know the history, and raised an eyebrow. Diokles, the man who had taken over when Kleitos froze, surprised Satyrus by taking his side. 'He's ready now,' Diokles said.

Satyrus nodded. 'Very well. Give him the *Hornet*.'

'Oar master?' Kleitos asked.

'Oar master, helmsman, navarch – call yourself what you will. It's going to be you and Master Theron taking the *Hornet* all the way to Rhodos. You up to it, mister?' Diokles raised an eyebrow.

Kleitos stood straight. 'Aye!'

Diokles cast Satyrus a look that suggested he had his doubts, but—

'Thrassos of Rhodos,' Theron said, calling another man forward. He was often a boat master, and he'd been slated for command back in Alexandria.

The big, red-haired man stepped forward. He looked like a barbarian, and he was, despite his Greek name. He wore a leather chiton like a farmer and had tattoos all over his arms. 'Aye?'

'You'll have the deck with Master Satyrus,' Diokles said. 'Can you handle it?'

Thrassos smiled. 'Nah,' he said. 'Nah. Serve good, eh?' His Greek had a guttural edge to it. Slaves washed up as free men at Rhodos, because their little fleet took so many pirates and freed their slaves. Thrassos was clearly a Dacae, or even more of a stranger, a German like Carlus in the Exiles.

Satyrus clasped hands with him anyway. 'Keep me alive,' he said.

Thrassos smiled. 'Me, too.'

Two weeks in Tomis and the weather broke, with two days of sun drying the hulls and more promised in Satyrus's broken bone. His hip was almost healed, and he found himself trapped in endless erotic dreams, as if, having come near death, he needed to mate. It made him feel as if he was still a boy, and at Calchus's symposia he struggled to hide his instant reaction to the man's slave girls and their admittedly pitiful dances. Satyrus's opinion of the man went down again at the sight of these girls – bruised, stone-faced and too young. His mother's commands about sex with slaves seemed perfectly tailored to them, despite the urges of his sleeping mind and Calchus's broadest urgings. 'Take one? Take two – they're small!' Every night, the same joke.

'I need to get going,' Satyrus said to Theron. 'Help me! I'm too damned weak to get it done.'

Theron clasped his shoulder softly and moved around, giving the necessary orders and placating Calchus with promises of future visits.

On the beach, with a fair north wind blowing as cold as Tartarus, Satyrus embraced his host. 'Thanks for your hospitality,' he said. 'Aren't you worried about Eumeles? He'll need a reprisal.'

'Not before spring,' Calchus said. 'And we're Lysimachos's men, here. We'll get him to send us a garrison. It may even mean war.'

'How will you send him word?' Satyrus asked, chilled to the bone already.

Calchus looked uncomfortable. 'Fishing smack to Amphipolis, perhaps,' he said. 'Or a rider overland.'

'We'll take the news,' Satyrus said. Theron raised an eyebrow. Satyrus looked at his former coach. 'Actions have consequences,' he said, thinking of Penelope lying dead in a pool of her own blood, all her courage snuffed out by violence.

Clown-voice killed Penelope, and I kill him to settle the score, and Eumeles sends a fleet to Tomis to settle that score. Or perhaps I sail to attack Eumeles, and he forces me to flee, and clown-voice pursues me, and thus kills Penelope – on and on, to the first principle of causality. Satyrus was lost in thought until Theron nudged him.

'We'll pass the news to Lysimachos,' Satyrus said.

'You have our eternal thanks already, benefactor!' Calchus said. 'Your father was the best of men and you follow him.'

Satyrus was tempted to say that the best of men would not have caused Penelope's death, nor Teax's. But he held his opinions close.

'Goodbye, guest-friend,' Satyrus said. He waved to the other townsmen on the beach – a thin crowd, because many of the freemen's ranks were empty.

They ran the ships into the surf and got under way quickly, fearing a turn in the weather.

The weather held for three days, and they sailed south and east without touching an oar. But just before beaching on the third evening, Theron's ship suddenly turned into the wind, the signal for trouble, and Satyrus got the *Lotus* alongside as fast as he could. Apollodorus led the marines aboard at a run, and then ran down the central deck, scattering mutineers. Ten men were killed, and Theron shook his head.

'I tried to reason with them,' he said thickly. 'They knocked me on the head.'

Kleitos had put the ship into the wind and held the stern for several long minutes, alone.

Satyrus clasped his hand. 'Well done!'

The man looked stunned. 'Didn't even know what I was doing!' he muttered. 'One against so many.'

Apollodorus came back with a dozen oarsmen under guard. 'Taken in arms,' he said. 'No question. Kill 'em?'

Satyrus shook his head. 'Exchange them for a dozen of our rowers in the *Lotus*.'

They made a poor job of landing the ships for dinner, and the officers gathered in a worried knot by a fire.

'My arm says we're in for a weather change,' Satyrus said. 'Nothing good there.'

'Somebody's spreading the word that we're going to have 'em all killed,' Kleitos said. He looked bashful and surprised that he'd spoken out, but he stood his ground. 'I heard it when they were getting ready to rush me. They asked me to join 'em.'

'You know them?' Satyrus asked.

Diokles laughed bitterly. 'We all know somebody over there. Professional seamen and rowers? Small world, Navarch.'

Satyrus rubbed his beard – he hadn't shaved since he took his wound. 'Seems to me we should talk to them,' he said.

Theron snorted. 'My head still hurts,' he said.

'Promise them wages and a fair landing at Rhodos,' Satyrus said.

'Rhodos is death for some of 'em,' Diokles said. He handed Satyrus a cup of warm wine and honey. 'That's why they're antsy.'

'Lysimachos could use them,' Satyrus said, considering the words even as he said them.

'That'd turn some heads,' Theron said. 'Those men are as good as pirates. Leon is the enemy of every pirate on the seas.'

Satyrus shrugged. 'It isn't *right* to kill them, but it isn't *right* to release them where they'll serve pirates? Is that it, Master Theron? I hear Philokles in your voice, sir.'

Theron shook his head. 'My head's too thick to argue moral philosophy, lad. And I see your point.'

'I need Lysimachos,' Satyrus said. 'He's supposedly our ally – he's Ptolemy's ally, but Alexandria is far away and Lysimachos is close.'

'Lysimachos might take these men – and the ships they crew – and tell us that we're lucky to be alive.' Theron looked around at the other men in the firelight, but the sailors were quiet. Most of them were lower-class freemen, and they weren't about to intrude on a political argument between two gentlemen.

Satyrus looked pointedly at Diokles. The Tyrian nodded slowly. 'So? I mean, begging your pardon, but if he does that, he's no good ally, and we're still richer by the *Golden Lotus* and our lives. And frankly, gents – you can't build a fleet on these hulls. We captured a few old triremes. Only *Hornet* is worth a crap. There's worm in the other two.'

Theron nodded. He slapped Diokles on the shoulder. 'That'll teach me to talk about things I don't really know,' he said. 'In future, don't hold your tongue.'

The dark-haired Tyrian's earrings twinkled in the firelight. 'So?'

'So – let's muster the lot of them – our oarsmen too. We'll tell it to them straight.' Satyrus was nodding as he spoke. 'And, Apollodorus, marines, full armour. So they see the other choice.'

Apollodorus nodded. 'Just for the poets, Navarch – I'd rather you executed a couple first. That's a message the rest will understand.'

Theron looked away in distaste, but Diokles nodded. 'I agree. Kill a couple of the louts who were caught with weapons today.'

'In cold blood?' Satyrus asked.

'I wasn't planning to give 'em swords,' Apollodorus said. 'Don't worry, Navarch. I'll do it.'

'No,' Satyrus said. He swallowed, feeling trapped. Feeling as if something was moving on the dark beach. Furies. Curses. His oath to avenge his mother. He shook his head. He thought of Teax. Of the consequences of being a king.

'Muster the men,' he said.

It took only minutes – the captured rowers had their own fires, watched by tired oarsmen in captured armour.

'At least they're all fed,' Satyrus said to Diokles.

'Your friend did us proud,' Diokles said. He was chewing on a pork bone.

'Do these men have to die?' Satyrus asked.

'Zeus Soter, Navarch! They rose in mutiny against you, tried to kill Theron and tried to take one of our ships.' Diokles looked at Satyrus from under his black eyebrows and spat gristle in the sand. 'You plan to be a king? I'm no tutor, like your Spartan, nor an athlete, like Theron. Bless 'em both – fine men. *Good* men. But – if you plan to be a king, people are going to die. And you are going to kill 'em. Get me? Maybe you need to lesson yourself on it. Or maybe ...' The Tyrian didn't meet Satyrus's eye. 'Maybe you oughtn't to do it. At all.'

Satyrus stopped walking and stared at his helmsman. 'Philokles told me once that he thought that good men – truly good men – neither made war nor took life.' He sighed. 'And then he said that it looked different from the front rank of the phalanx – both good and evil.'

'Aye,' Diokles said, nodding. 'I hear that.' He gave a pained smile and took another bite of pork.

'We'd have done the same to them,' Satyrus said. 'If we were taken, we'd do our best to fight back.'

'And I'd not squirm when the sword bit my neck, eh, Navarch?' Diokles shrugged. The contempt in his voice wasn't strong, but it was there. 'Let Apollodorus do it, if you have to.'

Satyrus shook his head, watching Theron, wondering how much of the man's good opinion he was going to forfeit. 'No,' he said. He loosened his sword in the scabbard and walked forward, where the marines had dragged the prisoner oarsmen to kneel in the sand.

He felt as if his feet were loud on the sand. He could feel the Furies gather.

Satyrus walked up their ranks. Several were boys. The rest were long-armed, hunch-backed rowing professionals, with massive necks and heavy muscle. A few raised their heads to look at him. None of them looked like evil come to earth, or like servants of dark gods, or any comforting, easy, evil thing he could name. They looked like beaten men, cold and empty of hope, kneeling on a beach, waiting to die.

The whole beach was silent, as the fires crackled, dry oak and beech and birch driftwood from the north. Satyrus could smell the birch, the smell of his childhood fires.

If it was not just one Penelope, but a generation of them? Not just one Teax, but a thousand?

A few steps from the end of the line of prisoners, he drew and killed one like a sacrifice, an older man with a cut on his forearm, and then the younger man next to him, blade sweeping across his throat on the back stroke from the first cut so that the two dead men fell almost together. Satyrus stepped clear of the flow of blood. He cleaned his sword on a scrap of linen from his *doros* and continued to walk towards the crowd of enemy sailors.

'Don't be fools,' he said. They were so quiet that he didn't need to raise his voice. 'I am taking these ships to Lysimachos, just around the horn of the Propontis – Amphipolis in Thrace. I'll leave you all ashore there. No Rhodian navy to try you. No one else has to die.'

There was a buzz, and he raised his voice. 'The men at Tomis wanted to butcher the lot of you. I could still do it.' His voice was hard, as hard as a man who has just killed in cold blood – who might do it again, just for the pleasure of the power. 'Row me round to Lysimachos and I'll put you ashore with silver in your hands. Trifle with me again ...' He paused, took a deep breath and raised his voice to a storm-roar, 'And I'll kill the lot of you and burn the bodies in the extra ships. Clear?'

The utter silence that followed his last words was its own testament.

'Excellent,' Satyrus said. He walked off into the darkness.

Theron held his hair while he threw up. The big Corinthian didn't say anything. And Satyrus put it away, with Teax and Penelope and the dead girl by the Tanais River. Now he had a name for it.

The price of kingship.

That night, he took a dose of poppy juice in secret, and he felt better.

The next day, they raised the Thracian Bosporus with dark clouds gathering in the north. Far off, they saw the nick of a white sail on the horizon, and as the *Golden Lotus* entered the still waters of the Bosporus itself, they passed close to a fifty-oared pentekonter hull, turtled in the water and covered in weed – weeks old.

'Pirates?' Satyrus asked.

'Poseidon,' muttered the harsh voice of his helmsman.

They swept south. Now the oarsmen had to labour, the wind veering around in minutes so that it pushed right in their faces and the sea rising behind them, even with the narrow channel and protected water.

Lotus had a third of her benches empty and more only half-filled, and her crew had to struggle to keep the big ship head up to the growing wind and moving steadily down the channel.

The other ships had captured oarsmen but nearly full crews, and whatever the men had taken from Satyrus's brutal display, they rowed well, so that the squadron moved in a crisp line-ahead, *Lotus* followed by *Falcon* followed by *Hornet* and then the two smaller triremes.

Stades passed, and the oarsmen of the *Lotus* laboured on. Satyrus walked amidships.

'Friends,' he called, 'we've a storm behind us and forty stades into Byzantium and safe harbour. I'll row with you, but row we must – all the way down the gullet.'

He sat on a half-manned bench and took the oar as it came over the top. Thrassos sat opposite him and did the same.

Good rowers – and Uncle Leon took only the best – have their own rhythm, and don't need a timoneer unless they lose the stroke. Satyrus rowed until his palms bled, and then he rowed further – penance, at the very least. But the men on the benches around smiled at him, and the great loom of the *Golden Lotus*'s oars wove on and on and the stades flowed by. Above, the deck crew took every scrap of canvas off the masts – the wind was head-on. And then the deck crew joined the rowers.

Satyrus's left arm throbbed, and then it burned, and then he sobbed with pain. He took a nip of the poppy juice from his little perfume flask and was instantly better. The pain still filled his head, but he floated on it instead of swimming in it. He wasn't actually doing much rowing any more; mostly his hands just went around with the oar. The three-week-old break was too raw, and the pain too much, for his muscles to have much purchase, but he kept the oar going.

One of the deck-crewmen – Delos, a snub-nosed man who had a reputation for impudence – came and lifted him away from his oar. 'Need you to steer,' the man said. He gave Satyrus a tired smile that was worth all the courtly courtesy in the world. Then he sank on to the bench where Satyrus had been and took the oar at the top of its swing.

Satyrus stood at the rail and heaved for some time. When the red haze left his vision, he was looking at the walls of a city rising over the bow of his ship.

'Herakles and Poseidon and all the gods,' he breathed. He

picked up the wineskin that sat under the helmsman's bench in the stern and poured all the contents over the side into the sea.

The oarsmen cheered, and even after thirty stades into the wind, their cheer carried and they came down the last of the channel in fine shape, the bow cutting into the wind as they began to round the harbour point.

Satyrus turned the ship with the steering oar, his left arm throbbing so that he choked, and only then did he see that the beach was packed with ships – fifty warships, and ten more anchored out.

'Poseidon,' he said. He slumped.

But right at the edge of the beach, he could see *Labours of Herakles* drawn up, his bronze prow gleaming in the winter rain.

He looked at the rest of the fleet for ten laboured breaths, and then his heart beat again. He didn't know them. Except for *Herakles* and a penteres that might be the *Fennel Stalk*, they were someone else's ships.

He didn't know them. Whoever's fleet that was, it wasn't the fleet of Eumeles of Pantecapaeum.

'Hard to find a place to drop our anchor,' Satyrus managed to quip. He hoped that he sounded confident.

He needn't have worried. Sailors swarmed out of the town to help his men anchor out – there wasn't a spot on the beach, but the tavern emptied to help, and his ships were moored fore and aft, often moored right against the other ships, so that their anchors shared the load. It was only as the first gusts of hail-tipped storm wind bit into them that Satyrus raised his voice to ask where all these ships were from.

'Hah!' laughed a big black sailor in a fancy chiton and wearing a one-hundred-drachma sword. 'We serve no man!'

Satyrus sat down on his steering bench and laughed. He had moored to a pirate fleet.

The first man to meet him ashore was Abraham, lean and bronzed, his long hair in wet ringlets. The man threw his arms around Satyrus and they embraced for a long time – long enough for sailors to call and make salacious comments.

'I thought you were dead,' Abraham said. 'But I hoped – and

prayed. And I decided to wait here. Daedalus gave me hope – he came in a week after me and swore he'd seen you get free of the enemy line. But Dionysius said that he saw you sink.'

'We sank another boat. Easy mistake to make.' Satyrus let his friend lead him by the hand to a harbourfront wine shop – the kind of place that no Athenian gentleman would ever enter. The doorway was the stern gallery of a trireme, and the benches inside, worn smooth by a thousand thousand patrons, were oar benches, and the walls were covered in bits of wood, nailed to the wall with heavy copper nails. Satyrus slumped on to a bench and looked around.

'I need you to meet someone,' Abraham said quickly. 'Then you can rest.'

The place was quiet, yet *packed* with men – two hundred in a place meant for thirty. 'Zeus Soter!' he said, looking around. 'Is this a tribunal?'

'We don't swear by Zeus,' a burly old man said. 'Only Poseidon.' He sat on the bench opposite Satyrus. His face was scarred and he'd lost an eye so long before that the pit of his lost eye was smooth, as if filled with wax. He wore his hair long, in iron-grey ringlets, as if he was a young aristocrat in the agora of Athens. His linen chiton was purple-edged, like a tyrant's, and he wore a diadem of gold, studded with five magnificent jewels.

'I'm Demostrate,' he said. He nodded at Abraham. 'This young reprobate told me that you're Kineas's son. And that you might be dead. But this afternoon, it turns out you're alive. Eh?'

Satyrus tried not to nurse his arm. He waved at Diokles, who was pushing to get in. 'That's my helmsman. Get him a place,' Satyrus said. His voice snapped with energy, despite his fatigue. He thought that he had the measure of the place. 'Demostrate. The pirate king.' He looked at Abraham.

Abraham shrugged. 'Not all merchants can afford a squadron of warships to escort their cargoes. My father pays his tenth to Demostrate.'

Satyrus shrugged, although it hurt his arm. 'My uncle does not.' He looked at Demostrate. 'What can I do for you?'

Demostrate's chin moved up and down – either with silent laughter or in silent affirmation. Perhaps both. 'You have your father in you, and that's for certain-sure. I gather you just got your arse handed to you by Eumeles' shiny new fleet.'

Satyrus rubbed his new beard and managed a smile. 'Well – they *did* outnumber us three to one.'

Demostrate nodded. 'See, I thought that if Leon and Eumeles fought, I'd just sit and rub my hands in glee.'

Satyrus nodded, wondering if he was a prisoner now. It seemed to be a situation that called for some bluff. Satyrus didn't feel as if he had any bluff in him. He looked around at the hundreds of eyes watching him in near perfect silence. The place reeked – tallow candles, oil lamps, hundreds of unwashed bodies and old, stale wine and beer. 'But?' Satyrus prompted.

'But it turns out that I hate fucking Eumeles worse than I hate Leon. Leon's just a man with goods I covet. He's put some mates of mine under the waves, and I'll repay him in time. But Eumeles used to be a creepy lad named Heron, and he had me exiled.'

Satyrus grinned and shot to his feet. 'Zeus's – that is, Poseidon's balls! You're Demostrate of Pantecapaeum!'

'Aye, lad, that I am!' the old man said. He had a pleasant voice, not at all the gravelly rasp that his face would lead a man to expect.

'You were my father's admiral!' Satyrus said. His smile filled his face as he saw the possibilities – and the dangers. For this was a truly dangerous man – a man who'd refused alliance with any of the parties in the struggle of the Diadochoi, who preyed on all comers.

He sat down, his right hand automatically loosening his sword in its sheath, and rested his shoulders against the wall. His right hand cradled his injured left arm.

'Not really.' The old man shrugged. 'Nah. Nothing so fancy. I covered the coast for him one summer while he made war on the Macedonians. And the next year I guarded his merchantmen while they moved his army. To be honest, lad, it was dull, dull work for a sailorman, and damn little plunder.' He shrugged, and the gold beads in his locks winked. He had heavy amber earrings. 'So – how'd you come to get beaten?'

Satyrus was suddenly struck by the fitness of it – that Demostrate was talking to him – his father's ally. Who hated Eumeles for his exile. Of course, Leon would *never* stomach alliance with the man who controlled the entrance to the Propontis and preyed on every merchant who didn't buy his favour.

Clearly time to start thinking like a king.

'Sheer folly,' Satyrus said. As he spoke, Diokles shouldered a man aside and sat heavily next to Satyrus on the bench. 'And bad intelligence.'

'Tell it,' Demostrate said. He motioned for a man to bring wine. 'The lads like a good sea-fight story. What do you drink?'

'Wine,' Satyrus said, and got a ripple of chuckles and smiles from the hard men packed around him. 'I've had a long eight weeks.' He looked around. 'Where should I start? We heard that Eumeles had two dozen ships, and we headed north with twenty – not to fight him, but simply to land at Olbia.'

'Aye, where yer father was archon. Olbia would be yours just by landing there. I understand that.' Demostrate nodded.

'Eumeles knew we were coming,' Satyrus said. 'He was in the mouth of the Borysthenes with eighty ships. When we retreated, he followed and forced us to battle against the coast, eighty ships to twenty.'

Mutters, whispers and a catcall from the men around him. Demostrate merely turned his head and the silence returned. 'The battle story I've heard – from Daedalus of Halicarnassus. He says you fought well. Care to tell it?'

Satyrus shrugged. 'Not well enough to win, or to rescue my uncle.'

Demostrate nodded. A boy came up with a heavy bronze wine krater and cups. He put them on the table and served the wine. Demostrate poured a full cup on the floor. 'Not in the sea!' he said as he poured his libation.

Dozens of voices echoed his prayer.

Satyrus took a cup and drank, and it was good Chian wine – as good as anything on a dandy's table in Alexandria. 'Welcome to my town, Satyrus son of Kineas,' Demostrate said, still standing.

'Care to buy a pair of small triremes?' Satyrus asked. 'They have a little worm, but nothing a pirate king can't fix with his arsenal.'

Men laughed, but Demostrate sat and laughed louder. 'They're mine now, don't you think?'

Satyrus shrugged. 'By that logic, your life is mine now, don't you think?' Without shifting his weight, his right hand, which had been cradling his left arm, reached over it and he drew the short sword from under his arm in the motion practised a thousand times – the blade out, the tip precisely at the bridge of the pirate's nose.

Demostrate didn't move. 'Now that's a point of what people call *philosophy*, don't you think? I can possess myself of your ships, but you can only *take* my life. You can't keep it.' The old man grinned. 'And thankless as these scum are, I don't think you'd live long to brag of it.'

Satyrus was proud that, despite the last eight weeks and everything he'd been through, the point of his sword wavered less than a finger's width. 'The thing is that if you take my ships, I have absolutely nothing to lose.'

'You'd be killing the young Jew here and your helmsman, too. Maybe every man in your crews.' Demostrate still didn't move.

'That's a risk I'm willing to take,' Satyrus said. 'The last eight weeks have taught me quite a bit about the price of kingship.'

'So you'd sacrifice your own friends and your whole life for the gratification of instant revenge,' the pirate said.

Satyrus shrugged but his sword point did not. 'No. I'd *wager* my own life and that of my friends that you are a reasonable man. With the full knowledge that if my bluff was called, I'd have to pay the wager. Revenge,' and here, Satyrus shrugged again, and his point twitched as his hand tired, 'is a luxury I can't yet afford.'

'I won't bargain while you threaten me, lad. It'll look bad for the scum.' Demostrate met his eye and winked.

Satyrus sheathed his sword with the same economy of movement he'd used to draw it. 'Replace the ram on my *Black Falcon* and you can have both ships and all the men that rowed them,' Satyrus said. There it was. The knuckle bones were rolled.

The silence was as thick as the smell. Satyrus had time to think of how much his arm hurt, and to wonder if he was about to be relieved of the pain – for ever.

'Find us a base in the Euxine and we'll rip Eumeles a new arsehole together,' Demostrate said. 'Every city on the Euxine is closed to me.' He shrugged, rose to his feet. 'I like him. What of you lot?'

The two hundred laughed and muttered – no roars of acclaim, but few hoots of derision, either.

The old man leaned down. 'Finish the wine and my compliments, lad. You've all winter to get a new ram – and I'm quite happy to have a new pair of light triremes, although I have the better of the deal. But I have thirty ships that can stand in the line of battle with you, and maybe I know where there's more. Right now, you need to sleep.'

Satyrus nodded heavily. 'Thanks,' he said.

Most of the two hundred men followed Demostrate out of the arched door, and Satyrus was left in a dockside tavern with Diokles, Abraham and Theron, who had lurked at the edge of the door.

'Leon hates him,' Theron said.

Satyrus gulped wine. What he needed was water, and the wine went straight to his head.

'Where are our men?' Satyrus asked.

'Drunk as lords, somewhere dry,' Diokles said. 'I promised a muster for pay tomorrow. Do you have coin?'

'Not a silver owl,' Satyrus said. 'However much Leon hates this man, I suspect his credit is good here.'

Abraham leaned forward. 'I'm made of money. I have silver to hand and I can get more.' He raised an eyebrow. 'Even though you just wagered my life.'

Diokles shook his head. 'Demostrate! I thought we'd all be gutted on the spot.'

'We may yet,' Satyrus said. 'I liked him.'

Theron sighed. 'He's a hard man, Satyrus. You think you're hard?'

'I suspect he'll keep a deal when he makes one,' Satyrus said.

'He left Lysimachos high and dry two years back, you'll recall,' Theron shot back. 'Bought and paid for, he deserted – and took this town. From Lysimachos. Who hates him. Whose alliance you crave. And Amastris? Her father Dionysius, whose alliance you desire, hates this pirate for closing his trade.'

Satyrus nodded. He was drunk on two cups of wine. His arm

throbbed, and he was high on the adrenaline of having drawn on the greatest pirate in the world – and lived. 'Tomorrow,' he said unsteadily. 'Abraham, do you have a bed for me?'

Abraham put an arm around his shoulders. 'You poor bastard. I didn't think he'd come the moment you landed.'

Theron finished his wine. 'He wanted to find you weak. To see what you are made of. Satyrus, it's the law of the wild, here. It's like living with lions. If you bind yourself to these men, you are outside the laws of men.'

Satyrus waved his hand. 'Tell me tomorrow,' he said. He stumbled out into the dark with Abraham's arms around his shoulders.

'You look like shit,' Abraham said as they walked through the rain.

'I'm drunk,' Satyrus said.

'No, worse than that,' Abraham said.

'I'm drunk, and I got some people killed, and then I killed some more people all by myself,' Satyrus said. 'Other than that, I'm fine.' Then he stopped against a building and threw up all the wine and everything else he'd eaten for a day.

Abraham held his head and said nothing.

Abraham had made his father's factor's house into a headquarters for his crew, and he had cleared the warehouse for his wounded when he came in. What Isaac Ben Zion would make of the loss of profits was another matter.

It was a two-storey house with an enclosed yard and an attached warehouse, common across the Hellenic world, but it was comfortable in a way that Calchus's house never had been. The slaves were sleek and well fed, and the yard was full of sailors and oarsmen at all hours – noisy, singing, sometimes vicious but never dull. The house itself held all the officers of two ships, and with Satyrus's arrival, it held the officers of four ships.

On his first morning there, Satyrus awoke to hot, heavily spiced wine and barley gruel, which on later days he would eat while listening to reports from his officers in the biggest room on the ground floor, a room utterly devoid of the decorations that Greeks preferred – scenes of the gods, heroes, slaughter. Instead, there were carefully painted designs along the borders, and blank walls in bright colours.

On the first morning, Satyrus sat drinking hot wine and looking at the blue wall. 'You need a scene painter.'

'I'm a Jew,' Abraham said. 'Remember? No nymphs will be raped on my walls.'

'Can't you have Jahveh – I don't know – smiting his enemies?' Satyrus wasn't trying to mock, but it sounded that way.

Abraham made a peasant sign to avert ill-luck. 'No,' he said firmly. 'No, we can't.' Then he grinned. 'Listen – with blank walls, you can imagine any scene you want!'

Satyrus watched the walls and sipped more wine, and he felt the mirth drain out of him. 'Listen,' he said. 'When I stare at these walls, right now I just see people being killed. Killed by me – one way or another.'

'You're the one ready to make an alliance with a pirate,' Theron said, coming in. He had fresh oil on his skin. 'Mind you, the pirate has a gymnasium and a palaestra.'

Satyrus looked up in irritation. 'I was speaking to Abraham.'

Theron sat and poured himself hot wine. 'Exercise cleared my head. I have things I want to say to you.'

Abraham rose. 'I'll leave the two of you.'

Satyrus frowned. 'No.'

Theron shrugged, and Abraham sat.

'I was appalled when you killed those men,' Theron said. 'But I was appalled when you marched the phalanx away and left Philokles bleeding on the sand.'

Abraham looked from one to the other. 'Killed what men?' he asked.

'I executed two mutineers,' Satyrus said. 'Myself.'

Abraham nodded, his face closed.

'I think you are what you have been trained to be. I think that I helped to train you.' Theron shrugged.

Satyrus nodded. 'Hardly a day passes when I don't think of it,' he said. He leaned back on the armrest of his kline and put his feet up. 'The day my world changed. I still wonder about Phiale, too.'

'You let the doctor live,' Theron continued. 'And he repaid you badly.'

'Yes,' Satyrus said.

Theron said, 'I love you. I hope that when I have a son, he's like you. I remain yours, and I'll stay by your side, if you'll have me. But – Satyrus, please listen.'

Satyrus was staring at the fire on the hearth. 'I'm basking in the first compliments you've ever paid me, pighead. I'm listening!' He turned and smiled at Theron.

Theron smiled back. But after a moment, his smile faded. 'But I want you to ask yourself if this is really the path you want. Kingship? Will you really wade in blood all the way to the ivory stool? And who will you be when you get there?'

Satyrus felt the tears well up in his eyes. He rolled over to hide them. 'Abraham, do you think you could find me a physician to reset this arm?' he asked.

Abraham rose, looked at both of them silently and left the room.

When he was gone, Satyrus sat up. 'You were right, Theron. This is between us. He is a different kind of confidant.' He looked at his right hand, as if searching it for bloodstains. Was there blood under the nails? Did it show?

'Your father refused the stool and the diadem,' Theron said. 'I didn't know him – but I know that of him. He refused.'

Satyrus sat looking at his hand, and then he raised his face. 'I'm sorry, Teacher. But that die is cast. I made that decision on the beach, two nights back. Or perhaps when I watched a house burn at Tomis. My world is changed. It is not the world my father lived in.' He spoke slowly, as if he was a magistrate reading a sentence. 'Philokles told me to examine myself. It's like a curse. Does Demostrate ever examine himself? I doubt it.'

Theron shook his head. 'I don't judge other men,' he said. 'Not that way.'

Satyrus raised an eyebrow. 'You judge me,' he said. 'Because I'm young, and you helped shape me. And right now, I think you'd like me either to give up my desire to be king, or to tell you *why* I should be king. But I can't. I can't even be sure that I will be a better king than Eumeles.' He leaned forward, and put his good right hand on Theron's. 'But what I can tell you, Teacher, is that I will examine myself, day by day, and judge myself by the standards Philokles taught. And Eumeles will not examine himself. He will simply act, and act. As empty of worth as an actor pretending to be a hero.'

Theron took a deep breath. 'Who gave you so much wisdom?' he asked.

'You,' Satyrus said. 'You and Philokles. And Sappho and Diodorus and Leon and Nihmu and Coenus and Hama. And perhaps Abraham, as well.'

Theron drank the rest of his wine, clearly overcome by emotion. 'So – the end justifies the means?'

Satyrus shrugged. 'I don't know. I think about it every hour. Are all lives of equal worth? I doubt it. Did those two men deserve to die in the sand under my blade? Yes – and no. Would it change your view if I said that they did not die in vain?'

'Would it change their view?' Theron asked. 'They're the ones who are dead.'

Satyrus nodded. 'I know. Remember the girl by the Tanais? The one I gut-shot?'

Theron shook his head. 'Can't say I do – but you've spoken of her before.'

Satyrus nodded. 'I put her down, like a wounded horse. Except that she wasn't a horse.' He shuddered. 'I think the road to kingship started there, in that meadow. The beach the other night was merely a signpost.' He squared his shoulders. 'Fine. I'm ready. If I have to wade in blood, as you said, then I must simply work harder to put something on the other side of the balance.'

'And Demostrate? The end justifies him?' Theron leaned forward. 'You feel guilt for killing two men – two criminals.' He shook his head. 'A complex act – but hardly a vicious one. But if you get into bed with this pirate, you share the responsibility for every slave he takes, every home he burns, every merchant he ruins, every man he kills.'

Satyrus nodded. 'Yes,' he said. 'Yes, I do.' He stared off into space, reviewing his dead. 'So be it.'

'Bah – your youth is speaking!' Theron made a motion of disgust.

'Perhaps.' Satyrus didn't feel particularly young. His arm hurt, his whole body ached and he wanted to sleep for a day or two.

But other things pressed on him. He sipped hot wine. 'Listen, Theron – my sister must think me dead. Sappho – Diodorus – all of them.'

Theron rubbed his chin, his anger deflated. 'You're right, of course.'

'I should sail down to Alexandria as soon as I make my bargain with Demostrate. If I can get him to agree.'

Abraham came back in. 'Am I welcome back?' he asked from the beaded doorway.

Satyrus nodded. 'Yes,' he said.

'Are you two still friends?' Abraham asked, looking from one to the other.

'Yes,' Theron said. A small smile started at his lips, and spread like the rise of the sun to his face and eyes. 'Yes,' he said, 'we are.'

'Good,' Abraham said. 'Because if our moral philosophy hour is over, there are officers waiting for instructions and an invitation from Demostrate to the public dinner. Work to be done.'

Satyrus turned to his friend. 'Care to travel home?'

Abraham raised an eyebrow, and his dark-brown eyes sparkled. 'No, thanks.' He smiled. 'Once home, I may never actually be allowed to leave again.' He shrugged, a particularly Hellenic gesture. 'I like it here.'

Satyrus nodded, seeing his friend in a different light. Abraham was suddenly *not* the conservative Hebrew businessman of his adolescence. War had changed him. Satyrus noted that Abraham had earrings and a thumb ring and was wearing a sword – in his own house.

Eventually, that might merit comment. For the moment, Satyrus confined himself to saying 'I understand' with a quick smile. He turned to his former coach. 'Theron?'

Theron rubbed his chin. 'I'm of a mind to be your envoy to Lysimachos,' he said. 'If you'll have me.' He looked up and met Satyrus's eye. 'But we need to rescue Leon,' he said. 'Much as I want to go to Lysimachos, I'm the man you can spare to effect a rescue.'

Satyrus shook his head. 'No, Theron. You are not a spy or a scout. You are a famous athlete and a known associate of Lord Ptolemy.'

Theron looked away. 'You know that we are – sworn?'

Satyrus nodded. 'I know that all of you are Pythagoreans,' he said.

Theron took a deep breath. 'Do you know what the first principle of Pythagoras is?' he asked.

'I feel as if I'm back in school. Yes, Theron. I know. You swear friendship – and the first principle is that each will lay down his life for his friend.' Satyrus leaned forward, speaking forcefully. 'I'm telling you that this is not the moment and that Leon would not expect you, his most famous friend, to attempt to rescue him single-handedly.'

Theron sighed. 'So what will we do?'

Satyrus put his forehead in his hands. 'I don't know. I don't think there's a prisoner in the world important enough that Eumeles would trade him. But it may be that Sappho or Nihmu have already received a ransom demand, and until we have been to Alexandria, I don't wish to jump the wrong way.'

Theron rested his heavy arms on the table. 'I have no interest in going to Alexandria,' he said.

'Nor I,' Abraham said. 'Must you go?'

Satyrus was watching the fire on the hearth. 'I must. In fact, everything springs from Alexandria. First of all, money. If I raise a fleet, I will start spending money at a rate that will threaten even Uncle Leon's treasure. Second, Melitta. Third, the rescue of Leon. Fourth, or perhaps first, Diodorus and the Exiles. If I have a fleet, I need them ready.'

Theron nodded. 'We can write to Diodorus from here,' he said.

Satyrus sat up. 'Now that's a good idea. I can send the letter myself and it will be with him in three weeks.'

Theron nodded. 'And he won't know yet that Leon is taken.'

Abraham nodded. 'He can take your soldiers to Alexandria and wait for the fleet.'

Satyrus was looking into the fire. Suddenly, he felt as if the god was at his shoulder, warming his hands at the fire, whispering in his ear – for in between two licks of flame, he saw his campaign unfold. 'No,' he said. His voice trembled.

'No, what?' Abraham asked.

'No. He won't march to Alexandria. That's the wrong way.' Satyrus sat up. 'He'll march to Heraklea. I've got it. I have most of it. Theron, trust me, I'll find a way to rescue Leon. He was taken *for me*. I won't forget.'

'But you still need to go to Alexandria?' Theron asked.

'For all the reasons. I'll go as soon as I've got Demostrate's word on alliance.' He nodded. He still felt the god at his shoulder. Despite his arm, he felt almost greater than human.

'Pay my regards to my father,' Abraham said. 'I won't be going home soon. As I say, he wouldn't let me go again.'

'I'm proposing a trip to the most exotic city in all the seas, our home and native land, or at least our collective adoptive polis, and you two plan to while away the winter in a town full of pirates,' Satyrus said.

Abraham smiled, and his earrings twinkled. 'Wait until you attend their parties.'

Satyrus met his smile. 'I can imagine.'

Abraham shook his head. 'No. No, you can't.'

As soon as the officers were gathered, Satyrus composed his letter to Diodorus. He wrote it out on papyrus, and then he took a wax tablet and melted the wax from the frames. On the bare wood, he wrote his message.

Dear Uncle

Our scout of the Euxine ended in disaster. Uncle Leon was taken and we lost twelve ships. I have made a plan to win the Euxine back, and I will need you and every man you have – if Seleucus will spare you. I plan to be at Heraklea at the spring equinox. I ask – nay, Uncle, I beg – that you meet me there with all your force. I will have a fleet to transport you.

Uncle Leon is in the hands of Eumeles. I have prevented Theron from going to his rescue by promising that we will all bend our every effort that way in the spring. I rely on you to support us in this.

I will proceed immediately to Alexandria to speak to Melitta and to your lady wife concerning our plans. Please respond to me there, or at the Temple of Poseidon at Rhodos, or to Amastris, Princess of Heraklea, who I believe would be a reliable letter box.

At the thought of Amastris, Satyrus smiled. Passionate, headstrong and perhaps a bit fickle – a mistress who could never be taken for granted. Satyrus loved her, even the fickle and the self-centred. She was a prize worth winning, and he meant to win her. And she would love to receive a secret letter.

A symposium in a pirate town was a riotous affair, with twenty couches in a huge circle and women on half of them with their men, loud songs and louder laughter. A symposium in honour of the feast of Cypriot Aphrodite was several degrees further down a scale which ran from salacious to riot, and worse.

'This is *not* like home,' Abraham commented, as they walked through the streets of Byzantium. Every house had a goddess out front, most decorated with saffron, some with real gold. 'These parties are scarier than battles.' He waved at an Aphrodite who was obviously using her hands to pleasure herself. 'This is *not* Alexandria.'

Satyrus, his left arm wrapped tightly by a physician and a few drops of poppy in his veins, felt capable of anything. 'Like Kinon's at home?'

Abraham shook his head. 'No. Not at all like Kinon's. Like – well, like what my father *thinks* goes on at Kinon's. They play games ...'

Satyrus hugged his friend with his good arm. Abraham had always been something of a prude, by Hellenic standards. 'I'm here to make a deal with Demostrate,' he said. 'I'll survive some games.'

Abraham coughed politely into his fist.

Before the sun was fully set, Satyrus lay between Daedalus of Halicarnassus, living proof of how thin was the line between piracy and mercenary service, and Abraham, the eldest son of a Jewish merchant in Alexandria and yet already accepted in this world as a man of worth. The men were well dressed, oiled and in some cases perfumed like the gentry of any town of Hellenes, although they came in more skin colours than were normal in Athens or Miletus. Their common livelihood crossed the barriers of race or riches, in the form of scars and a certain complexion that could only be earned by years at sea, and gave the skin the look of old leather, whether that skin was ink-black or milk white. And every man present wore a sword strapped to his side, even on a kline at a symposium.

Beyond Daedalus was Aeschinades, one of the most famous captains in the Aegean, and he lay with a beautiful woman with dark tan skin, her breasts under his hands, her back to him and her face towards Satyrus. Satyrus wasn't sure whether he was actually copulating with her or not, but he didn't look too closely. Her face was curiously blank – Satyrus looked twice, almost involuntarily, wondering why the woman did not even simulate pleasure.

On the other side, beyond Abraham, lay Manes, the terror of the coast of Phrygia, a man who had gobbled up more shipping than Poseidon, or so he claimed with open hubris. He shared his couch with a veritable Ganymede, a boy so attractive and so openly, brazenly sexual that *his* expression made Satyrus uncomfortable, as if he sought by his antics to make up for the lack of emotion on the dark woman's face.

'I warned you,' Abraham said from beside him.

'I didn't pay enough attention,' Satyrus conceded. 'I've never seen this kind of behaviour, even at Kinon's. I confess my error.'

Abraham grinned. 'Wait until the wine goes around and the flute girls come out. Ever played "feed the flute girl"?'

Satyrus felt himself blush. 'I've heard—'

'That's what I mean. You won't "hear". I've been here four weeks – I'm used to it. To them.' Abraham held out his cup for wine. 'I have to admit, I like the bastards. They say what they mean, and they are afraid of nothing.' He shook his head. 'Actually, most of them are afraid of Demostrate, and of Manes. Other than that ...' He grinned. 'But you are either with them or you aren't.'

'You fed a flute girl?' Satyrus asked.

'Yes,' Abraham said. He blushed. 'And I will again.'

'They prey on the weak for money,' Satyrus said. 'All these women are chattel slaves.'

'So do the Diadochoi,' Abraham said. 'And I say again – either you are with them or not. They will ask you to play – and if you will not, they will never deal with you.'

Satyrus watched one of the captains further around the circle strike a slave sharply, a casual blow that knocked the slave flat. He breathed in and out slowly, as if preparing for combat.

Abraham leaned over. 'Many of these men have *been* slaves,' he said. 'This is not our world.'

Dinner was excellent – young kid with saffron, a simple rabbit stew with beans that was nonetheless delicious, and oysters, thousands of them, brought in with a nude Aphrodite on a giant shell, and the whole carried by four big men.

The captains began to stamp and cheer, even as they poured oysters down their throats.

She was a beauty – not in the first blush of youth, but tall, strong and well-breasted. Her hair was dyed almost white-blonde, like the goddess, and her nipples were gilded. She held herself like a goddess, not a slave.

The oysters went down noisily, and Satyrus found that Aphrodite intended to share his couch. 'I come from Demostrate,' she said in a deep, clear voice. Her Greek had no more accent than she had raiment.

'Take her, lad!' Demostrate shouted. 'I'm too damn old!'

'Feast of Aphrodite!' Manes shouted. He waved his cup. 'Do her honour!'

The other men shouted and the calls became louder. The singer gestured to her musicians and began to sing in a stronger voice – a hymn to Aphrodite. Sappho, in fact – a piece that Satyrus knew.

Abraham touched his shoulder while the rest of them shouted. 'I warned you,' he said.

Satyrus rolled back, and Aphrodite ran her hand up under his chiton, grabbed his penis and pulled it sharply. Satyrus was amazed to find that her fingers cut straight through the poppy in his blood and the pain in his arm.

'They mean for you to – copulate. With her. Now.' Abraham's face was carefully neutral. 'I warned you!'

Aphrodite flicked her thumb across the tip of his manhood and he was hard. Just like that.

'Relax,' she said. 'Would you prefer me on top or beneath you?' she asked, her right hand working his penis like raw dough.

Simple courtesy came to Satyrus's rescue. 'The goddess must be on top,' he said, and rolled under her. 'Please mind my arm.'

The other men roared to see her straddle him. She squatted and impaled herself on him, and then lay along his length. 'The longer this takes,' she said, 'the better they will like you, and the more luck you bring us.' She moved slowly up and down, and then bent her head so that her white-gold dyed hair covered his face. He could hear the roar of the captains, but he couldn't see them – he felt his response quicken.

He noted that her gilded nipples left traces of gold across his chiton.

'Unpin my chiton,' he said up into her hair. 'I don't stand a chance of lasting—'

She pressed a hand on his left arm, and pain welled up like water from a spring. 'If you let me, I can make you last a long time,' she said in his ear, her breasts moving along his chest.

Outside the tent of her hair, they were pounding their couches, singing the hymn to Aphrodite, and Satyrus could hear Demostrate's voice raised the loudest. The man was a fine singer.

She had his chiton unpinned, and he used his right arm to strip it over his head – more distraction, and more pain in his left arm, and more cheering.

'Second time!' Demostrate shouted, and the hymn began again.

'You are very beautiful,' Satyrus said. 'Are you a slave?'

Aphrodite breathed out suddenly, raising her face from his. Her lips were so precisely formed that they looked as if they were *sharp*. 'I am yours,' she said. 'Demostrate has given me to you.' She sank along his length, rose up and gave a shout – simulated ecstasy, Satyrus suspected, having seen Phiale do the same – but brilliantly simulated. The room roared and the hymn rolled on.

'Third time!' Demostrate shouted, and the hymn began again.

'Hurt me again,' Satyrus said into her hair. The hair was saving him – he could see neither the lush provocation of her skin nor the leering faces of his dinner companions, and he kept it that way, confining himself to the privacy she made him.

She rubbed her thumb with deadly accuracy along the line of

the break on his forearm, and then her other hand rubbed up between his legs as the pain rolled through his body, compensating – what kind of a life gave a woman this sort of skill? Satyrus was no longer fully in the symposium, instead hovering in a separate world, a place that smelled of spice and perfume and sex, where wine and poppy filled his head, pain and pleasure ran together – he had no control over his body, and it made him *afraid*, more than battle, so that his manhood began to wilt, and she writhed against him and hissed, and his hips rolled in response to her, and he grabbed her head and his mouth closed on hers. She gasped, as if being kissed shocked her, and he reached down and ran his hand between them, and she gasped again into his kiss.

'Fifth time!' Demostrate yelled, and the room cheered as if they had just won a fight. Satyrus wondered where the fourth time had gone and suddenly passed the point of control and finished, his body arching into hers, his hands clenched in her flesh, and she shouted again, and this time he neither knew nor cared whether her pleasure was simulated.

She moved to roll away, but his right arm crushed her to him. 'Don't move,' he said.

She rode him for part of another verse, laughing softly against him, and then he pulled his chiton – his best – from the floor and wiped both of them clean while the other guests hooted and cheered and the woman who had sung the hymn looked away in distaste. Satyrus got up, naked, and walked over to Demostrate, his member still tumescent, usually a social gaffe at a symposium.

'That may have been the best gift of my life,' Satyrus said. 'But you still owe me a ram for *Black Falcon*.'

Demostrate laughed. 'Was that five times, or six?' he asked. 'Good luck either way. You are a cunning one, lad. I saw you!' He laughed and pulled Satyrus down on to his couch. In a whisper, he said, 'You think we're fucking barbarians, lad. And maybe you're right. But now we all know that *you* are, too.' He sat up. 'Can you get us a port on the Euxine?' he asked. Sitting on the edge of his kline, he took a heavy silver *mastos* cup two hundred years old, dipped it in a krater held by two slaves and drank it off.

'Yes,' Satyrus said.

Demostrate handed him the cup.

Satyrus drank all of it, every drop, and turned it, licked the nipple and rattled the bead, and men cheered him.

'Then let's go and fuck Eumeles as hard as you fucked the goddess, lad. I think the boys fancy you.'

Satyrus couldn't stop the bitter smile that crossed his lips. 'The feeling is not mutual,' Satyrus said.

Demostrate had his diadem on his head, the jewels winking in the firelight. He grabbed Satyrus and pulled him close, so that their naked shoulders rubbed against each other. The pirate king's skin was a loom of scars, a far cry from the cream and doeskin of Aphrodite, and an odd contrast to Satyrus, whose mind was running too fast. The old man thrust his face into Satyrus's face.

'Good,' Demostrate said. 'They're scum. Never forget it – they're all circling, ready for me to die.' He laughed. 'And not one of them could keep all this together.' His breath wasn't foul. It smelled of cloves and wine. 'You could command them, in a few years.'

Satyrus shook his head. 'No,' he said.

Demostrate leaned close. 'When you have a chance, kill Manes.'

Satyrus looked at the old pirate, as shocked as when the goddess's thumb had flicked his penis. The effect of his words was physical.

Demostrate laughed. 'Welcome to Tartarus, lad. If you want us to fight for you, you'll have to do more than make love at a symposium. Manes needs to die, lad. And if you kill him, the others – well, many of them are sheep, for all they're the terror of the seas.' He laughed. 'Now go back to your own couch before the others decide that *you* have to die.'

Satyrus rose. Demostrate kissed him – a man's kiss, no different from any kiss that any guest would get at a symposium, but it chilled Satyrus. And as he began to walk back across the tiled floor, he happened to look at Manes, where he lay entwined with his seductive Ganymede. The man looked back at him like a beast in a cage. Satyrus looked away – made himself look around, as if amused at the whole scene, and then back into Manes' animal eyes.

He had no trouble seeing why all these hard men feared Manes.

He walked back to his couch. Aphrodite rolled off, but he grabbed her hand. 'Honour my couch, Goddess,' he said.

She smiled. 'If you ask,' she said. 'My, you have nice manners.'

'I'm from Alexandria,' he said. Then he set himself to talk to her, because her tent of hair had kept him sane.

Hours later he walked home naked under his chlamys, cold and damp, and halfway home he stripped the cloak over his head and stood in the marketplace with the icy rain running over his skin.

Abraham stood by him, and when he felt that he had punished himself sufficiently, he followed Abraham, and they walked home together, with Aphrodite following them, her belongings balanced on her head. She followed Satyrus into the house.

Theron was surprised by his nudity, but not for long. 'Looks like quite the party,' he said. He looked at Aphrodite. 'You were a party favour?' Theron asked. 'Wish I'd been invited.'

Satyrus threw himself into one of Abraham's comfortable chairs – heavy wooden ones, like the Nabataeans used. 'You're free. And you have my thanks. You played your role beautifully.'

Aphrodite smiled. 'Free? Are you serious?'

Satyrus couldn't help but smile at her joy – so much more real than her gasps in his arms. 'Who would tease a slave that way? Yes, of course.'

She stood, her eyes downcast. She was as old as Satyrus – perhaps nineteen. Quite old, for a sex slave. Her body was superb, muscled, fit and well-kept, but her face was showing signs of her profession.

Theron raised her chin. 'You are Corinthian!' he said.

She smiled. 'Yes,' she said.

He laughed. 'You actually *are* a priestess of Aphrodite,' he said.

'Yes,' she said. 'I was. I ran away. The goddess followed me.' She looked down again, her cheeks red.

Satyrus wanted to be sick. 'You are free. And if I can do anything for you – passage, perhaps? Or a place in a household?'

Abraham put a hand under her elbow. 'Let me find you a place you can sleep,' he said. 'I have a friend upstairs who will be happy to meet you.'

Satyrus had had no idea that Abraham had a *friend*. He put his head in his hands as soon as she was gone. 'Oh, gods,' he said.

Theron said nothing.

After a while, Satyrus looked up. 'We need an allied port on the Euxine,' he said.

Theron sighed, and said nothing.

After a while, Satyrus went to bed.

10

When she awoke, she had lost years of her life, and she was a child in her mother's felt yurt, camping on the sea of grass. Gryphons and eagles warred with stags and leopards on the worked felt hangings, and pine resin scented the air. A brazier of worked bronze hung from the central poles over the hearth, and the air was warm, like summer. She was wrapped in fur. The woman by the brazier, in her white deerskin coat, was her mother.

In one great rush, all her life came back to her, a single cascade of memory, so that her mother died and she gave birth in a single instant, and she wept for her distant son and her dead mother with the same tears.

'So,' Nihmu said. She was sitting on her knees, wearing a robe of white deerskin worked in red and blue patterns with dyed hair, with rows of golden plaques at the seams and golden cones with dyed deer-hair tufts tinkling as she raised her arm to feed hot wine to Melitta. 'So – you are back to us.'

Melitta drank the wine, smiled at Nihmu and was gone again.

When next she awoke, Nihmu was kneeling by her, arranging crisp wool blankets and a clean fur. 'Hush, child,' she said.

Melitta sat up so suddenly that her head spun, and she lay back on her side. 'I'm awake!' she said.

'Yes,' Nihmu said. She was speaking Sakje. They both were. Melitta got her head up again. 'I almost died, didn't I?'

'Some of the people think that you did die.' Nihmu frowned. 'I find the people – different. But it is I who am different.'

'You seem the same to me,' Melitta said.

Her appetite returned like her memories, and she ate and ate. It was two days before her fingers explored the stiffness of her face. She felt a chill despite the fur robe that wrapped her.

'Aunt Nihmu?' she asked. 'How bad is my face?'

'Were you planning to be a Greek matron?' Nihmu asked. 'If so, I suspect you'd have some difficulty.'

Coenus pushed through the flap of the yurt. 'I will go and sacrifice – something. By Hermes and all the gods, Melitta – I'm sorry to have lost you. It must have been brutal!'

'Brutal?' Melitta was fingering her cheek. 'That's exactly what it was,' she said. She sat up. 'I felt that I was being tested,' she said.

'Perhaps you were,' Nihmu agreed. 'She's worried about the scar.'

Coenus kissed her. 'No man worthy of the name will think less of you for the scar,' he said.

Melitta frowned. 'That bad?' she asked. She could see in their eyes that it was bad. 'May I have a mirror?' she asked.

'How did you get it?' Nihmu asked her. She took a mirror out of her sleeve, as if she'd been waiting for this moment.

'Did my good horse make it? The one with the gryphon brand?' Melitta asked.

Coenus nodded. 'Yes,' he said. 'Quite a horse.'

'I killed the last owner. He was trying to put an arrow on his bow when I jumped him.' She looked away. 'His arrow scratched me.'

'It was poisoned,' Nihmu said.

'I think it saved me,' Melitta admitted. 'I was in a haze – almost living in the spirit land. I might not have made it in this world.'

Coenus made the face he always made at barbarian notions of reality. 'It almost killed you, girl.' His protestation sounded odd, and Melitta realized that he too was speaking in Sakje.

Samahe came in through the tent flap. 'Now we shall rejoice,' she said. She came and folded herself into the space between Nihmu and the bed of furs. She took both of Melitta's hands in hers, and Melitta had another moment of memory, because Samahe's hands were the same rough and smooth that her mother's had been, ridges of callus and muscle and the backs as soft as any woman's. She saw the mirror and shrugged. 'You look like a woman who is ready to be a war queen,' Samahe said. 'Not like some soft Greek girl. Take the mirror and look. Then put it away. There is much to do.'

Melitta picked up the mirror – a Greek one, with a bronze and ivory handle and a silver reflector. The image was true, even in the firelight of the yurt. The same slightly upturned nose, the same black hair. And on the left side of her face, a black line like a tattoo, jagged like a lightning bolt, from the corner of her left eye to her chin.

No person with great beauty ever fully values it, the sheer attraction, the pleasure of it, until it is lost. Only then did Melitta admit to herself that she had been beautiful. The kind of girl for which fashionable Alexandria boys wrote poems.

'I have a feeling that my future as a valuable hetaira has taken a death-blow,' she said, to mask her inner scream. She looked like something that had been dead.

'How many men did you kill?' a new voice asked, and a small man pushed into the lodge. Everyone shuffled to make room around the fire and the brazier as Ataelus sat cross-legged, his fierce face unusually happy. 'You came back to us!' he said.

Melitta took his hands and kissed him on the cheek. 'Ah! Now I think I will live. My mother's best warrior.'

'You are like your mother born again,' Samahe said.

'Six,' Melitta said. 'At least six. I tried to let one live, but the gods took his life anyway.'

'Aiyee!' Ataelus shouted. 'Six Sauromatae!' He leaned back and laughed so hard that he had to cross his hands on his stomach. 'Six, and took their horses and arms and brought them here! I have singers already singing it, lady.' He leaned close. 'I ask you – I have to ask you. You are here to raise the tribes?'

Melitta thought of her new face. 'Yes,' she said.

'Good,' Ataelus said. 'My name is not enough. You – and Nihmu, and even Coenus, back from the time of Kineax – together, we will raise the tribes. You must grow well, so that we can ride. We will ride far.'

Samahe nodded. 'Too long, we have been outlaws on our own grass.'

'This winter, we take it all back,' Ataelus said. 'Upazan killed your father. Somehow he must die, despite the prophecy. Perhaps you will kill him.'

'Prophecy?' Melitta asked.

Nihmu looked at the ground. 'Upazan may not die by a man's blade,' she said.

Melitta was going to say something derisive about superstition, but she knew that this was the wrong place. *These are my people now,* she thought.

'We start with Marthax,' Melitta said.

All the heads in the lodge turned to her. Ataelus shook his head. 'I hear the voice of the Lady Srayanka – but I had thought to win over Parshtaevalt of the Cruel Hands first, and then the Grass Cats. Urvara is close to Olbia. She will be your friend.'

Melitta sat up straight. She looked at Nihmu. 'The eagles are flown, Ataelus. When Marthax submits, all the tribes will come over, and we will not have civil war.' She used the Greek word for internal strife, because Sakje lacked a way to express it. 'It is the prophecy – which many should know. And should be in your song.'

Ataelus nodded and scratched his chin. 'I will not treat you like a girl in council again. Marthax? He is old. His sons are all dead.' Ataelus rocked back and forth. 'Perhaps it could be done.'

Nihmu spoke up. 'When I was a prophet, I sang it,' she said. 'But Melitta, I didn't say that it had to be Marthax first.'

'Melitta,' Ataelus said, and shook his head. 'Such a kindly name.'

'Srayanka chose that name,' Samahe said, with a dark look at her husband.

'The people have chosen another. Just as Srayanka was "Cruel Hands" at war.' Ataelus shrugged. 'The people make names. I have one. You have one. She is a warrior – she came in with her kills and her spoil, and she was named.'

Samahe frowned.

'What is my war name, Uncle?' Melitta asked Ataelus.

'Srakorlax,' Ataelus said. 'The scent of death.'

It was two weeks before she was ready to ride, and she still had spells of dizziness. But every day they came to her yurt, and in those two weeks, she felt herself change, as if her mind was moving to meet the new face that had been cut into her old face.

She had imagined, when leaving Alexandria, that she would have to prove herself to the Sakje – that she would have to win Ataelus, and then, with him at her back, impress the other Sakje.

It wasn't like that at all. Instead, they were *instantly* her people. As if she had been awaited. Perhaps she had. And perhaps the gods had given her the trial so that she and her scar could ride into their camps and lead them. But she sensed who they needed her to be, and every day she allowed herself to become that person.

After all, the person they needed was her mother. And she remembered her mother well.

So they sat in her yurt, and planned.

'What of the Sauromatae?' she asked.

'We leave them to their stolen land,' Ataelus said. 'For now. First we ride west. Then, when we are strong, we ride back east.'

'My brother intends to be king of the Bosporus,' Melitta said. 'He intends to make war on Eumeles.'

Ataelus nodded. 'He will make war to win his father's portion, as you will make war to win your mother's. This is just as it should be – and you will be strong allies. But his road and ours are not the same. Marthax has taken the people too close to the cities, and the result is not good. I ask that you take the people back to the grass.'

'Is that all you ask?' Melitta said.

The others, warriors and friends, fell silent.

Ataelus gave a half-smile. 'Too long, I have been the only voice to command.'

Melitta shook her head. 'No. I speak no hidden censure, Ataelus. I have been gone for years. What else do you ask? What else do the people need?'

'If we go back to the grass, as it was in Satrax's time, all will be well,' Ataelus said.

'It may be that the wine cannot be put back in the flask,' Samahe said to her husband. 'The people like living closer to the settlements. What woman wears hides when she can have cloth? What man wears iron when the settlements sell fine bronze armour? Good Greek helmets?'

Ataelus made a face. 'It is true,' he said ruefully.

Nihmu sat forward. 'Now that you can speak, it is time that you rejoined the worlds of the people – both worlds. Will you come into the smoke with me?'

Samahe frowned. 'It is too soon.'

Nihmu shook her head. 'It is *not* too soon. The lady almost lost herself in the spirit world coming here. This is because she has been too far from the spirits for too long.'

Melitta had always enjoyed the smoke, although she seldom, if ever, had the kind of revelations that the *baqcas* like her father and Nihmu derived from it. 'I will come with you,' she said.

Samahe frowned again. 'Nihmu, are you baqca? I thought that your powers left you.'

Coenus put a hand on Nihmu's shoulder, but she shook it off. 'I am baqca!' she said with too much emphasis.

'Perhaps you should go and speak with Tameax,' Samahe said.

'He is?' Nihmu asked, haughtily.

'He is my baqca,' Ataelus said, looking elsewhere. 'He is young, but he does not lack power. He might guide you.'

'I need no guidance, much less from a man,' Nihmu shot back. 'My prophecies are known in every tent on the plains.'

'It is true,' Samahe said. 'But you were a virgin girl when you spoke those words, and your father spoke through your lips. Or so the people say.'

Melitta sensed pressures that she did not yet understand, a fracture among her closest friends. 'Let us sit in the smoke,' she said. 'Then let us see your baqca. We will need the omens tested before we ride.' She hardened her voice. 'But before the midwinter feast, I want to find Marthax.'

Sakje people took smoke by erecting small tents of hide, shaped like the pyramids of Aegypt, the seams sealed with good pine pitch from the northern forests. Then they lit small braziers – ornate works of bronze and brass, many made by Greek smiths in the towns, with refined charcoal made by the Sindi charcoal-burners in the valleys. When the brazier was hot, the Sakje would throw handfuls of seeds – mostly from the wild hemp, but some from other plants; every man and woman had her own particular choices, for scent and depth of dreams – and the smoke would fill the tent, and people would sit and dream, or walk the spirit ways.

As a child, Melitta had thought nothing of the smoke, because every Sakje took smoke, her mother included. But after exposure to Alexandria, to the Aegyptian temples of Hathor and Bast, she saw the smoke with two sets of eyes. Greek Melitta saw it as a drug, little different from the poppy that both healed and destroyed, that gave beautiful dreams and nightmares, that both aided the physician and was the physician's despair. Indeed, watching three prostitutes share poppy by turning it to smoke in the night market of Alexandria had opened her eyes. To what the smoke might contain.

Yet in her heart, she was still a Sakje girl, and she did not doubt that the visions and pathways of the smoke were true ones, even if she understood the agency of the smoke better than others. So she lay curled on the floor of Nihmu's smoke tent, sometimes raising the flap to draw a breath of fresh, sweet air, but mostly breathing deep of the pungent stuff, like burning pine boughs but somehow more deep.

For a long time, the smoke only reduced her pain, but then … *she was standing on the sea of grass in summer, and a red wind played among the ripe seed heads of the grass, so that ripples moved and swayed – the time of year when the Sakje said that the grass was alive.*

And she saw Samahe's yurt standing exactly where it stood in the waking world, but there were no other yurts and no horses, only the single structure. And in the centre of Samahe's yurt there stood a tree, and that tree filled the yurt and rose through the smoke hole and away into the heavens.

And at the base of the tree stood a dead man, his bone arms crossed over the white ribs of his chest, his bony rump leaning on the tree, so that even in death he conveyed both impatience and arrogance.

It was not Melitta's habit to be afraid, in the world of waking or in the spirit world, and she walked up to the dead man. 'Why do you wait, dead man?' she asked.

The skull of the dead man laughed, a hollow sound. 'For you,' he said.

'Do I know you?' she asked, and then, feeling a prick of fear, 'Did I kill you?'

'Do my bones still bear the meat and gristle of life, girl? Your dead still seek the tree, and their bones still seek to lose the meat of life. They would make a worse sight than me.'

Melitta found a skull impossible to read.

'What do you want? This is my dream!' she insisted.

'You have walked far from the people, that you can argue with a spirit guide. Do you still speak the tongue of the people in your head? Because all I hear from you is Greek.' The skull smiled – but the skull always smiled.

'I speak Sakje!' she insisted, but even as she said the words, they came from her mouth in Greek, and she watched them form into Greek letters and float towards the skeleton and the tree. A bony hand rose and waved them away, as if they were insects in high summer.

'Not really,' the skeleton said. 'You know the words, but not the way.'

'Am I supposed to climb the tree?' Melitta asked.

'You? All I see here is a Greek girl who can kill men.' The skull's hollow laughter rang out.

Melitta stepped up closer to the self-professed spirit guide. 'My father was a Greek man, and he climbed the tree. I wonder if you are a guide. Not all spirits in the world of dreams are beneficent.'

The skeleton shook with the force of its laughter, and her dream rang with it, like a gale on the plains. 'Get hence, usurper!' he roared. 'I came to warn you, but you have failed the test.'

Melitta didn't flinch. 'I need no more tests,' she said. 'Be gone, spirit, before I break your bones.'

She awoke with a foul taste in her mouth and a pounding in her head, as if her temples were the tight-stretched skin of a drum and the drummer's sticks beat her head in time to the pulsing of her heart.

Nihmu was weeping.

Melitta curled around her and stroked her forehead. 'What's wrong, Auntie?'

Nihmu rose suddenly, throwing Melitta back against the leather cushions on the floor. 'Nothing!' she said. 'There is nothing wrong. I saw many spirit guides, and I have received much news. I must think.'

Melitta's head hurt too much to ask further questions. She let Nihmu go, and then she breathed deeply of the fresh, cold air outside the tent. Her headache was banished in minutes and she knelt in the new snow outside, collecting the cushions, stripping the brazier and dumping the coals to hiss and steam in the snow.

Then she knocked down the hide tent and folded it quickly, before it grew too cold and stiff.

All of these things, she realized in putting them away, were Samahe's, not Nihmu's. She took them back to Samahe's yurt.

The Sakje woman was sitting cross-legged on the floor of her lodge, working by the light of two Greek lamps. She was weaving thongs through small bronze scales, repairing an armour shirt.

This was work that Melitta knew well from her youth, and she sat down with the other woman and began to cut a leather thong from a patch of caribou hide, holding the tough hide in her teeth and cutting with a sharp knife. They worked in silence because both women had their mouths full. After some time, Samahe spat out the last of her thong. 'You took smoke?' she asked.

Melitta gave a wry smile. 'It took me, more like.' She started a new thong, cutting the edge of the hide carefully. A skilled man, or woman, could make a single thong many horse-lengths long, all a single thickness. Melitta wasn't that good, but she was pleased to see that her thong was not like a child's, full of knots and bumps. She still had skill.

Samahe nodded. 'I don't like the smoke any more,' she said. 'When I was a maiden, the smoke was good. Now it brings me only dreams of all the men I have killed.' She shrugged. 'The last few years, I have killed many and many.' She did not say this with the pride of a warrior, but merely with weariness.

'I met a guide,' Melitta said. 'Or a demon. He barred me from the tree and mocked me as a Greek.'

Samahe's eyes met hers. 'I wouldn't share that with other people,' she said.

Melitta shrugged. 'It makes no sense,' she said. 'My father was Greek. By all accounts, he seldom even accepted that he was baqca. Yet no spirit guide ever blocked him from the tree!'

'That is Greek talk,' Samahe said. 'The spirits do as they do, and it is not for us to question.'

'Bah,' Melitta said. 'That is tyranny. It is illogical.' Even as she spoke the Greek word, she understood how deep this conflict would run, and it made her angry. 'I am Sakje!' she said.

Samahe looked up from her work. 'I don't doubt it, lady. Do not let any other of the people doubt it, either.' She chewed on the thong for a dozen heartbeats, softening the stuff. Then she leaned forward. 'And Nihmu?' she asked.

'I couldn't say,' Melitta answered. 'She mentioned many spirit guides.'

Samahe shook her head. 'Why must she be baqca?' she asked. 'She cursed the gift when she had it, and rejoiced when it left her. Where is her mate? Why has she returned?'

Melitta was used to the gossip of women. She enjoyed it when it was well meant, and she judged Samahe's comments as kindly. 'Her mate is captive to Eumeles at Pantecapaeum.' She took the hide from her mouth. 'But it is many years and she has no child, and in Alexandria, we wondered if the lack of a child was weighing on her.' And then, unbidden, thoughts of what she had seen between Nihmu and Coenus on the trail came to her, and she frowned.

Samahe shook her head. 'I don't think she should have returned,' she said.

The next day, Melitta sat in another yurt with Tameax, the youngest baqca she had ever met. Nihmu had refused to come.

'You are no older than I am,' Melitta said, after clasping his hand and sitting down. She saw that he had a fine drum – indeed, it looked to her to be Kam Baqca's drum, an artefact from her youth, with tiny iron charms hanging all around the rim. He tapped it idly with a long bone as he looked at her.

'I am older than you by a number of cycles,' he said with a smile. 'But I won't expect you to believe it.'

'Really?' she asked.

'I have not always been a man. At least, I think I can remember being a fish.' He shrugged and smiled.

Melitta laughed. 'Most men claim to have been some great and noble animal, like an eagle or a bear.'

'Most men are liars,' he said.

'Perhaps, by claiming to have been a small thing, you seek to disarm me into believing other things,' Melitta drawled. He had deep cushions, leather ones filled with horsehair, and she allowed herself to slip back on to them. In a curious way, it was like debating with Philokles.

'You are not like a Sakje,' he said. 'Your brain runs like a river that has many channels.'

'I have been in many places,' Melitta said. 'Yet I am a Sakje.'

'I have seen this same thing in Ataelus,' Tameax said. 'Why do the Greeks think so differently?'

'I wish I had Philokles here to tell you,' Melitta answered, and found her eyes filling with tears. 'He was my teacher, in a kind of learning called "logic".' She sat up. 'He spoke at length with Kam Baqca, a whole winter.' She felt it important that he see that the greatest baqca of the current age had approved of the Greek thinking. 'You understand what the Greeks call mathematics?'

'Understand? No. But I know to what you refer.' He smiled at her. 'Did you really kill six Sauromatae?'

She nodded.

He shrugged. 'I will tell the spirits. Some spirits object to you, as an alien. Others call you the daughter of Srayanka. Others say you will kill the people.' He laughed, and he had a clear laugh. 'Spirits are all a little mad – how can they be otherwise, when they are already dead?'

'I met one in the smoke,' Melitta said. Samahe had advised her to keep this to herself.

He leaned forward. 'Yes?'

'A skeleton,' she said.

'Bah – most of them have but naked bones, until you clothe them with your own dreams. Who was he?' The baqca was intensely interested, quivering like an Aegyptian cat watching a mouse in a grain sack.

'I didn't ask.' She shifted uncertainly on the cushions. 'He annoyed me and I threatened him.'

Tameax laughed his clear, silvery laugh. 'You may be Sakje,' he said. He rocked back on his heels and poured herb tea from a kettle on his tripod. 'Nihmu is avoiding me. She is *not* recovering her powers. Why would she, who had so much power, pretend? All here honour her.'

Melitta felt that she was on dangerous ground. 'She seeks more than honour,' she allowed. 'I'm not sure that I understand her.'

'You treat me as an equal,' Tameax said.

Melitta met his eye. 'How should I treat you?'

Tameax shook his head. 'The people have two ways to deal with me,' he said. 'Some deny that I have power, insisting that I am too young, that I have not given my manhood for power, that I cannot be real. Others treat me as an object of fear. No one treats me as an equal. Yet you, a queen, speak to me as if I am your brother.'

Melitta shrugged.

'Will you treat all the people this way, even when you are the war queen of the Assagatje?' he asked. 'The scar on your cheek says that you could be a hard queen to follow.'

'What is your place in all this?' she shot back.

He nodded, pinching his lips. 'If you become queen, I will become your baqca.' He handed her a cup of tea. 'I seek to know what kind of queen you might be. Ataelus will follow you whatever I say, and my loyalty to him is depthless. So I will not leave your side. I come with Ataelus, his horse and his bow – part of his equipage.' He used the Sakje word that meant the same as the Greek panoply – all the war things. 'You do not fear me, or despise me. This will mean much to me.' He nodded. 'Why will you ride against Marthax, and not to the tribes that will support you?'

Melitta raised her head and looked away from the intensity of his blue eyes, at the hangings behind his head. She thought for a time that seemed to her long. 'There are many reasons, all true, and yet some are more true than others,' she said.

He nodded.

'If I ride to Parshtaevalt or Urvara, I will build an army. In answer, Marthax will *also* build an army. When armies are built, they fight. Once that battle is fought, it will no longer matter whether I win or I lose, because the people will have split.'

Tameax fingered his wispy black beard. He was remarkably handsome. The remarkable part is that he was a baqca, and they were usually ugly men, or mad ones. He was strictly sane, and had the straight nose and blue eyes of the Medes and the Persians. 'This seems true to me. Did you dream it?'

'No,' she said. She shrugged, wondering why she was being so honest. She'd considered her strategy again and again, and it had occurred to her to tell the people that she had dreamed it, but his eyes disarmed her.

The shadow of a smile touched the corners of his mouth. 'Perhaps I will,' he said. In another man, it would have been an admission of the falsity of his dreams, but that was not how it came from him. 'But there is more.'

'You are – very like my tutor.' She sat up fully and crossed her legs. Then she picked up her tea cup – a beautiful thing of pottery, unlike any other cup she had ever handled. 'If I go to Parshtaevalt, he will advise me. And Urvara – she will advise me. And each will have their own needs and desires and they will quarrel, and I will lose by it. And each will expect my mother – always my mother. When I go straight to Marthax and ...' She paused, having almost revealed her entire plan. Not even to this handsome young man. She took a breath. 'When I win him over, *I* will be queen. By my own hands.'

Tameax nodded. 'Would you take me as a lover, Queen of the Assagatje?'

Melitta felt herself blush. 'No,' she said with real regret. 'Not if you are to be my baqca.'

Now it was his turn to flush – clearly, it was not the answer he expected. 'Maidens seldom refuse me,' he said.

She shrugged, smiling at him. 'Many of your maidens are not queens, I expect,' she said.

'We will see,' he answered. 'I am a patient man. And to be honest, right now we sit in my yurt on a field of new snow, far from our lands, the enemy of every man and horse in the vale of the Tanais, and part of my mind imagines what it might be to be baqca of a queen, but the other says that we will never be anything but a band of brigands, and that you dream big dreams for nothing.'

'This from a baqca?' she asked. She rose to her feet. 'Is the cup from Qin?' she asked.

'Yes,' he said. 'I had four, and now I have but two.'

'Perhaps we will go there one day.' She touched his hand in giving him the cup. 'Nihmu went with Leon.'

'I have been to the grass that laps on the shores of Qin,' he said. 'I would like to go again. Indeed, it was that trip that made me baqca.' He put the cup reverentially into a small lacquer box and then he took her hand. 'You see deeply,' he said.

She took her hand out of his and stepped away. 'You say that to every spear-maiden who comes to this tent,' she said.

His eyes sparkled. 'I do too.'

'Keep it for them and be my friend,' she said.

'The cycle will bring what it brings,' he said.

11

AEGEAN, WINTER, 311–310 BC

The days after the feast of Aphrodite were full of work. Satyrus heard the views of each of his officers and then made his own decisions, and it was a week after the mad symposium that he briefed them all on how he saw the winter.

'I am going to take the *Golden Lotus* to Alexandria,' he said. 'My people deserve to know that I am alive. Further, I need money in quantity and counsel. If I'm lucky, Diodorus will be home for the winter. We need our hired Macedonians – as marines first, and then as the core of our army.'

Theron nodded. None of the other officers had any comment to make.

'Theron will go to Lysimachos as my ambassador in the *Herakles*.' Satyrus was satisfied with the condition of the *Herakles*. 'We need to choose a crew from our own sailors, Abraham's and any of the captives who will take service with us for the *Hornet*.'

Diokles nodded. 'Most of them still come around to the warehouse every morning,' he said. 'You paid them. They're like stray cats when you give them a bowl of milk.'

Theron shook his head. 'You threatened to kill them all!' he protested.

Diokles grinned. 'He's got quite the reputation now,' the Tyrian said.

'Daedalus should be here,' Theron said.

'He's a mercenary and what I need to discuss is still too raw,' Satyrus answered.

Theron shook his head in disagreement. 'Daedalus has been loyal ever since we got here. And he commands a powerful ship and a good crew. And despite what men say, he's no pirate.'

'And what of me?' Abraham asked.

'You're my ambassador to the pirates,' Satyrus said. 'And you get the *Hornet* for your own, if you want him.'

'Nice.' Abraham smiled. 'That's the best present I've ever had. Mine to keep?'

'Unless you lose him to one of Eumeles' cruisers,' Satyrus shot back.

Abraham shook his head. 'Thanks,' he said again. Then, after a moment, 'You'll go to Rhodos?'

Diokles shook his head. 'I've sailed for Rhodos most of my life,' he said. 'They won't like it, that you came from here. And there must be rumours in every port in the east now – that we're here.'

Satyrus leaned back until his head was against the Sakje tapestry that hung behind him. 'I've thought about this for a week,' he said. 'Hear me and tell me if I'm in the grip of delusion.' He gave them a rueful smile. 'We need Rhodos *and* the pirates. *And* Lysimachos. We need them all.'

Diokles smiled. 'Pigs can't fly,' he said.

Theron shook his head. 'Hear him out,' he said.

Abraham rubbed his chin and looked at his friend. 'Do they have a common interest?' he asked.

Satyrus nodded at Abraham. 'Give that man a golden daric. Rhodos wants the pirates gone. *We can take them away.* If we defeat Eumeles, Demostrate will return to Pantecapaeum and the pirate fleet will disperse. At the very least, they'll be out of the Propontis and the grain fleets will move.'

Diokles whistled. 'Just like that? And Rhodos will just let them go?'

'Rhodos is facing extinction,' Satyrus said. 'They are trying to be the balance point in the war between One-Eye and Ptolemy. They need peace for their hulls to carry cargoes, and they need peace to be able to apply their sea power to the pirates. Instead, they have war all around them and their losses mount. At any moment, one of the adversaries is going to take a fleet and have a go at laying siege to Rhodos. If, at the same time, the pirates are ravaging their merchants – they're dead.'

'Indeed,' Theron said. 'In fact, Antigonus One-Eye is trying to hire pirates on the Syrian coast to serve in his fleet.'

'And while the pirates sit in the Propontis, Lysimachos lacks the power to go into the Euxine and defend his satrapy against Eumeles,' Abraham said. 'I see it! Whereas, when you offer to take the pirates out of the Propontis, you actually turn them into a navy that, to all effects, serves Lysimachos against Eumeles!'

Diokles shook his head. 'But they all hate each other!' he said.

Satyrus sat up, the claw feet of his iron chair smacking the floor with a crack. Then he stood. 'Exactly. They all hate each other – so without a fourth party, they'll never make common cause.'

He looked around at all of them. Kalos sat silent, interested only in returning to his new girl, or to sea, and indifferent to all the politics. Apollodorus had a new bronze *thorax* with silver inlay and buckles that was attracting most of his attention. Neiron listened attentively, as did the much younger Kleitos, still unsure of himself in such august company.

'Listen,' Satyrus said, and even Apollodorus sat up. 'This planning is just so much dreaming of farms in Attica until they all sign articles. It may be more than we can manage, but it will cost us nothing but a winter under sail. We'll ship small cargoes and turn a profit like good Alexandrian merchants, and if this fails, we will start hiring mercenaries until we can fight Eumeles beak to beak. But this alliance is *now*. And it will serve Ptolemy as well as it serves us, by freeing Rhodos and empowering Lysimachos, his ally.'

'Too fucking deep for me,' Kalos said. 'You lead, I'll sail.'

Satyrus looked at Theron. 'Is this too complex to succeed?' he asked.

'You need three groups of men to see clearly to their own best interest, past a web of personal loves and hates,' the athlete replied. 'And then you need a port on the Euxine, or have you forgotten? Do you expect Lysimachos to give you Tomis as a base?'

Satyrus nodded. 'I haven't forgotten,' he said. 'I have hurt Tomis too much already. I'd rather not go there again.' He looked around. 'I will if I must. But I have another plan for a port, which I'll share in time. Until then, I think I'll keep it to myself.'

'What of Manes?' Abraham asked. 'Or is he too small for us to worry ourselves with?' He was already drinking wine.

Satyrus addressed all of them again. 'Demostrate ordered me to rid him of Manes.' He shrugged.

'His sailors are making trouble for ours whenever they meet,' Diokles said. 'Ask Neiron.'

Neiron rubbed the back of his head, looked around and

shrugged. 'In Rhodos, I'd call the watch. Here, I asked the lads to carry sticks.' He grinned.

Satyrus looked at Abraham. 'So – tell me about Manes.'

'He sees himself as Demostrate's heir,' Abraham said. 'He's a vicious animal without the leadership skills of a shark. Men fear him. Rhodos has a tremendous price on his head.' Abraham shrugged. 'He scares me – he'd do anything to achieve power. The other captains walk around him.'

'Why is he making trouble with us?' Satyrus asked.

Abraham looked at Theron. They shared a look, and then Theron spoke up. 'Already, there's word on the streets here that Demostrate has offered you an alliance. Or perhaps ...' Theron grinned. 'Perhaps you are lovers. Don't look shocked – sailors love a good sex scandal. Or perhaps he's naming you his heir. Maybe all three.' Theron shook his head. 'Manes is reacting to all these rumours. Which may come straight from Demostrate, who's pushing him to violence and hoping you'll get rid of him.'

Abraham leaned in. 'Or hoping that Manes will get rid of you,' he added. He shook his head apologetically. 'They're pirates!' he said, as if that explained any amount of treachery.

'I want to sail before the end of the week,' Satyrus said, 'and I don't want Manes interfering with me, here or at sea.'

'Kill him,' Diokles said.

Theron nodded. 'Public service,' he said.

Abraham looked around. 'Goodness,' he said. 'And I thought *I* was getting coarse here.'

Satyrus walked to the sideboard and poured himself more hot wine. 'The cost of kingship,' he said. The wine he poured was like blood flowing into a cup, and the gesture wasn't lost on any of them. 'I'll fight him man to man, but I want him trapped into it and I want his sailors helpless. Any suggestions?'

Abraham nodded. 'It has to be man to man,' he said, 'if you want these criminals to follow you.'

'I see that,' Satyrus said, betraying his impatience. 'Although I won't hide from you that this Manes scares me, too. He's the sort to walk down your spear and kill you when he's dead himself.'

Diokles was nodding to himself. 'I don't know about any

of that,' he said, 'but Manes is claiming that you're actually a prisoner held for ransom, not a free captain.'

Theron scratched under his beard.

'So he'd have to prevent Satyrus from leaving,' he said slowly.

Satyrus agreed immediately. 'Neat. So our next action will precipitate his. How do we trap him?'

'He doesn't look very bright,' Kalos grunted.

'Takes one to know one,' Diokles quipped.

'Pipe down, you two,' Satyrus said. 'He's got the largest contingent after Demostrate. He can't be a fool.'

'Fear has its own courage. Perhaps it also has its own intelligence,' Theron said.

'I have an idea,' Kleitos said quietly. 'Listen – you'll need to build new crews. Yes?'

Satyrus nodded.

'Here's what we could do,' Kleitos began.

The next day, Satyrus promoted Kalos to trierarch aboard *Golden Lotus* and then promoted all the other officers to fill the gaps in his flotilla. Neiron was to be helmsman on the *Lotus*. Kleitos received the *Hornet* under Abraham, and Diokles became helmsman on the *Falcon* – helmsman and trierarch together. Theron went back to his *Labours of Herakles*, which hadn't taken the casualties of the other ships and had all her standing officers intact – Antiphon of Rhodos was his helmsman, a steady man who disliked Byzantium and the pirates so thoroughly that he only came ashore to buy supplies.

The promotions were private, but the men in question made sacrifices at the Temple of Poseidon – except Diokles, who made sacrifice at the Temple of Zeus Casios, the conqueror of the oceans. The sacrifices were public knowledge and led to a certain amount of gossip – more, when they began laying in stores of amphorae and purchasing supplies – and cargoes.

Byzantium was glutted with grain – the result of the repeated seizure of cargoes coming down the Euxine from Olbia, Pantecapaeum and the northern grain fields. War galleys make poor cargo ships, but the *Golden Lotus* with her three and a half oar decks and deeper draught was designed to fight and carry cargo, and he at least could take a respectable amount of grain.

The other crews mocked Neiron as he loaded the *Lotus*. Most of his men were former captives, and they did not bear the taunting well, lacking the discipline of the old crew. There were fights.

There were worse than fights, as it turned out that some of the grain was rotten, or rat's dung, and Neiron felt that he'd been taken. He remonstrated with a merchant, who laughed in his face and snapped his fingers. 'You bought it,' the merchant said.

Another day and one of Neiron's senior rowers was killed – gutted in the agora by one of Manes' men.

Satyrus complained to Demostrate, who told him that he should look to his own.

Manes' men began to prowl close to the warehouse, smashing the *Lotus*'s boats when they were left on the beach and beating any oarsmen from the *Lotus* that they caught alone.

The new crew of the *Lotus* grew more and more resentful – first, that they were treated so, and second, that their enemies received no punishment. By contrast, Manes' men grew louder and more determined.

A careful observer might have noticed that neither Abraham nor any of the veteran crewmen of the original *Black Falcon* were anywhere to be seen, on the streets or in the wine shops. They played no role in the fighting and they suffered no indignities.

Four days after the new captains made their sacrifices, Satyrus attended another symposium – this one considerably less colourful than the last. He lay on the same couch as Daedalus. The Halicarnassian seemed surprised to find him there.

'I heard that you were lading your ships,' he said. He was more than a little distant.

Satyrus ate a grape. 'Listen,' he said, 'tomorrow there will be some trouble. I'm keeping you clear of it. After tomorrow, I'd like to invite you to return to my table – and my council.'

'*After* the trouble? This isn't a bid for my aid against Manes?' Daedalus asked, clearly incredulous. 'He's out for your blood, lad. Your uncle would have my arse if I didn't help you.' He shook his head. 'I've expected a message from you for a week.'

'After the trouble,' Satyrus said. 'I'll explain tomorrow. For the moment, it would be enough if you'd give me a good, sharp shove off the kline.'

'Are you a fool? I'm most of what is standing between you and Manes ripping your guts out!'

Satyrus had to smile – Daedalus, the mercenary, was living up to his high reputation as a man who, once bought, stayed bought. 'I know that,' Satyrus said. 'Believe me, you don't want to be involved,' he said.

Daedalus shook his head. 'But after tomorrow, you'll explain?'

'By this time tomorrow, it'll all be clear as a new day at sea,' Satyrus said.

Daedalus shook his head. And put his elbow into Satyrus's gut, shoving him brutally to the floor, so that Satyrus's chiton was fouled with old wine and worse.

'Keep your juvenile plotting,' the mercenary growled.

Satyrus hoped that he was acting. He got up, rubbing his ribs – that was real enough – and slunk back to his own couch. On the way, Manes glared at him with his bestial glare, and Satyrus avoided his eye.

'Look,' Manes growled. 'It's the prisoner! Buying grain for a long captivity, boy?' he asked, and his own adherents laughed.

Satyrus stepped back, putting more distance between Manes and himself. 'I'm no man's prisoner,' he said. His voice wasn't as firm as the other pirates would have liked to hear, and there was some mockery.

'We'll see in the morning,' Manes said. He laughed. 'What a ransom you'll fetch!'

'I'm a captain, not a prisoner. Talk to Demostrate if you doubt my word,' Satyrus said.

'Your word is worthless here, captive.' Manes looked around. 'And Demostrate is a captain among captains. If he spurns your ransom, the more fool he.' Manes laughed, a hard sound for most men to hear.

Satyrus appeared to force himself to stand firm. 'Prove it,' he said mildly. 'Fight me.'

Manes sat up. 'Fuck you, boy. I may bugger you in the street, if I want.'

'Afraid of me?' Satyrus asked, conversationally. Now, the tide was turning. Men didn't mock Manes, and this was too rich.

Manes swung his feet off his couch. 'I fear *nothing*. Not you, not Demostrate, not Rhodos. I am the terror of the coasts, the lord of the sea.'

Satyrus gave him a mocking bow. 'Really? So – you'll fight!'

Manes reached for his sword and Satyrus's fingers ached for his own hilt. Manes *was terrifying* and his arms were long. If he drew first ...

Ganymede reached out and touched his master's arm and whispered in his ear.

Manes stopped, and breathed deeply. 'I do not need to fight you, boy.'

Satyrus gave the beast a mocking smile. 'I think you'll find that you'd have done better to fight me,' he said.

Manes growled, and the hair stood up on Satyrus's neck.

Demostrate was watching, but he took no action. Again Ganymede took his master's arm, and this time he whispered furiously in his master's ear. Manes shook him off, but then he turned his back on Satyrus and stomped off, head high.

'Coward,' Satyrus said, loud and clear.

Manes paused, his foot actually in the air, and then took the next step. He walked from the symposium, accompanied by a roar of comment.

Satyrus grinned at the other drinkers, and then headed after him. He didn't follow Manes all the way to the outside door – he was quite sure what reception would greet him there. Instead, he walked down the slave stairs and through the kitchen, emerging from the slave entrance straight into the midst of Apollodorus's marines, who ran him through the streets to Abraham's. They battened down the hatches.

Despite all of Satyrus's precautions, Manes made no provocative move during the night.

'By Apollo, that man scares me,' Satyrus said, as he sipped hot wine. The sun was still under the lip of the world, but the warehouse was lit from end to end as the sailors prepared to man the *Lotus*.

'He is one of those men who seem to be greater, or less, than human,' Theron said.

Satyrus nodded. 'He must die. When he goes down at my

hand, there will be no more tests – no more humiliations, and no more slave girls on my couch.'

Theron shook his head. 'Lad, you are about to try to kill a monster to avoid having to make love to beautiful women. I don't have to be Philokles to point out the fallacy of your position.'

Satyrus didn't turn his head. 'I will not be mocked about this.'

Theron shrugged. 'We go to dice with Moira,' Theron said. 'I won't offend you more.'

Satyrus nodded. 'Good. Are we ready?'

'We're ready. You are sure he will attack us?' Theron asked. He closed the last clasp on his breastplate.

'Short of leading him on a rope, I've done all I can to provoke his attack. His minion spent the last minutes of the symposium reminding him that he was going to kill me in the morning, and there was no need to risk himself in the night. It must be now. We've all but advertised our sailing time.' Satyrus shook his head.

'Who are you reassuring?' Theron asked.

'Myself,' Satyrus said. 'He terrifies me. But this must be done.'

'Would it make you feel better if I said you were like a force of nature yourself?' Theron asked.

Satyrus nodded. 'Yes,' he said, and smiled.

Satyrus need not have worried. They were two streets from the beach when he saw the two-wheeled cart pushed across the narrow street and men with torches began to fill the space around his column of sailors.

Satyrus was at the head of the column, with Theron and Neiron. He stopped. He was in full armour and had an aspis on his shoulder. His helmet was already closed over his face.

'Satyrus!' Manes roared. He stepped out from a side street. 'Throw down your weapons. Or I'll kill all your men.'

Indeed, the whole crew of his four ships could be seen, every man of them carrying a torch and a club or a sword. They outnumbered the crew of the *Falcon* by two to one or more.

'I doubt that you could,' Satyrus said. He raised his aspis, expecting an arrow from the dark. 'Why don't you fight me, man to man?'

Manes laughed again. 'In the dark? Anything can happen in a

fight in the dark. That's what you want, isn't it? I want something different.' He laughed again. 'Last chance. Throw down that toy shield and be a slave. The way you should have been from the moment you arrived.'

Satyrus didn't lower his aspis. 'Last chance, Manes. Walk away.' In a loud, clear voice, he bellowed, 'Kill his archers!'

Even inside his helmet, he heard the arrows coming. Several struck his shield, driving him back a step, and one rang off his helmet, and another stung him along the back of his knee. Behind him, a man screamed.

That was not according to plan.

Then, a little late, his own archers rose up from ambush in the darkness and shot – mostly at a range of a few feet. Manes' men screamed as they died.

Manes froze, a snarl on his face. He was a beast – but a cunning beast.

'So,' he spat.

Satyrus's shield arm hurt. He had a lot of poppy in him to keep himself steady, and he needed to get this over with. But even through the drug, Manes scared him.

'Sword to sword, Manes. Right now.' Satyrus stepped forward, swinging his aspis into line despite the pain in his arm.

Manes backed away in the flickering light. 'Just so your archers can shoot me in the back?' he said. 'No chance. Your day will come, little fucker. And then I'll do you. Maybe I'll use you for a while before I kill you – how's that?'

Satyrus pressed forward and raised his voice. 'Sounds like a lot of talk from a man who won't stand and fight.'

Manes' eyes were everywhere, and his paramour caught his sword hand and pulled him back, back again, into the wary circle of his men.

'Fuck you, boy!' he shouted at Satyrus.

Satyrus shouted back, 'Twice you've backed down, cur! Dog! Coward!' He laughed. 'And the other scum are afraid of *you*?'

But Manes' crews were backing away in the street, a strong shield wall facing Satyrus and another facing to where the crew of the *Falcon* had appeared on their flank.

'Do it,' Neiron said at his side.

'No,' Abraham said. His armour was so well polished that it reflected every pinpoint of light in the street. He looked like something superhuman. 'No. If you start a battle here, we'll lose men, and Manes will escape anyway. And the pirates will hate you. You have to get him to fight.'

'Ares, I tried,' Satyrus said.

Abraham laughed. 'We heard. He'll be a long time living this down. Hurry back.'

Satyrus frowned. 'He'll try for you,' he said.

Abraham hugged him. 'I can ride the lion,' he said. 'Go and do what you have to do. And give my regards to my father.'

12

SEA OF GRASS, NORTH OF OLBIA,
WINTER, 311–310 BC

The wind flowed over the plains from the north, carrying the floating feathers of snow that so impressed Herodotus and cutting through any garment a Sakje could wear, so that warriors wore their armour over their fur jackets just to cut the wind.

Melitta wore a new armour shirt: a pair of sheepskins, the inner quilted with wool, the outer covered in alternating bronze and iron scales that winked dully in the winter light. She wore the scale shirt over her fox-fur jacket and sheepskin trousers tucked into sheepskin boots, and her shapeless fur hat covered her whole head, and still she was cold. Between her legs, her temple hack, borrowed what seemed like a lifetime ago on the east coast of the Euxine, plodded tirelessly into the wind. Her opinion of the horse had risen during her flight north – nothing much to look at, and worthless in a fight, the stoop-backed horse had an indomitable spirit. She had come to trust him, and so he had a name – Turtle. The name made the other tribesmen laugh, but by now, two snowstorms into their trek across the sea of grass, they knew his merits. Slow, but sure.

Behind her walked six Sakje ponies, most of them carrying her spare tack, her war gear, a small tent and all the goods she needed to make a camp. Samahe and Ataelus had outfitted her well, by Sakje standards, although many of her items were the plunder of the men she had killed, a palpable reminder – for her and for the others – of her skills. And at the back of her string of remounts walked Gryphon, one of the tallest warhorses among the Sakje.

Ataelus interrupted her thoughts about her horses when he appeared from the snow and waved his whip. 'Time to camp!' he said with his usual ruthless cheerfulness. 'Snow's getting worse.'

It took two hours to get the camp built. The biggest issue was wood for warmth and cooking. While one group of Sakje tramped the snow flat and raised yurts, another trudged north and south along the riverbank, searching for trees that had succumbed to the spring floods and not yet been pillaged by other travellers.

Melitta found a big tree toppled by what appeared to be the hand of the gods – the great ball of its roots still attached, so that the ground under them appeared to be a cave. Melitta walked along the trunk with her light bronze axe in her hand, tapping the wood as she went, but it was all sound, and the trunk rang when she tapped it as if it too was made of bronze.

The big oak had grown at a bend in the river and its companions still stood – including a middle-aged willow that had been struck by lightning when young and had grown with a deep double trunk. Melitta set to breaking smaller branches in the willow, hauling the heavier wood to the breaking cleft and throwing her whole weight against each branch.

After she had built a considerable pile, Ataelus rode up. With him was the youngest of his warriors, a Standing Horse exile called Scopasis. He was young and sullen and bore a scar that ran across the bridge of his nose, which he was continually touching. He had been cast out of his clan for a murder, and Ataelus had sunk far enough to take him in, but never let him out of his sight.

Ataelus descended on the great tree with all his usual energy and a heavy iron axe, product of a Sindi smith. Scopasis sat on his horse and watched.

Melitta kept working as Ataelus brought her branches already trimmed, but eventually she had a considerable pile of branches too big for her to break.

She waved at the hunched figure of the young man. 'I need your strength,' she said.

He grunted and rolled off his horse.

'Help me break those,' she said.

'Uh,' he said. Moving with deliberate slowness, he picked up the smallest branch and broke it. Then he stopped and looked at her.

Sighing at men everywhere and this one in particular, Melitta collected a heavier branch from the pile. 'Come on,' she said. 'I don't bite.'

Ataelus chuckled and kept cutting with the axe.

Scopasis came and joined her. He pushed sharply against the butt and it didn't break. He stumbled back.

'Fuck!' he said.

'Push with me,' Melitta said. 'Come on.'

'Fuck that,' the boy said, and turned away.

Melitta smiled to herself. She'd served as an archer in the army of Ptolemy, and she'd spent quite some time studying – and aping – the ways of young men. She cut patiently at her desired breaking point with her small bronze axe, put it in the fork of the tree and pushed. There was a crack, and she pushed again – a sharp sound, and she was lying in the snow.

Scopasis laughed. Melitta laughed with him. 'Come and lend me your strength,' Melitta called.

Again, the boy walked over. This time he chose a bigger branch. He put it in the fork of the tree and waited for her to join him, and together they pushed. It took several tries, but they broke the branch, and then reset the shorter pieces and broke them again. Then Scopasis went and got another branch without being prompted.

Scopasis worked steadily for over an hour, until Tameax rode up and laughed. 'You got the boy to do some work!' he said.

Scopasis dropped the branch he was carrying, leaped on to his horse's back and rode away without a word.

Melitta walked up to the baqca. 'Never let it be said that you see everything in the future,' she commented. 'You just undid an afternoon's work.'

Tameax shrugged. 'Bah – if he's so thin-skinned, he's useless.'

'That is why you are a baqca and not a king. Go and find him, apologize and bring him back.' Melitta smiled. 'Please.'

'Why?' Tameax asked.

Ataelus watched, his axe raised.

'Because I ask,' Melitta said.

Tameax narrowed his eyes, and suddenly Melitta understood what she saw there. 'Don't be a fool, baqca,' she shot at him. She walked up closer. 'I do not need to walk the spirit world to see that you are *jealous*. Jealous that I cut wood with an exiled *boy*?' She walked up close to him, and then closer, and he stepped back. 'You presume, baqca. Your feelings are a presumption. Perhaps you are too small a man to be my baqca, eh?'

Tameax's face filled with blood and a vein on his temple throbbed. 'I cannot help my feelings,' he said.

'You remind me of that boy,' Melitta said. 'He cannot control his feelings either. The difference is that he's been mistreated his whole life – for being the smallest, I expect. What is your excuse?'

Tameax made an effort – an effort that showed through his heavy furs in every line of his body. He stood straighter. 'I'll go and fetch the boy,' he said, his face still red.

'Good,' Melitta allowed, and went back to breaking wood.

That night, Ataelus and Samahe's son Thyrsis came in with a dozen more warriors – all young men and women, from a mix of tribes, although Standing Horses seemed to predominate.

Thyrsis was a handsome young man with excellent manners and the kind of physique that boys his age dreamed of. He excelled at games, he had killed Sauromatae on raids, and his brown eyes were capable of assessment and analysis – she'd watched him consider how to mend a scabbard, his careful cutting, his fine work with a sheet of scrap bronze.

In fact, his superiority in all things was obvious, and all the young warriors of both sexes accepted it apart from Scopasis. Scopasis, though younger, would accept no order from Thyrsis, nor ride with him.

Thyrsis came and sat by Melitta, who was adding scales to the shirt that Samahe had made her, putting shoulder-plates on the yoke. Her back was to Nihmu, who was sewing a soft deerskin shirt. They leaned their backs against each other for warmth and stability. On the other side of the fire, Ataelus went through his arrows, peering along their lengths, while Coenus cast lead sling balls in a stone mould and the metallic tang of the hot lead filled the yurt.

Samahe had scouted all day, well ahead of the clan, and now she was asleep in her furs and blankets.

'Greetings, lady,' Thyrsis said, respectfully. He was a very polite young man.

Melitta made room for him. There was something about him – perhaps his respect for her – that made her feel much older than him.

'I brought new warriors,' he said, looking at his father.

'And no meat,' Ataelus said wryly.

'Word of your coming is spreading like flame on dry grass,' Thyrsis said. 'If you would ride two days to the Grass Cats' winter town, we might raise a hundred riders – or twice that.'

Melitta smiled, coughed when a gust of wind somewhere managed to push smoke into her eyes and mouth, and shook her head. 'And then?' she asked.

'Why, then we can fight Marthax,' Thyrsis said.

'Marthax has half a thousand knights, every one of them with three warhorses as good as Gryphon or your father's charger, Eagle. The last thing I want is to challenge him to battle.'

Thyrsis shook his head and began shedding fur – a minute by the fire and outdoor clothes caused a sea of sweat. 'Then what do we go for? Will Marthax cravenly hand you the kingship?'

'Why would that be craven?' Melitta asked. Behind Ataelus, the tent flap opened and Scopasis entered. He went and sat by Ataelus. Melitta turned back to Thyrsis. 'Perhaps Marthax will do what is best for the people. He has no other heir.'

Thyrsis watched the fire. 'But – I promised them a fight. They are young and hot.'

Melitta glanced at Ataelus. Being the lady was already far more complex than she had expected, and she wished her brother, who thought deeply and read people well, was there with her. 'You want a fight,' Melitta said. She tried to keep her voice kind. 'You recruit young fighters because you want to be a chief, like your father, and lead them in war.' Melitta sighed. 'We will have war soon enough.'

Thyrsis nodded. 'Will you ride with my young warriors to-morrow?' he asked.

'I look forward to meeting them, Thyrsis,' Melitta said. 'But I am here to be the lady of all the Assagatje, not just the young.'

Scopasis watched her the way an eagle watches a rabbit. Annoyed, she went back to her armour, carefully running a fresh thong through the next scale and fixing it in place, then tying the knots. No one else spoke.

'How much further to Marthax?' Nihmu asked.

'Ten days' ride, and then some searching to find him. He may be at the Royal Winter Town, and he may not.' Ataelus shrugged.

Melitta had never come so far west in her youth. 'He must have word of us by now,' she said.

Ataelus nodded. 'You said to go straight to him,' he answered.

Mere days from meeting the king of the Assagatje, Melitta's doubts rose like a choking cloud to overwhelm her hopes. 'So I did,' she said.

'It is not too late to turn south and find Urvara,' Ataelus added. 'She would escort you with a thousand warriors.'

Melitta shook her head. 'In the spring. No one can ride with a thousand warriors in the winter unless they have Greeks to supply them. And my brother will come in the spring – I can feel it, as if I can see his mind. We must be ready when he is ready or we'll both fail. I must unite the Assagatje before the snow melts and the ground hardens.'

'You take a mighty risk,' Ataelus said.

Melitta looked up to find Scopasis's eyes on her. 'Yes,' she said.

The next day, Scopasis emerged from a snow squall, riding hard. 'Horsemen behind us,' he said to Melitta, and then to Ataelus. 'Moving fast. At least fifty.'

Ataelus rubbed his scraggly beard. He raised an eyebrow.

Melitta shrugged. 'Who can it be, coming from the south, except Urvara?'

Ataelus said, 'You don't want Urvara?'

Melitta shrugged right back. 'Perhaps the gods have taken that decision from me,' she said.

They formed up anyway, the bulk of the warriors under Ataelus's wolf's-tail banner, three crisp ranks. Ataelus had served for years with Greek commanders, and he had learned a great deal of their ideas on shock, on tactics, even formations. His clan of outcasts was yet a formidable fighting force. So they formed at the lip of a snow-covered ridge, and the other party rode slowly up the ridge, their horses black against the white snow until they were quite close.

Scopasis had pushed his warhorse in behind Melitta in the formation. Now he leaned forward. 'That is Urvara,' he said.

'Do you hate her?' Melitta asked without turning her head.

Scopasis paused. 'No,' he said, with no tone at all. 'No. I killed the man. What other sentence could she give?'

Melitta wondered. Scopasis was no ordinary killer. Two days had sufficed to teach her that.

No time to consider him now. 'Stay here,' she said to the boy. The last thing she needed in a parley with the biggest clan on the steppes was one of their own angry exiles at her side.

She collected Nihmu and Coenus, Ataelus and Samahe by catching their eyes, each in turn, and then she cantered Gryphon down the hill, snow flying around her, until she reached the tall blonde woman who sat under the Grass Cat banner in a scarlet cloak of Greek wool, trimmed in ermine. She looked like a queen. At her side sat a man who could rival Coenus for his Hellenic stubbornness, in a Thracian cloak and wool chiton, boots and no trousers.

Urvara didn't hesitate, but pushed her horse forward and embraced Melitta as soon as she picked her out – and then the queenly woman embraced Nihmu with the same savagery.

'Eumenes!' Melitta said. Eumenes was a fixture of her childhood – and her adolescence. 'Aren't you supposed to be in the field with Diodorus?' Only after she said the words did she realize that she hadn't spoken Greek for a month.

Eumenes laughed. 'I might ask you the same! I feel like a slave sent to fetch the master's truant boy from the agora. Sappho sent me!'

Urvara looked at them both. 'There will be time for this later. Melitta, none here will stand against your claim. I will put my hands in yours this minute – but why would you not come to me?'

Melitta took both of Urvara's hands – hard and soft, like Samahe's and her mother's. 'I do not want war with Marthax,' Melitta said. 'I want him to give me his title without war.' Melitta shrugged. 'He hates you.'

Urvara shook her head. 'Bah – Marthax and I have cooperated well enough for ten years, although there is little love between us.'

Melitta brushed snow from her hood. 'If I arrive at his camp with a thousand horses, he will have no choice but to fight. If I arrive with fifty horses, he will talk.'

Urvara shook her head. 'No, my dear. I'm sorry – but no. He'll just kill you and hide the body. He is not the man he once was.'

'And yet you say you cooperate,' Melitta shot back.

'He cooperates with me because he needs my warriors. My tribe has grown – thanks to my Eumenes and his Olbians, we are rich, we have children and we grow.' She reached out a hand, and Eumenes took it.

Melitta shook her head in frustration. 'So?'

Ataelus shrugged. 'For riding,' he said in his usual broken Greek. 'For snowing.' Ataelus pointed at Urvara's escort, fifty knights in full armour. 'Not enough for making war, but enough for making peace,' he said, his pronunciation of *eirene* almost comical.

Eumenes nodded. 'Marthax won't dare murder you with us as bodyguards,' he said.

Melitta couldn't help but feel relieved. 'Let's ride, then!'

They camped that night on the Borysthenes, just twenty stades from the battlefield at the Ford of the River God. There was wood aplenty.

Eumenes watched with Melitta as the camp went dark. Tonight, there was no question of her breaking wood. Her status had changed again with the addition of Urvara.

'How do you come to be here?' she asked him in Greek.

Eumenes snuggled deeper into his cloak. 'I was wounded in the summer fighting and Diodorus sent me back to Alexandria with his dispatches. It was all luck – I arrived to find you and Coenus two weeks gone, and a letter from Lykeles asking me to come to Olbia if I was available. I was – so I followed you out.'

Coenus appeared as if cued by his name. He had killed a buck and the dead animal was roped to the rump of his horse. 'What did Lykeles need?'

Eumenes grinned. 'Me. He's been archon three times, as has Clio. And Urvara wanted me home.' He smiled. 'I doubt I'll campaign again, Coenus. I'm archon of Olbia.'

Coenus grinned back and embraced the younger man. 'Your father's dream,' he said.

'My father was a traitor,' Eumenes said. There was little bitterness in the statement, just cold fact.

Coenus shrugged. 'He sought power and failed.' Coenus shook his head. 'The wheel turns, eh?'

Eumenes shook his head. 'Not far from here, Kineas taught me to fall off a horse without hurting myself.'

'We should ride to the battlefield tomorrow,' Coenus said. 'We should make a sacrifice.'

Eumenes brightened. 'That is a noble idea,' he said.

'I'm a noble man,' Coenus answered. He laughed.

Melitta watched them with pleasure. 'He's still here, for you, isn't he?' she asked Coenus.

But Eumenes answered. 'Every day. He formed us – really, he formed all of us. I hear him in your voice – sometimes in Urvara's. He made her the lady of the Grass Cats, just by refusing to accept her contenders. He made me a troop commander. He made Petrocolus the head of the *Kaloi* in Olbia. His hand is still on every part of our lives.'

Melitta felt tears fill her eyes. 'That. I know all that. But it is in the way you mock each other – and yourselves.'

Coenus nodded. 'Odd, as we seldom teased him. But true, nonetheless. You are wise.'

'I'm working on it,' Melitta said.

Over dinner they agreed to go together to the battlefield and offer sacrifices at the shrine and the trophy, despite the weather. Tameax felt that such respect for the past would please the spirits, and Coenus insisted the Greek gods and heroes would have the same opinion.

The next day they were up early, the wet yurts stripped off their poles in the dark and made into ungainly bundles. Horses struggled to drag the travois made of tent poles, and Coenus led a party of hunters away upstream before the last animal was packed. He returned in the first light of dawn with another buck on a spare horse, and with a pair of goats in baskets from the Sindi village at the river bend.

'There wasn't a village there twenty years ago,' he said to Eumenes, who was adjusting his girth next to Melitta in the early light.

Eumenes yawned and shook his head. 'No. In another generation, this valley will be full.'

'The Sindi must be breeding like rabbits,' Coenus said.

Urvara laughed bitterly. 'Perhaps,' she said. 'But many of those "Sindi" are my people, settling down to farm the soil. Sky people making themselves dirt people.' She sighed. 'It has always happened, but never in such numbers.'

It was mid-morning when they arrived at the shrine. Melitta had heard all her life about the great battle at the ford, but now Eumenes and Samahe, Urvara and Ataelus, Nihmu and Coenus rode her through it as if she had been a participant.

'Here, Kam Baqca rode to glory!' Samahe said, and Nihmu wept. Melitta noticed that Tameax writhed at the mere mention of the great shaman. Samahe didn't notice, or didn't care. 'She and her knights were like an arrow of gold, and they cut the Macedonians the way that an arrow enters a caribou, and the beast runs on, seeming to be alive, when really it is already dead.'

And later, Coenus showed them on a field of snow how the last charge of the Greeks and the Sakje had folded the Macedonian flank, so that when Srayanka cut her way through the ford she met Kineas in the middle of the field.

'We penned them against the river, and killed them until the sun slunk away to avoid the smell of death,' Ataelus sang. It was a Sakje epic. Most of the other warriors knew it, and they sang it as the sun rose.

'Bah!' Coenus said. 'Philokles must have stood just here.' His voice cracked a little. 'Really, honey bee, your father always said that Philokles won the battle. He and his young men held one of the Macedonian taxeis for an hour – maybe more. With their bare hands.'

At the trophy, raised by the old shrine to the River God, Olbia had built a marble altar with a relief of a man on horseback and another of a set of arms and a shield with the star of Macedon. Coenus smiled. 'Nice,' he said.

Eumenes nodded back, overcome with emotion. 'Lykeles ordered it built. I've never seen it before. It is well done.'

Then they all dismounted. Even Scopasis, who did nothing willingly, slid off his horse. They ringed the Greek altar, and

Tameax killed one goat, and Coenus killed the other, and the blood steamed like a new-lit fire that breeds more smoke than flame, rising to heaven in the crisp morning air.

Coenus made a fire and they roasted the meat, burned the bones and the hide, and then, after Eumenes poured libations, Coenus handed cooked meat to every man and woman. 'Eat and drink,' he said. 'Remember those who died here, and those who stood their ground. Remember Satrax, king of the Assagatje, who died for his victory, and Kam Baqca, and remember Ajax and Nicomedes.'

The older Sakje cried, and so did the Greeks, while the younger ones looked on, wondering to see so many hard men and women weeping.

'I lost my father here,' Urvara said.

Tameax cleared his throat. 'As did Nihmu,' he said.

Nihmu was being held by Coenus.

'As did I,' Eumenes said. 'Although he fought on the other side.' He poured more wine in the snow. 'Gods, I beg forgiveness for the shade of my father.' And he wept as well.

They were gathered like that when they heard hoofbeats. Warriors scattered – no one had kept a watch, their emotions were so high – and knights ran for their warhorses like ants from a shattered anthill.

Urvara watched the oncoming riders without fear. 'It was wise to come here,' she said. 'This is sacred ground, and it reminds men of who you are.' She pointed at the riders coming over the river. 'That is Parshtaevalt, and his banner of the Cruel Hand.' She looked at Melitta. 'Whether you wanted us or not, lady, we'll all go together to see Marthax.'

And minutes later, Parshtaevalt embraced Melitta. Then he knelt, as Sakje never do, and placed his hands between hers. 'I am your man, for ever, as I was your mother's,' he said. He looked at the remnants of the sacrifice and shook his head. He looked at Coenus. 'Did you save any for me? I fought here, too.'

Coenus laughed. 'Do you still eat whole horses?' he asked.

The lord of the Cruel Hands laughed like a boy. 'This one taught me my Greek,' he said, pointing at Coenus, 'when Kineax was too busy making calf-eyes at your mother!'

Eumenes took meat from the altar and brought it to Parshtaevalt, and he ate it and drank some wine. Then he looked around at all of them, and his own knights. 'Can you feel the thing?' he asked, in Greek.

Eumenes was next to Melitta. 'I feel it,' he said.

Coenus embraced him. 'I feel it,' he said. 'If only Diodorus were here.'

'Crax,' Ataelus said. 'Sitalkes.'

'They will come,' Eumenes said.

Parshtaevalt nodded. 'All of us will come,' he said to Melitta. 'All of your father's men, and all of your mother's. And we will show these newcomers how war is made.'

13

Lemnos, Lesvos – a night in Methymna, and fresh lamb – and down the sea to Chios, past Samos to a day of fevered trading in Miletus while his arm throbbed as if his wound was new, and then down the Sporades to Rhodos. The wind didn't always serve, but they were in the most protected parts of the sea, and they could make a good anchorage and a town every night.

Satyrus needed a town every night – his arm was so bad that he began to wonder if it would have to be rebroken and reset, and he had a fever, which didn't seem possible from such an old wound. At Miletus, he went to the old Temple of Apollo and made a sacrifice, and only willpower kept them at sea past the sanctuary of Asclepius on Cos.

Byzantium had left other scars as well, and Satyrus could neither sleep nor rest without his mind running off along his various choices, the paths of his own choosing and the choices thrust upon him. He felt himself grow sullen. He regretted the lack of Theron, or even Diokles. Neiron was older, cautious, proud of his new rank and determined not to lose it. Where Diokles might have censured his acerbic comments, Neiron bore them with a patience that simply stung Satyrus to further annoyance.

The entrance to the harbour at Rhodos was framing the bow when he boiled over.

'Oars! Stand by, all tiers.' The oar master was Neiron's replacement. His voice didn't carry authority, and his sense of timing was poor. He was a master rower, and had sat the stroke bench in two triremes, and yet he wasn't good enough to make the next step. Satyrus was sorry for him – he was a good man, and a loyal one – Messus was his name, and he was Tyrian, like Diokles, although older and greyer.

'That man has no authority,' he said.

Neiron's eyes were on his landfall and the harbour entrance.

'I'm speaking to you,' he barked.

Neiron's eyes never moved. 'Sorry, sir. I'm conning the ship.'

That stung Satyrus. Feeling foolish – hurt, angry, off centre and foolish – he sat on the helmsman's bench and watched the Temple of Poseidon grow larger.

'All benches! Oars – in!' Messus called. His rhythm was no better than it had been in the other harbours, and the starboard oars were slow coming in, turning the ship slightly, so that Neiron had to compensate.

Messus hung his head. He turned red in the face and looked anywhere but the stern.

The *Lotus* was coasting, losing speed against the water but still moving quickly enough, and the beach under the Temple of Poseidon was crowded.

'We're going too fast,' Satyrus said.

Neiron was watching the beach.

Satyrus knew that he was angry, that his decision-making wasn't its best, but he was also an experienced trierarch now, and he knew when *Lotus* was going too fast. 'Reverse your benches!' he called. He ran forward, heedless of his arm. 'Reverse your benches!'

Messus shrank against the mast, clearly unsure what to do next.

Satyrus ignored him. He looked down at the *thranitai*, the upper-deck oarsmen, and the stroke oar nodded.

'Give way, all!' Satyrus called. The oars went up to the catch and down, and the blades bit the water. 'Mind your helm, Neiron. We'll birth between the two warships.'

Neiron's face grew dark, but he obeyed. The flush was still in his cheeks when Satyrus returned to the stern.

'I was intending a different landing,' Neiron said carefully. 'Among the merchants.'

Satyrus saw, suddenly, that Neiron had seen a berth – a distant berth that needed more momentum.

Neiron continued: 'I didn't know that we had the right to put in among their warships.' He was angry, but his anger showed only in the careful enunciation of his Greek.

Satyrus clutched his arm. 'My – apologies, helmsman. I see it now.'

Neiron shrugged. 'No matter,' he said.

'I feel like an idiot. I'll apologize in front of the men if you like.' Satyrus was miserable.

'No matter, I said.' Neiron slapped his oars to get the bow to move – threading the needle of the narrow space between a pair of Rhodian triemioliai, the same burthen and design as the *Lotus*, just as Messus called for the oars to come in, his voice tremulous.

Satyrus went ashore in the ship's boat, the throbbing in his arm just an echo of the throbbing in his head. He shook it to clear it. Rhodos was a beautiful town, cleaner and better tended than Alexandria, *old* in a way that lent dignity rather than squalor. Neiron followed him up the steps to the temple. Satyrus wanted to say something – wanted to clear the air – but Neiron's rebuff to his apology left him nowhere to go.

At the top of the steps, Timaeus of Rhodos waited, his broad hands tucked into a girdle made of hemp rope. At his side stood the other navarch for the year, Panther, son of Diomedes, a man who had killed more pirates than any other.

'There are few men in the circle of the world who would dare to sail direct from Demostrate to Rhodos and then berth in my harbour among my ships,' Timaeus said.

Satyrus was winded just from climbing the steps of the temple. He made himself stand straight.

Satyrus let himself breathe. 'I need a favour,' he said.

'You need a doctor, lad,' Panther said.

That was the last thing Satyrus remembered.

When he returned to consciousness, he had no idea of the passage of time and felt panic until a stranger – a woman – came into the room and took his hand.

'Who are you?' he asked.

She ignored him and put a cool hand on his, then turned it over and placed a thumb on his wrist. 'Lie down,' she said, in the same tone that Diokles used on drunken sailors, if quieter.

'How long have I been out?' Satyrus asked.

'How long have you been taking poppy juice for pain?' she asked him.

He tried to think. 'A week's sailing to reach Rhodos – sparingly the two weeks before that, and then perhaps two more weeks before that.'

185

'You took poppy for five weeks for a broken arm and a fevered wound?' she asked. 'What fool advised that?'

Satyrus felt too weak to argue.

'Your body now craves the poppy as much as it craves healing,' she said. 'Your arm is so badly hurt that it must be rebroken – which will be excruciatingly painful. For which I will have to give you poppy.' She shrugged. 'I recommend that you find a proper physician – preferably one with the same training I have – and let him take the poppy from your body.'

Satyrus sighed. 'I have a great deal to accomplish this winter.'

'You may find things harder if you are dead. Or permanently enslaved to the poppy. But – that is not my business. I have said my piece.' She poured a spoon of clear liquid that smelt of sugar and almonds. 'Drink this.'

'What is it?' he asked, and then he was gone.

Colours – an endless language of colours and shapes, smells, and an explosion, even in his dreams, of meanings so intense that he experienced an endless, fractal emotion, as if he was creating and destroying everything in the universe – gods, ships, monsters – and he swam inside his own body, which was itself as great as all the cosmos – what would Heraklitus say?

And then he sat in a meadow that rolled to every horizon, with a clear blue sky above and flowers like a carpet under him. He rose to his dream feet and looked around.

'You are nearer death than your physician seems to know,' the big man next to him said. Indeed, he was too big to be a man – Satyrus's head came only to the man's pectoral muscles, which were enormous. He had a lion skin on his shoulder and a wreath of laurel in his hair and he smelled like a farmer.

Satyrus bowed his head. 'Lord Herakles!' he said.

'Do I look like a lord?' the man in the lion skin asked. 'Are you mindful of my city?'

Satyrus nodded. 'I am. I intend to ask the tyrant—'

'Ask nothing. As the city will never give you the prize you desire, so you must not give it aught.' He yawned. 'Let us fight a fall. On your guard!'

Satyrus was suddenly naked, facing this giant on the sands of an eternal palaestra. He took his guard position and the moment that

both of them acknowledged the contest, Satyrus shot in, powered by
his legs, reaching for a lock on his opponent's knee.

He got his right arm behind those mighty thews and pulled, and
then his left arm was caught in a stronger grip.

'Well fought,' his opponent said, and he felt all the bones in his
arm shatter . . .

And he awoke to sunshine on his face. His left arm was hurting.

'He's back with us,' a male voice said. 'Get the lady.'

Time passed – a minute, a day? – and again he felt the cool
hand on his wrist and then on his forehead. 'Hmm. Less fever.
Hard to tell, with so much poppy. How do you feel?'

'Herakles broke my arm,' Satyrus said, before he realized what
he was saying.

'Really?' she asked. She turned away, outside his line of vision,
and came back with a five-page wax tablet, on which she wrote
furiously, her stylus moving like the shuttle on a loom. 'What
were you doing?'

'Fighting the pankration,' Satyrus said. He felt silly now.

'Wonderful!' she said. 'I do not need to consult a professional
astrologer to say that this bodes well for your healing.' She reached
for something. 'Drink this,' she said.

Time went away again.

Neiron came and went, and Panther, and he bathed every night
in the colours and the gardens of the gods. Time flowed away
from him – sometimes, he could see time itself, the stream that
Heraklitus had described, flowing by him, and every drop was
itself a sea of human deeds and choices, and yet once it flowed by,
none of it could be caught.

Rhodos – a perfect landfall.

He killed the Sauromatae girl in the meadow, over and over
again, and the two men on the beach. He watched Teax being
raped, and he heard Penelope killed. Over, and over. And he
wrestled with a god. He saw Eumeles kill his mother. He watched
Philokles die. He imagined the Sauromatae chief, Upazan, killing
his father, who he had never seen.

After a time, none of them were events of horror, but simply
drops in the stream that ran through the field where Herakles
stood in his lion skin.

And then he was awake, and the field and the wrestling and all the life and death flowed away and became dreams.

'Two weeks?' he asked. 'Despoina, I don't even know your name!'

'You may call me Aspasia,' she said. 'I am a doctor. Indeed, I am the only Asclepius-trained physician in Rhodos. And you may leave my house whenever you like, but if you want that arm to hold a shield again, you will remain here, taking only light exercise, eating the diet I prescribe, and perhaps reading, for two weeks.' She was tall – as tall as a man, and well formed, but her air of authority and the grey in her hair put her a little above his level, as if she was an officer and he was an oarsman.

On his third day of wakefulness, during the hours that were mostly normal, before he was dosed with poppy, he met her husband, a Rhodian captain and amateur scholar. He was dark-skinned, tall and broad, named Memnon.

'My father had a friend who was Memnon of Rhodos!' Satyrus said.

'It is a common name here, especially among those of us of Libyan and Ethiopian blood,' Memnon said. 'But surely you mean Memnon, the polemarch of Olbia?'

'Is he yet?' Satyrus was lying on a couch, his head propped on pillows. 'He must be quite old.'

'Is fifty old?' Aspasia asked. 'In Aegypt, a peasant would be ten years in his grave – but among Greeks, it is no great age.'

Satyrus was determined to show that he, too, had an education. 'Not too old to serve in the phalanx, at least in Sparta,' he said. 'I stand corrected.' And then he looked at Memnon the captain. 'Do you know Memnon of Olbia?' he asked.

'I do. It is a small world – and really, Rhodos is but a small town. He is my cousin. He has just written to me.'

'Will you write back?' Satyrus asked. 'May I include a note?'

'Of course!' Memnon said.

The relationship established, Memnon was quickly a friend, whereas Aspasia kept her distance. She was always courteous but never friendly. She would spend an hour by Satyrus's side, mixing drugs, and yet communicate only on medical matters. At first he took her distance for disapproval. Only with time did he see it for what it was – the mask of authority. She was a woman who gave orders to men. She was not a friend to them.

When he finally understood, he nodded in appreciation. Lying on a couch for two weeks, awake and mostly in command of his mind, left him with too much time to think, and much of it was spent considering the manner in which *he* commanded.

That evening, he brought it up with Memnon as they shared a game of shells and ships – a game that, at least symbolically, represented a naval battle. Memnon's board was carved of lapis and marble, so that it looked like squares of the sea, deeper and shallower, and a master had carved his ebony and ivory triremes. Each ship was different, so that some were twenty-oared boats and others were pirate *hemioliai*, biremes, triremes.

'Do you befriend your officers?' Satyrus asked.

Memnon laughed. 'Not as often as I'd like. It can be lonely on a long voyage – as you well know. I'm not used to a twenty-year-old trierarch. Anyway, I like to be friends with my helmsman, but it isn't always that way.'

'Ever try too hard?' Satyrus asked.

Memnon laughed. 'Maybe you should be talking to my wife – or a priest. Certainly, Satyrus, I have tried too hard. When you are my age, though, it all seems less important. I have my friends – I am who I am. Some men like me and others cross the street to avoid me, and that's as it is.' Memnon shrugged. 'I care less and less as I grow older.'

Satyrus shook his head ruefully. 'I seek humility, not further advice towards insularity.'

'Or arrogance?' Memnon asked. He laughed. He was a man who laughed easily, even at himself. 'You aren't arrogant. You are just used to being obeyed. It's a good thing in an officer. Perhaps a little difficult in a friend, eh?' He sat back, made his move and drank some wine. 'So, you really stared Manes down and called him a coward?'

Satyrus nodded. 'I did.'

Silence lay between them, and then Satyrus made his move. He was going to lose – and knowledge that he had lost made him play better, so that his ivory fleet might minimize its losses.

'Most boys – men – your age would have quite a tale to tell,' Memnon said.

Aspasia entered with his dose. She mixed the poppy and the almond juice by his bed, and Satyrus felt the craving rise in him as he smelled it.

Satyrus tried to push the desire down, wondering at the same time how he would ever stop using the stuff. He thought about his dose twenty times a day. More. 'I arranged an ambush, and it didn't go as well as I had expected. This happens to me – I make plans, and they never carry quite as well as I expect.' He shrugged. 'I tried to make him fight me. In effect, he ran away. That made him the victor and me the defeated. I was not ... careful enough.'

Memnon smiled into his wine cup. 'You would have taken Manes all by yourself?' he asked.

Satyrus nodded. 'To get what I want from the pirates, I will have to kill Manes,' he said. 'All by myself. Or die trying.'

Memnon smiled at that and poured a libation. 'To Apollo, and all the gods. Here's to living to tell our stories, even if we add a little to them with the passage of years.'

'If you will pour libations on my new floor, you can fetch a slave to clean it up,' Aspasia said. But she smiled at her husband. He smiled back, and Satyrus was – jealous? Not jealous, precisely. He felt that they had something that he was missing. Something he really only shared with his sister. He took his dose and drifted off, thinking of Melitta.

The next day, Timaeus and Panther came with Neiron. Memnon came in, too, although Satyrus knew he had a ship in lading. They crowded around Satyrus's bed while cold winter rain lashed the pebbles of the beach outside.

Timaeus took a cup of wine from a slave, saluted his hostess and nodded to Satyrus. 'Only the man who called Manes a coward could get me out on a day like this, lad,' he said.

Panther went straight to the point. 'Neiron here says that you have a proposition for us.'

Satyrus gave his helmsman a brief look. He couldn't imagine Neiron approaching the Rhodians. The man didn't have that much initiative – unless Satyrus had badly misjudged him.

Neiron shrugged. 'If I was out of line, I beg your forgiveness, lord. But these men have your trust, and they asked a hundred questions about Byzantium. It seemed easiest just to tell them.'

Satyrus nodded. 'No apology required. Timaeus, I have come in hopes that Rhodos will loan me a powerful squadron – in exchange for my clearing the Bosporus and the Propontis of pirates.'

Panther leaned forward. 'And how, *exactly*, will you do that?'

Satyrus met Panther's eye. 'I'll lead them into the Euxine and use them against Eumeles of Pantecapaeum.'

Timaeus laughed. He was heavily bearded, and men said that he was the avatar of Poseidon, and today, with rain in his curly hair and the summer tan gone from his skin, he looked the part. He laughed like a god as well – a heavy laugh that shook the rafters. 'You are bold!' he said.

Satyrus laughed with him. 'Laugh all you like,' he said when they were done. 'My way will not fail. If I win, the pirates are gone – employed by me. If I lose, they are still gone – to the bottom of the Euxine.'

'But you want a squadron from us,' Panther said.

'I will not win without a disciplined core,' Satyrus said. 'The pirates have thirty or forty ships that can stand in the line of battle, but they are not a fleet. I will have a few ships of my own, and I hope to add a few more from Lysimachos. None of my ships – except perhaps the *Lotus* – is as good as a Rhodian.'

'We have steered well clear of helping any of the Diadochoi,' Timaeus said. 'Why would we help you?'

'Because I will reopen trade into the Euxine – a grain trade that Rhodos needs and Athens needs. Lysimachos needs it and so does Cassander. Because I will get rid of more pirates in the spring than your whole fleet in a year's campaign – just by taking them away.'

'Yes, lad – but why would we serve with you? You'll take them away whether we come along for the ride or not.' Timaeus laughed again. 'And personal feeling aside – if you plan to take them to fight Eumeles, perhaps we should prefer that he then triumph over you? Then the pirates are dead, and we haven't lifted a finger.'

Satyrus nodded. 'Two points, Lord Navarch. First, one of

morality. Some of the pirates are vicious men – look at Manes. But more of them are merely displaced. Alexander built fleets and now all the Diadochoi follow suit – they use them and then discard them.'

'Hence our distaste for them, lad,' Timaeus said.

'But the pirates themselves – many of them – are scarcely to blame.' Satyrus could see that this point was of no interest whatsoever to his audience, so he waved negation. 'Never mind,' he said. 'Second point. The day is coming when your neutrality will be tantamount to declaring a side. Already, twice, Antigonus and his son have blockaded you. If they'd had the siege machines, they'd have attacked. If Antigonus ever tries for Aegypt again, he must have your alliance or your submission.'

'True,' Panther said.

'And I am *not* one of the Diadochoi. I am Leon's nephew, and when I am king of the Bosporus, I can guarantee you a friendly fleet and a constant grain supply. When Antigonus makes his move and Rhodos is besieged, you will need me.' Satyrus sat back and crossed his arms.

Now Panther stroked his beard.

Timaeus shook his head. 'Pirates!' he said.

'Mercenaries,' Satyrus shot back. 'Daedalus is an exile from Halicarnassus, and Demostrate is an exile from Pantecapaeum. Why is one a mercenary and the other a pirate?'

'You might yet have a career as a sophist,' Timaeus answered. 'A pirate is a pirate. You may call sheepdogs the same as wolves, but when the real wolves come, everyone knows what they smell like.'

'The ally we need is Lysimachos,' Panther said. 'And he hates Demostrate as much as we do.'

'If I can show you an alliance with Lysimachos?' Satyrus asked. 'I have asked him. Eumeles has attacked his Thracian possessions in the Euxine – only raids now, but he will land to stay in time. As long as Demostrate holds the Bosporus, Lysimachos cannot reinforce his garrisons. But if I take Demostrate away, instantly Lysimachos is master of his own shores.'

Panther looked at his co-navarch. 'I see this,' he said.

Timaeus shook his head. 'It is complex.'

Memnon, silent until now, leaned forward. 'I'm sorry to betray a confidence, Satyrus, but I'm a Rhodian first. You said yourself that your plans are often too complex.' He shrugged. 'Can you carry this off?'

Neiron shook his head. 'His plans are excellent. No man – not even the gods – can plan for everything.' The Cardian looked around. 'He planned the ambush of Manes, and failed. But none of your captains brought the Terror to heel. This man will.'

Satyrus looked at his helmsman, vowing to give the man anything he asked. Neiron spoke out better in this foreign council than even Diokles might have – Diokles would have been handicapped by service to Rhodos. 'I do make complex plans,' he admitted. 'I am one man, trying to restore my kingdom. If Olbia had a straight road from Alexandria, I wouldn't trouble you – or Demostrate.'

Timaeus nodded. 'Fair enough. You've given us something to consider. When do you sail?'

Satyrus managed a smile. 'I sail when Aspasia says I sail.'

Timaeus and Panther exchanged a long look. 'Alexandria?' he asked.

'Yes,' Satyrus answered.

'Perhaps you could pick us up a cargo? And we'd meet again in a month,' Timaeus suggested.

'A cargo from Alexandria? In winter?' Satyrus asked. The seas south of Cyprus were deadly in winter. 'I'll charge you a bonus for every mina of grain.'

Timaeus shrugged. 'We'll take it out of our fee for the squadron,' he said. 'If we agree.'

Alexandria spread before him like a basket of riches, the greatest harbour in the world surrounded by a city expanding so fast that a man could sit on the stern of his ship and watch the suburbs grow. At the end of the Pharos peninsula, a long spit of land that protruded like a caribou horn from the curve of the shore, workmen toiled with great blocks of limestone, laying the foundations of Ptolemy's proposed lighthouse even as thousands of other labourers carried baskets of earth from the mainland to widen and firm up the ground.

Satyrus stood by Neiron and watched Pharos slip past as his oarsmen dipped, paused and dipped again, bringing his ship slowly, carefully through the mass of shipping that filled the roadstead and crowded the beaches.

'There's Master Leon's house,' the lookout in the bow called.

Satyrus had a feeling of dread wash over him. He had no reason to feel that way, and he made a peasant sign of aversion.

'We'll land on the beach by the house,' he said.

Neiron nodded.

Satyrus had his rebroken arm splinted and tightly wrapped against his chest, but it hurt all the time. He watched the shore, attempting to rid himself of his mood and trying not to dwell on the pain in his arm.

Neither was particularly successful.

'Guard ship!' the lookout called.

'Messus has to go,' Satyrus said to Neiron.

'I'll see to it,' Neiron said. He shrugged. 'Messus is just as unhappy as you are.'

'I don't see him growing into the job,' Satyrus said, shaking his head.

'No,' Neiron said. He stroked his beard, his eyes on the approaching guard ship. 'Leon has merchant hulls – some of them quite fast. Like *Sparrow Hawk*. He could handle one of those, I think.'

Satyrus shook his head. Annoyed at always having to be the hard voice. 'He lacks authority.'

Neiron looked as if he was going to disagree.

'He lacks authority!' Satyrus snapped. Then he slumped. 'I'm becoming a bloody tyrant.'

'You do have a certain sense of your own importance,' Neiron said carefully.

Satyrus shook his head. 'It just goes on and on,' he said, but he didn't specify what it was.

'Oars – in!' Messus called. His timing was poor, and the oarsmen, who liked him, tried to compensate, but a hundred and eighty oarsmen can't all pretend that an order is properly given, and the *Golden Lotus* looked a far cry from her legendary efficiency as her wings folded in.

The guard ship coasted alongside and her trierarch stepped aboard trailing the smell of expensive oils. 'Cargo?' he demanded as his crimson boots hit the deck. 'I'm Menander, captain of the customs. Please show me your sailing bills.'

'Alum and hides,' Satyrus said.

'Hides for Aegypt? Leon's nephew must have lost his mind!' the man said. He made a note on his wax tablets.

Satyrus was growing angry again, but he knew that to lose his temper would be to act like a fool. He caught Neiron's look. 'I am injured, and not my best,' he said with a bow. 'My helmsman will handle this business.' Satyrus withdrew to the helmsman's bench. Neiron handed over a purse, and Menander peered into the hold, as if he could see past the lower-deck oarsmen and into the earthenware amphorae and the bales. 'All seems to be in order here,' he said, the purse bulging inside his chiton. He stepped back into his ship and they poled off, pulling strongly for their next victim.

'Now that's piracy, if you were to ask me,' Neiron said.

'Thanks,' Satyrus said. 'I'm in a mood to do harm. Something is wrong – I can feel it.'

Neiron shook his head. 'No – it's the poppy, Satyrus. That's all – throws your mind off. Sometimes a wound will do it alone – but a wound and the poppy can be deadly friends. I've had a few wounds.' He shrugged. 'Took one in my scalp – siege of Tyre, when I was young. It wouldn't heal, and the bump grew and grew. I thought I was going mad.'

'But you didn't,' Satyrus said.

Neiron stared at the approaching shore. 'Well – I did, for a bit. But that's not what I mean.'

Satyrus had to smile. 'This story is supposed to cheer me up?'

Neiron shrugged. 'I was saved by a good healer. And the gods, I suppose. You need to get to a doctor, just as Lady Aspasia said.'

'What did the doctor do with you?' Satyrus asked.

Neiron shook his head. 'Tied me down while I pissed the poppy out. Ares, it hurt. And that was after he cut a piece from my head, so that my skull felt odd for two years. I still rub it all the time.' He shrugged. 'That's what I mean, though. A bad wound changes you.'

Satyrus nodded. 'Everything looks right,' he said, cradling his arm. In his mind, there was a black smudge on the sky over the city.

Neiron sighed.

They went ashore beneath Satyrus's old bedroom window, and slaves and freemen were waiting on the beach with Sappho, having seen the famous *Golden Lotus* in the bay. Sappho smiled at him from the moment she caught his eye.

'We heard that you'd retaken the *Lotus*,' she said, and kissed him.

'I got him captured,' Satyrus said. He hugged her, and she responded fiercely. 'I'll free him in the end.' He looked around. 'Where's Melitta?'

'This is Kineas,' Sappho said. She held up a plump, round baby with huge blue eyes that wandered all around, as curious about the ship and the sky and the birds as about this strange man who'd taken him in his arms.

'Melitta's son! He's beautiful! Hello, nephew! Goodness!' Satyrus laughed. 'I feel quite old.'

'Melitta has gone to the Euxine to raise the tribes,' Sappho said quietly. 'I sent Coenus with her, and Eumenes when he came from Babylon.'

'Herakles!' Satyrus said. 'She left her son?'

Sappho's eyebrows made a hard line and the beauty of her face vanished in a mask. 'She did not run away,' Sappho said. 'Men tried to kill her – and me. This is war, Satyrus.'

Satyrus watched his sea bag going ashore. 'Aunt Sappho, you remember Neiron? He's my helmsman now. He proved himself this voyage. I hope he can stay in the house.'

Neiron bowed. Sappho inclined her head. 'Welcome to our house, Neiron.'

'Master Satyrus needs a healer,' Neiron said pointedly.

Sappho nodded. 'You look – pinched. Are you drinking too much, boy?'

'Poppy,' Neiron said. 'For a wound.'

'Herakles!' Satyrus didn't know whether to laugh or weep. 'I'm right here. I'm a grown man and I can see to my own needs!'

'So I see,' Sappho said, in a voice that suggested the opposite.

She was already giving orders with her hands, and maids came running.

Nearchus read the note from Aspasia. He scratched the bridge of his nose and smiled. 'Aspasia herself?' he said. Then he shook his head. 'You are in for a bad few weeks. Let me see the arm.'

He undid the bandages and the splints, and then replaced them. 'Beautiful, of course. Aspasia wouldn't do poor work. But she has left me the hard part. The night market is full of men who can set a bone.' He looked at Sappho, who had insisted on being present. 'I want him fed like an ox for sacrifice for a week. Satyrus, take what exercise you can with that arm. Because the next two weeks will be brutal.'

Satyrus shook his head. 'So you all keep telling me,' he said.

Nearchus scratched his nose again. 'We aren't kidding.'

Satyrus ate, and walked. He sacrificed at temples. On the third day he went across the city to the Aegyptian quarter, escorted by Namastis, a priest of Poseidon who had served with him at Gaza.

'You're sure they can forge the true steel?' Satyrus asked.

Namastis rolled his eyes. 'As you tell the story, a priest of Ptah made the sword in the first place. Yes?' Namastis grinned. 'You Greeks and your arrogance. You call us "Aigyptioi" – yes?'

Satyrus was watching the whole world of the Aegyptian quarter, and he nodded perfunctorily. It smelled different. It looked different. The people on the street seemed younger – vibrant with energy, fast-moving, alive.

A pretty girl flashed him a smile – not a common experience in the Greek streets.

'Do I have any of your attention?' Namastis asked. He paused and put his hand on the girl's head, and she accepted his blessing with a mixture of pleasure and impatience, like a child being praised by a parent.

'We call you "Aigyptioi",' Satyrus said in sing-song repetition.

'All you are saying is the "home of Ptah" or the "home of craft".' Namastis led him up the steps of the temple, where a very normal-looking god in robes presided – a god without the usual animal head.

The priests were immediately interested, thanks to a few words in private from Namastis, and when Satyrus unrolled the shards of his father's sword, they gathered around like dogs with a bone, whispering and touching the steel.

Namastis took him aside. 'They say many things. Mostly, they say that Sek-Atum made this, and he is old, but still the best. He is downriver at Memphis. How long will you be here?'

Satyrus shrugged. 'Until I am no longer friends with the poppy,' he said.

Namastis nodded, the import striking deep. 'Oh, my friend,' he said, and put a hand on Satyrus's shoulder.

He spoke to the priests. They looked sombre. The eldest among them came and put a thumb on Satyrus's lips, surprising him, and then looked deeply into his eyes. He nodded brusquely and stepped away, speaking quickly to Namastis.

'They will send the hilt and shards downriver to Memphis today. They say that the breaking of the blade and your health are one – that the blade must be reforged or your health will be broken like the blade, and the poppy in your body is the flaw in the blade. They say many things – they are priests.' Namastis shrugged. 'They say that the blade should have gone into your father's grave. Does this make sense to you?'

Satyrus thought of the kurgan by the Tanais River. It had a stone at the top, like every kurgan. 'I know what they speak of, yes,' he said. 'But they will reforge the blade?'

'As soon as it can be done. A donation would not be unwelcome. A mina of silver would be appropriate.'

'I will send them a mina of gold, if they are successful.' Satyrus hugged Namastis. 'This means a great deal to me.'

'It is well that you brought me. And it is good that you respect the ways of this land.' Namastis led him by the hand down the steps of the temple of Ptah and out of the Aegyptian quarter. They shared a meal and then Namastis had to go back to his duty at the temple.

'I will pray for you. Come and visit me!' Namastis said.

Satyrus went straight from the Temple of Poseidon to the palace. At the palace, he made an appointment with Gabines, the steward of the lord of Aegypt. He listened to the news in the agora and spread some rumours of his own.

On the fourth day, he visited Abraham's father, Isaac, who met him in the courtyard and had him in to drink *qua-veh*.

'How is my scapegrace son?' Ben Zion asked.

Satyrus drank the bitter stuff carefully. He realized that he had hoped that Miriam, Abraham's talkative daughter, would put in an appearance, although he had come to recognize that the poppy, when present, muted all such longings, and when absent, accentuated them. Right now he was as far from his last dose as he ever got, and thus on edge.

'He is well,' Satyrus said carefully. 'He sent a cargo, which I carried in the *Lotus* and sold at Rhodos. I brought alum from Rhodos – here are my bills. And that sack has the silver.'

Ben Zion waved a hand at two weeks of winter sailing. 'I would rather have my son. He is playing pirate while he ought to be getting married.'

Satyrus had a vivid image of Abraham playing 'feed the flute girl' at the symposium of Aphrodite. 'He will come back in the summer,' Satyrus said. 'I only came to assure you that he is well.'

'Well? He is fornicating like a stallion amongst heathens who would murder him for his curly hair. He is playing pirate with men who would eat his heart when they cut it out – and you took him there.' Ben Zion didn't seem particularly angry. He said these things as simple facts.

Satyrus met his eye. 'He is my best captain – my right hand. In a year, I will be king, or not.'

Ben Zion nodded. 'Listen, Satyrus son of Kineas, who would be king. If you fall, my son's head will lie beside yours. If you triumph, what value to me? What value to me if my son dies? I would rather that he came back here to his own and left your world of *adventure*. When he is dead, it will be too late for him to repent.'

Satyrus stood up. 'He is my best friend,' Satyrus said. 'I am sorry you don't value his accomplishments. He is as brave as a lion – thoughtful in council. He sees far, and he does not hesitate to do what must be done. If he were my son, I would be proud that he was accounted a great captain. They know his name in Rhodos and in Byzantium.'

'You are a young fool, like my son, Satyrus son of Kineas.

What makes you think that I am not proud? I was proud when he came home from the fight at Gaza, like a young David in his pride. Men come to me and say, "Your son took an enemy galley in a fair fight, when the battle was lost," and again, "Your son saved his ship, and his friend." I hear these things, and I rejoice that my son is made of such stuff. *And I still want him back here, where I can love him, and not dead with you.*' Ben Zion held up the pot. 'More qua-veh?' he asked. 'We Jews speak our minds, young Satyrus. Don't bother to be offended. Bring him back to me.'

He walked Satyrus to the gate, and Satyrus felt better than he'd expected. He smiled at the older man, who tugged his own beard and laughed.

'How long will you be here?' Ben Zion asked. 'Surely all your busy schemes need you?'

Satyrus looked up at the exedra and saw movement behind a curtain. He looked back at Ben Zion, moved somehow to simple honesty.

'I took poppy for a wound and I've had too much of it. My physician is going to take it out of me. This will take more than a week.' He smiled ruefully.

'God be with you, then,' Ben Zion said. 'It is no small matter.' The older man took his elbow. 'You are looking for my daughter, I think.'

Satyrus nodded. 'I liked her.'

Ben Zion shook his head. 'She is married now. You have enough of my family already.' He guided Satyrus out of the gate.

Miriam married. Well, he scarcely knew her really, and that only to be annoyed at her. 'And how is the machine?' Satyrus asked.

Ben Zion tugged his beard again. But the smile that came to his lips was unforced. 'Magnificent. Lord Ptolemy has been here – to my house! To see it function. He wants one for his library. The tyrant of Athens has sent me a letter about it.' Ben Zion shook his head. 'I am one of the greatest grain merchants in the world, and no one knows my name outside the trade. But now that I have financed this machine – now men know me. What is the Greek word I am looking for?'

'Irony?' Satyrus asked.

'You have it, young man. The irony threatens to overwhelm me.' Ben Zion nodded to himself. 'There is a lesson there somewhere. Perhaps about the futility of human striving.' He studied the ground and then, raising his eyes, he seemed to study Satyrus. 'Two of the philosophers who worked on the machine are coming to Alexandria – indeed, I expect them any day. They come from Syracusa – students of Pythagoras and Archimedes. Would you like to meet such men? Or are their mathematics too academic for an adventurer such as yourself?'

Satyrus clasped the older man's hand. 'I would be delighted. It will give me something I can look forward to – while I lie on a bed and curse the poppy.'

'Good. I will send word to Leon's house. You will rescue him?' Ben Zion asked suddenly.

'Yes,' Satyrus said.

'Good. For that, I loan you my son. Leon and I are partners – it is fitting that my son help his nephew.' Ben Zion squeezed his arm and went back through his gate, leaving Satyrus wondering whether Ben Zion was speaking to himself or to Satyrus.

The next day, Nearchus pronounced Satyrus fit.

Satyrus lay on his bed with a bucket of scrolls.

'Read while you can,' Nearchus said.

And so it began.

14

NORTH OF OLBIA, WINTER, 311–310 BC

Melitta's first debate, first council and first absolute commands as lady of the Assagatje involved sending her allies home to their yurts. The irony was not lost on her.

The presence of Parshtaevalt and Urvara had exactly the effect she had anticipated. They treated her like a particularly wise child – they spoke carefully, they laid out their plans and expected her immediate approval. They, and their people, camped a few stades from the field of the Ford of the River God, and tribesmen began to join them. Just as Ataelus, Urvara and Parshtaevalt wanted. By their very inaction, they were gathering an army.

On the third day after the sacrifices, Melitta arose from her pallet of furs determined to take command of her own people – and her destiny. She dressed carefully and went to Nihmu, who now openly shared a lodge with Coenus. She brushed new snow from the flap and opened it, holding the stick carefully so that it did not dump more snow on the carpets inside.

'I desire to summon all of the leaders in camp,' she said.

Coenus was boiling water in a small bronze pot balanced on a tripod. He was naked from the waist up, the grey hair of his abdomen criss-crossed with scars. She had seldom seen a body so scarred.

He was unembarrassed. 'Lady,' he said. He inclined his head. He, at least, treated her as an adult – and as his commander.

Nihmu was wearing only a wool shirt. She came and knelt by Melitta and gave her a cup of warm cider from the fire. 'Lady?' she said. 'I am neither a commander nor your baqca.' She shrugged. 'How would I summon your council?'

'Stand outside and yell?' Melitta asked. 'I don't know. But if you won't summon them, I'll stand in the snow and yell. Yesterday's council was summoned by Ataelus. I was *invited*. Today, I'll do the inviting.'

Coenus nodded. 'I'll do it, lady,' he said. 'I am friends with all, and yet your man. I will go from yurt to yurt and invite them to come – where?'

'To my yurt,' Melitta said. 'Now. I want Ataelus and Samahe, Urvara and Eumenes, Tameax, and Parshtaevalt – and his tanist, if he has one. That handsome boy he had at his tail yesterday? His son?'

Nihmu shook her head. 'Sister's son,' she said. 'Gaweint, by name.' She smiled. 'He is handsome,' she said, more to Coenus than to Melitta.

Coenus shrugged. 'If you say so, my beauty.'

Melitta was – outraged was too strong, but surprised, even shocked, that they should flirt openly in front of her. 'Nihmu!' she said, before her political mind could stop her. 'You have a husband!'

Nihmu smiled a cat's smile. 'So I do. He is a prisoner with the enemy, and I bend my efforts to his rescue.'

Melitta flicked a glance at Coenus, who was equally unperturbed at this almost open accusation of adultery. 'If she thinks ill of us—' Coenus began.

'Ill?' Melitta asked.

There was silence in the tent.

'I wish Sappho were here,' Coenus said.

Melitta looked at both of them. They looked back at her. Melitta knew enough about emotion and body language to know that they were neither embarrassed nor defensive – an attitude which enraged her.

'Very well,' she said. 'Summon my leaders.' She turned on her heel and then scrambled to get out of the tent flap with dignity. *What are they doing? Their actions will reflect on me!* she thought, and then decided that was unfair. Most Sakje didn't know anything about Nihmu's husband – and fewer would care. Sakje women did as they pleased. Sex was seldom the driving force among the nomads that it was in the cities.

She went back to her yurt and sat, waiting for them to come. The time stretched on and on – in some ways, the longest wait of her life. Early on, she began to wonder what she would do if they did not come.

But a yurt's walls are thin, and even as she fed her anger with thoughts of their disobedience, her ears told her that they were coming – Parshtaevalt shouted for his clean fur tunic, and sent another rider to find Gaweint, who was hunting.

And then they came, all together, which led her to believe that they had met somewhere else. Urvara entered first. She bowed – a rare gesture – and when bid, seated herself at the fire. One by one, the other senior chiefs entered and sat.

Melitta smiled and offered them wine. Coenus slipped in – Coenus, the Megaran aristocrat – and he served them each in horn cups that held the heat. Nihmu came and sat at the fire, and Melitta allowed her, although she was not sure what Nihmu's role was, nor what her arrival presaged.

'Let me speak to the point,' Melitta said when they were seated. 'It was never my desire to gather an army. You are gathering an army. Send them home.'

Ataelus nodded. 'We do it for you.'

Melitta kept her voice even. 'Send them home.'

Urvara smiled. 'Melitta, we understand that—'

Melitta cut her off ruthlessly. 'I care *nothing* for your understanding. Send them home, or I will ride away and you can rot in the snow. Either I am to be the lady of the Assagatje or I am not. *My name* draws these riders. *My name* alone will bind the Assagatje.' She looked around, pushed down her nerves and her quickened heartbeat and forced herself to sound calm. 'I do not intend to be *saskar* – a tyrant. But in this first thing, I will be obeyed, or we will part our ways.'

Ataelus shook his head. 'Marthax will not bow his head to a girl.'

Melitta shrugged. 'Then I will kill him in combat, one to one.'

'Why should he agree to such a combat?' Urvara asked.

'Is he a fool?' Melitta asked. 'Really? This camp – in winter, in the open – proves that my name will gather an army. His name *will not.* He knows this as well as I. Let us give him dignity – to acknowledge me if he will, or to die under my knife if he will not.'

Parshtaevalt stood up. 'Lady, he was – and remains – the deadliest lance on the plains. Marthax will kill you – and that is the end of our hopes.'

Melitta shrugged. 'No,' she said. 'He will not kill me.'

Nihmu leaned forward. 'All here love you, honey bee. You must listen—'

'No,' Melitta said. 'No. I will not listen any more. Each of you may keep twenty-five knights. That is all. We will ride for Marthax's camp in the morning, and if I am not obeyed, I will ride for the coast.'

One by one, they shuffled out – anger written on every face. *Who likes to be given orders by a younger woman?* she thought. But she kept her face impassive.

When they were all gone, Coenus cleaned her wine-heating pot with a coarse linen rag. He looked at her, waiting for her to speak. When she did not, he finally put the pot on the pile of her dishes and stood up.

'It had to be done,' he said.

'Are you the only one truly my man?' she asked.

Coenus smiled. 'Far from it, lady. I have known you every day of your life – they know you only from afar. So they will worship you, where I already know what you will do. As does Nihmu. And none of us offers you anything but respect.' He gave her his lopsided grin. 'But – it had to be done. Even parents must eventually relinquish control of children.'

She smiled back. 'Is this, too, something about which your Xenophon wrote?'

He shook his head. 'He never wrote on the magic of command,' Coenus said. 'I learned those lessons from your father, and I have little to teach you. Why are you so certain that you can put Marthax down? Is it the prophecy?'

Melitta sat on her furs. 'Yes and no. I *know* it.'

Coenus came and sat next to her. 'They don't know it.'

'They must trust me,' Melitta said.

Coenus stared at the coals of her fire. 'Lady, they *know* that in a trial of arms, their faction – your faction – will triumph. Any other method has elements of risk. Their logic is almost Greek – their way *will not fail.*'

'Listen to me, Coenus,' Melitta said, in Greek. She spoke fast, the way Philokles taught when making an argument. 'That logic is false. In a trial of arms, we would win *for a day*. Marthax would lose a battle, or refuse it, and ride away to the north, unbeaten, to gather tribesmen and be a thorn in my side. And my people and his people would fight for a generation – perhaps more – while the Sauromatae creep into our eastern door and the Cruel Hands and the Grass Cats settle in the rich river valleys and become Sindi. His people and my people – raid and counter-raid – and never would we be *one people* as we were in Satrax's day. But if I succeed, in a month, I am queen of the Assagatje. And when the ground is hard, *all* our horses will go east against the Sauromatae.'

'Your mother followed the very strategy that you say Marthax would adopt,' Coenus said. 'She rode away and formed her own alliances.'

'I know it,' she answered. 'I grew up with it. I have thought about it all my adult life. I think that she did what she did for my father. For him it was right. For the war against Alexander, it was right. But – for the Assagatje, it was wrong. And I will remedy that.'

Coenus got up. 'You think deeply. I don't know which party has the right of it, but I will help to see that they obey you – if only because that is the way it must be, or your role has no meaning.' He reached out, and they clasped hands.

At the tent door, she stopped him. 'You have never held a major command,' she said. 'And yet my father loved you, and you are the best of warriors.'

'I dislike ordering men to do things I do not do myself,' Coenus said.

Melitta raised an eyebrow. 'You are an aristocrat. You give orders with every breath.'

'I will order a cup of wine from a slave. I will not order the slave to face a cavalry charge.' Coenus smiled. 'I'm not even a good phylarch. I end up pitching the tents and cooking the food – myself.'

'I would give you a command,' she said. 'I would form a group of my own knights, and have you as my commander.'

Coenus nodded. 'For a time,' he said. 'For this summer, I would be honoured. But when you are victorious, I will take my horses and go and rebuild my shrine to Artemis. I will tend my wife's grave, hunt animals and die content. I am tired of war.'

She smiled. 'I must be content, too. From the warriors now in the camp, find me a trumpeter and five knights – just five.'

Coenus nodded. 'As you command, lady.'

She frowned. 'And Nihmu?' she asked.

'Nihmu struggles,' Coenus said.

Melitta crossed her arms. 'I was not asking about her ... spirit.'

Coenus shook his head. 'If you are asking about our sleeping arrangements, I can only suggest that it is none of your business. Lady.' He held her eye effortlessly. 'And it is *not* your business.'

Melitta actually shook with the repressed urge to stomp her foot. 'Very well,' she said archly. 'You are dismissed.'

'Have a care, lady,' Coenus cautioned. 'Sakje rulers do not "dismiss". That is for Greek tyrants and Medes.'

Melitta slumped. 'Point taken.'

Coenus nodded. 'Good.' He slipped through the flap, and was gone.

Just after the golden rim of the sun crossed the horizon the next morning, they left the camp. Hundreds of tribesmen still milled about. More than a few mounted and rode alongside the column, but Melitta could see that they were not packed to travel, so she ignored them except to accept their good wishes. Urvara and Parshtaevalt had twenty-five knights each, and a few more riders as heralds and outriders – strictly speaking, neither had *exactly* obeyed.

Ataelus had twenty-five riders, precisely, and he grinned at her and invited her to count. Instead, she embraced him on horseback.

Coenus led six knights of his own choosing. The only one she knew was Scopasis, who wore a new scale shirt, a little big, but a beautiful piece, and a bronze Boeotian helmet that he hadn't had the day before. All six of her knights could be identified by the crown of fir tree wrapped around their helmets, which gave them a curiously organic appearance – but made them appear as a unit. They fell in around her and rode at her side.

'Introduce me,' Melitta said to Coenus.

Coenus nodded. 'My phylarch is Scopasis. He is an outlaw,

and has no other loyalty. He is *your* man. Besides,' Coenus flashed a smile at the small man, 'I like him.'

Scopasis spoke up from under his new helmet. 'I will follow you to death, lady.'

Melitta grinned. 'That's not exactly my plan. But I, too, like Scopasis. And the others?'

'Laen here is actually your cousin – the son of Srayanka's half-sister Daan.' Coenus pointed Laen out. He was a tall young man with a gilded-bronze muscle cuirass and an ancient, and beautiful, Attic helmet with silver mounts. 'Nihmu chose him – they're related. I could have had fifty men if you'd wanted so many. There was a disturbance!' Coenus laughed. 'Nearly a melee. I wish I could have held games. This young troublemaker with the blond moustache is Darax, and the one whose nose scrapes the sky is Bareint. The two hiding in Bareint's mighty shadow are brothers from the Standing Horse tribe – Sindispharnax and Lanthespharnax, or so I understand their names. Sindi and Lanthe, to me. The lanky one with the extravagant moustache is Agreint.'

Melitta's head whirled at so many new names. 'Sindispharnax?'

'Lady?' the warrior asked. He pushed his horse forward.

'Hardly a Sakje name?' she asked.

'My mother was a Persian captive,' he said proudly. 'She sits still with the elder matrons, and she gave us Parsae names.' He leaned forward. 'My father served yours on the Great Raid east, lady.'

She nodded. To Coenus, she said, 'So, how did you choose them?'

'I asked any man who wanted to join your escort to meet me at my yurt with his best horse,' he said. 'I simply inspected the horses. I chose the six best. Their riders came along for the ride, so to speak.'

She curled her mouth and made a face. 'Perhaps we should be more attentive to men?'

Coenus leaned close. 'Am I the commander of your knights, lady?'

'You are,' she replied. And nodded. 'Point taken. And my trumpeter?' she asked.

'Unless you take Urvara's, there's not a trumpet in the camp.' Coenus flicked a Greek salute. 'Take Marthax's.'

She nodded. 'Good thought.'

That night they made a cold camp, and Melitta regretted that she hadn't a sleeping companion to keep her warm. She piled every fur and blanket she owned on a cleared place in the snow, and eventually, after walking until her feet were warm, she got to sleep.

In the morning they rode on, into the north. It snowed twice, the first a matter of little moment, the second putting a fresh layer on the grass as deep as the hocks of a horse. None of the horses were struggling yet, but a few more inches on top of what had already fallen and travel would begin to become dangerous.

Ataelus went out with scouts as soon as the sky was grey. His riders and Samahe's came in all day, reporting on the distance to Marthax's camp. At noon, when the sun was a pale silver disk in the sky, Ataelus came in himself.

'Marthax awaits us on the Great Field,' he said. 'I saw him, and he saluted me. We did not speak. He and all his knights are armed.'

'How many?' Urvara asked.

'All of his three hundred,' Ataelus said, with a significant look at Melitta.

'We have fewer than a single hundred,' Parshtaevalt said.

'We won't need them,' Melitta said, and hoped that her voice carried sufficient authority. 'Ride on.' She motioned to Ataelus to stay at her side. 'What is this Great Field?' she asked.

Ataelus laughed. 'Here in the north is the city of the Sakje, yes? You know it? Not a city at all – some temples, mostly built by Greek craftsmen, and the houses of the big traders. And walls, and corrals – pasturage for ten thousand animals in time of war, all closed in walls. The Sindi dug it for us. And outside the main gate is the Great Field, where all the people gather sometimes.'

'To name a king?' Melitta asked. Her stomach was turning over, and she felt the same ice in her spine that she'd felt in her first fight – and the first time she made love to Xenophon.

Ataelus shook his head. 'To talk. To trade. Sometimes to fight.'

He shrugged. 'I am from the east, lady. We have different ways. Your people inherit the rulership – mother to daughter, father to sister's son. Mine fight for it.'

'We are not so different,' Melitta said. Her hands were cold.

The sun had gone well down the sky when their column arrived in the Great Field. Immediately, her clan leaders formed their knights. She was in the centre, with hers, and she put Ataelus on the far right, Urvara on the right and Parshtaevalt on the left. They formed their line a stade apart, and Marthax's riders watched them. Most of them weren't even mounted – they stood by their horses, blowing on their hands. Melitta slipped off her riding horse and climbed up on to Gryphon.

'We should all change to our chargers,' Coenus said.

'No,' Melitta said. 'They're not mounted on chargers. Only Marthax. And me.'

Coenus grunted. 'Would it be so wrong if we had some advantage? They outnumber us three to one.'

'Yes,' Melitta said. She was cold right through, and her hands were shaking. It all came down to this, and suddenly she was robbed of her certainty. All these people – people she loved, for all she quarrelled with them – had followed her to this field, with the icy north wind blowing horse-tails of snow. What if she was wrong?

'I wish I had a trumpeter,' she said, and rode forward alone. After two paces, she pulled up and turned. 'No one is to follow me!' she called, her young voice carrying on the wind.

Coenus made a noise, and Parshtaevalt's horse fidgeted, demonstrating his rider's feelings. Somewhere in the line, a horse farted and Melitta smiled. Then she turned and gave her horse a nudge, and she was walking, alone, across the field.

Gryphon was as calm as if they were riding in Ataelus's camp, although his ears were up and he was looking at the opposing line. He was a tried warhorse – he knew what combat was.

Melitta wished she had grander clothes. She wore a good wolf-skin cloak worked in caribou hair, and her mother's helmet, the aventail sparkling with gold and silver scales and a row of blue enamel scales where the aventail met the bronze bowl. She had her mother's gorytos of gold – but her boots were shabby and her trousers were plain hide. And her gauntlets were those of Gryphon's last owner – magnificent, but dirty with a month's riding and camp work.

Marthax – the man she assumed was Marthax – was on a big grey in the middle of the line. He had a helmet of gold, a gold-washed scale shirt and a heavy scarlet and fur coat, Persian style, across his shoulders. His beard was heavy and rolled over his breastplate, and it was so shot with grey that it appeared white at a distance. His boots were red, and his trousers were red with gold plaques.

He touched his stallion's sides and came to meet her.

He had a hand on his hip and held himself erect, and he *looked like a king*. In fact, his dignity was palpable. She wanted to hate him – her mother's original enemy, although not the man who had killed her. But he had helped – or he had stood aloof. And yet, at ten horse-lengths' distance, he looked too noble to be an enemy.

Will my brother ever attain that sort of dignity? she asked herself. *Will I?* Her hands would not get warm, and they shook – and her shoulders shook with cold and nerves.

She thrust her chest out and straightened her shoulders, and met his eyes – both of their faces hidden in the depths of helmets. His were bloodshot and blue. Close up, his dignity was unimpaired, but his strength was less.

'You came,' he said, when they were three horse-lengths apart. His breath rose like the steam from the blood of the sacrifices. His horse's breath rose with it.

'As did you,' Melitta said. 'I ask you to name me your heir.' Just like that. The Sakje way – no Persian meddling with wine and small talk.

Marthax pulled his helmet off. Under it, he wore a small arming cap of linen and wool. He scratched his head. 'No,' he said. He sounded genuinely regretful. 'No. I can't.'

She took her helmet off as well, and her hair fell from under her cap. A sigh arose from both lines as it became obvious that they were going to talk and not fight. 'I would never humiliate you,' she said. 'But the whole people must ride to war in the east, to face the Sauromatae.'

'Listen, girl,' he said, and his horse did a curvet, and pain showed in his face. 'Listen while I talk. I have an *agreement* with Upazan of the Sauromatae. You do not. I can never go to war with him and not be an oath-breaker. I will keep my oath. Will you fight me hand to hand instead?'

'You acknowledge my right?' she asked.

'Bah! Of course. I have no other heir.' For the first time, his impatience showed, and Melitta wondered why he was impatient. He pushed his horse forward and she flinched, fearing treachery, but he pushed his face close to hers. His breath was foul. He was, in fact, a sick man. A sick, old man. 'Listen, *girl*. I made a mistake with Upazan. You will make mistakes, too. But I bought the people time, and now I will fight you for the kingship. *Do you understand?*' he asked.

Melitta straightened her back. 'I understand, O King.'

That made him smile. 'I'm sorry about your mother, lass. I didn't understand how easy it is to share, and how foolish it is to crave power.' He was looking at the setting sun. 'I have but one request.'

Melitta nodded.

'Build me a good kurgan. Do it in spring, when you rally your army, and no man will say you are not the queen. Any ills will be healed.' He looked around. 'I hated being king, but by all the gods, I love life. Don't fuck up, girl.' His voice choked a little.

He put his helmet on his head. 'Can you fight?' he asked. 'I hear that you can.'

She piled her hair on to her head again, and pulled her fox-skin hat over it. 'I can,' she said.

He nodded. 'I'll ride back to my own lines. You do the same. When I raise my sword, we charge.'

Melitta nodded. Then she turned her horse and rode slowly back across the snow-covered ground to her own lines, where all the chiefs had gathered around her knights.

'We fight,' Melitta said.

Parshtaevalt shook his head. 'Let me fight him,' he said. 'It is allowed.'

But Urvara had been watching. 'You *will* win,' she said. 'I see it now. At the last, Marthax is, in fact, a good king.'

And Melitta nodded. There were tears in her eyes. 'My mother said that he was a great man, before he turned on her.' She shrugged. 'I suspected that man was still there.'

Urvara nodded. 'I should have seen sooner, lady.'

Melitta thought of saying something ... authoritative. About trusting her the next time. But she decided that nothing needed to be said. Instead, she took her best spear from Coenus.

'He is ready,' Urvara said. She had been watching over Melitta's shoulder.

'As am I,' Melitta said. She settled her helmet, clenched and unclenched her hands, and raised her spear.

All the Sakje in both lines cheered and the two riders began to move.

He was big and well armoured. He had a war axe with a spike, a vicious weapon, and he was holding it out at the length of his arm, pointing the spike at her eyes. He had a small shield with a running stag in bronze over iron scales, and he was coming at a flat gallop.

There were no rules in the kingship duel, although it was said that anyone who took the kingship with a bow in their hand would fail as king. It was said.

She held her spear overhand, as if to throw it, and she pointed Gryphon's head at the middle of Marthax's horse's chest and gave him both heels. He leaped forward and the snow blurred past his feet as she seemed to ride the wind.

Marthax raised his shield against her throw a few strides away, and she twirled the staff in her fingers and brought it under her arm, the point in line all the way, so that her spear struck his shield and he was out of his saddle and she barely kept her seat, her knees locked around Gryphon's barrel, the horse himself responding to the shock of impact with long training.

She brought Gryphon around in a long circle. *Stay down,* she thought. *Stay down and live!* But another part of her said, *I unhorsed Marthax, and I will be queen!* Around she came, and he was up on one knee, using the axe to raise himself. There was blood flowing from under his helmet, but he was on his feet.

She reined Gryphon to a stop a few horse-lengths from him.

'Don't be a fool, girl,' he snapped.

She slipped to the ground and drew her plain-hilted akinakes, the same one she'd carried at Gaza and in every fight on the plains. She put her spear into her left hand.

He came for her without another word, trudging across the snow as fast as his wound would allow.

She threw the spear left-handed, and it hit his knee above the armour and he was down in the snow again.

And he laughed. 'Arggh!' he growled.

She circled warily, because he still had the axe and he was *getting up*.

'Aye, you can fight,' he said. 'A good kurgan!' he said, and he stumbled at her, his axe raised for a powerful swing.

And she stepped inside his swing, took the weakest part of the blow on her shoulder and back, faked her brother's favourite Harmodius overhand – and rammed the whole length of her sword up under his arm in a rising backhand thrust. It was a move that she had practised with Satyrus and Philokles and Theron a thousand times, and it seemed fitting that he should have it, because when well done, it granted instant death.

Her blade went in to the hilt, and the king was dead before he slumped to the ground, the weight of his fall pulling the sword from her grasp.

She bent over him to retrieve her sword, and the pain of his blow to her back sprang at her like an ambush and she almost fell. Had he changed his mind at the last? Or had he granted her a fair fight because he had her measure?

He was dead. She failed to pull the blade free on the third tug, and it snapped in her hand. She dropped the worn hilt in the snow and realized that the riders were cheering her – from both sides of the line. Just as she had foreseen.

At her feet lay an old man, his beard red with blood, his lined face freed from his helmet by her last blow. She bent down, and closed his eyes.

Coenus rode up, having collected Gryphon's reins. Behind him were Urvara and Parshtaevalt, and across the field, Marthax's commanders were surging forward as well.

'Hail, Queen of the Assagatje,' Coenus said.

'He gave it to me,' she said.

'Aye. Well, he was always one of the best,' Coenus said. 'We'd never have beaten Zopryon without him.'

Other men and women were surrounding her. She got herself up on Gryphon with as much struggle as she'd ever had in her life. 'Listen!' she shouted, and they were silent.

'Srakorlax!' Scopasis called. Other Sakje took up the name.

'Listen to me!' she shouted. Gryphon stood as steady as a rock between her legs. 'Marthax died the king of the Assagatje – the heir of Satrax. In the spring, we will build him a great kurgan on the riverbank. Every man of his knights will give a horse, and I will give a hundred more. He was the lord of ten thousand horses!'

Four hundred voices should not be able to fill the icy wastes of the sea of grass in winter, but their roar echoed joy – and relief that there was to be no bloody civil war.

'And then we will gather our might, and the Sauromatae will feel the weight of our hooves!' she called.

And again they roared.

15

ALEXANDRIA, WINTER, 311–310 BC

*H*erakles stood naked except for his lion skin, towering over Satyrus's supine form. At a distance, Satyrus regretted his own death, and his spirit hung over the room, watching the hero-god standing beside his body.

Thanatos entered from the floor, striding into the room as if climbing invisible steps from Hades below.

'Mine,' he said.

'No,' Herakles said.

'Mine!' Death hissed, and his voice was the voice of every creature of the underworld, and the stench of death and the flat smell of old earth accompanied him. His garments were of rotted linen, and his crown was gold so long buried as to have a patina.

Herakles stood between Death and the bed. 'No,' he said, and crossed his mighty arms.

'Ten times over!' Death hissed. 'Am I some demi-mortal, to be treated so?'

'Begone,' Herakles said.

Thanatos was no coward. 'Bah,' he spat, and sand dribbled from his mouth. 'Let me see how much of you remains mortal, little godling.'

Herakles shrugged. 'I have tried your strength, Uncle.'

Thanatos struck suddenly, with a sword shaped like a sickle, the kepesh of Aegypt. Herakles caught the wrist of the hand that held the sword and lifted the god and his sword clear of the floor and walked out of the room, on to the balcony over the sea.

'Cool your head in the kingdom of your brother, Poseidon,' Herakles said.

'I took your father in his moment of triumph, boy! And I'll do the same to you!' Thanatos said, and his dreadful eyes crossed with Satyrus's and he knew that was meant for him.

And then Herakles turned and threw the god of death over the balcony.

There was no splash.

And in the way of dreams, Herakles led him along the river many parasangs, until they came to a temple, and Herakles led him to the altar – but it was no altar, and an old man, supported by two brawny apprentices, was forging iron on an anvil, and the scene was lit in the red of the forge, and as Satyrus watched, the bent blade was quenched, and Satyrus smiled in his dream, and then he was being pulled by the hand through the tangled ways of the night market, passing whores and rag-pickers and basket-weavers, passing a baker who did his business at night for the greater profit, and a man who sold stolen goods, and a woman who claimed her mother was Moira, goddess of fate, and that she could see the future. Herakles walked past them all, and none of them saw him, except the daughter of Moira, who raised her eyes from a fraudulent fortune and drew her stole over her head in terror.

They entered a tavern, and men moved out of the way of the god of heroes without knowing that they did so, stepping aside at a movement in the corner of the eye, and Satyrus moved in his wake. He could smell the sour wine, and smell also the tang of the poppy juice that the innkeeper kept in a glass bottle – real temple glass, worth its weight in gold. He almost lost the god in his sudden flood of desire to possess that wretched stuff, to change this dream of sordid reality for the colours that spoke like gods.

He balanced between two steps, one of which would lead him, invisible and wraithlike, to the bottle, the other of which would follow his god. And then he followed Herakles through a curtain of soiled leather, and then through a wall of dry stone chinked with mud, to a filthy room that might once have been whitewashed and now stank of old wine and rotten food.

He knew the man at the table instantly. It was Sophokles, the Athenian doctor-assassin, and he had four men crouching on the dirt floor and a fifth person, a woman, standing by the door, her arms crossed over her breasts. They all turned their heads as the god stepped among them, and Sophokles stood suddenly, took a breath and looked around him.

'Something – has come,' he said. 'Damn Aegypt and her walking spirits!'

Herakles didn't speak, but pointed mutely at the woman by the door.

Satyrus knew her, and he ...

Awoke. He was covered in sweat, and weak – so weak that he couldn't raise his arm to wipe the sweat from his face.

Nearchus sat by him. 'You are awake?' he asked.

Satyrus willed his arm to move, and it was as if his paralysis lifted even as he forced that first movement – and a sharp pain shot through his arm, a cramp like the ones that a poorly massaged athlete can get after pushing himself too hard. An experience that Satyrus had had many times.

Another cramp hit him and he rolled on his side and retched. Nearchus held a basin for him, but nothing came out but a thin stream of bile.

When the cramps released their hold of his muscles he relaxed and a slave wiped his chin with a cloth. He breathed in, then let the breath out, testing his gag reflex.

'Was I dead?' he asked.

Nearchus shook his head. 'Not at all. You did quite well, young man. Although, to be honest, the habit was scarcely ingrained – a mere matter of weeks. My brother, for instance ...' Nearchus shook his head.

'Where is Phiale?' Satyrus asked.

'She visits often, I believe,' Nearchus said. 'Young master, I cannot imagine that you fancy her services in your current state.'

'On ... contrary, doctor. Song ... Phiale ...' He took a breath and managed to speak clearly. 'Will do as much to restore my health as—' A cramp hit his stomach, and he rolled into a ball. When he could breathe, he continued, '... all your ministrations.' He gave a ghost of a smile. 'I ... do not mean it. You – how can I bless you enough?'

Nearchus rolled his shoulders. 'I am a family retainer. I do my duty. I must allow that I have always enjoyed serving Master Leon.'

The next two days saw Satyrus recover and retch by turns, his muscles refusing their duty in the middle of the simplest actions. He spent the daylight hours lying in the pale winter sun on his balcony. Sometimes he imagined that he could see the incorporeal image of his god standing over him, and other times he shook his head at the curious effects of his illness on his mind. Nearchus had found him a boy-slave, Helios, a native of Amphipolis enslaved when his parents took him on a sea voyage, and the boy waited on him with a solicitousness seldom found in a slave.

Satyrus sat in the sun, a scroll of Herodotus in his hands. He couldn't get through the words, even the words that dealt with the stand of the Hellenes at Plataea, the climax of Herodotus's great work.

'How long have you been a slave?' Satyrus asked.

The boy considered. 'Four years,' he said. 'I was taken in the spring of the year that Cassander killed the queen.'

Satyrus smiled, because even in his current state, he knew that the boy meant Olympias, the witch-queen of Macedon. An enemy. One enemy fewer.

'Were you – ill-used?' he asked. 'By the pirates?'

'Not by the pirates,' Helios said in a matter-of-fact voice. 'But they killed my parents.'

Satyrus nodded. 'Do you know the name of the pirate who took you?' Satyrus asked.

'Oh, yes,' the boy said. 'We were taken by Demostrate. His crew killed my parents because they fought. He apologized to me.' The boy gave a steady smile.

Nearchus and Sappho were sending him a message. His brain took this in through the fog of pain and wretchedness – this boy was their vote of disapproval of his alliance with the pirate king.

'Would you care to come to sea with me, boy?' he asked.

Helios beamed like his namesake, the sun, and his Thracian-blond hair glowed in the sun. 'Oh, yes!' he said.

Satyrus lay back, exhausted by the exchange. 'If I take you to sea, and teach you to fight, will you serve me for four years?'

Helios shrugged. 'I'm a slave,' he said. But then he smiled. 'I'd love to go to sea,' he said.

Satyrus realized that he'd left the important part of the offer unsaid. He tried to formulate it in his mind, but it was slipping away. 'Never mind,' he said, and fell asleep.

The next time he was awake, Nearchus sat by his bed and fed him soup – wonderful goat stew, with spices and dumplings.

Then he threw it all up.

Helios cleaned him.

Then he threw up again.

Helios cleaned him again, patiently getting every fleck of his disgusting vomit out of his long hair, his eyelashes, his pubic hair.

Satyrus drank water and went to sleep.

Later he awoke and it was dark. He moved on his couch, and he heard an answering movement and felt the boy's body move against him. 'I'm sorry,' Helios said. 'You were shivering.'

Satyrus stretched – and was not hit by a muscle spasm. 'Helios,' he whispered, 'do you think we could try a little soup?'

Lamps were lit all over the house before ten minutes had elapsed on the water clock. Nearchus came in, wearing a Persian robe. He put a hand on Satyrus's forehead, and then on his stomach. 'By Hermes and all the gods,' he said.

Helios came in from the kitchen with a bowl of soup. He sat on the bed and spooned it into his master.

Satyrus ate sparingly, although he wanted to drink the bowl and call for another, and he lay back on the bed consumed with hunger.

Half an hour passed, and the food was still in his stomach.

Nearchus shrugged. 'I was off by a day,' he said. 'You'll recover quickly now.'

Helios brought a brazier and lit it to heat a copper pot with stew brought from the kitchen. Every half-hour he gave his master another twenty spoons of soup.

'Free you,' Satyrus said. 'If I – free you? And take you to sea? Four years? Need a servant,' he said.

Helios grinned. 'Of course,' he said. And more quietly, 'I knew what you meant,' he said. 'I just had to hear you say it.' He burst into tears. 'People make promises,' he said.

Satyrus found himself patting the boy's head. *I hated it when Philokles did this to me,* he thought.

Helios looked up. 'A man came – an Aegyptian man in the robes of a priest. He brought you a bundle.'

'Go and fetch it for me,' Satyrus said.

In moments it was unrolled, to reveal his father's sword – perhaps just a touch shorter, Satyrus thought, but it was superb, and the metal was now a bright blue, almost purple at the point, so that the blade glittered with icy malevolence.

'Run me an errand?' Satyrus said to Helios. 'Go to Sappho and get a mina of gold. Take Hama and two soldiers as an escort, and go to the Temple of Poseidon. Deliver the gold to Namastis, the priest. If he wants you to come, escort him wherever he leads you.'

Helios was staring at the sword. 'One day, I want a sword like that,' he said.

'One day, I'll get you one,' Satyrus allowed. 'Now run along.'

The next day, Nearchus sat on an iron stool in his room, grinding powders at his window. 'I use this room to make drugs when you are away,' he said. 'I hope you don't mind. You have the best light.'

Satyrus grinned. 'I'm not really in a position to resent anything you do, doctor.'

Nearchus nodded and kept grinding. 'So I assumed. Do you still want Phiale?'

Satyrus's grin fled. 'Yes,' he said grimly. 'Has anyone ever been convicted on the evidence of a dream, do you think?' he asked.

Nearchus shrugged. 'I would assume it happens,' he said. 'Dreams have power.'

Satyrus's eyes grew hard. 'I wish to investigate the course of a dream,' he said. 'Does Phiale still keep the same maidservant at her house?'

Nearchus looked up from his pestle and mortar. 'Yes,' he said.

'Same woman she had when I was – that is, when I was a client?' Satyrus asked.

Nearchus was back at his work. 'I wasn't in this household then,' he said. 'A small woman, dark hair, would be pretty if she did not look so hard?'

'Fair enough description of Alcaea,' Satyrus said. 'She's got a tattoo on her left wrist.'

Nearchus shrugged while working. 'I've never examined her wrists.'

Satyrus waved to Helios, who was sitting against the wall. 'Can you read and write, boy?' he asked.

Helios nodded. 'Well enough,' he said. 'Greek and a little of the temple script, as well.'

'Really?' Satyrus asked. 'How nice. You are full of surprises. I need you to run me an errand.'

Helios nodded. He stood.

'Go and find Alcaea. She works for the hetaira Phiale. See if you can get to know her a little. Then see if you can find out where she was, hmm, perhaps two nights ago.'

Nearchus raised an eyebrow. 'That's a tall order for a slave.'

Satyrus lay back. 'I've promised him his freedom,' he said. 'Let him earn it.'

He ate more soup, and Nearchus changed him – yet another humiliating small service the man performed for him. Satyrus thought that he himself would make a poor doctor. He hated touching people, hated the foulness of his own excrement, the bile from his stomach, the thousand details of illness. 'How do you stand it?' Satyrus asked, when he was clean.

'Hmm?' Nearchus asked. 'I'm sorry, what did you say?' He was looking out of the window.

Satyrus shook his head. 'Nothing,' he said.

In the morning, he awoke with the sun and tried to get off his bed. He walked a few steps and discovered that he lacked the strength, and he tottered back to bed without hurting anything. He ate an egg for breakfast, and then another.

'You're done,' Nearchus said at noon, when the egg hadn't come up. 'I want you to be very, very hesitant to take poppy again. Even for a bad wound. The next time will be worse. In fact, you'll always have a craving for the stuff. Understand?'

'Yes,' Satyrus said.

'Good,' Nearchus answered. 'Sappho has wanted to see you for days, but you don't like to appear weak – I know your kind. And she's busy with the baby.'

'Where's Helios?' Satyrus asked.

'Haven't seen him. You have only yourself to blame – you gave him a task like the labours of Herakles.' Nearchus shrugged.

Satyrus read Herodotus while the doctor ground bone for pigment and then burned some ivory on a brazier outside.

'Phew!' he said, coming back. 'Sorry for the smell.'

Satyrus made a face. 'I've made a few smells myself, the last week,' he said.

Nearchus nodded, fanning himself. 'Let's get you dressed,' he said with a glance at the water clock. He refilled it, restarting its two-hour mechanism, and then found Satyrus a plain white chiton and got him into it and back on his couch.

'I'm sorry I sent Helios away,' Satyrus said. 'I hadn't realized you'd be stuck with his work.'

Nearchus shook his head. 'I made that decision. We have rules in this house – since the attacks when young Kineas was born. Slaves are taken on only after we check their histories. We do most work ourselves and we don't encourage visitors. There's a rumour in town that you are here – but we still haven't confirmed it. It may be you, or it may be Leon who brought the *Lotus* in to port. See?'

Satyrus nodded. 'I do see.'

'And Hama has contacts in the – how shall I say it? – the underworld. Among the criminals of the night market. We hear things. There are men in this town who offer money for your death.'

Satyrus smiled. 'Stratokles is dead, and his plots continue to roll along.'

Nearchus scratched his nose. 'Sophokles the Athenian is more to the point.'

Satyrus nodded. 'I know,' he said.

Even as he nodded, Sappho swept into the room with Kallista at her heels, cradling a baby.

Satyrus smiled at both of them. Sappho bent and kissed him, and so did Kallista.

'I never figured you for a nanny,' Satyrus said to Kallista. She was also an active hetaira, formerly his sister's slave and now a freedwoman and her own mistress.

'Hmm,' Kallista said, archly. 'I'm sure you are an expert on women, young master. I'm a mother now, thank you.'

'What do you think of young Helios?' Sappho asked. A maid-servant placed a stool behind her and she settled into it.

Satyrus reached up and took his nephew, and cradled him to his chest. The boy was just old enough to sit up under his own power, and he blinked around at the world. 'He's excellent. I've promised him his freedom already.'

Sappho arched her eyebrows. 'Really? I thought perhaps you needed a servant.'

'I do. I'll get four years out of him – but apparently he's been promised freedom before. I thought I'd give him the bone first.' He smiled at Sappho, who nodded slowly – a nod of agreeable disagreement.

'And you know that he was taken by pirates,' she said. 'His parents killed, sold to a brothel, used like a whore for two years until an Aegyptian priest – a customer, of course – bought him to use as a scribe – and a bed-warmer.' Her voice grew harder and lower as she spoke. Like Uncle Leon, Sappho had been sold as a slave and used brutally before she was freed. It was the fate that every free Hellene dreaded – and the inevitable cost of a world that ran on slavery. But Leon and Sappho acted on their hatred. Both bought parcels of slaves, especially those who had been born free, and found them situations that would free them.

'By my ally, Demostrate,' Satyrus said.

'Your "ally" is a very titan of Tartarus,' she spat.

Satyrus shrugged. 'Auntie,' he said, 'I have learned in the last year that if I intend to be king, sometimes I will have to do things that are, in and of themselves, despicable.'

Sappho remained stone-faced, but behind her, Kallista nodded.

Satyrus held out his finger and young Kineas latched on to it, pulled it, tried to swallow it. 'I can't win you over,' he said. 'So I have to ask you to trust me. I know what I'm doing.'

'Your mother made a pact with Alexander,' Sappho said. 'I never forgave her. I never could. It is one of the reasons we settled in Alexandria. And now you – you who are virtually my child – will sell yourself the same way.'

'My mother dealt with anyone who would deal with her, for peace. For security. Even Alexander.' Satyrus had no idea that there was bad blood between his mother and Sappho, but he kissed his nephew and then shook his head. 'I'm sorry. Really sorry. I feel dirty whenever I spend time with him. But he was my father's admiral. My father used him, and I'll do the same.'

'He wasn't covered in the blood of his victims then,' Sappho said.

Satyrus lay back. 'Hello, little man,' he said. 'Don't be in a hurry to grow up.'

Kineas made some gurgling sounds and stretched out his arms

for Kallista. Kallista came and took him with the air of a woman who distrusts that any man can entertain a baby.

'Does he have a wet-nurse?' Satyrus asked.

'Me,' Kallista answered.

'You?' Satyrus asked.

She laughed, a low laugh, the seductive laugh that brought customers to her at five and ten minae a night, and sometimes twenty times as much. 'I think you know how babies are made,' she said.

Satyrus decided it would be indelicate to ask who the father might be. But the question must have shown on his face, for Kallista laughed aloud, not an iota of seduction to it.

'Not a client,' she said. 'A friend.' She put the child to her breast. 'They can grow up together,' she said.

Later that afternoon, Helios came in with a clean blanket and wrapped Satyrus up.

'Any luck on your mission?' Satyrus asked.

'I found her.' Helios nodded. 'I'm meeting her again tonight. She goes out at night – often. She's very trusted in that house – almost the steward. She's the sort of slave that scares other slaves. Hard to tell which side she's on, if you take my meaning.'

'I do,' Satyrus said. 'Need money?'

Helios nodded. 'I'd like a few darics,' he said. 'I'd like to appear a trusted slave myself.'

'You are no longer a trusted slave,' Satyrus said. He picked up a scroll that Nearchus had brought him. 'There you are,' he said. 'A free man. Not a citizen – although I'll see to that when the four years are up.'

Helios flung himself on the scroll. He unrolled it, and Satyrus saw him mouth the words of the scroll as he read. He read it twice.

'I still have to present myself to the chief priest,' he said.

'Better hurry.' Satyrus nodded. 'About an hour before ...' He laughed aloud, because he was speaking to an empty room. 'You need Nearchus as a witness!' he called after the boy.

Nearchus came in after half an hour, looking flustered. 'I've been kissed by that beautiful boy in public,' he said. 'Believe me, it's quite an experience.' Nearchus raised an eyebrow. 'You've made him very happy. But – won't he wander off? He's free.'

'I can tell you've never been a slave,' Satyrus said. 'I'll spend four years teaching him to be free. If he wanders off, he'll be a slave again in a week. And he knows it. Where will he work? At a brothel? As a free man?'

Nearchus nodded. 'I see.' He scratched his beard. 'He could go to the temples and sign as an apprentice. Perhaps as a doctor.'

'He'll be the handsomest oar master in Leon's fleet in four years,' Satyrus said. 'Or dead.' He gave Nearchus half a smile. 'I think he fancies revenge, and I don't mind handing him the means and the opportunity.'

Nearchus stopped grinding his powders. He turned his head. 'You would betray your ally?'

'Betray?' Satyrus asked. He laughed. 'Really, Nearchus, what a sheltered life you've lived.' Then he changed his tone. He picked up a barley roll – one of the cook's best – and ate it, staring at his scroll. 'Can you take a letter for me, Nearchus?'

'I'm a doctor, not a scribe. And Helios has a nice clear hand.' Nearchus's pestle continued to scrape.

'I'm already fond of the boy, but I can't trust him with a letter for Diodorus,' Satyrus said.

Nearchus nodded sharply. 'I understand,' he said. 'You're a lot of work, you know that?' he asked with a mock frown.

The letter took most of the afternoon. At some point, Sappho became involved, adding her own instructions and best wishes for her husband, and adding news that he might use, far away in Babylon with Seleucus – news that Satyrus wanted as well. Kallista sat with the two babies, a slave-nurse taking them in turn, and Satyrus was quick enough to realize that Sappho was passing him news as she wrote, without having to speak it aloud. They were writing in black ink on the boards of a wax tablet, where all the wax had been stripped away. She wrote in her firm, square hand:

Ptolemy is preparing for a naval campaign against Cyprus. Antigonus is in Syria, firming up his support with the coastal cities, while his son Demetrios rebuilds his power base in Palestine after last year's defeat. Cassander is trying to gain control of young Herakles, the last son of Alexander – whether to make him king of Macedonia or to murder him, no one can say. And Lysimachos works to build his own city, to rival Alexandria and Antioch. Every one of the Diadochoi seems to need to have his own city.

And Satyrus wrote:

I hope you have had my first letter by now. I will have need of the Exiles and our phalanx in the spring. If Seleucus can spare you, I will await you at Heraklea on the Euxine by the spring feast of Athena. Please send my regards to Crax and Sitalkes, and also to Amyntas and Draco, and tell them that Melitta has gone east to raise the Sakje.

She read what he wrote. 'You are that sure,' she said.

He nodded. 'No,' he said. 'My sister may already be dead. Or my naval alliance may fail. Or Dionysius of Heraklea may refuse to let me use his town to base my army – or we may just lose.' He shrugged. 'So many things can go wrong – the word "sure" never enters my mind.'

He took the ink and wrote carefully:

Please send me a reply as soon as you receive this. If you can spare the time, send a duplicate to Sappho and another care of Lady Amastris, Heraklea, and a third care of Eumenes, the archon of Olbia (if you can believe such a thing). A fourth via Panther, navarch of Rhodos, at the Temple of Poseidon, would give me the widest possible notice of your reply, as I will be a bird on the wing.

'Have you ever thought that if you succeed, my husband will lose his command? The Exiles will no longer be exiles.' Sappho laughed. 'I don't mean it. But – if Tanais is restored – what will we all do?'

Satyrus shook his head. 'No idea, Auntie,' he said. 'But I'd be delighted to find out.'

And later, much later that night, Helios came in. He smelled of a discreet perfume.

'Well?' Satyrus asked. 'Did you spend a pleasant evening?'

'Not particularly,' the boy said. His voice was set, his face carefully blank. 'She's as dumb as a post, for all her hard-arse ways. She offered me a hundred gold darics to kill you.' The boy dropped a purse on the sideboard, so heavy that the cedar creaked. 'I told her a sad tale of your misuse of me, and she told me I was soft.' Helios looked at the floor. 'But after I pleasured her, she sang another tune, and there's the proof. And yes – she's out most nights. She has a taste for boys, like most women of her type.' His own self-loathing was obvious, but so was his dislike of her. 'She thinks she owns me!' he spat.

Satyrus shivered. 'I – thought that you were too young. To – I'm sorry, Helios. I've put you in a position ...' Satyrus thought that killing the innocent was hardly the only price of kingship.

Helios blinked his long blond lashes and shrugged. 'I haven't been too young – never mind. It's nothing I haven't done before, and in worse causes.'

Satyrus kept his voice neutral. 'Where'd the money come from? She can't have a hundred gold darics on her own?'

'No,' Helios said. 'And I don't know myself. Is her mistress in the game? I don't know. She's coming tomorrow, by the way. To sing to you.'

Satyrus nodded. 'We leave in three days. You should get yourself a blade, a helmet and a light cuirass. Have you ever worn armour?'

Helios blinked. 'No,' he said.

'Go to Isaac Ben Zion and ask his steward to sell you armour. How old are you, really?' Satyrus asked.

'I think I'm fourteen,' the boy answered. 'I lost some time – in the brothel.' He looked at the floor.

Satyrus put a hand under his chin and raised his head. 'Didn't anyone tell you the rule of Leon's house?' he asked. 'No man need regret what he did before he came here – only what he does here. You are free. Free yourself.'

Helios gazed at him with uncomfortable admiration.

Satyrus looked away. 'If you are fourteen,' he said, 'get the

Aegyptian linen armour. You'll grow too fast to be worth bronze or scale.' He pointed at the gold darics. 'You can use those, if you like. But only after Phiale visits.'

'What will you do to her?' Helios asked.

'To her?' Satyrus said, and his voice was hard. He was surprised at the feeling in his heart – more like hate than he had expected. 'Nothing,' he said. 'I will do nothing to her.'

Phiale came in just behind her scent – a touch of mint and jasmine that clutched at his heart. She whirled her fine wool stole over her head and tossed it to her maidservant, who caught it in the air and stepped over to the wall.

Satyrus watched the maidservant exchange a glance with Helios, who was already standing against the wall. Then he allowed himself to kiss her on the cheek. Her breath on his face ought to have excited him – the subtlety with which she used her body was the height of her powers, and she felt his control immediately.

She stepped back and crossed her arms. 'You are angry with me?'

Hama came to the door with Carlus, the biggest man among the Exiles, a giant German with scars that mixed with the tattoos on his face. He entered the room, drew a short sword and stood with it balanced across his hands.

'Where is Sophokles, Phiale?' Satyrus asked.

Her hand went to her throat. 'I am a free woman. You may not restrain me.' Her eyes reproached him.

'Take the slave,' Satyrus said. 'Do not touch the mistress.'

Carlus closed his hand on Alcaea's hair. Her hand came up with a knife, and he slammed her against the wall. She dropped the knife.

'I accuse your slave of plotting against my life.' Satyrus waved at Helios. 'Freeman Helios will testify that your slave offered one hundred gold darics to kill me.'

Phiale shrunk back into a corner. 'Sappho!' she screamed. 'Satyrus has lost his wits!'

'Listen to me, Phiale. Stratokles and Sophokles bought you. But I cannot prove it, and besides – you are for sale. Who could blame you for being bought?' Satyrus struggled to keep the bitterness from his voice, and he thought how much amusement his sister would draw from the situation. She had never liked the hetaira, and had warned him repeatedly about engaging his feelings with her – she had mocked him, in fact.

'You are insane. The drug has addled your wits. Let me go.' She stood straight. 'I came to sing for you!' she said.

'If I ordered you stripped, what interesting vials would I find? A quill full of poison, perhaps?' Satyrus shook his head.

'I demand—' she began. Satyrus rose to his feet and she was silent.

'You mistake me for a much nicer boy you once knew. There will be no demands, Phiale. Today – this very hour – you will board a ship for Athens, after you reveal every iota of your plots. You will go there and you will never return to Alexandria. And you will write a letter for me, to your master.'

Phiale was white now. But she held his gaze. 'You are delusional.'

'Entirely possible,' Satyrus said. 'But not in this.'

Sappho came in, with Nearchus behind her. 'You have her!' she said.

Phiale's eye widened. 'We are friends!' she said.

'You have spied on my house for the last time,' Sappho returned.

'Hypocrite!' Phiale spat.

'Not, perhaps, your best defence.' Satyrus walked over to Alcaea.

'Why would I go to Athens?' Phiale asked.

'You lodge all of your earnings with Isaac Ben Zion, do you not?' Satyrus asked. 'I think that when I tell him you betrayed his business partner into captivity, he will perhaps seize your fortune.' Satyrus smiled. 'It was – short-sighted, shall I say? To leave your money where it could be used against you. By tomorrow, every obol will be locked in my aunt's coffers. If you ever want it again, you'll have to obey *us*. Go to Athens. Stay there. Hate us if you will – but hate us from a distance. And if we ever, ever catch you acting against our interests again – spying, muttering, gossiping – some men like Carlus will appear at your house, seize you and carry you off. And they will take you to Delos – and sell you into slavery. Am I clear? You are not young any more. I do not think you could earn your way free again.'

Phiale began to sob. She went straight from imperious to broken without passing through another emotion. 'It is not fair! You are not fair! You, who were my lover – who has defamed me like this? You would exile me on the word of a *slave*?'

Alcaea spoke up. 'What of me, lord?' she asked.

Satyrus nodded. 'Death, unless you tell me everything. And I already know a great deal. So much that I have little reason to offer you leniency unless you tell me things that I don't know. Let me offer you a beginning. You meet with Sophokles in the night market, behind the false wall of a certain tavern—'

Phiale's hand went back to her throat, and Alcaea threw herself on the ground. 'I am a slave, master! What else can I do but obey her?'

Sappho crouched on the floor next to the abject slave. 'Obey who, my dear?' she asked.

'My mistress!' Alcaea wailed.

'She will say anything to be saved,' Phiale said.

'I have her notes to the doctor,' Alcaea said, clasping Satyrus's knees in supplication. 'She wrote to him – every week, reporting on your household.'

Satyrus nodded. 'And who have you suborned in this household?' he asked.

Sappho started, and Satyrus put a hand on her shoulder. 'Who provides you with information from within this household?' Satyrus asked.

'I don't know,' Alcaea answered. Seeing Sappho's face, she wailed, 'I don't know! There's a wax tablet left under the rain barrel at our house every week. It's almost always there.'

Satyrus nodded. 'That, I did not know. It is possible you will live. Hama? Would you care to question her?'

Hama nodded. 'At your service, lord.'

Satyrus turned to Phiale. 'Will you go to Athens, despoina? Or shall I take another action?'

She shrugged. 'I will not go.'

'Really?' Satyrus asked. 'I am not sure that my *eudaimonia* would survive killing you. But please don't mistake me, despoina. I will kill you if I must. I *will* be king in the Euxine. I will not be stopped by a provincial hetaira and a hired killer. Where do I find Sophokles?'

She shook her head. 'I don't know,' she said. 'I deny your charges. You have no evidence. I will go to Athens and hate you from there.'

'Choose,' Satyrus said. 'Tell me everything, and live. Where do I find him? If you tell the truth, you are off to a new life in Athens.'

'I *deny* your charge. I don't know *anyone* named Sophokles. Stratokles hired me as a courtesan and you, apparently, have a mad resentment about it. How could I know? I am a hetaira!' Phiale stood tall.

'I have her notes to him,' Alcaea spat.

'You lie!' Phiale said. 'How could you?'

'You ordered me to burn them,' Alcaea said. 'I kept them against such a day as this.'

'Bah – she could write them herself,' Phiale said. 'She does all my writing for me anyway.'

Satyrus shook his head. 'I don't think you are taking me seriously,' he said.

Phiale crossed her arms over her chest. 'I will not be tricked into condemning myself.'

Hama spoke regretfully. 'I can have her speaking about anything in an hour,' he said.

Nearchus stepped forward. 'I will not be party to torture,' he said.

Satyrus looked around at all of them. 'Once, when I did *not* kill Stratokles, you all advised me to strike first in the future. Aunt Sappho, this woman is a viper who will hurt us any way she can. Even now, an assassin – her ally – stalks us. He tried to kill Lita, and you took a dagger in the chest to save her. This woman provided the information that prompted that attack, and the information that led to Leon's capture – and she has perhaps done as much against Lord Ptolemy and Diodorus. *This is not the time to be soft.*'

Nearchus looked at Phiale. Her eyes implored him. 'I am innocent,' she said to him. 'Satyrus is mad.'

Nearchus turned back to Satyrus. He shook his head and turned to Phiale. 'I will not see you tortured,' he said. 'But you, not Satyrus, are mad.'

'I know where you can find Sophokles the physician,' Alcaea said from her position of supplication on the floor.

'As do I,' Satyrus said. He did *not* want to kill Phiale. But he didn't see much choice. It was the situation on the beach again – more deaths to haunt him. But Satyrus had begun to understand people. If he didn't break her, the hetaira would come back for him.

And then he thought, *What would Philokles do?* And he saw it. Philokles would never kill her. Philokles would simply draw her fangs and leave her. The moral act.

'Bring her,' he said.

They missed Sophokles by the thickness of a door. The Athenian physician vanished into the tunnels behind the tavern even as Satyrus's men broke down the false wall. Hama had his sword at the innkeeper's throat and they flooded the streets with soldiers, but they still missed him. Carlus dragged Phiale wherever they went, on every search, so that every denizen of the night market saw the hetaira's presence with the Exiles.

Later, over hot wine, Satyrus shook his head. 'I was precipitate,' he said. 'I allowed my need to get back to sea to drive my actions. I should have let her develop her plot and taken her in commission. And the same with the doctor. I see that now.'

Hama, sitting by the hearth with his Thracian boots up on the hearth's lip, grinned. 'But every thief, pimp and whore in the market thinks she gave us the doctor, eh?' he said to Neiron, who laughed grimly. His oarsmen had swept the streets with Hama's soldiers.

Satyrus nodded. 'That part went well,' he said.

Sappho came in with cheese and olives, which she set by the men. 'What of the maidservant?' she asked.

'I leave Alcaea to you, Aunt. Kill her, torture her, sell her – her utility to us is done.' Satyrus shrugged.

Sappho looked at him. 'She is a person, Satyrus. She has an existence beyond her *utility*.'

Satyrus shook his head. 'Perhaps,' he allowed.

'If you propose to become Eumeles, I see no reason to support you,' Sappho said.

'Aunt! I have acted only to save this family! To protect you!' Satyrus was stung – the more so as his aunt said things that he wondered about himself. The Stoics said that no insult hurt you unless you already believed it.

Sappho came and stood before him. 'You are working on making yourself a monster,' she said. 'You were preparing to kill Phiale in cold blood, like a tyrant. I saw it in your eyes. Had you done so – despite her evil actions, despite everything – many of us would not have forgiven you. Theron is far away, and Philokles is dead, and my husband is off fighting. It is left to me to discipline you – and I am not any softer than you, *nephew*. You are working on making yourself a monster. Wake up!' she said.

Satyrus tried to swallow his wine, and it stuck in his throat. Hama looked elsewhere. Nearchus nodded at every word, and Neiron looked like a man who wanted to hide under his seat.

'Hama?' Satyrus asked. 'Do you think I did wrong?'

The Gallic officer looked at his boots. He shrugged. 'In war, men do hard things,' he said. 'Such things are – uglier – in peace.'

Satyrus stood up, suddenly angry. 'We are at war!' he said.

Sappho shook her head. 'No, we are not. *You* choose to make war on Eumeles. My husband and Leon support you because of their love for your parents – and for you. And such a war will take lives, nephew. People *will* die. If you are no better than Eumeles – a selfish, grasping man, but a competent administrator – if you are another of the same, who sees his own interest as the height of all law, who kills women to make sure that his path to power is secure – then all those people die for *nothing*.' She slumped. 'She is despicable. But her bad actions would never excuse yours. I saw your eyes – you were *that close* to killing her.'

'She might have killed us all!' Satyrus yelled.

'Eumeles could *say the same of your mother*!' Sappho shouted back. 'He killed her because he feared her!' She came and took his hands. 'Do you honestly fear *Phiale*?'

Satyrus stood with his hands on the back of his chair, clenched as if his ship was in a storm and he was clutching the rail to keep from being swept overboard. His eyes flicked from man to man to woman around the hearth, and his rage soared – and then sank away, like flames on damp wood. He loosed his grip on the chair. 'What would you have me do?' he asked.

Nearchus shrugged. 'Send her to Athens,' he said. 'And wash your hands of her.'

Sappho shook her head. 'Leave her here,' she said, 'and I will watch her. With Alcaea.' Sappho raised a manicured eyebrow. 'I will purchase Alcaea's interest, and put her back with her former mistress as our spy.'

'And Phiale will kill her, or avoid her,' Satyrus said.

'I doubt it,' Sappho said. 'And I think that you should let me try.'

Satyrus looked at Hama. 'Well?' he asked.

Hama shook his head. 'Lord, don't involve me in this. I obey. I would kill her for you, if you asked. And yet – I agree with the lady, too. About what a chief can become. I have seen a good chief become a bad chief, but I have never seen a bad lord become a good one.' He shrugged. 'For me, I wish we had caught the doctor.'

Satyrus flicked his eyes to his helmsman. 'And you, Neiron?'

Neiron shook his head. 'Land has problems that don't exist at sea. I prefer the sea. But I'll say this. When we go to sea – no enemy here will be a danger to us unless they have a faster ship and a better crew. We'll be gone with the tide. By the time this woman has power and money again,' the old seaman shrugged, 'we'll feed the fishes – or you'll be king.'

Satyrus nodded. 'Good advice.' He looked at his aunt. 'From all of you,' he said. And sighed. 'I do not want to be a monster.'

'Good,' Sappho said.

Satyrus took a deep breath. 'But – word of our sailing must not leave the city when we go. Hama, Sappho – can you keep Phiale from sending a letter? A tablet? A scroll? One slave, slipping out on a merchanter? And Sophokles—'

Neiron put a hand on his navarch's shoulder. 'They can't. But they can try – and they can, by the gods, make it harder.'

Satyrus shook his head. 'We need time. If Eumeles is warned ...' He shook his head. 'Life is risk.' He managed a smile. 'I'm twenty, and I'm losing my nerve. Very well, Auntie. You have her.'

'Thank you.' She touched his cheek. 'Hama and I will do our best.'

In the morning, Satyrus presented himself to Gabines, Ptolemy's steward, for his appointment. He expected to wait – in Aegypt, no one was ever granted his first request to meet the lord of the land.

To his own surprise, he found himself ushered immediately to the lord of Aegypt's presence. Ptolemy sat under the magnificent fresco of the gods and heroes, on a carved ivory stool, as if he was just the archon of the city and not its uncrowned king.

'Satyrus!' he said, rising from his stool to clasp Satyrus's hands. 'We feared the worst. And we still miss your uncle.'

Satyrus bowed his head. 'My lord, I am working to remedy my uncle's absence. And I am preparing a spring campaign to topple his captor.'

Ptolemy settled and Gabines motioned at the slaves for wine. 'See to it that your planning is better than the last time!' Ptolemy said.

Satyrus flushed. 'We had a spy in our midst,' he said.

Gabines, the lord of Aegypt's spymaster, leaned forward. 'Do tell, young man.'

Satyrus took his wine, tasted it appreciatively and nodded.

'A stool for the prince of the Euxine,' Gabines ordered.

Satyrus had to smile.

'And we hear that you won yourself several victories,' Ptolemy said. 'After your initial defeat. Eumeles is reported to be beside himself.'

Gabines raised a hand. 'My lord, I would like to hear of this spy,' he said.

Satyrus nodded and sat on the stool that was brought for him. 'You know Phiale, the hetaira?' he asked.

'Not as well as I would like,' answered the lord of Aegypt. He laughed loudly, showing all his teeth.

Satyrus frowned. 'She spied for Eumeles, with Sophokles, the Athenian physician.'

Gabines nodded. 'Sophokles is gone,' he said. 'I had him at a certain location, but now he has fled. My informant puts him on a ship to Sicily.'

Satyrus's head snapped around. 'You knew he was in the night market?' Satyrus asked.

'Yes!' Gabines said. 'And if your uncle had been here, he'd have had enough sense to ask me before he acted.'

Ptolemy nodded. 'You are not king, here, lad. You were pre-cipitate.'

It is not easy to keep your temper when you are young, and everyone older than you seems to be in a conspiracy to put you in the wrong. Satyrus flushed, and he felt the heat on his cheeks. He covered the onset of anger by sipping more wine.

Gabines shook his head. 'Next time, you'll know better, lad. Can you *prove* the involvement of Phiale?'

Satyrus nodded. 'I think so, although Philokles would say that it depends on what you require as a standard of proof. Her slave attempted to suborn mine. We have this slave, and she has writ-ings of her mistress – writings which Phiale says are forged.'

'Circumstances are against the woman,' Gabines said, scratch-ing his beard. He glanced at his master. 'I don't recommend that you get to know her any better, my lord.' He looked at Satyrus. 'What do you propose to do to her, young man?'

Satyrus sat back and smiled. 'Nothing.'

The lord of Aegypt and his steward exchanged smiles. 'Really?' Gabines asked.

Satyrus nodded. 'My aunt his given her word that Phiale will cause me no more ... discontent.' He savoured his wine. 'Can you tell me of Eumeles?'

Gabines was silent for a long moment. Satyrus noticed that he could hear the slave behind him, breathing. It was that quiet.

'Eumeles is incensed that you destroyed his squadron at Tomis. And he has had word of you from Byzantium, and from Rhodos. And from here.' Gabines raised his eyes. 'But he is far more afraid of your sister. We hear that he is hiring mercenaries already.'

'Where is my sister?' Satyrus asked.

'We don't know,' Ptolemy put in. 'Somewhere in the back-country. There's a song in Pantecapaeum, or so my agent there tells me – a song about her killing seven men in single combat.' Ptolemy shook his head. 'I remember her as such a nice quiet girl.'

Satyrus couldn't help but grin. 'That's Lita.' He nodded to Gabines. 'By spring she'll have an army. When the ground is hard, she'll have a go at Marthax – the king of the Assagatje. By high summer, if all goes well, she'll be ready to face Eumeles.'

'If Eumeles doesn't make an alliance with this Marthax,' Gabines said. He shrugged.

'And you, lad?' Ptolemy asked.

'I have asked Diodorus to meet me at Heraklea on the Euxine,' Satyrus said. 'I intend to raise a fleet and go over to the attack when the weather changes.'

'Just like that? Raise a fleet?' Ptolemy asked.

'I have an agreement with Demostrate, the pirate king.' Satyrus sipped his excellent wine. 'And with Rhodos.'

'Pirates and Rhodos don't mix, lad!' Ptolemy said.

'And I'm hoping to add Lysimachos.' Satyrus leaned forward. 'He has few ships, but I need his good will – and I can clear Eumeles off his part of the seaboard. And move the pirates off his lines of communication. He needs me.'

Gabines nodded. 'We need him as well. Without his little satrapy, Antigonus One-Eye can move freely between Asia and Europe – and Cassander is doomed.'

'Yet Cassander supports Eumeles,' Satyrus said.

Ptolemy shrugged. 'We're allies, not brothers. Eumeles is no friend of Aegypt's – as you well know.'

'You have the lord's blessing to take the Euxine – if you can,' Gabines said. His eyes flicked to the slaves. 'But our hand cannot be seen in it. We cannot spare you any ships.'

'Really?' Satyrus asked. 'I thought that you might lend me—'

Gabines shook his head. 'Lord Ptolemy needs every oar in the water for his expedition to Cyprus,' he said.

Satyrus looked at Ptolemy, not his steward. 'Is this true, lord? I had counted on ten or fifteen triremes from here.'

Ptolemy leaned forward. 'You failed,' he said bluntly. 'You had a go at Eumeles, and failed. He captured two of my ships and the repercussions were annoying. I can't afford to go through that again – with Cassander.'

Satyrus nodded. 'I need ships,' he said. Then he shrugged. 'Very well,' he said. 'But I have your permission to proceed?'

Ptolemy shook his head. 'I give no permission,' he said. He shrugged as broadly as an actor. 'I can't control you!'

Satyrus couldn't help but laugh. 'My lord, it seems to me that if I succeed, you'll claim to have been my benefactor, and if I fail, you'll disown me and show how you offered me no aid.'

Gabines nodded. 'Precisely, young man. What we will do,' Gabines said, 'is to cover your back. We were,' he cleared his throat, 'embarrassed by the attacks on your sister. Nothing like that will happen again.'

Ptolemy nodded.

Gabines leaned forward like a conspirator. 'But I will keep a man on this Sophokles. And I will ensure that no agent of Eumeles can communicate from here – for ten days after you sail.'

Satyrus nodded. 'That is worth some ships,' he said. 'May I ask how you can do that?'

Gabines shrugged. 'We are ready to send our first scouts to look at the coast of Cyprus – and a diversion up the coast of Syria. We will stop all shipping for ten days.'

Satyrus whistled and shook his head. 'The blessings of my patron, Herakles, attend you in every endeavour,' he said.

Ptolemy grinned. 'My patron as well, lad.'

Satyrus nodded. 'I still need the ships. I believe that my uncle Leon would say that promises are easy.'

'When you are a king, you'll quickly get the hang of this posturing,' Ptolemy said. He rose and clasped hands with Satyrus like an equal. Then he leaned forward and whispered into Satyrus's ear. 'May Tyche bless you,' he whispered. 'I have two ships – good ships, quadriremes with heavy hulls – going at auction later today. And a pair of triremes that my architects have condemned as too small for modern war.' He stepped back and winked. 'They will all four be sold at salvage rates.' He held Satyrus's hand in his. 'It's the best I can do.'

Satyrus grinned. 'Bless you, lord,' he said.

Ships sold for their wood are rarely auctioned off with all their rigging and oars – nor do their crews ordinarily stand by the auction, waiting to be hired by the new owners – yet these things happened. Satyrus and Isaac Ben Zion were the only buyers at the auction.

'Don't bid against me on the big quadrireme with the engine in the bow,' Ben Zion said. 'It's for Abraham.'

Satyrus stripped Leon's establishment of officers without hesitation, taking the cream of his merchant captains, helmsmen and oar masters for the new ships. He was delighted to find a captured trireme, the *Wasp*, lying on the beach.

'How'd he come here?' Satyrus asked, and sailors scrambled to tell him how Sarpax had taken him with a pentekonter at the mouth of the Euxine. Satyrus tracked Sarpax to a brothel and recruited him to command the *Wasp* for the summer, against Eumeles.

'Can you shoot as well as your sister?' Sarpax asked. He laughed, and the pearl in his ear glowed. 'Will it bring Master Leon back?'

'Yes,' Satyrus said, and they clasped hands, and the thing was done.

Satyrus also took the *Hyacinth*, sister ship to the *Golden Lotus*, another triemiolia out of Rhodos, the flag of Leon's Massalia squadron, bringing his squadron to seven.

He had dinner with his officers – all men he knew from Sappho's table. '*Oinoe*? *Plataea*?' Sappho asked from her couch. 'Those are the names of nymphs.'

'No – battles at which Athens did well.' Satyrus raised a cup of wine. 'Here's to the Painted Stoa, friends. And to Philokles' friend Zeno. He gave me the idea for the names. *Oinoe* and *Plataea* are the fours. *Marathon* and *Troy* are the threes.'

Sandokes, the new navarch of the *Oinoe*, was an Ionian from Samothrace. He had beautifully curled black hair, a pair of gold chariots hung from his ears, and his body showed the muscles of a man who took special care at the gymnasium – despite which, he was one of Leon's favourite captains, a man who had made the run to Massalia four times and had once taken a merchanter outside the Pillars of Herakles. He knew Sarpax of old, and the two shared a couch.

Aekes, who also had the reputation of being Sandokes' friend, was of an opposite temperament. He had salt-washed hair and wore a simple leather chiton made of two deer skins sewn together, like a farmer. He was clean enough, and his arms and legs showed the muscle of a working seaman, but no earrings graced his ears, nor did he appear to have any special clothes to wear to a symposium. What he did have was a long Celtic sword in a bronze scabbard that rested against his couch, and a reputation as a successful pirate-hunter. He commanded the *Hyacinth*. He was said to have been born a Spartan helot, but no one ever questioned him about it. Satyrus knew that he had been close to Philokles, and had donated a hefty sum for the Spartan's statue in the library – as yet uncast.

Dionysius – one of dozens of men in Alexandria to bear that name, or perhaps hundreds – was one of Satyrus's childhood friends. He lay near Sandokes, whom he idolized. He was taking the *Marathon*. Satyrus had hesitated to take him again – Dionysius had almost lost his ship at the battle off Olbia, and he'd spread the rumour of Satyrus's death. But Dionysius had paid the cost of the ship and the rowers from his father's fortune, in hard cash – and the truth was that Satyrus's fleet was beginning to cost so much that he could see the bottom of Uncle Leon's coffers.

Anaxilaus was a scientific captain, a friend of many of the philosophers at the library, a man of education who nonetheless followed the sea. He had red hair, which alone enabled him to stand out among guests, and his excellent manners betrayed his Sicilian origins. His father and grandfather had both been tyrants in Italy, and Anaxilaus often joked that he'd gone to sea because it was safer than staying at home. He had *Troy*. His younger and much handsomer brother Gelon would have the *Plataea* until he got him to Byzantium for Abraham. He'd been promised a trireme there. He lay opposite Apollodorus, who fancied himself a gentleman and insisted on naming his pedigree to the Sicilians – in detail.

They were social men – sailors are social by nature – and if the conversation was loud and nautical, it was also well-bred. Sappho was still smiling at Anaxilaus's gallantry as she escorted the last of the guests to the door. 'Sicilians have the very best manners,' she said, as her steward closed the garden door.

'I think Philokles would have argued that Spartans have the very best manners,' Satyrus said. They walked back to the main room together and lay on adjacent couches.

'Are you still angry with me?' she asked.

'No,' Satyrus said. 'No. You were right, of course. I miss Philokles. He used to say that it is sometimes easy to mistake the hard thing for the easy thing.' Satyrus could feel the wine in his brain. His aunt was really quite beautiful – not the first time he'd noticed. He banished the thought as unworthy. 'It is easy to kill, and difficult to find another way – but it is difficult to make myself kill, and that clouds the issue.' Satyrus took a long drink of wine. 'I think I killed two men in the Euxine to show myself that I could.'

Sappho rolled on to her stomach – not the posture of a well-bred woman of Thebes, but of a hetaira. 'Dear nephew, we all do things we regret – often merely to prove things to ourselves. May I say that I think you are lucky in your captains?'

Satyrus smiled and tried to dispel the heaviness in his brain – and his heart. 'I agree. Fine men – and a good party, too.'

Sappho smiled into her cup. 'As the veteran of a few parties, my dear, I can tell you that good men are what make a good party – not the quality of the lobsters or the antics of the flute girls.'

Satyrus smiled at her. 'Philokles might have said the same.'

Sappho nodded. Her laugh was self-mocking, and Satyrus didn't know what to make of it, so he tried to change the subject. 'You are satisfied that you can restrain Phiale?' he asked.

She nodded. 'Gabines sent me a note,' she said. 'We will watch Phiale. And Sophokles has gone to Sicily. He won't return unless you do. *I* am not a worthy target.'

Satyrus snorted. 'That just shows what a fool he is. You command me and my sister. You direct the finances of the Exiles and as far as I can discern, it was you, not Coenus, who dispatched my sister to take the leadership of the Sakje.'

Sappho raised her wine. 'Flatterer!' she said.

'Men are strange,' Satyrus said. 'Greek men pretend that women are inferior, when it seems to me that you, who are the daughter and former wife of boeotarchs, wife now of a strategos, are the match for any man in a contest of wits.'

'I have had a triumph or two,' Sappho said. She drank again. 'All flattery gratefully accepted. I've passed the age when men will be stopped in the street by my looks.'

He got up unsteadily, having had too much wine for a man so close to his recovery. 'You are wrong, Aunt! Men still praise your beauty.' He walked towards her unsteadily. She had seldom been so beautiful.

Sappho rose from her couch and straightened her chiton. 'You are the image of your father, Satyrus. Right down to his clumsy, but welcome, flattery. Your feelings for Phiale have left you vulnerable. Be wary.' She embraced him, and he felt her warmth, the press of her breasts against his chest – and then she stepped away.

He flushed, because as usual, his aunt was dead on the mark. 'Will I ever grow up?' he asked.

Sappho laughed, her eyes sparkling, until he laughed, too. 'A good party brings out the lechery in all of us,' she said. 'Go and conquer the Euxine,' she added. 'And get your sister to come back for her son, before I decide to keep him.'

'You said you wanted no more children,' Satyrus said. 'I remember you saying it to us.'

She shook her head and turned away. 'I have seen men who have a will of iron where women are concerned – until one takes them by the hand, and at the first touch, they become clay in her hand.' She shrugged. 'Women can be that way about children.'

'But—' he began.

'Shush, nephew,' she said. 'Go and conquer the Euxine. I'll see to the child.'

In the morning, his squadron came off the beach all together. Leon's officers – Satyrus's officers now – were all professionals, better officers, man for man, than Ptolemy's navy had available to them. Satyrus lounged against the rail of the *Lotus* and listened to their orders, watched the rowers and the deck crews race to get the ships down the beach and into the water. The two light triremes were easy, but the heavy quadriremes with their bow catapults and their heavy crews were slower to launch, and Diomedes, the new helmsman of the *Plataea*, could be heard from a stade away.

But their hulls were newly cleaned. The *Lotus* had been scraped and dried while Satyrus lay in his bed shouting at visions in his head, and the rowers pulled him north along the coast of Palestine at a fair clip.

Satyrus watched the coast go by, his eyes always flicking to the empty horizons to the west, where Cyprus lurked out of sight. But winter – high winter – was not the time to risk a heavy blow on the open sea south of Cyprus.

They beached at Ake, the northernmost outpost of Ptolemy's power, and rested a day and a night before racing north with a rare favourable breeze. They passed Tyre in the full light of day, and saw the inner harbour crammed with military shipping, but all their masts were down and most of the hulls were stacked out of the water. And three hours later, they blew past Sidon, their sails still full of their good north wind. The helmsmen and the trierarchs all offered libations to Poseidon, and they stood on. If a pursuit was launched, they never saw it.

'I thought Ptolemy had a squadron moving up this coast as a feint,' Neiron said. 'We should have seen it.'

'I have a growing suspicion that *we* are Ptolemy's feint,' Satyrus answered. He looked at the land in the ruddy light of a winter evening. 'We might not get weather this good again for ten days. It is too good to stop for the night.' He looked at Neiron. 'I'm of a mind to try to get north of Laodikea before we look for a beach.'

Neiron nodded. 'Ask me to solve your land quarrels and I'm all at sea,' Neiron said. He nodded and scratched under his beard. 'Here, I'm happy to give advice. We'll have this wind until at least the rising of the morning star. The sky is clear and the men are still fresh – no one's touched an oar all day.' He frowned. 'Besides – you want them ready for anything by the time we enter the Euxine. Some small risks now will give us better crews.'

They passed Laodikea in the dark, its position marked only by the dull glow of a town at night – and even then, most of the light came from the Temple of Poseidon's eternal fire on the height behind the town.

The morning star was rising when they passed the headland

at Gigarta and Neiron indicated the darkness of the open ocean. 'There's a set of islands north and west of Tripolis,' he said. 'If I line up the Kalamus headland with the North Star, we should be on a beach in an hour.'

The wind was dropping, and the sails flapped every few minutes as the wind backed and spat.

Satyrus nodded. 'Weather change?' he asked.

'Like enough,' Neiron answered.

'Do it,' Satyrus ordered, and an hour later he was eating hot stew on a beach just big enough for seven warships and their crews. And he noticed a certain regard among the helmsmen and trierarchs. Night sailing was not for the weak of heart.

In the morning, they rowed away north, with the wind blowing from off the land. The triemiolia could sail on a broad reach, but the triremes and quadriremes couldn't, and their rowers got plenty of practice.

Noon saw them north of the old pirate haven at Arados, and they ate their evening meal on the beach at Gabala on the coast of Syria.

In fact, they spent three days on the beach at Gabala, lashed by winds and heavy rain that made launching the light triremes impossible, and Satyrus was forced to use his manpower to pull the ships clear of the water, high up on the beaches. And he had a thousand rowers to feed, so that his men were roaming the countryside for food before the winter storm ended, every scrap of provision consumed.

On the fourth day, he got them under way with empty bellies and some empty benches where men didn't return. The *Plataea* made heavy going of the launch, and laboured in the waves, because his upper-tier rowers had eaten something bad and dysentery was rife.

They'd been at sea less than an hour before Satyrus saw the squadron astern. He pointed, and Neiron swore. 'Poseidon's stade-long member,' he said. 'Where'd they come from?'

Satyrus shook his head. 'Tyre? Sidon? I always knew there was a risk, coming up this coast. We're sailing right through Demetrios's fleet.' He shook his head. 'Ptolemy has a lot to answer for.'

Noon, and they passed the headland at Posideion, and every man threw a handful of barley into the sea if he had any grain. The squadron behind them was just a series of nicks on the horizon, and even those sightings were occasional. No one had a mast raised on a day like this, with the wind blowing more north than anything else, and all the rowers cursed their lot at every stroke of the oars.

In early afternoon, the wind shifted back to the east, blowing off the land, and the pursuing squadron began to gain ground, their fresher rowers and more recent food beginning to tell.

Satyrus watched as they drew closer. He stood in the stern and watched the pennants of the mast as they fluttered back and forth, showing every wind-change. 'Neiron?' he called.

'Sir?' Neiron woke up fully alert. He had the oar master at the helm and he himself was asleep on the helmsman's bench.

'I intend to turn west, put the wind at our sterns and sail for Cyprus,' he said. 'What do you think?'

Neiron licked his fingers and raised them, and then looked at the clouds. 'Risky,' he said.

Satyrus pointed astern, and Neiron's eyes followed until he saw the pursuit. 'They may not be after us,' he said, stroking his beard.

Satyrus nodded. 'They are persistent, though. There's another blow coming up, and these gentlemen are still at sea.'

'And they *do* look like warships.' Neiron looked under his hand. 'Six hours to the first sighting of the Temple of Aphrodite Kleides.' He shook his head. 'If the wind changes, we're in the open sea at night with a storm rising behind us.'

Satyrus nodded.

Neiron shook his head. 'Do it,' he said.

Satyrus took the helm himself. Neiron went forward and ordered the deck crew and the sailors to raise the mainsail, and as soon as it was laid to the mast, Satyrus gave the orders and the *Lotus*, still under oars, turned from north to west in his own length. Satyrus was pleased to see that the next ship in line, the *Oinoe*, was prepared, and although he took longer to get his mast up, he made the turn in good order. Behind him, *Plataea* redeemed himself from an earlier poor performance and made the run with alacrity, and the two light triremes turned like acrobats and raised their masts even as they turned.

Hyacinth was late in his turn, and lost ground as he rowed slowly north, his helmsman apparently asleep at his oars.

But however slow the *Hyacinth* was, the pursuers were slower. They continued north so long that Satyrus began to wonder if he was fleeing from shadows. Only when they had cut Satyrus off completely from the coast did they turn their bows out to sea – but they didn't raise their sails.

'I count ten,' Neiron said. 'Heavy bastards. Everyone's building bigger and bigger – is that a *hepteres*? A seven?'

The largest pursuer towered over the others, with three decks of oars and a wide, heavy hull that nonetheless seemed to sail with speed.

'That's Demetrios, or his admiral,' Satyrus said. He shook his head. 'He must think we're the long-awaited raid out of Aegypt.'

'So he's kept us off his coast,' Neiron said. 'And now he leaves us to Poseidon's mercy.'

'I wish you hadn't said that,' Satyrus said.

They drove on, into rising seas, with the wind howling behind them.

But they had good ships and good officers, and before the last pink rays of the winter sun set behind the mountains of Cyprus, the *Lotus* had his stern on the black sand west of Ourannia, with a promontory between them and the east wind's might. Cypriot peasants came down to the beach with baskets of dried fish and fresh crabs, and Satyrus paid cash for a feast even as the wind rose and the rain began to fall.

For three days they crawled along the coast of Cyprus, with their bow pushing straight into a fresh westerly that followed the storm, and they continued along the coast all the way to the beach at Likkia – a beach Satyrus had used before. He provisioned his ships there, paying on credit with his uncle's name, which was good for anything here. He waited for two days for an east wind, and when it rose, he made sacrifice on the beach and launched his ships.

'Straight west for Rhodos,' he said.

Neiron shook his head. 'Why risk it?' he asked.

'I can feel the time slipping away from me,' Satyrus said. 'Any day, word of our departure will get out of Alexandria.'

'Anyone going north has to go the way we've gone,' Neiron said.

'And I've done it before,' he said.

Neiron nodded. 'So I've heard,' he answered. 'Isn't once enough?' Most ships stayed on the coast, sailing from the point of Cyprus north to the coast of Asia Minor and then crawling west from haven to haven.

'If this wind holds for twelve hours, we'll raise Rhodos before the stars show in the sky,' Satyrus said.

'If the wind drops, we'll be adrift on the great green and praying for Poseidon's mercy.' Neiron shrugged. 'But you are the navarch. I just hope that when Tyche deserts you, I'm already dead.'

Satyrus smiled, but his hands remained clenched and his stomach did back-flips until he made his landfall that evening. The crew cheered when the lookout sighted the promontory at Panos, and again when they glided down the mirror-flat water of the city's inner harbour, past the Temple of Poseidon. Satyrus didn't hide the libation he offered to the waters of the harbour.

'All that to save a day?' Neiron asked.

Satyrus finished pouring the wine into the sea and stood up. 'My gut tells me that every day matters,' he said.

'Do you think they'll accept your offer?' Neiron asked.

Satyrus pointed at the beach under the temple, where a full dozen Rhodian triemioliai lay on the beach. 'Can you think of any other reason they'd prepare a squadron in midwinter?' he asked.

Neiron smiled. 'The gods love you,' he said. He nodded grimly. 'Use it while it lasts.'

PART III

THE EAGLES FLY

16

PANTECAPAEUM, LATE WINTER, 310 BC

'And how is our august prisoner?' Eumeles was in rare good humour. He sat on his iron stool and looked out over the battlements of his citadel at the Euxine sparkling in the late winter sun. Or was it the early spring? The weather was mild, and the sun shone.

Idomenes had a list of important issues, and Leon, the prisoner, was not one of them. 'He's alive. Do you really need to know more?'

Eumeles shrugged. 'I wonder how young Melitta will feel if I send her a hand or an eye?'

Idomenes shut his eyes for a moment and then opened them slowly. 'I wouldn't recommend it, lord. She has our farmers in her hands already.'

'If that fool Marthax had come to me ...' Eumeles shook his head. 'But she has no fleet, and the only infantry she'll get are those mutinous dogs from Olbia. Our army will eat her – and while we're at it, we'll make Olbia loyal. Once and for all.' Eumeles smiled. 'That's a campaign I really look forward to. No more two steps forward and three steps back. When Olbia is crushed, I will actually be king.'

Idomenes nodded. 'Yes, lord,' he said automatically. 'In the meantime, the Athenians want their grain quotas filled or they threaten to withdraw our loans.'

'Where, exactly, do they expect this grain to come from?' Eumeles shook his head. 'How can they expect to fill their ships twice a year, where they used to fill them once?'

'You sold them the second cargo last autumn, lord.' Idomenes shouldn't have said that – he'd allowed his actual views to colour his voice, and his master whirled on him, his pale eyes murderous.

'I'm sorry,' Eumeles said, his voice just above a whisper, 'I must be mistaken. I think I just heard you offering to *criticize my policies.*'

Idomenes opened his tablets and ran his stylus down the list of action items. 'Lord, the fact is that the Athenians demand more grain immediately. And if they are not satisfied, your mercenaries will not be shipped – and we will have nothing to pay the men we have. On the same subject, Nikephoros requests audience. He intends, I assume, to demand payment. His men are three months in arrears.'

Nikephoros was Eumeles' exceptionally competent strategos. He was both loyal and intelligent, a remarkable combination.

Eumeles nodded. 'Let's see him, then.'

'You understand that we have no money?' Idomenes asked.

Eumeles looked at him and laughed. 'You have a hard life, Idomenes. Criticize the tyrant and live in fear. Fail to advise him and if he falls, you fall.' Eumeles shook his head. 'Listen – I was riding this tiger when you were a pup. My father was tyrant here. Have a little faith. Things have turned for the better this winter. I can feel the end of the worst part. These money matters are never that difficult to solve. And once the barbarians on the sea of grass are in their place – then we will see power. Real power. I don't think Lysimachos and Antigonus and all the busy Diadochoi actually understand how rich we are up here.' Eumeles smiled. 'I intend to be very strong indeed before I let them discover that I can buy and sell the lords of the Inner Sea.' He looked at Idomenes' tablets and sighed. 'I just have to get through the usual sordid details to reach the good part.'

Idomenes went to fetch Nikephoros. He preferred his master in the darker and more pragmatic moods. His ebullient moods were the most dangerous for his clarity.

'How is he today?' Nikephoros asked. He had a magnificent bronze and silver breastplate under his Tyrian crimson cloak.

'At his best,' Idomenes said.

Nikephoros raised an eyebrow. 'You always say that. It is not always true.' He shrugged. 'I speak no treason. We need him at his best. I do not like the reports from the *georgoi*. We could lose the countryside to this witch.'

'Farmers are notorious for their superstitions,' Idomenes said.

Nikephoros stopped just short of the citadel doors. 'Listen, steward. I pay you the courtesy of discussing matters of state with you like an equal, because I think that you are a man with your master's best interests at heart. Do not mutter platitudes to me.'

'I must take your sword, Strategos,' the guard said. His voice was apologetic.

Nikephoros didn't take his eyes off the steward as he handed his plain, straight sword to the guard.

'The georgoi have reason to fear,' Idomenes admitted.

'Exactly.' Nikephoros nodded. 'Let's go.'

He inclined his head to the tyrant, and no more. Eumeles returned this with a civil bow. 'You've come for money?' Eumeles began.

'The lads are three months in arrears. You know that, so I won't belabour it. If the new phalanx arrives and *they've* been paid, there'll be a mutiny.' Nikephoros crossed his arms. 'Not why I came, though.'

'Your men haven't yet been called on to fight.' Eumeles seemed to think that this was an important point. 'They're fed and warm. I'll pay them when I need them.'

Nikephoros rolled his eyes. 'Lord, save it for the assembly. My men expect to be paid. You tasked me to find you soldiers – real soldiers, not Ionian crap. I hired them away from Heraklea and even from Lysimachos, and now they want cash.'

Eumeles looked down his nose at his strategos. 'Very well. I need them to find the means of their own pay. An elegant solution. Send the phalanx into the countryside and collect the grain – all of it. Anything these georgoi have in their barns. Send a taxeis to the Tanais back-country first – we'll not pick on our own farmers until there's nothing left on the Tanais.'

'You want me to take their *seed*?' Nikephoros asked.

Eumeles nodded. 'Yes. Every grain of it.'

'But—' Idomenes began.

'Do I look like a fool?' Eumeles shouted, and rose to his feet. He was taller than most men, rail thin, and the hair was gone from the top of his head. He looked more like a bureaucrat than a terrifying tyrant, until he rose to his full height. 'Take their *profits*,' he said. 'Take their means of supporting this petty princess, this Melitta. And take their means of farming, and they'll *starve*.'

Idomenes shook his head. He caught Nikephoros's eye, and

they agreed, silently. 'Master – lord, if we strip the farmers on the Tanais, we cast them into her arms.'

Eumeles nodded. 'I see how you might think that. But frankly – and let us not delude ourselves – these peasants are lost to us already. They are all traitors – why not take their goods?'

'As soon as I withdraw the men from gathering this tax, the whole region will go up in flames,' Nikephoros said.

Eumeles shook his head. 'No. You are wrong. As soon as you gather this tax, they will become refugees, homeless men wandering, scrubbing for food. After I beat the barbarians, I will come back and give my soldiers grants of land – big ones, complete with an abject and starving population of serfs. I will have a loyal and stable population of soldiers, the soldiers will, overnight, become prosperous landowners and the fractious peasants will be reduced to slavery – as is best for them. And the only weapon I need use against them is hunger.'

Nikephoros scratched his chin. 'It becomes a matter of timing then, lord.'

Eumeles laughed. 'Yes – and the timing is all mine. Listen – this girl cannot rally the tribes in a matter of days. Before her "army" is formed, we will flood her with useless mouths – Sindi and Maeotae peasants, starving, desperate men. And their useless families. As soon as the money is in, we pay our men, our new troops arrive and we're away after her. We crush her as soon as the ground is dry, and we're done. The peasants have nowhere to turn – and we've changed the basis of landownership. The way it should have been from the first.'

Idomenes nodded. 'It is – well thought out.' He nodded again. 'I acknowledge your – breadth of vision, lord.'

Nikephoros gave half a smile. 'I have to admit that it will go over well with the lads. Gentlemen farmers? What Macedonian boy doesn't fancy that? But I have two issues, lord. First, the kind of campaign you envision against the georgoi – that's the death of discipline. Bad for 'em. Second, these ain't Spartan helots. They have arms – bows, armour, big axes.'

Eumeles nodded. 'Are those military problems?' he asked.

Nikephoros nodded. 'I suppose they are, at that.'

Eumeles sat down again and drank some wine. 'Get me a

military solution then. But I need that grain on the docks in a month. And no excuses.'

'What of the brother?' Nikephoros asked. 'Satyrus?'

Eumeles raised an eyebrow at Idomenes. He flipped through his tablets. 'Five weeks ago he was in Alexandria.' Idomenes couldn't help but smile. 'Being treated for dependence on the poppy.' He snapped his tablets closed. 'No more reports.'

'It is winter,' Eumeles said. 'He may have the balls to try again in the spring. He may become a lotus-eater. It matters not. Either way, I'll have crushed the girl in six weeks, and there's nothing he can do to stop me.' Eumeles raised his cup. 'Here's to an end of this petty crap. Here's to the kingdom of the Bosporus.'

Idomenes poured wine for Nikephoros and for himself. They all drank, and only Nikephoros seemed to worry that no libation had been poured.

17

'He's seen us,' Neiron said. He was looking into the late winter sun, and the sparkle on the wave-tops was enough to fool most eyes. 'Coming about.'

Satyrus got a hand on the standing shroud and pulled himself up until he was standing on the rail. The speed of their passage – crisp west wind heeling them over – raised his chiton and he slapped it down.

Far off, almost to the horizon, the other ship's masts were narrowing, coming together.

'Yes,' Satyrus said.

A week on Rhodos and ten days to Byzantium – a meal, a hug from Abraham and from Theron, an exchange of orders and off again, leaving Sandokes and Panther of Rhodos to bring the fleet along after the interval he had commanded. He had hoped to slip by the picket at the Bosporus – indeed, he'd counted on it.

Abraham and Theron had been successful – and that meant that he needed an anchorage in the Euxine – an anchorage to windward of Pantecapaeum. Lysimachos had contributed a mere three triremes and a hundred marines – but his alliance meant a great deal more than that. Theron had done well.

And Demostrate, the pirate king, was still in hand – thanks to Abraham, the old man clasped hands with a wary Panther, as if he had always been a friend of Rhodos. Satyrus had left them watching each other warily.

Manes had glowered, his eyes doing everything but glow red. But his ships had followed as well.

Satyrus had passed the Bosporus as fast as his rowers could manage and the gods favoured him with a perfect wind, so that the moment the *Lotus*'s bow had passed the rocks at the exit to the channel, he had spread both his sails and turned east, the wind astern. Everything had been perfect for a fast passage – except the warship to windward.

'He'll never catch us,' Neiron said after the sand-glass was turned.

Satyrus shook his head. 'He doesn't have to catch us.' He stamped his foot in pure annoyance. 'Never, ever underestimate your opponent. I didn't think Eumeles had the captains to keep the sea all winter. Listen, Neiron – we're in the *Golden Lotus*. Every sailor in the Euxine knows this ship.'

Neiron nodded. 'In other words ...' Neiron said, his eyes now rising to the sky and the weather.

'In other words, we have to take *him*,' Satyrus said.

An hour later, they had their pursuer dead astern, a heavy trireme or perhaps a decked penteres with extra rowers – hard to tell. Whichever warship he might be, he had a heavy crew and a deep draught for a galley, and carried his sail well.

Golden Lotus might have had no trouble outrunning the heavier ship, if that had been his aim. Instead, Neiron had the mainsail badly brailed and the boatsail set nearly fore and aft, drawing as little wind as he could without attracting attention – and the big leather sea anchor was being dragged in the wake, which made Satyrus's job at the helm far more difficult. The *Lotus* was labouring like a plough horse, and Satyrus's arms were taking the whole weight of the struggle. He was out of shape – he was feeling the effects of weeks in bed. Wrestling sailors and eating like a bull were helping, but he'd lost muscle and he knew it.

Astern, their pursuer had his lower oar deck manned, and they were pulling like heroes racing for a prize – which, in fact, they were. The lower deck pushed the ship just a little faster and kept her stiff and upright.

'That's a right sailor,' Neiron said approvingly. 'Knows his business.'

'Too well,' Satyrus said. He pointed to where a scarlet chiton could be seen standing on the enemy ship's bow. 'He's looking at our wake. Stesagoras!' Satyrus called to his new Alexandrian deck master. 'Look alive, Stesagoras! Get ready to cut the sea anchor free. At my command, Philaeus! Prepare to go about – oars in the water.' Philaeus was his new oar master, one of Leon's professionals.

Philaeus could be heard relaying the commands and adding his own – reversing the port-side benches.

Lotus had all his benches manned, despite the fact that his sides were closed. For now.

The pursuer was manning his upper benches. 'He wants to surprise us when he turns away,' Satyrus said.

'He knows his business,' Neiron said again.

'Show them our oars,' Satyrus called.

Philaeus had a beautiful voice – deep and melodious, like a priest. 'Open the ports! In the leather! Ready, and steady, and oars!'

All together, like a peacock's tail, the *Golden Lotus* showed her oars – all three decks at once.

'Turn to port!' Satyrus ordered.

The port oars on all three banks were already reversed. From the first stroke, he leaned on the steering oars.

Stesagoras severed the sea anchor himself with one shrewd blow of a fighting axe. The whole hull rang and the *Lotus* went from plough horse to racehorse in a single bound. Then the deck master ran down the central fighting deck. 'Sails!' he called. 'Brail up tight and drop the yards. Look lively, lads!'

The wind on the sails pushed against the rowers for precious seconds, but then the yards came down – the advantage of a triemiolia was that his masts could stand even during a fight, allowing him to carry sail longer and drop it faster. The dropped yards covered the half-deck and not the oarsmen, who rowed on.

The sailors and the deckhands laboured to get the mass of flapping linen canvas under control – but the ram was already halfway around.

'Poseidon!' Neiron shouted.

'Herakles,' Satyrus said. He picked up a wineskin that the helmsman kept under the bench and flung it over the side full, without even pulling the plug. 'We need all the help we can get,' he said, but he laughed and felt the power on him.

Stesagoras waded into the mainsail, his long arms gathering material as he went, and suddenly there were ten men visible on the canvas, and then – just like that – the mainsail was half the size, a quarter, and then the heavy bundle was being lashed to the mast. The boatsail was already gone.

Their pursuer was just starting his turn, his oars out and rowing crisply, his port-side benches reversed – but the range was short and the larger ship was having his own troubles.

Satyrus's archers shot a volley of arrows and received a volley in return. There were screams from forward.

'Oar-rake and board,' Satyrus said. 'Neiron, take the helm.'

Neiron's hands shot out and took the steering oars. 'I have the helm,' he shouted over the screams from the bow.

'You have the helm,' Satyrus said again and relinquished control. Helios had his breastplate in its bag out from under the bench and he pulled it on, somewhat surprised to see that despite the weather, the breastplate gleamed like gold and the helmet was as silver as the moon. His arming cap was damp and cold, but the breastplate was colder.

An arrow glanced off his backplate and stung his arm, scarring Helios along the thigh before vanishing over the side. He looked up from the buckles to the fight.

'They're shooting downwind,' Neiron said. Another arrow passed so close that Helios ducked.

'Archer captain's down!' Stesagoras passed from amidships.

'Any time, Navarch!' Neiron said.

'Take him,' Satyrus said. 'I'm away.' He turned to Helios, who was fully armed. 'With me, lad,' he said. He ran forward even as he heard Philaeus call for the ramming speed. The enemy galley, having passed from hunter to prey, was turning away towards the south coast of the Euxine, obviously intending to save himself by beaching.

An arrow passed so close to Satyrus's helmet that its passing sounded like the ripping of fine linen. The ship leaped forward between his feet – he could feel the change in motion – but the enemy ship was turning, faster. And faster. Satyrus ran forward as Philaeus bellowed for the starboard-side rowers to back water – a chancy manoeuvre, but one that was faster than actually reversing benches. The deck shifted under his feet.

Satyrus got forward and found his new archer captain dead with a Sakje shaft just over his nose and another under his arm.

The archers were all down with their heads safe under the bulk-heads. 'They murdered us!' one called.

Satyrus counted three dead – of eight archers. As he counted, a blow rocked his helmet and he saw stars and fell flat on the deck – but his helmet turned the arrow. Helios gave him a hand and he got to his feet. Then an arrow hit the boy and stuck in his quilted corslet. Helios gave a whimper and then clamped down on it and crouched beneath the bulkhead, trying to get the arrow out of his side.

'Son of a bitch!' Satyrus said. He picked up a fallen bow, raised his head and shot. He had no idea where his arrow went and immediately reached for another arrow.

He looked, shot – this time at a robed Sakje warrior just two horse-lengths away – and his breastplate turned *another* arrow and he sat down suddenly.

'They're too damned good!' he joked to Apollodorus.

The marine captain didn't answer. He was sitting against the bulkhead, leaning forward, and Satyrus realized suddenly that he was unconscious – or dead.

'Marines!' he called, and suddenly the ship turned again, and he was thrown into the gutter at the edge of the deck. He scraped his face on Apollodorus's scale armour and came to rest against Helios, whose eyes were as big as copper coins. Philaeus was roaring for all rowers to back oars, and Satyrus forced himself to his feet and looked aft. Neiron was leaning hard on the steering oars, and forward the stern of the big penteres was passing down their side, just a ship's length away and getting farther – and then the enemy ship seemed to pitch both of its masts over the side as if he'd been bitten by a sea monster.

'What in the name of Hades?' Satyrus rolled to his feet and ran to the command platform. The arrows had stopped coming.

Stesagoras had an arrow through his bicep. 'Poseidon's mercy, your honour. She was a monster and no mistake.' One of his mates broke the arrow and the Alexandrian forced the shaft out of the entry wound and fell in a faint.

Satyrus looked over the side – and understood. The enemy ship was already breaking up, having run full tilt on to a rock in the shallow bay that their captain had taken for a beach. There was no beach – just a row of breakers and a cliff ten times the height of a man.

'There he goes,' Neiron said. 'Poseidon, and all the sea nymphs.' He waved. 'The Thinyas rocks. Almost ran on 'em myself.' He made the peasant sign to avert ill-fortune.

Satyrus looked at the sky and then astern. 'Can we save their people?' he asked.

Neiron grinned. 'Now you're talking.' Then he sobered. 'Mind you, they galled us hard.'

Satyrus shrugged. 'Once they're wet, a rower is a rower,' he said, quoting an old proverb about the brotherhood of the sea. There were some men – Phoenicians, for the most part – who believed in letting drowning seamen die, to propitiate the sea. But Greeks tended to rescue men if it could be done.

'Shall I put about, then?' Neiron asked.

'Marines!' Satyrus yelled. He nodded. 'On me!'

They rescued half a hundred men. Helios, in addition to his other talents, could swim, and he fearlessly leaped into the freezing sea and dragged men out – first a ship's boy and then a small, wiry man.

After Satyrus watched him pull the second man to the side, Neiron got his attention and pointed at the shore. Satyrus saw twenty more men make it to shore and vanish over the cliff at the water's edge.

'Shall we hunt them down?' one of his marines asked.

Satyrus shook his head. 'I wonder how long they'll take to get home?' he mused.

They spent the night on an open beach, a hundred stades short of Heraklea. The night gave Satyrus time to daydream about his lady love, whom he hadn't seen in almost a year. Amastris of Heraklea was beautiful – as well as being intelligent, rich and the only niece of the Euxine's second most powerful man, Dionysius of Heraklea.

Satyrus sat alone on a lion skin – a present from Gabines when they sailed, straight from old Ptolemy, or so he said. He had a big black mug of soup and he was wrapped in his two warmest cloaks, and still the wind cut at him.

Neiron clambered up the rocks to him. 'I'm too old to go looking for a sprite like you,' he said.

'That was a first-rate ship,' Satyrus said. He took a swig of scalding soup. Down on the beach, the survivors of the *Winged Dolphin* – for so he proved to be named – huddled around a fire. 'If all of Eumeles' ships are that good, we're in for a fight.'

'Captain was from Samos. He got away. The rest was good sailors. All pirates.' Neiron shrugged. 'You need to eat. And, if I may say so, you need to walk around the men.'

Satyrus nodded. He got to his feet and drank more soup. 'Tomorrow I roll the dice. I'm scared.'

Neiron said nothing.

'Stesagoras and Philaeus are good men,' Satyrus said. 'So are you, Neiron.' He held out his hand.

Neiron seemed surprised. But he clasped hands. 'Why – thank you, Navarch.'

'Call me Satyrus,' he said.

Neiron smiled. 'Well – never thought I'd see the day.' He laughed. More soberly, he said, 'We'll need more marines, a new marine officer and a peck of archers. Those Sakje raped us.'

'They hurt us off Olbia, too.' Satyrus shook his head and finished his soup. 'My people,' he said bitterly. 'Apollodorus deserves a proper burial.'

'Aye.' Neiron looked away. He and the marine had never exactly been friends. 'At Heraklea?'

'Have to be.' Satyrus nodded. 'Thanks. I feel better.'

'Talking often has that effect, sir – Satyrus,' the helmsman said.

The harbourmaster at Heraklea stepped aboard and his eyes widened. 'Satyrus of Tanais?' he asked.

Satyrus remembered him. It had only been four years – he remembered the man from the heady days of intrigue and assassination at the court of Heraklea. The months just after his mother had been murdered.

'Bias?' he said, and offered his hand.

'Lord!' Bias responded. In Heraklea, they had had tyrants and aristocrats for so long that Greek men might bend the knee like barbarians, to a man of better blood.

'Is Nestor still the tyrant's right hand?' Satyrus asked.

'Isn't he my son-in-law?' Bias asked, and laughed. 'Pretty bold, just sailing in here, lord. The tyrant is no friend of yours these days. There's a rumour in the agora that you – um-hmm – have spent too much time with his niece. And the tyrant of Pantecapaeum wants you dead. We have peace with them.'

Satyrus nodded. 'I need to see Nestor,' he said. 'And then I will make it right. And Bias – I love Amastris. I would never trifle with her.' He felt a little odd as the lie rolled out of his mouth. But it had been her – or so he told himself. And there had never been any *trifling* about it.

Bias didn't even bother to look at the bill of lading. 'If you want to see Nestor,' he said, 'come ashore in my boat.'

Satyrus considered the possibility that he would be taken, alone, and killed to satisfy the obligations of statecraft. Then he shrugged. 'Neiron, take command,' he said. 'If I don't return by nightfall, take the ship out of the harbour. You know what to do then.'

Neiron nodded.

As they rowed ashore, Bias leaned forward. 'What is your helmsman to do if you don't return, lord?' he asked.

Satyrus watched the rowers. He flashed the older man a smile. 'Fetch my fleet,' he said. 'And burn the town to ash.'

Bias sat down on his thwart.

'Just so that we understand each other, Bias. I love Amastris – not Heraklea.' Satyrus shrugged. 'I mean no ill. But – if I am taken, there will be a consequence.'

'Where is your fleet?' Bias asked. He tried to sound offhand.

Satyrus waved a hand vaguely. 'Close enough,' he said.

They landed by the customs wharf and Satyrus was left alone. There was some discussion in whispers around him, and he began to regret the boldness of his arrival. He wished he was surrounded by marines.

After an hour, a strange man, obviously a slave and terrified, came and ushered him into a very comfortable house, largely empty of furnishings, near the wharves. Satyrus was sufficiently scared that it took him some minutes to realize that it was Kinon's house. Kinon had been Leon's factor in Heraklea, and had died in a night of blood and terror, when Eumeles' paid assassins came for the twins. Satyrus had to fight the temptation to look for bloodstains on the flagstones.

He waited an hour, by the old water clock in the garden. The rose bushes were dead. Satyrus got wine from the terrified slave and loosed the sword in his scabbard, increasingly convinced that he'd made a mistake. Better to have come with the fleet at his tail and no negotiations.

But he'd promised himself – and his aunt – to try other ways. And Amastris – how could he use force against her city?

More time passed. The old slave brought him more wine – excellent wine, for all that the house was drab.

'Is this still Master Leon's house?' Satyrus asked.

'Yes, lord,' the old man said.

Satyrus considered that this might have been courtesy, not entrapment.

Satyrus had time to consider quite a number of things. The sun set and the stars rose, cold and clear, with a promise of colder weather – but good sailing.

'Would my lord like dinner?' the old slave asked.

'What do you have?' Satyrus asked.

'I brought lobster,' said a soft voice from the direction of the garden. 'I remember that you liked it, in Alexandria.'

Satyrus sat up and straightened his chiton at the neck. 'I didn't really dare hope that you would come,' he said.

She was always more beautiful than he remembered. He stood up, and she swept in under his arm and kissed him. Her mouth touched his neck, his chin – and then he bent to her lips and forgot all his busy plans.

'Stop!' she said, after the lamps had begun to gutter. The slave had not come back to fill the oil.

He had no idea how much time had passed, and his hand was on her naked hip, her Ionian chiton hiked up to her bare stomach. She smiled in the near-dark and her eyes sparkled. 'Stop!' she said again.

Satyrus stopped, although he pressed a kiss to the place where her shoulder met her neck. She turned and bit his thumb, rolled

264

off his lap and pulled her chiton sharply down over her knees. He feared her anger for a moment, but she was smiling.

'I am the tyrant's heir, here. And if I make love to you, I'd like it to be on a broad couch with a flask of good wine at my elbow, and not in this sarcophagus of a house.' She shook her head. 'I can feel their ghosts. Can't you? They died in pain – in fear.'

Satyrus took a deep breath and let it out slowly, clearing his head. 'I was here, Amastris. I remember it too well to fear the ghosts.'

She touched his lips with her fingers. 'Sometimes you scare me, Satyrus. Your life has been – death. What scars do you carry?'

'You have seen them all, I think,' he joked.

'That is not funny here. Much as I fancy you, my dear. Someone has talked. Nestor takes my side, and yours. He brought me. But he made me swear not to – well ... not to do anything to make him a liar.' She smiled at him, and then shook her head. 'I'm cold,' she said. 'I have a letter for you – from some perfume merchant in Babylon.' She smiled. 'The Persian who brought it is perhaps the handsomest man I've ever seen.'

Satyrus sat up. His heart stopped, and then started again – *thud, thud.* 'In Babylon?' he said.

'Yes,' she said, settling next to him again. 'Is that important? Did you buy me some fabulous present?'

Satyrus ran a hand up her arm – to her side and to her bare breast. 'Perhaps,' he said.

She pushed him away. 'I'm serious. But ...' She stood and retreated. 'Bias seems to think you have a fleet.'

He nodded. 'I do.'

She clapped her hands. 'So you intend to try again?'

Satyrus nodded.

'Then go and do it! My uncle will have to receive you when you are the tyrant of Olbia!' She pulled a dark cloak over her shoulders. 'Oh, I ache for you. Get a move on!' She grinned, and she seemed like the girl he remembered from his first visit here. 'Just like a man, to stop to see a girl on his way to being a king.'

'I'm afraid that I came for more than a kiss,' Satyrus said. His mind was clear. 'Is Nestor outside?'

'What does Nestor have to do with it?' she asked. Her tone was not all Satyrus would have wished, but she'd always been difficult when she found that she wasn't the centre of attention.

'I need an audience with your uncle,' Satyrus said.

'You? He's as likely to take you as a criminal as to talk to you.' She drew herself to her full height. 'Talk to me instead.'

Satyrus shook his head. The room was dark, and the gesture was probably lost. 'Oh, my darling. I mean no – no disrespect. But I need an anchorage for my fleet. Your uncle has the best anchorage on this coast. The winds blow from here to Pantecapaeum.'

'You did not come for me?' she asked. She stepped back again.

Satyrus spoke slowly. 'No. Nor did you come down here to let me take you away.'

He saw her adopt the mantle of the outraged woman. 'I might have,' she said.

Satyrus took a step.

She turned away.

'Nestor!' Satyrus called.

She whirled. 'What are you about?' she asked. 'Nestor wants no part of you!'

'I need a friend here,' Satyrus said. 'I think Nestor is that friend.'

'A moment ago I lay in your arms. But *I am not that friend*?' she spat at him.

Satyrus always regretted the clarity of his vision, because too often he saw things he was not supposed to see. 'You do not want to be my friend with your uncle,' Satyrus said. 'I hear it in your voice.'

'You lie!' she said.

Satyrus tried to catch her hand – failed – succeeded. 'Listen!' he said. 'I love you.'

'You do not,' she cried.

'I do. But in this – you want me to be the secret lover, and I must play the public ally. This is the game of the world, love. I need your uncle's harbour. Without it, I will not succeed.' Satyrus drew a breath, but she cut in, even as he heard the ring of hobnails on flagstones.

'You need my harbour more than you need me?' she asked, and Nestor came into the dark with a torch in his hand.

As big as Philokles had been, Nestor emerged from the dark just the way Satyrus had seen him the first time – covered in bronze from head to toe, with ornate greaves, foot-guards forged like naked feet, a magnificent muscled cuirass and arm-guards to match.

'I see that Eutropios is still working,' Satyrus said.

Nestor clasped his hand. 'I knew you'd come back, boy. I'm glad to find both of you dressed.' He grinned. 'I hadn't expected you to call for me, boy!'

Satyrus grinned. He took the torch and used it to light lamps. 'You must be the last man on earth to call me "boy",' he said. 'I need to see Lord Dionysius.'

'Offers of marriage are not going to be acceptable just now,' Nestor said. 'He believes that you might have taken – liberties. At court.' Nestor shrugged. 'And you are known here as "that adventurer".'

Satyrus nodded. 'I need the anchorage. For ten days. And the town's field of Ares. Again, for ten days.'

'Zeus Soter, boy!' Nestor shook his head. 'What?'

'I need Dionysius's alliance,' he said. 'Or at the very least, his acceptance.'

'He's mad,' Amastris said. 'And I thought he came for me!'

Nestor shook his head. 'You are mad.'

'Let me see Dionysius,' Satyrus said. He could see the knuckle bones spinning in the air.

'You accept the consequences if he decides to dispense with you?' Nestor asked.

'I will if he does,' Satyrus answered.

Dionysius might not have moved in four years. He lay on his great bed, his massive body stretching each leather band of the mattress so that his every move was accompanied by tortured stretching noises.

This time, no one asked Satyrus for his sword – a remarkable oversight. This time, he was not offered a chair or a couch. Instead, he stood in front of the tyrant.

'What on earth are you doing here, boy?' he asked. 'I don't recall inviting you back.'

Satyrus pasted on the smile of gentle confidence that he'd practised for the last five years. 'I came back to thank you for the lessons in politics,' he said.

Dionysius laughed. 'I do remember offering you some instruction, at that.' His chuckles creaked and wheezed the bed on which he lay, so that he seemed to be a comic chorus. Then he stopped. 'There's a rumour from Alexandria that you debauched my niece,' he said.

'No,' Satyrus said. Philokles had taught him that a direct negation was a more effective denial than any amount of excuse. 'No. But I do wish to marry her.'

Dionysius nodded. 'No. Anything else?' He raised his head. 'I do hear that you've become quite the warlord,' he said. 'You took Eumeles' squadron on the other coast – by yourself, or so we are told. Amastris actually clapped her hands when she heard. Of course, she didn't clap so hard when we heard that you massacred the prisoners. Yourself.'

Satyrus shrugged, as if the massacre of prisoners was of no moment. 'If I may not have her hand in marriage,' Satyrus asked, 'perhaps you would consider a treaty of alliance – offensive and defensive.'

'Really?' Dionysius said. 'Gods below, boy – you don't lack balls. But – no. Eumeles is no friend of mine, but your next failed expedition won't come from here.'

'I'd ask you to reconsider,' Satyrus said. 'Because, if you won't, the consequences will be – severe.'

Dionysius sat up. 'Are you threatening me, boy?' he asked.

'Yes,' Satyrus said. 'Yes, I am.' The smile remained fixed in place.

Behind him, Amastris choked a sob. 'What are you doing?' she asked.

'My uncle, Diodorus, is twenty days' march away. He'll be coming over the mountains from Phrygia. Just the opposite of the way I fled – five years back.' Satyrus held the grin on his lips by force of will. 'He has a thousand horse and four thousand foot – more than enough to maintain a siege here.'

Nestor raised his arm, but Satyrus pushed on. 'In five days, the whole fleet of Demostrate will come up the coast from

Byzantium,' he said, while Nestor rose to his feet. 'You can give me an alliance and allow me to use your harbour, or take the consequence.'

'I can put you to death this hour!' Dionysius roared.

'And take the consequences,' Satyrus said. Nestor's hand was on the collar of his cloak, and Nestor was pinning his sword expertly against his side, but Satyrus didn't struggle. There was no point. The dice were spinning, bouncing – the moments before they stopped – is that a six? A one?

'This town has never fallen to assault,' Dionysius said, but there was hesitation in his voice.

Satyrus kept his eyes on the tyrant. 'And it need never. If you support me now – just with your harbour, and you can pretend that I forced your hand – I will be your loyal ally for ever. Refuse me – and you may as well kill me.'

'Your naked threat is an ugly weapon,' Dionysius said.

'Sometimes the ugly is the beautiful,' Satyrus said.

Dionysius laughed. He laughed so hard that his bed-frame shook. Nestor let go of Satyrus's cloak and stepped away.

The fat man laughed, and laughed, and then he drank some wine. 'I lay here, on this very couch, and listened to you announce that you would make yourself king,' he said. 'And Eumeles is a threat to me and to every city on the south coast. Do you actually have Demostrate?'

'I do, my lord.' Satyrus nodded.

Dionysius nodded, his chins still quivering. 'You have wit, lad. But I'm not sure I believe that you have an army.'

Satyrus had nothing to lose. 'Amastris? You said you had a letter for me?'

Amastris stepped past Nestor. 'You will help him?' she asked her uncle. She sat on his couch and ruffled his hair – an oddly ugly gesture. Then she sent a slave for the letter. Time passed slowly. Satyrus had time to review all the other options he had had. And then the local helot came running back down the hall, her bare feet a whisper on the stone floors. She bowed to the tyrant, who waved his hand.

And she handed Dionysius the tablets.

The tyrant opened them – a two-fold tablet, with wax inserts on each side, four pages in all. The wax was inscribed, and he cast his eyes over it. '"Amion, merchant of Babylon, sends word to Satyrus, merchant of Alexandria, that he will send the Lady Amastris the required perfumes, and further stipulates against future payment ..."' Dionysius looked up. 'I fear you will insist that this is a code.'

Satyrus shook his head. 'No,' he said. 'If you will permit me?' He reached out, and Nestor took the tablets from his master and put them in Satyrus's hand. Satyrus got a twinge from the bruise where one of the arrows had struck his breastplate. Then he had the tablets. He flexed the light wood between his hands, and popped the wax pages, one by one, from their frames.

And there was writing, small writing, covering the revealed wood. Satyrus sighed, and it seemed as if every muscle in his body relaxed. He handed the waxless boards back to Nestor, who passed them to the tyrant.

'You are full of surprises,' Dionysius said. He nodded. '"Diodorus to Satyrus, greetings. Ares and Athena bless your enterprise – I received your message today, less than a week after Seleucus paid us off for the winter. As soon as the men are sober, I will march. I will come up the royal road as far as I may, and then by the old road to Heraklea. Expect me as soon as the passes are clear. Sitalkes and Crax and all our friends speak of nothing now but our return from exile, and all of the omens are favourable."' Dionysius raised his eyes. 'Of course, you might have planted this.'

Satyrus nodded. 'I might, at that.'

'Bah – I cannot bear to execute him. And as he says himself, that is the only other choice.' Dionysius nodded. 'Nice trick with the boards, young man. From Herodotus, I believe. But – very well. I don't care to face a siege from the age's finest captain. I will be your ally. But – if you fail, boy – don't come back here.'

Satyrus bowed again. He thought of the state of his treasury and the thin balance of good will in his fleet. 'If I fail,' he said, and the mask finally slipped, and his voice trembled, 'if I fail, lord, I will feed the fishes.'

Dionysius pursed his lips and drank some wine. 'Good,' he said. 'So we understand each other.'

18

Melitta put her little army in motion while the steppe was still frozen. The winter wind continued to blow, although it was becoming warmer every day and the sun shone longer, and the shadows along the riverbanks grew shorter and smaller. Deer began to move. It was a matter of a week or two until the ground became a sea of mud.

It was her second great gamble, and her second demand that her captains trust her. This time, after one brief speech, they obeyed. It was that easy.

The Grass Cats and the Cruel Hands came in by the hundred, led by the best armoured knights, the richest clan warriors, some owning three or four hundred animals, and their wagons rolled along at the tail of their columns. Young women, bundled in furs to the eyes, rode on the flanks, eyes alert for wolves, because the horses were thin and slow after a long winter on the sea of grass – now the sea of snow.

'There will be grain aplenty in the valley of the Tanais,' Melitta said. 'And when Upazan's riders come, we'll meet them horse to horse.'

Eumenes shook his head. 'I can possibly have the Olbians together to march before the feast of Athena,' he said. 'Even then, I'd be taking farmers away from their planting.'

Melitta nodded. 'I wish I knew where my brother was,' she said. 'And what he planned. But in this, my heart tells me that speed is everything.' She tried not to admit, even to herself, that she held Gardan and Methene in her heart – and all the farmers.

Coenus, at least, was solidly behind her. 'With your permission,' he said, 'I'll take a few of Ataelus's scouts and ride ahead. I fancy that I can find Temerix. And I think we need him.'

Ataelus nodded. 'Better I go too,' he said. He shrugged. 'Temerix and I for friends – for fighting Upazan, many years. Eh?'

Coenus grinned. 'Like old times.'

'Raise your hoplites in the spring, when the seed is in the ground,' Melitta said.

'The campaign may be over by then,' Eumenes said.

Urvara hugged him. 'You are still a young man in your heart, my love. Listen – if we go east, fast as the wind, we will still have to fight Upazan – and then Eumeles. Yes?'

Eumenes nodded.

Coenus rubbed his chin. 'Eumenes – how powerful is Olbia these days?'

Eumenes spread his hands. 'I've been archon for a winter,' he said. 'I imagine we can marshal three thousand hoplites and as many *psiloi*.'

'And for ships?' Coenus asked.

'Eumeles has forbidden us to have a fleet,' Eumenes said. 'So – nothing but a dozen merchant triremes that could be refitted for war.'

Coenus nodded. 'Let me put an idea in your ear,' he said. 'We both know that Satyrus will not sit idle. He'll raise a fleet.'

Nihmu agreed. 'He loves the sea.'

Parshtaevalt made a motion of disgust. 'But it is true,' he said. 'My daughter and her war party found him far down the Bay of Trout, with a ship.' He smiled. 'He made a spear-girl pregnant.'

Melitta blushed for her brother. 'Yes, he loves the sea,' she said. 'Coenus, what is on your mind?'

Coenus laughed. 'Listen to me, the great strategos. Nonetheless – as soon as Eumeles hears of Satyrus's fleet, he'll have to go and face it.'

Urvara nodded. 'Fleets are like armies that way,' she said.

Coenus shrugged. 'So you take every man in Olbia and make a grab for Pantecapaeum,' he said.

Urvara gasped at the boldness, and Eumenes clasped his former phylarch's hand. 'You are a great man, and when Melitta makes you the strategos of all her armies, I hope you remember the little people.' He laughed. 'The risk would be immense,' he said. 'But the gain ...'

'By all the gods,' Ataelus said in Greek. He laughed. 'Imagine Eumeles for waking up – for finding no kingdom he is having?' The Sakje chief roared. 'Maybe I'm for staying here, sailing on a ship for Pantecapaeum.' His face grew still. In Sakje, he said. 'But no – I will go where I may find the man himself.'

'Eumeles?' Melitta asked.

'I will kill him,' Ataelus said. 'I was there when he betrayed your mother.'

'I know,' Melitta said. 'But your arrow will have to race mine.'

The first two days away from the Borysthenes were the worst, because the weather away from the great river was colder and harsher, and the animals suffered. After the second night, she rode out with Scopasis in the morning and saw rows of dead horses, older beasts who had perished at their pickets in the freezing rain, and others too sluggish to move with them.

The people were pragmatists. They butchered the dying horses and carried the meat, steaming, on the rumps of their horses. Then they moved on, at times riding with their heads down, directly into the ferocious winds of the central plains.

'Fucking wind comes from Hyrkania!' Parshtaevalt yelled.

'Bactria!' Nihmu called back.

Melitta felt dwarfed by the size of her responsibilities – and by the stature of her 'subjects'. Every one of her chiefs had served her mother and father – had ridden east to fight Iskander, had ridden at the Ford of the River God. And she – half their age, veteran of one great battle – was expected to *lead* them.

On the third day, Marthax's war leaders joined them. She had left them at his camp, with a promise of future obedience, but she had never expected them to come so swiftly. Graethe, now chief of the Standing Horses, rode to her and made the sign of submission, and she took his hands between hers – warm hands – and he swore by the three great Sakje gods to be her man.

'The baqca says that you ride straight to war,' he said. His beard was full of snow, but under the snow there was as much white as black. She could remember him as Marthax's emissary to her mother – a loud young man, capable of violence.

'The baqca is correct,' she said. 'I go to drive Upazan from the Tanais.'

'Good!' Graethe said. 'You promised Marthax a kurgan.'

'We will build to the skies,' she promised. 'When Upazan is driven from the mouth of the Tanais.'

'We have brought him,' Graethe said. He pointed at a travois, dragged by two tired horses.

She looked at the frozen blood on the hides, but there was nothing to be seen of the dead king except a corpse-shaped bundle of furs.

They rode east, across the rising ground, and back to the coast at Hygreis, the first town of Srayanka's eastern kingdom that had been.

The Maeotae greeted them with open arms. Her outriders paid hard gold for grain and she camped for two days. The weather was milder on the shores of the Bay of Salmon.

'The world will be mud in ten days. Or less,' Urvara said.

Melitta nodded, sitting her horse on the high dunes north of the town. 'I know, lady. But from here, we could ride the dunes and the hard sand all the way home.'

Urvara laughed. 'Too easily, I forget that you grew up here. With your foreign words and your face, I forget that you really are one of us. Ride the dunes! The sea road. Inland clans like mine forget these things.'

'I am not the first lord of ten thousand horses to launch an early campaign,' Melitta said.

Parshtaevalt laughed. 'No, you are not. In fact, Satrax did the same to the Getae, with your father holding his hand – after the Getae did the same to us. Oh, how they burned us! We fought that whole war before the grain came in.'

Melitta nodded. 'Four days to Tanais.'

Urvara's horse began to shy at the smell on the wind – roast pork. 'Then?'

Parshtaevalt shook his head at Urvara. 'What do you think? Then we fight.'

Melitta shook her head. 'I don't think so. It will take another ten days of sunshine to make the grass dry enough to ride – maybe twenty. We will build a kurgan for Marthax – next to my father's. And a fortified camp – a base. Food, grain, shelter.'

Graethe laughed. 'The Sakje don't need a shelter,' he said. 'We have four thousand riders. Twenty thousand horses. In less than a month our horses will be fat.'

Melitta shook her head. 'This will not be a war like any other the Sakje have fought,' she said. 'I am young, but I remember that in my youth, my mother alone could lead five thousand riders into the field. Now the whole fighting strength of the royal Sakje – the keepers of the western gate – is ten thousand horsemen. How many Sauromatae are there?'

'Too many,' Urvara said. 'I already miss Ataelus.'

'He'll meet us at Tanais,' Melitta said.

Urvara said nothing.

Tanais had stood on a bluff above the river. In her youth, Melitta remembered the hippodrome and the temples – a beautiful marble temple in the Ionian style, dedicated to Athena Nike by her father's friends and Uncle Leon, who had paid for most of it. She remembered the buildings laid out in a neat grid, new and clean, and a statue of her father mounted on a horse, cast in bronze, his sword pointing east at the lands where they had fought Iskander.

It was all gone. The pedestal of the statue – a big marble plinth with scenes from the battles in the east carved around the base – still sat alone at the top of the bluff, but mud and snow covered the scars of burning, and the statue itself was now armour and arrowheads and a thousand other bronze implements.

She sat on Gryphon, his feet planted in the midst of the ruin of her childhood, and all the dreams her parents had shared, and she wept. In some complex way, she hadn't quite believed that Tanais was destroyed until she saw it. She realized that she had awakened that morning, eager to ride, expecting – what? Expecting to find the old freedman in the hippodrome? Bion waiting in his stall?

In a way, it made her job easier. She didn't hesitate to order the top of the bluff scraped clean. The plinth from her father's statue went into the wall that her Sakje constructed, aided by the farmers of the surrounding country. They came in with their grain within hours. She had them build her a granary in the Sindi way – they burned a huge fire to thaw the ground, and then dug the dirt out, digging down many times the height of a man and lining the pit with stones. Then they covered it with a thatch roof, supported by beams floated down the river.

As the Sindi and the Maeotae worked, the Sakje built another great fire on the shore. When the embers began to cool, they dug a tomb chamber deep into the dry dirt, and more logs went into a wooden house in the dirt. They laid Marthax in the house and killed a hundred horses in the trench outside. Every man and woman brought a square of turf, and many of the Sindi and the Maeotae came as well, and the kurgan went up and up.

They had been ten days at Tanais when Ataelus rode in with a hundred riders at his back, and four hundred grim-faced men on ponies with bows and axes. They had Sauromatae ponies and Sauromatae coats of hide, and they sang as they came.

The Maeotae farmers came out to line the roads to greet them. The roads were swampy, and women cursed the cold mud on their legs, but they cheered as Ataelus rode by.

Ataelus dismounted by Melitta and embraced her. 'You remember Temerix?' he asked.

Temerix was the same – a figure of menace. He was older but no smaller. He had a new scar on his face. 'I hear you cut a path to us,' the smith said. 'I was behind you two days – they were too thick, and I had to ride away.' He laughed, and it was a fell sound. 'But I raised the northern valleys,' he said. He pointed at the men behind him. 'Upazan's tax collectors won't be riding home.'

'And – Lu?' Melitta asked. Lu was another fixture from her childhood – her nurse, her confidante. Temerix's wife from far to the east.

'Lu sends her love,' Temerix said. 'Love' sounded odd in his mouth. But he smiled, and years fled from his face. 'By all the gods, Srayanka's daughter, we will have good times now.'

Melitta hugged Ataelus again. 'I worried you were gone so long,' she said.

'Upazan's men were already in the high ground when I found the smith,' he said. 'They thought that we had fled! Hah! The ground is strewn with corpses.' He looked to the side. 'Coenus is wounded.'

'That is hard news. He is – the captain of my guard.' She almost said *the man I trust the most.*

'He is forming the men of the upper Tanais into a militia,' Ataelus said in Sakje. 'The wound is not so bad.'

Melitta chewed on her hair. 'We have a secure base, and grain,' she said. 'As soon as the ground is dry, let us ride up the valley and see what Upazan has.' In private, she worried that Ataelus, Temerix and Coenus had shown her power to Upazan too early.

Ten days of spring breezes. Ten days of watching farmers scratch their heads, of watching the more daring lead their oxen into the fields and all but vanish in the rich, black mud, the great beasts scarcely able to walk for the clods adhering like melted cheese to their hooves.

Even when many of the farmers began to plough in earnest, breaking the new soil once, and then again, and a third and even a fourth time before planting their seed, still she waited, because Ataelus was tireless, and Samahe rode the hills with her maidens, and spring came slowly there.

In the valleys, girls danced the spring dances under the trees, and seeds were planted that needed no dirt to grow, and laughter filled the air as the first green shoots leaped from the ground as an answer to Demeter's prayer and Persephone's return. Melitta, who had not thought about sex in five months, felt the pangs of interest, first in one boy, then in another, until the urge of spring was so powerful that she took refuge in being the queen. She began to dress the part, and she put her bodyguard and Urvara, who was in most ways her first minister, between her yearnings and her body.

Even with the knights of her bodyguard, she was short and direct, and she did not encourage discussion.

And then came a day, when the first roses were budding, when the Athenaea had been celebrated, that Ataelus and Samahe pronounced that the ground was hard. Melitta rose to her feet and flicked her riding whip. 'Send for my horses,' she said.

The army was away that day.

They rode with spare horses to hand, a vanguard commanded by Temerix well in advance against ambush and a rearguard trailing well behind the main body against disaster. They took no wagons, and they rode two hundred stades a day or more – even over the high ground.

Melitta made time to ride with the maidens – young women, all painfully younger than she was herself, and she was angered at the loss of youth and freedom. At first they were quiet and foolishly respectful, and then they were boastful and foolishly loud, bragging of the men they would kill and the others they would bed, or playing at sex among themselves, and she resented them.

She also resented Nihmu, who since Coenus's absence had withdrawn more and more into the spirit world, taking smoke every day or more, and speaking of her dreams as if they were the premonitions of her youth. Her assumption of the mantle of a baqca angered some and pleased others, as the tides of tribal politics ran, but Tameax avoided her and refused to lend her a drum or speak her rituals with her.

She confronted Nihmu in the fake privacy of her smoke tent, forcing herself through the deep, rich fumes to speak her mind. 'I need you as a counsellor,' Melitta said. 'I have a baqca.'

Nihmu gave a dreamy smile. 'I will never again lie with a man,' she said, 'and then I will recover all my powers.'

Melitta wriggled out of the tent, enraged, as if the smoke had fed her anger as wood feeds a fire.

Ataelus was gone from dawn until dark, hunting the high ridges. Samahe rode with him. Coenus was still ahead, training farmers in his beloved valley – where he had built the temple to Artemis. Urvara, Parshtaevalt and Graethe each had their own clans and their own factions.

Melitta stopped wanting to weep. She stopped wanting to cry, to fuck, to have friends. In a matter of days, in the same way that she had made herself hard in order to survive, she made herself into the queen – silent, careful and exact. She became the woman she remembered standing silently by her bed in the firelight of the hall – hair wrapped in gold braid-cases, body hidden by the white doeskin jacket with its gold plates and careful caribou-hair embroidery.

Sometimes, while holding her, her mother had wept. Those tears had always puzzled Melitta when she felt them on her cheeks when she was six years old. But now, standing alone, her hair in the same gold braid-cases and her breasts held in the same caribou coat, she felt the same emptiness – she knew it was the same.

'I miss my son,' she said to the wind.

'Where is Satyrus?' she asked the newborn sun.

'Is this all there is?' she asked the new flowers.

And the army moved north.

At the Temple of Artemis, she allowed herself the luxury of hugging Coenus.

'My apologies, lady,' he said with a deep bow. His left arm was in a sling. 'I took a wound in the first fighting and I thought I might as well recuperate here.'

Melitta had to admit, despite her annoyance with him, that his farmers looked dangerous. They were the only armoured infantry of her whole army, five hundred men in scale armour or heavy leather, with bows and spears and crescent-shaped shields like Thracians. 'You are making them into Greeks,' she accused.

'I'd kill for half a hundred hoplites,' Coenus allowed.

'You are the captain of my guard,' she said, pointedly.

'I am,' he allowed. 'I apologize, lady.'

'Very well,' she said. 'You have trained them. Now let us march. And you can return to your duties.'

He nodded brusquely and took his place, and his men joined the column, kissing their wives, embracing their children and marching away to the north. And that night she pounced on him in the relative privacy of her tent.

'Have you seen Nihmu?' she asked.

'She no longer ... has need of me,' Coenus said. He narrowed his eyes. 'Not that you have done anything to help her.'

'I?' Melitta asked. 'I can't even get her to talk. The moment the army halts, she is off her horse, taking smoke. She all but lives in the spirit world.'

Coenus shook his head. 'That is her choice. She wants back the powers that – that I'm unsure she ever had. I can't stomach it. I rode away to leave her.' He raised his head, and Melitta could see the tears. 'I'm sorry, Melitta. I can't watch her kill herself. Send me away again.'

She shook herself. 'You left me because of *Nihmu*?' she asked sharply. 'Coenus, I am twenty years old, commanding an army of strangers in a land that is often foreign to me.'

'Could have fooled me,' Coenus said. 'They love you.'

'They have no idea who I am. I'm not sure that *I* know who I am. I will soon be what they make me – the virgin goddess. Artemis come to life. My mother.' She shook with fury. 'And you rode away to avoid the consequences of seducing Nihmu from her husband!'

Coenus stood up. 'I don't have to listen to this,' he said. 'And I didn't seduce her from my friend. Much the opposite.'

'Listen to me! I need you, damn it. But you – you led her astray. Admit it!' Melitta didn't like that Coenus was human – and she didn't like the look on his face now.

'*I* led *her* astray?' Coenus spat.

There was a commotion at the edge of the darkness beyond the fire. Hoof beats, and shouting.

'We will talk of this later,' Melitta said.

'Where is the lady?' a rider asked, and more hoof beats in the dark.

Melitta raised her voice. 'Here!' she shouted, and even as she called, Coenus drew his sword and stepped between her and the rider.

'You trust too easily,' Coenus said.

The rider stayed clear of the sword. 'I am your sworn man,' he said. 'Lady, the camp at Tanais is under attack – Eumeles' men are landing from ships!'

'What is this?' she asked.

'A taxeis of Eumeles' foot soldiers landed from ships,' he said. 'We surprised them on the beach and killed dozens, but they drove us back into the fort.'

Melitta shook her head to clear it. 'Get me my chiefs,' she said.

Coenus sheathed his sword. 'Artemis stand with us. They can't have enough men to take the fort – we left half a thousand farmers to hold it.'

Parshtaevalt came up first, tying his sash. 'The farmers won't hold unless they know we are coming,' he said. 'The dirt people don't expect to fight alone – and who can blame them?'

'How close are we to Upazan?' Melitta asked Ataelus when he came.

He looked at Samahe. She shrugged. 'We haven't found a single rider in the high ground,' she said.

Ataelus shrugged. 'I think it was a mistake to attack his riders at the end of winter,' he admitted. 'But they were under my hand, and I took them.'

'So Upazan has slipped away,' Melitta said.

'Back to the sea of grass north of the Hyrkanian Sea,' Coenus said. 'To raise his own army, I suspect.'

All of the tribal leaders nodded.

'And he'll return when he wants, on his own terms,' Urvara said. 'While we have to fight to defend the farmers, he'll hit us as he likes.'

'And Eumeles can play the same game with his ships. If we rush to every town he threatens, he'll sail away.' Coenus smacked his open palm with his fist.

Graethe scratched at his moustache. 'What do we do, then? You Greeks are good at this sort of war – many fields, and many foes. Me, I want to ride, to feel a foe under my iron.'

Melitta poked the fire with a stick and then recalled her pose as the unflappable queen. 'We will have to relieve the fort at Tanais,' she said. 'How many soldiers were there?' she asked the Sindi rider.

He shook his head. 'Many,' he said.

'A thousand?' Coenus asked. 'How many ships?'

'Many,' the boy said. 'I was sent to find the queen, and no one told me to count the ships.'

'Let's say he sent half his fleet – forty ships. At most, one taxeis of pikemen – perhaps with the best of the oarsmen as *peltastai*.' Coenus spat on the grass. 'I'm tired of being cold all the time,' he said, as if this was germane.

Parshtaevalt laughed. 'You are unchanged by the passing of years,' he said.

'How could Eumeles be on us so fast?' Urvara asked.

Melitta shook her head. 'It takes too long to move troops – and ships,' she said. 'This is some planned movement that we have interrupted.'

'What if the rest of his army is coming behind?' Graethe said.

'We must relieve the fort,' Melitta said again. 'If we fail to save these farmers, the others will never trust us again.'

And just like that, her notion carried. The chiefs walked off into the dark to ready their warriors to turn around in the morning.

'Why are you so angry?' Coenus asked. 'They obey – better than they obeyed Satrax, as I remember.'

'There is more to life than being obeyed,' she said.

She heard Scopasis laugh, close at hand. 'People laugh,' she said. 'I seldom laugh any more. My mother never laughed, and now I know why.'

'Then perhaps you know why I, an aristocrat, refuse to command,' Coenus said.

'I need you,' she admitted, looking up at him.

'I'll see what I can do with Nihmu,' he answered.

The next morning, they rode back south, and the ground it had taken them seven days to cover was dryer, the mud hardened to dirt, and by the evening of the fourth day, their outriders were skirmishing with foragers from the enemy camp. The Sakje went right in among them, killing the mercenaries and driving the survivors back over the damp ground into their camp.

Melitta went with Temerix, despite the advice of her chiefs. Coenus forced her to take Scopasis as a bodyguard, and together they rode with Temerix's warband on their stout ponies. Then they took their bows, slung their axes and moved forward carefully, staying in the trees on the high ridges. Below, in the valley's fields and meadows, she could see the horsemen moving, cutting off parties of Greek soldiers and shooting them full of arrows. There were burning farmhouses throughout the Tanais Valley. The sight sickened her, as if her valley had a deadly disease that had transmitted itself to her blood.

Four hours they walked the ridges, and never saw an enemy except in the valley below, and Temerix grunted every time he saw a devastated farmstead. And while they never saw an enemy, Temerix's men found dozens of farmfolk, Sindi and Maeotae, living in small caves or dirt hollows where they'd fled the depredations of the enemy.

Melitta wanted to weep at every group of them. They reached out to touch her, and she smiled for them instead, and told them that it would be all right.

And then they moved on – closer and closer to the enemy camp. By afternoon, the camp was visible, just a few stades from her mother's city on the bluff. They were camped at the foot of her father's kurgan, in a big rectangle of earth and wood stakes.

She lay with the Sindi smith, on earth still wet enough to soak through her clothes and armour, and watched the gates of the camp. There were two, and both were guarded. Parties of the enemy were coming down both roads to get in their camp as quickly as possible.

Temerix nodded. 'Now we fight,' he said.

Unlike her other chiefs, he didn't ask her permission. He spoke in Sindi, and men jumped to do his bidding. He turned to her. 'Go to kill Greeks,' he said. 'You?'

She got to her feet, adjusted her gorytos and her akinakes, and nodded. 'Me too,' she said.

Temerix's eyes flicked over to Scopasis and back to her. 'Loose five arrows and run,' he said. 'Understand?'

Scopasis nodded.

Melitta nodded. It was not her first ambush, but Temerix had no way of knowing that.

'I shoot first arrow,' Temerix said. And then he was off, running down the hillside.

The Sindi were fast on rough ground – as fast as horsemen, or even faster, at least for short bursts. And their progress was eerie – almost inhuman, as she had to watch them carefully not to lose them in the scrub and tree cover of the hillside. Their ragged cloaks and dun colours vanished against the valley's spring green.

The soldiers on the road were too fixated on the horsemen behind them. They were well formed, and they held together, but they had no flank guards and no advance party – just sixty men under a senior file-leader, moving at a jog back along the road, with another twenty light-armed men – peltastai, probably rowers from the fleet, armed only with javelins and knives.

Temerix had chosen to catch them on the same stretch of road where Melitta had had her first taste of combat, all those years before. Where her brother had saved Coenus. Where Theron had proven to be a friend. It seemed odd, to be fighting on the same ground again, as if her life was going around some sort of loop.

She put herself behind an oak so big that she and Scopasis wouldn't have been able to encircle it with their arms. She could hear the Greeks on the road.

'Give me a hand up,' she said quietly.

Scopasis frowned, but then he made a stirrup and she stepped up into his hands, on to his shoulder and up into the tree's first big joint. Her guess was that the Greeks saw nothing but the mounted Sakje pursuing them.

She got into the joint, scraping her knee and cursing the weight of her armour, which made everything harder and served no purpose in this kind of war. Then her bow was in her hand and she had an arrow on the bow and her whole focus was on the Greeks coming down the road. They were trotting, and their officer had a big plume.

'Not far, boys,' he shouted, in Macedonian-accented Greek. 'Two stades. Keep it together.'

The file-closers nearest to Melitta were middle-aged men with hard faces and grey in their beards, but the middle-rankers were children wearing helmets that were far too big for them, padded in sheepskin that showed around the edges of their high-peaked helms. Of course, they were the same age as her spear-maidens and their brothers.

Armies of children, killing each other so that adults can wield power, she thought.

Temerix's first arrow screamed as it flew, and it took the officer high on his unarmoured thigh. He went down in a clatter of bronze. Before his men could react, two dozen shafts flew, buzzing like wasps aroused by foolish children, and men fell.

Melitta shot a file-closer in the neck and felt a burst of pleasure at the fine shot.

Another file-leader waved his sword. 'At 'em, lads!' he shouted, and died, several arrows in him. But *another* leader got them moving, and they rushed down the road at the ambush. Now their shields were facing the right way and the next volley of arrows from the ambushers had little effect.

Melitta shot twice and had no idea whether her arrows were going home. She had the third arrow drawn, her right thumb just brushing the outward edge of her lip as her mother had taught her, when she realized that Scopasis was fighting hand-to-hand at her feet. She leaned out and shot *down* at a boy in leather armour. Her shaft glanced off his Thracian helmet to bury itself in his foot, and he yelled.

Scopasis was fighting with a long-handled cavalry axe, the kind that the Greeks called a *sagaris*, and as soon as he saw the boy stumble, he cut at him, and the axe collapsed the dome of his helmet.

Melitta drew again. This time the Greeks were looking up and had their shields ready – but they couldn't watch her and Scopasis at the same time. There were three more of them, and the biggest one had a long sword.

'On my count, boys,' he said. 'One – arrggh!' He fell as if the axe had taken him, an arrow in his back.

The other two broke. Melitta shot one, low in the back, so that he fell and kicked and screamed. The other tripped and fell on a root, and Scopasis killed him while he cowered and begged.

Melitta looked up and down the road. There were Greeks still alive – they were running at full speed for their fort.

'Jump,' Scopasis said. 'I'll catch you.'

Melitta dropped her bow into its scabbard and jumped.

He caught her with an audible grunt, and he sank to one knee with the effort, but he did catch her. The scales of her thorax caught in the scales of his for a moment, and their faces were close.

'Thank you,' she said, far more stiffly than she had meant. Scopasis had clear green eyes, like the glass the Aegyptians made. She hadn't noticed that before. Then she was out of his arms and moving.

Heartbeats later, and Temerix's horn was sounding on the ridge. She and Scopasis were the last ambushers to rejoin the smith, where he sat on a stump, sharpening his axe.

'Why do we run, when the enemy is beaten?' she asked.

Temerix shrugged. 'Because I say,' he answered with a grim smile. Then he shook his head. 'Kill – run. Always. Sometimes enemy runs too. But sometime, someday, enemy has ambush of his own – yes? Sure. My men live and not die. Yes?' He looked around and spoke in Sindi, and the men nodded and laughed. 'You fight well, and you *obey*,' Temerix said. 'Queen of Assagatje *obey* a Sindi.' He nodded. 'It is good.' He spoke again, the men around her laughed, and the nearest, a small man with tattoos around his eyes, slapped her on the back.

On the way back, they collected their refugees and sent them to strip the dead in the valley. In camp, Urvara was beside herself with worry when she saw Melitta, and she was visibly reining in her temper.

'I had to,' Melitta said.

Temerix slapped her back and headed off with his own. Urvara watched him go, and then kissed her brow. 'I guess you did, at that,' she said in Sakje. 'You know that if you die, this comes to an end.'

'No,' Melitta said. 'No, Auntie. I have a brother, and a son. If I die, they'll ride the horse.'

The next morning, it rained – cold rain that seemed like a last touch of winter's icy fingers. She sat in the cold rain with Coenus on the same low ridge where Temerix had rallied them the day before, opposite the enemy camp. The enemy ships were drawn up on the muddy beach – twenty triremes and forty more small merchant ships and big fishing smacks, all capable of carrying forty or fifty men.

Coenus peered at them under his hand in the rising sun. 'Nikephoros,' he said. 'Good officer. Look at the camp – and the sentries.'

'You know him?' Melitta asked.

'Don't spend your life on the stage without getting to know the chorus,' Coenus said. 'There he is!' He pointed to the line of ships.

Melitta had no idea what her captain was pointing at. Coenus's eyes had always been godlike. 'Will he fight?' she asked.

Coenus saw her puzzlement. 'No,' he said. 'Whatever he came for, he's too smart to fight. He made a grab at the fort, destroyed some farms, got his fingers burned and now he's re-embarking.'

'He built that fortified camp and now he'll just *leave it*?' she asked.

'That's right, honey bee,' Coenus said. He rubbed his beard and then snuffled. He had a cold. Most of them did. Spring had come and the ground was drying, but the nights were still damp and cold. 'I would. Camps are easy to build. He can't afford losses. And if he lost a battle here – we'd kill every man in his force and burn his ships.'

Scopasis, normally silent, was moved to speak. 'Send us, lady. We will storm his camp *now*.'

Gaweint seconded him. 'Send us!' he said.

Melitta looked at Coenus, expecting a rapid negation. Instead, the Megaran scratched his beard, and then pulled his helmet off and his wool cap and scratched his head more thoroughly. 'Creatures of icy Tartarus,' he cursed. 'Lice. Lice are supposed to come with *warm* weather. Scopasis, you may have something – and I don't mean more lice. Lady, how many dead can you tolerate?'

Melitta felt her stomach contract. 'What are you saying?'

Coenus smiled grimly. 'Did I mention how all my life I've refused command? This is it. Scopasis is right. They've just started to load.' He crushed a bug between his nails. 'Right now, if we go for them, we'll wipe them out.' He smeared the remains of the bug on his horse's withers. 'It'll cost you a thousand warriors.'

'Unacceptable,' she said. Coenus's tone horrified her.

'It'd change the war,' Coenus said. 'In one blow, we cripple his fleet and get his best general and a third of his professional soldiers.'

Scopasis pulled his horse in front of her. 'I would be proud to lead,' he said. 'I will die here.'

Gaweint threw his sword in the air. 'Hah!' he said, and caught it.

Urvara came up with her bodyguard and Parshtaevalt followed, dickering with Graethe over the price of a horse. They fell silent as they saw the enemy camp.

Melitta looked down at the enemy ships and the files of rowers going aboard, the men on the walls looking up the hill at the Sakje and over their shoulders, already nervous that they might be abandoned.

'No,' she said. 'It is enough that they board their ships and sail away.'

'Tomorrow, they will land a hundred stades from here. They will burn the Temple of Herakles, or kill your friend – that farmer up on the Hypanis. What's his name? Gardan.' Coenus shrugged. 'Right now, we have them under our hands.' Coenus pulled his wool arming cap back on to his head. 'I don't want to order it, either. But this is what war is. And if you order it, I will lead it.'

'A thousand riders?' Urvara asked. 'Dead?' She looked at Coenus. 'This is some Greek madness. The people would never recover.'

'And Upazan would still come,' Parshtaevalt said. 'But – oh, Coenus. It is a hard thing, but even if it is my clan that dies, I see the merit in your words.'

Coenus nodded. 'Don't mistake me, friends. I don't *want* this battle. But mark my words – later in the summer we'll face Nikephoros on ground of his own choosing, with Eumeles and all his mercenaries and Upazan guarding his flanks.'

Melitta was sure that her answer was the right one. 'Friends,' she said, and all their heads turned. 'My friends, this is a battle I will never fight – a battle where I must expect a thousand empty saddles. Coenus – I understand. I am enough Greek that I understand, but I will find us another way.'

Coenus nodded. He tucked his helmet into the leather bag at his back and pulled out a Sakje fur hat. 'Good,' he said. 'It would have been horrible.'

Scopasis shook his head. 'Glorious,' he spat. Gaweint looked as if he might cry.

Ataelus came up last, heard the end of the debate and slapped his former outlaw on the back. 'Live a few more days,' he said. 'You may find that dying in battle is not the only joy.'

The Sindi and the Maeotae cheered like heroes as their queen rode up the bluff and entered the gates over the corpses of a dozen dead phalangites. Coenus congratulated the farmers on the spirit of their defence, and Ataelus already had two hundred riders across the river, riding the coast, trying to find out where the enemy fleet was heading.

'Where is my brother?' Melitta asked.

'If he is alive, he is coming,' Urvara said.

Coenus nodded.

But the enemy fleet sailed out into the bay, and Melitta suspected that perhaps an opportunity had sailed with it.

One boat returned, a pentekonter rowed by soldiers with a handsome older man in the stern. Melitta found Coenus overseeing the storage of yet more grain and pointed it out to him.

'Nikephoros,' he said. 'Must want to bury his dead. He's of the old school – quite an honourable man.'

'How can he stomach his master, then?' Melitta asked. She saw Nihmu – pale, thin and distraught. It took her a moment to realize that Nihmu was waiting on her – literally. Melitta had waited on Nihmu most of her adult life. It was odd to reverse the situation.

Coenus smiled at Nihmu and she looked elsewhere. He rolled his eyes. 'Listen, honey bee. Your father was lucky. His employer was a monster – but Kineas rose above him. Not every professional soldier can do the same.'

Melitta continued to watch the fifty-oared boat approach. 'Nihmu?' she said softly.

'Lady?' Nihmu came closer. 'Lady? I have come to crave a boon.'

Melitta tore her eyes from the approaching galley. 'Nihmu, I think you're being silly. I'm not the lady to you.'

Nihmu had tears in her eyes. 'You are, lady. Listen – I wish to leave.'

Melitta started. '*Leave?*' she asked. She glanced at Coenus – whose look of Laconic concern didn't fool her for a moment. 'Why are you leaving?'

Nihmu bit her lip. 'I am going to rescue my husband,' she said. 'Coenus and I feel that it won't be long before Eumeles executes him. He must be rescued.'

Melitta felt a void in her stomach as she realized that among all her busy plots and plans, Leon had vanished into obscurity. She looked at Coenus, who wiped sweat from his brow and shook his head. 'Nihmu and I agreed that it must be her. If I go, you have no military counsel that you trust.' His voice was flat, and she realized that he was making a sacrifice, and bearing it – rather the opposite of her first assumption.

'You would rather rescue Leon?' she asked.

Coenus nodded. 'Yes,' he said. 'This morning reminded me of why I do not wish to command.'

Melitta nodded and began to walk down to the beach beneath her father's kurgan. The pentekonter was coming ashore, and the first sailors to touch the beach had branches of olive in their hands. A herald came next. He wore green and walked up the beach to Coenus, and bowed. Coenus pointed to Melitta. The herald looked puzzled, but then he inclined his head.

In abysmal Sakje, he said, 'Master of many horses Nikephoros look to ask to make not war with you.' The man's nerves were betrayed by the way he clutched his staff.

'I speak Greek,' she said.

'Ah! My pardon, despoina. My strategos requests a truce during which he might bury his dead, or take their bodies.' The herald waved his wand in the direction of the fort.

'Let him approach me himself,' Melitta said. 'I see him standing in the stern. It is right that leaders should look each other in the eye.'

The herald turned and walked away. She saw him walk back the half-stade across the sand.

'Build a fire,' Melitta said. 'Fetch wine.'

The herald went aboard, and she saw Nikephoros look her way and shrug. Then he leaped down into the cold water and trudged up the beach.

Coenus worked his magic. In moments, he had a driftwood fire going. Nihmu came to her side with a heavy amphora of wine cradled in her arms like a baby, and Urvara came down on horseback, dismounted and joined her. Temerix walked up on foot.

'Parshtaevalt, Ataelus and Graethe are already out on the grass,' Urvara said. 'I gather that's Nikephoros.'

Melitta nodded.

Nikephoros walked the half-stade towards them, apparently indifferent to his wet cloak and the icy wind. He came alone.

'Please come and be warm,' Melitta said. 'There's wine.'

'I never refuse a cup of wine,' Nikephoros said. 'Hello, Coenus the Megaran. Your presence gave me hope that I could expect the courtesies of war.'

Melitta handed him a cup of wine. 'Did you know my father?'

Nikephoros was Boeotian. He had copper-red hair – what was left of it – and fine armour. He wore a full beard like a man of a bygone era, and he didn't waste words. 'No. Or rather, only by repute.' He poured a libation. 'To all the gods, and to the shade of your father. In his name, I ask you for a truce of one day, in which to recover and bury my dead.'

Melitta nodded. 'It is odd, Nikephoros. An hour ago, I was considering the storming of your camp. Now we drink wine. Yes – and no. You may have a five-day truce to recover your dead. There will be some by the outlying farms where we killed them yesterday.'

'I need only a day,' Nikephoros said.

'Five days, during which your ships remain in the bay where I can see them.' Melitta had to look up at him. He had a pleasant face, the kind of face she trusted. *Too bad*, she thought.

His anger showed in his face. 'You did not beat me badly enough—' he said, and his voice was hard.

She raised her whip. 'You serve a usurper, a tyrant who ordered you here to *burn his own farmers*. I owe you no courtesy at all. Because Coenus told me that you are a man of honour, I agreed to meet you. But hear me, Boeotian. My father would never have served a tyrant like Eumeles. Instead, he would have overthrown him. My uncles serve Ptolemy, who builds cities, and Seleucus, who liberates them. I judge you by the company you keep. To me, you are a mercenary who serves a rebel. Take my five days, or sail away. There is no bargain to be made here.'

Nikephoros shook his head. His anger had cooled. 'So you already know,' he said.

Coenus's face was carefully blank.

Melitta took her cue from him. She said nothing. But suddenly hope soared in her.

Nikephoros sipped his wine. 'Listen, lady. I expect no special treatment from you, but your request is unreasonable. To wait five days is to guarantee that I'm blockaded here. So I'll offer three days, and no more.' He addressed Coenus. 'Be fair, Coenus.'

Coenus leaned forward. 'Because if we keep you here five days,' he said, 'Satyrus's fleet will be here.' His voice cracked a little at the end – he could barely keep the smile off his face.

Nikephoros shrugged. 'I can't chance it. That boy moves fast. I got word this morning he's at Heraklea with a fleet. I assume that you heard the same?'

He looked around, and his face filled with blood. This time he was angry. 'You didn't know!' he said.

'I know now,' Melitta said. 'Three days has just become acceptable.'

Nikephoros spat. 'This is not how embassies proceed. Coenus, I expected better of you.'

Coenus shrugged. 'Neither you nor your herald has been threatened. You dickered over the days of truce. It all seems normal to me.' He turned to Melitta. 'Three days?'

Melitta nodded.

Nikephoros stood still.

'Three days' truce,' Coenus intoned. 'You may land up to fifty men at a time, and you may use the beach north of the old town to cook and eat.'

'We want our camp!' Nikephoros shot back.

Coenus shook his head. 'No, Nikephoros. There is no question of that. Nor will we allow you to fortify a new place.'

Nikephoros shook his head. 'No truce, then.' He turned on his heel and walked away.

Coenus held up his hand for silence. Then he turned to Melitta. 'You know what this means!' he said quietly.

Melitta nodded. 'Listen, Coenus. There are boats in the fort. Take one and a crew of Sindi – follow his ships out of the Bay of Salmon and run down for Heraklea. Tell my brother how it lies and we'll have Leon back in no time.' She looked around at her chiefs. 'Satyrus must have a fleet.'

'And here?' Urvara asked. 'What about us?'

Melitta nodded. 'I think we went about this wrong,' she said. 'We're Sakje. We leave the farmers to hold the fort – they know we'll come back. We scatter into war bands, across the whole of the east country, and we make war our way, preying on the Sauromatae wherever we find them, acting as our own pickets for either invasion – Upazan or Eumeles. We harry whichever comes first. We concentrate if we can defeat a detachment, and otherwise we are like snowflakes on an eastern wind. Let them strike at the snow.' She waved her whip at Nikephoros, who now stood still, half a stade along the beach, looking out to sea. 'The farmers can protect their grain until my brother comes, surely.'

Urvara started to speak, but Coenus cut her off with an exclamation. 'By the gods – the grain! Nikephoros is here for the grain! He must be poor.'

Melitta spat at the notion of a king who would steal grain from his own subjects.

Urvara's eyes shone, reflecting the fire. 'That is proper war,' she said. 'That is the war the people know.'

'One day's rest,' Melitta said. 'And then we ride.' She turned to Coenus. 'Will you go for my brother?' she asked.

'You can live without me?' Coenus asked. His tone held mockery – whether of her or of himself she couldn't reckon.

She chose to take his question at face value. 'I need you,' she said. 'But no one is irreplaceable. Not even me. So go. Who will command my guard?'

'Scopasis,' Coenus said without hesitation. 'He has a keen eye and a loyal heart. Don't take his advice on military matters – he seeks glory.'

Melitta swatted her dearest advisor. 'I know that!' she said. She had tears in her eyes. She took Coenus's hand and Nihmu's. 'Come back to me.'

Nihmu was looking out at the enemy fleet. 'I can't believe I am going to sea again,' she said. 'Bah.' But she smiled. 'We'll come back,' she said.

But Melitta was chilled to see that Nihmu would not meet her eye. 'What have you seen?' Melitta demanded.

'Seen?' Nihmu asked. She shook her head, still refusing to meet Melitta's eye. 'I no longer see. The spirit world is closed to me.'

Melitta put her hand on the woman's shoulders. 'No!' she said. 'I don't believe it. What did you see?'

'Nikephoros is coming back,' Coenus said. 'Look like a queen.'

Nikephoros stopped a horse-length away and tucked his thumbs in his sash. 'Three days,' he said. He shrugged.

Melitta drew herself up against the weight of the armour on her shoulders. 'Three days,' she said, as graciously as she could manage.

The Boeotian nodded. He turned to Coenus. 'Your men will know where mine are lying,' he said.

Coenus handed his wine cup to his queen. 'I'm at your service, Strategos. Shall we get to it?'

Nikephoros didn't smile. His face was closed and hard, and Melitta wondered what inner struggle had just transpired. She could feel his anger across the fire. She thought that she might have scored on him with her speech – but not in a way that would help her cause. And she could see that he loved his men.

She stood on the beach, in a light rain, watching as other Greeks came ashore. She continued to stand there as they gathered wood, as the first parties brought corpses down to the beach. She stood with Urvara as they watched a party bring a man who yet lived down the rocky path to the beach, and rowed him swiftly out to the boats.

And that night, Coenus and Nihmu sailed away on a triakonter, unmolested through the enemy fleet.

With the dawn, her army vanished into the spring fields and the new grass, searching for Upazan's raiders, for ships full of enemies coming from the sea. Herself, she took her bodyguard, now swelled to twenty warriors with a hundred horses, and rode for the Hypanis. To see to Gardan's family. And to raise the georgoi to defend themselves, because war was coming to her whole country.

19

Satyrus lay that night in the house that had been Kinon's, and the old slave – Servilius – served him a superior breakfast of lentils cooked in wine and jugged hare. Then he sent another slave to his ship, to bring his men ashore.

He was still wiping the hare out of his moustache when the old slave came back to his elbow. 'Your man,' he said. Helios was there, dripping wet and nearly blue with cold.

'You swam ashore,' Satyrus said. He shook his head. 'If you die, I freed you for nothing.' He turned to the house slave. 'Servilius, can you get him warm?'

The older man nodded. 'Freed you, eh?' he said. 'Lucky man.' His tone suggested that if he were freed, he wouldn't squander his freedom by jumping into the water and swimming a stade to shore for his master. He managed this in one tilt of the head and a flat tone that no master could have found rebellious. 'And there's a visitor,' he tossed over his shoulder, as he led Helios away into the house.

'Clearly Dionysius took all the *good* slaves,' Satyrus muttered, walking out into the courtyard. The last time he'd been here, it had been covered in blood – dead slaves who had been his friends, and dead men who'd tried to kill him. The day he found out why men thought Philokles the Spartan was the avatar of Ares on earth.

At the gate he found a Persian mounted on a tall horse. He looked up at the man – who wore a long Persian coat against the cold, and was on one of the most beautiful horses he'd ever seen. 'Yes?' he asked.

The Persian slipped down from his charger's back like a Sakje. He was handsome, even by Persian standards, and his smile filled his face. 'No need to tell me your name, son of Kineas,' he said.

'You have the advantage of me,' Satyrus answered. Then it struck him that this must be Diodorus's messenger. 'Do I know you?' he asked.

'I hope that you've heard my name once or twice,' the Persian said. 'I was your father's friend.'

'You are Darius?' Satyrus said. 'Leon speaks of you often!'

Darius embraced him. He wore scent, like most Persians, and his coat was made of a wool so soft that it was like rabbit fur. 'It is about Leon I have come,' he said.

Satyrus sat on a couch while Darius prowled the room, looking at the furnishings and cursing the worthlessness of slaves. 'Mine are no better.' Darius laughed. 'The moment I'm away from my home, nothing is done. The horses don't even foal when I leave.'

'You've been serving with Diodorus?' Satyrus asked.

Darius nodded. 'All summer. No great battles, Son of Kineas, but a great deal of scouting, patrolling and some routing out of bandits. We earned our keep. Babylon is secure, and now Seleucus is laying siege to one of Demetrios's forts in Syria. Diodorus finished his contract and left with Seleucus's full permission. Indeed, I believe our troops will be fed as far as Phrygia.'

'Where Antigonus is lord,' Satyrus smiled.

'Exactly. Where our troops may pillage as they please.' Darius was a Persian lord – he had no care for the sufferings of Phrygian peasants. 'He should be here in twenty days. If the weather holds as well as it has, perhaps half that. I have already waited three weeks here for you, and we set out together.'

Satyrus poured more wine. 'Sorry to keep you waiting,' he said.

Darius shook his head. 'No – nothing to be concerned at. I am here to try a rescue of Leon. It is my – hmm.– my speciality? To go unseen where other men do not go.'

Satyrus smiled at the richly dressed nobleman before him. 'Lord Darius, I can't imagine that you would go unnoticed anywhere.'

Darius laughed. 'You see what I want you to see, son of Kineas. But thank you for your flattery. I think.' He shook his head. 'No more wine for me. I gather that you were present when Philokles died?'

Satyrus told him the story. By the end, he had tears in his eyes and the Persian cried. 'He was the bravest of men,' Darius said. 'I honour him. Crax and Diodorus said to ask you of his end. Now – I do not want you to tell me *anything* of your plans. I may be taken. But I will ask this – where shall I meet you, if I recover Leon?'

Satyrus was pleased by the sheer confidence of the man. 'I mean to strike for Olbia,' he said.

'You know your sister is loose in the high ground north of Tanais,' Darius said.

'She moves fast,' Satyrus said. 'But sooner or later, we must fight for Olbia and Pantecapaeum.'

Darius shook his head. 'Eumenes – our Eumenes, the Olbian – he will have Olbia for you whenever you want it,' he said. 'He left us in the autumn to be archon.'

Satyrus had heard as much in Alexandria. 'So?'

'So – there's little need for you to go to Olbia. And if you were to appear off Pantecapaeum in, say, ten days?'

'Fifteen,' Satyrus said. 'I can't be ready before that. And I need marines from Diodorus.'

Darius nodded. 'So, say twenty-five days. I will be ready and then some.'

Satyrus raised an eyebrow. 'You are that confident?' he asked.

Darius had a curious facial tic – he could frown and smile at the same time, like a man who smelled something bad. 'I would never offend the gods with such a phrase,' he said. 'But I will say that Pantecapaeum, like all the Euxine cities, has a glut of Persian slaves. And I would assume that you would free any man that I said had aided me – true?'

'Of course,' Satyrus said.

Darius shrugged. 'Then the thing is as good as done. If you will appear off Pantecapaeum in twenty-five days from tomorrow, I will undertake to bring your uncle – my sworn brother – out to your fleet by late afternoon.'

'But ...' Satyrus shook his head. 'I want to know how.'

Darius got to his feet. 'We'll see.' He shrugged. 'To be honest, I don't know myself.'

It was four days before his fleet arrived, and Darius had already slipped away on an Olbia-bound freighter carrying copper from Cyprus and empty earthenware amphorae for the grain trade. Satyrus had seen him go – a nondescript figure, like a prosperous slave factor or a lower-class Asian merchant. His confidence in the man increased.

It was the next day that Bias reported forty sail in the roadstead, and by dark he had sixty-eight warships filling the harbour. Bias was ready, and he stationed the Rhodians and the Alexandrians at one end of the mole, and put the pirates at the other end, separated by a powerful squadron of Heraklean ships. Every one of Nestor's men was in the streets, and the first sign of pirate trouble was ruthlessly crushed, a message that was understood in every squadron.

In the morning, Satyrus met with all the captains in a warehouse – the only building that was big enough to keep them all out of the wind. There was no hearth, and the icy air got in through loose boards.

'My army will be here in ten days,' Satyrus said. 'And our presence here won't be a secret long. Demostrate – would you care to close the Bosporus to our enemy?'

'Poseidon's prick, lad. We had it closed from Byzantium!' the old pirate said.

'Rumour is that Eumeles has got a shipment of mercenaries and money coming from Athens,' Satyrus said.

'Now that's worth knowing,' Demostrate allowed. 'We'll find 'em.'

'Abraham, I'd like you to take our ships and Lysimachos's and visit the towns on the western shore – starting with Tomis. A day each – clear out any interlopers and do our part by our ally.'

Abraham might have wanted to sail with the pirates, but he didn't show it. 'At your service, Navarch,' he said.

Panther of Rhodos waited until the command conference was over. There was shouting and dickering and the pirates had to make a special treaty about the expected plunder from Athens before one of the captains would sail. Panther watched them with contempt. 'You kept us here,' he said.

'Your men won't make trouble in Heraklea,' Satyrus said.

Panther frowned. 'My men get bored just as quickly as a pirate crew,' he said.

'Ten days,' Satyrus returned.

*

Twelve days after Darius left, and no sign of Diodorus, even from the Heraklean scouts at the mountain passes. Abraham's squadrons returned in high sprits. They'd met a pair of Pantecapaean triremes and taken them in a very one-sided fight off Tomis.

'Calchus sends his regards,' Abraham said. 'I don't think he knew what to do with me, but he was courteous enough, once I said I was from Lysimachos. And he dotes on Theron.'

Theron smiled. 'I believe that I will retire to Tomis,' he said. 'I like it.'

They were still enjoying the triumph of clearing the west coast when Bias sent a slave to announce that Coenus had arrived. Satyrus had seldom spent a more uncomfortable half-hour than that one, waiting for news of his sister.

Coenus and Nihmu came in like lost relatives, escorted from the port by his friend Dionysius. Nihmu looked drained – her skin was grey and her hair lank. Coenus, on the other hand, looked like a man who had shed ten years of age. He fairly shone with health in the late-afternoon sun.

'Satyrus,' he said, taking his hands. 'Your sister sends her love.'

'She is well!' Satyrus said. He realized that he had been holding some part of his breath for an hour.

'She will not hold back from war. She has had some hard times. But she is well, and she misses you. And she has made herself queen of the Assagatje.'

'Marthax?'

'Dead at her hand.' Coenus shrugged. 'To tell it thus is to make him seem a blackguard. Marthax died like a king, and the manner of his death made sure she would be queen.'

Satyrus turned to his captains. He caught Neiron's eye, and Diokles'. 'No more archers on Eumeles' ships,' he said. Then, to his aunt and uncle, he said, 'Where is she now?'

Coenus shook his head. 'No idea. Listen – I see you have a fleet. Let me tell my news as quickly as I may.' He explained rapidly, and then explained again when Neiron provided a hastily drawn chart of the Euxine.

'When I left, Eumeles' general, Nikephoros, was in the Bay of Salmon. He was afraid you'd trap him there and end the war.'

'Poseidon's cock,' Diokles muttered, and many of the other captains, Rhodian, Greek and Alexandrian, muttered too.

'If Diodorus had been on time,' Satyrus said, 'the war would be over.'

Coenus laughed. 'Sometimes your age shows, lad. War is *all luck*. There's no use in whining about luck you didn't have. Stick with the luck you do have. Tyche has given you a fleet and your sister an army.'

'We need Diodorus,' Satyrus insisted. 'We need his men as marines. We can't face Eumeles' fleet without an edge.'

Coenus looked around. He knew most of Leon's captains, and his eyes settled on Aekes. 'And you, farmer? Do you need Diodorus's men?'

Aekes shrugged. 'Not for myself. But Satyrus has allies. We must wait for them. And they have no marines.'

'Pirates,' Panther spat.

Coenus looked around and laughed. 'You mean you have *more* ships?'

Two days of feverish planning and Demostrate sailed in with most of his ships. He was in a foul mood when he came ashore.

'I lost a pair of ships to one of Eumeles' hundred-handed spawn – gods, it was Dios's own fault, caught like a lubber in the fog. Where did Eumeles get these captains?' The old man drank off a cup of neat wine and threw it against the wall, where it smashed. 'But the worst of it is that the Athenian squadron got past us. Ten triremes and four troop ships, and all the cash.'

Satyrus felt the prickle of disaster – and suspicion. 'You had thirty ships!' he said, and regretted the words.

'Oh, if only you'd been there yourself, I'm sure you'd have done better!' Demostrate said. He stormed out of the door.

Coenus slipped away after him and brought him back. Demostrate's bad temper seemed dispelled by the Megaran, and they embraced warmly. Then the pirate admiral apologized.

'I'm a fool when angry, and no mistake,' he said. 'Coenus says your sister is up on the Tanais with an army,' he went on.

Satyrus nodded.

Demostrate looked around. 'Then we've got Eumeles,' he said.

Satyrus shook his head. 'We need Diodorus,' he said.

'Your sister is waiting for you,' Coenus reminded him.

Satyrus looked around. They were all there – his own captains, and Demostrate, and all the Rhodian officers. Nestor stood alone, representing Heraklea. Satyrus rose to his feet and they grew quiet.

'My sister isn't waiting,' he said. 'She has an army and she's on the move, skirmishing with the Sauromatae who are just as much my enemies as Eumeles and his ships. She can't wait for me. Her fort at the Tanais may be besieged by Eumeles at any time, for all that she left it provisioned and garrisoned.' He looked around. 'If we strike now, we show Eumeles our strength and he no longer has to guess. Without Diodorus, we are weak. Weaker than Eumeles. And if we lose at sea, we're finished – the whole war comes apart like scale armour when the cord breaks. Right?'

Even Coenus nodded.

'We wait,' Satyrus said.

Seventeen days after Darius sailed away, and a Rhodian officer killed one of Manes' oarsmen in a brawl on the waterfront. Manes led his men on a riot of destruction, killing a local man and two Rhodians and burning a warehouse.

Satyrus summoned the officers, but of the pirates, only Demostrate came.

Telereus, Lysimachos's navarch, began by suggesting that he'd had enough. 'This sitting in port accomplishes nothing,' he said. 'I will go to Tomis, and watch the coast.'

Panther shook his head. 'Any day now, if Satyrus is to be believed, we'll get our marines – and then we're off to find Eumeles.'

'This mercenary might never come. He could be forty days away. How long do we wait?' Telereus asked.

Satyrus held his temper. 'I ask you to wait five more days,' he said. 'In the meantime, I need your crews and my crews to share the duty of patrolling the wharves, and I'd like the navarchs to work out districts of the waterfront, so that I can confine the Rhodians and the pirates to their own neighbourhoods. Panther, I must inform you that Nestor, the tyrant's right hand, says that he must take your helmsman into custody.'

Panther shook his head. 'No,' he said. 'No man of mine goes to the axe for killing a pirate.'

'Let me be clear,' Satyrus said. 'You gave orders that this sort of thing be avoided. This man disobeyed you, and now you treat him as a hero?'

Panther pointed at Diokles. 'If Diokles there had done it, would you hand him over to this Nestor?'

Satyrus nodded. 'Yes,' he said.

'Not a helmsman,' Diokles offered. 'Lead oar, port side, on the *Lord of the Silver Bow*. And the other fool drew first.' He shrugged. 'And Manes killed two of theirs. He's the bugger that needs killing.'

Nestor pushed forward. Even among hard men like these, his size imposed. 'That is for me to decide,' he said. 'You are allies here, not conquerors. If your man is not given up, you are no longer welcome here.' Nestor didn't bluff, and he was looking at Satyrus. Satyrus knew that the killing was merely the last straw, after a week of theft, some armed robbery and scuffles in every market.

Satyrus spread his arms. 'Must I beg you, Panther? All my hopes come down to this. I sent them to sea to prevent this – but I cannot make Diodorus arrive on time. I know that your men and the pirates are oil and water. Help me here. I will offer private surety ...' He looked at Nestor to gauge his reaction. 'That the man will not be found guilty.'

Nestor offered the smallest fraction of a nod.

'Your word?' Panther asked.

And Satyrus knew he had kept the Rhodians. For a day or two. He turned to the pirate king. 'And you?'

Demostrate shrugged. 'Manes is his own law,' he said. 'He's worse every day. He wants to kill me – he certainly doesn't take my orders.'

And he commands five ships – ships that I need, Satyrus thought.

In private, he asked Nestor to ignore Manes. He sent his own marines to watch Manes, but the monster seemed glutted with his latest rampage, and sat in his ships. Satyrus paid restitution to the merchant whose warehouse burned and tried to think of a way to make this all better.

He tried to get the whole fleet to practise rowing, to practise the complex battle tactics that professional captains and crews used to win battles. The Rhodians were at sea every day, rowing up and down, and his own ships emulated them. But Demostrate laughed. 'We don't need any schoolbook tactics,' he said, and walked away, leaving Satyrus fuming.

According to rumour, Manes had farted when told of the orders.

Satyrus planned to dine that night with his own captains. He felt besieged – Amastris would not meet with him, and Dionysius the tyrant was daily less receptive to him as Diodorus failed to appear. Without marines, he had little chance of striking a firm blow, as his ships were outnumbered. Panther was too angry to be supportive, and Demostrate wouldn't meet his eyes. His fleet was divided and untrained. He wondered what Eumeles' fleet was doing. Drilling, no doubt.

Satyrus was in his room at what had been Kinon's, brooding, when there was a knock.

'Lord Satyrus?' Helios came in. 'Visitors, my lord.'

Out in the main room, Satyrus could hear the tone change – men were speaking happily.

He heard a man's voice, and then a woman's, and then he was there, embracing Crax and then Nihmu.

'By the gods!' he said.

In two hours he had the situation in his head, and when he was done drawing maps on the floor, he turned to them. Diokles and Abraham were on the floor with him, following the new campaign, and Theron lay above them on his couch. The other captains and some of his ship's officers ringed them.

'We'll have our marines in two days,' he said.

Coenus shook his head. 'Well done, Nihmu,' he said.

'I can still ride,' she said. 'Even if other things have left me.' She turned to Satyrus. 'As soon as we landed and Coenus told me, I rode for the hills. I took six horses and I rode them hard.' She motioned to Crax.

Crax gave his golden laugh. 'We've had the very Furies dogging us, Satyrus,' he said. 'Phrygia is full of soldiers. Half serve Demetrios and the other half are masterless men. Either way, they prey on each other.' He shrugged. 'There's no food and no maintenance for the roads. The peasants are gone or dead. The weather has been – brutal.' He looked around, acknowledging men he knew with a wave or a wink. 'But Lord Diodorus is over the mountains at Bithynia.'

'But Eumeles has his reinforcements and his money,' Satyrus said. 'We've missed one opportunity, or possibly two. I need to strike quickly.'

'Pshaw, lad,' Crax said. Then he smiled. 'You are no lad. Listen then. Diodorus is coming. And from what Coenus says, your sister is *fine*. She's every bit the soldier you are. She'll keep ten days – maybe more.'

'Darius won't keep,' Satyrus said. 'He expects me in seven days. I can't see being there.'

Nihmu raised her head. '*I* can be there in seven days,' she said. 'One barbarian woman – no one will notice me.'

Satyrus turned. 'How will you find Darius?' he asked.

Nihmu laughed. 'We are Pythagoreans,' she said. 'Even a barbarian like me. Trust me, Satyrus – I will find him.'

Satyrus sighed.

'I'll go back,' Coenus said, 'and find Melitta.' He glanced at Nihmu, and a long look passed between them. 'But first I'll have a word with Demostrate.'

That night, Satyrus dreamed that he was juggling eggs. One after another he dropped them – each containing a tiny man who died as his egg splattered on the cobbles of the street. At first the men were faceless, but then he watched Demostrate die, gasping for air like a fish, and Nihmu, her body broken. He woke to silence and lay awake for an hour, and then another. Eventually he rose and walked to the yard, where Coenus was putting his bed roll on a horse. He had another pair behind him. Satyrus recognized Darius's magnificent Nisaean charger.

'That's Darius's horse!' Satyrus said without thinking.

Coenus smiled. 'Darius is my brother,' Coenus said, 'as Leon is. As Philokles was and Diodorus. Surely you know that.'

Satyrus had never thought about it. In a heartbeat, he understood better what had been before his eyes all his life. 'You really do share,' he said.

Coenus ruffled his hair. 'Wish me luck,' he said. He vaulted into the saddle. 'Getting too old for this. Listen – my last military advice. Take your time. Force Eumeles to a battle on the sea if you can. But remember – it is the *sight* of your fleet that will aid your sister and crush Eumeles. Your sister will be pinched hard for the lack of you. Understand me? I'll go hard. If she's on the Hypanis, I'll find her in ten days – perhaps less.'

Satyrus nodded. 'I understand. And I know how you hate to give advice.'

'Bah, your sister's got me into the habit.' He used his knees to turn the Nisaean and made for the gate. 'Athena guide your guile, Satyrus.'

'And Hermes your travels,' Satyrus said. But the dream was still with him. And he shivered.

And in the morning, Nihmu was gone as well.

Twenty-three days after Darius sailed away, Diodorus's advance guard marched into Heraklea. Satyrus rode out to meet them, and he almost wept to see the men of his childhood – Sitalkes and the giant Carlus, the Keltoi, a handful of Olbians and dozens of men he knew by sight if not by name. Diodorus himself led the column in a plain breastplate, his copper and grey beard moving with his horse.

'You look like a king,' Diodorus said. He reached out and clasped Satyrus's arm. 'Sorry to be late, lad,' he added.

To Satyrus, his soldier uncle, the one who had always seemed the most vital, the most powerful, now seemed a husk of himself. He seemed smaller. He hunched his shoulders.

'Will of the gods,' Satyrus said. 'How much rest do your men need?'

Diodorus took a deep breath and exhaled slowly. 'The horses need a week of food and pasture. It's still winter in the hills. The infantrymen – they could march right up the gangplanks. Crax says you need our Macedonians for marines.' He waved at the infantry trudging along. They were four files wide on the road, two files of shield-bearers between two files of spearmen. The two officers at the head of the column looked familiar.

Satyrus touched his heels to his mount and trotted over to

the road. 'Amyntas! Draco!' he called, and the two mercenaries grinned at him.

'Thought you'd forgotten us,' Draco said.

'Although it didn't seem all that likely,' Amyntas said.

Satyrus slipped down and clasped their hands. 'I need your taxeis,' he said. 'I need them as soon as I can get them afloat. How much rest do you need?'

Amyntas stared at the sky and Draco laughed. 'I'd like to have a cup of wine and a fuck,' he said.

'He's old,' Amyntas said, as the soldiers behind Draco shouted their agreement. 'All I need is the fuck.'

'I'll take that as meaning you can sail tomorrow,' Satyrus said. He felt the weight of the world lifting away, to be replaced by a new feeling in his stomach.

He carried that feeling up the hill to the palace, where suddenly he was again welcome. Dionysius the tyrant received him like a peer, and he sat through a dinner on a couch at the man's right hand.

The tyrant mocked his former soldiers. Draco and Amyntas had left Heraklea years before as escorts and had never returned. Macedonian soldiers were too valuable to be allowed to wander about. 'Deserters!' he roared, and laughed to watch them flinch.

Satyrus watched Amastris. She looked everywhere but into his eyes until the meal was mostly gone, and then her gaze skipped over his – her eyes drew his to her maid-slave, who handed something to Helios.

She was a fine actress, his Amastris. She acted her indifference to him so well that he was coming to believe it, except for these notes.

'You'll sail tomorrow?' Dionysius asked, snapping him out of his reverie.

'With the favour of the gods,' Satyrus said piously.

'I'd swear you asked me for twenty days,' Dionysius said. 'And now you've been here twenty-five. You owe me, boy.'

Satyrus nodded. 'I do owe you, my lord,' he said. 'On the other hand, I have not stormed your city to pay my bills,' he added.

Dionysius laughed. 'Did I teach you to speak so?' he asked.

'Yes,' Satyrus said.

*

He swayed when he walked away from the symposium that followed the dinner, and Helios put a hand under his arm and helped him walk.

'What's Amastris say?' Satyrus asked. His head was swaying as if his ship was moving under his feet.

Helios stopped, propped him against an alley wall and reached in his script for a piece of papyrus. 'She asks if you intend to sail away without tasting her,' he said, his voice deadpan.

'Tasting?' Satyrus asked. 'Aphrodite – how does she expect me to get to her?'

Helios shook his head and held out the note. 'You read, lord,' he said.

Satyrus walked along the buildings until he came to a prosperous shop with a torch in a cresset. 'Aphrodite's long and golden back,' he muttered. *Do you truly intend to taste salt water before you taste me?* it said.

Helios stood still.

Alcohol swirled in Satyrus's head. 'I needed to see this before I drank so much,' he said. He looked up at the citadel above them, and he saw that a lamp burned on one of the balconies that hung over the sea. And that the rooms beyond the balcony were lit. He shook his head and there was anger at the bottom of his love. 'She treats me unfairly,' he said.

Helios nodded agreement.

'To Hades with her,' Satyrus said. He began to walk down the road, towards the house that had been Kinon's, and bed. Then he stopped and looked back. 'I love her, Helios,' he said.

'Yes, sir,' Helios agreed.

'What would you do?' Satyrus asked.

Helios shrugged.

'What if I command you to speak?' Satyrus said. He was mocking the boy. Picking on a freedman because he couldn't allow himself to be angry at his love.

'Then I will speak,' Helios said. His tone of voice suggested that he had something to say. 'Do you command me?'

'I command you,' Satyrus said, responding to the challenge in the boy's tone.

'Then I say that she demands you to visit to prove her power, not because her body wants yours. And I say that if you were caught, the tyrant would have you taken or killed. And that you are not a citizen of Alexandria, the city of love, but a king who goes to win his kingdom.' Helios shrugged. 'And if you need to lie in a woman's arms tonight, I can find you one who will not steal your kingdom.'

Satyrus stumbled. 'You don't like her!' he said.

Helios shrugged again. 'I am less than the sandals on her feet,' he said. 'My likes or dislikes are nothing to her.'

Satyrus looked up, and saw the light on the balcony. There was someone moving there, too.

'The fleet sails at dawn,' Helios said. 'You ordered it.'

Satyrus nodded. He turned away from the palace. 'To bed,' he said.

Dawn, and a warm breeze off the land carried the hint of rain. Diodorus, Crax and Sitalkes stood on the beach with a dozen other officers, telling off files of pikemen on to the pirate vessels and any other ship short of a full load of marines. The Rhodians were already in the water, and behind them, Satyrus's own ships were just getting their sterns off the beach.

Horse transports were loading the cavalry chargers – thin mounts who would die if too long at sea, and would need grain and rest when they landed. Satyrus was staking it all on this throw. He was out of time. He stood on the helmsman's bench of the *Golden Lotus* and looked aft. 'Good to have you aboard,' he said to Draco, who stood just behind him.

Draco laughed. 'Amyntas will be jealous that I have you all to myself,' he said.

'Theron needs him more than I do,' Satyrus said.

Stesagoras came up. 'Where do you see me stowing all these marines?' he asked. He was speaking to Neiron as helmsman and trierarch, but he pitched his complaint to carry to Satyrus.

Satyrus watched the panorama of his fleet forming for another few heartbeats and stepped back off the bench.

'Put the extra marines aft, with the helm,' he said. Twenty

marines to a ship was too many for fine fighting, but it would give them a decisive advantage in a boarding fight.

'We'll be low in the water,' Neiron said quietly.

'Poseidon has sent us a fine breeze and a beautiful day,' Satyrus answered. His eyes found Helios, standing by with a gilt-bronze shield.

'Give the signal!' he called.

Helios found the sun with the surface of the shield – a flash that could be seen for stades – and gave three long flashes.

Sixty-six warships. At least twenty fewer than his enemy had. And his decks were crammed with marines, which meant that he could not afford to be caught in a hit-and-run battle of seamanship.

Neiron had the helm. Up forward, Philaeus began to call the stroke.

'I'm impressed,' Draco said.

'You'd be more impressed if you were with Eumeles,' Satyrus said.

Draco grunted. 'No, lad. I'm impressed with *you*. But I'll bite – how many ships does he have?'

Neiron didn't take his eyes off the bow. 'Eighty-five. And perhaps more if the Athenian ships serve with him.'

Draco nodded. 'Aye, that's what the lads are saying.'

Satyrus was always impressed with the accuracy of soldiers' gossip. 'And what do they say our chances are?' he asked.

Draco laughed. 'Oh, the odds don't make no never mind, lad. Everyone knows you're Tyche's darling. Fortune's favourite, eh? Luck's better than numbers any day.'

Satyrus's stomach told a different tale. 'Luck can slip away,' he said.

Draco nodded, pursing his lips in approval. 'Aye. That it can, and no mistake.' He smiled. 'But anyone can see you still have yours.'

Satyrus had to admit that it was hard to remain worried when you could watch the four solid columns of triremes form up and sail away on a favourable breeze with stripped merchantmen as horse transports in between the columns.

Draco watched the coast and the citadel of Heraklea. 'But I'd swear we're going east,' he said.

'You may make a sailor yet.' Neiron grinned.

'Pantecapaeum is north!' Draco said.

'Too much of a risk. More than a thousand stades. With a wind like this, we might make it in a day – but more likely we'd spend the night at sea.' Neiron was the navarch's helmsman. He'd made the course.

Draco shrugged. 'So? We spend a night at sea.'

Satyrus cut in, 'Draco, a night at sea is no laughing matter. First, storms come up on the Euxine without any warning. A storm almost killed my father when he first came here, and we could get our fleet scattered in an hour – could lose half our ships. We only need to lose about ten and we've lost.'

Neiron nodded. 'Aye – and we can't cook at sea.'

Draco grinned. 'Of course. I'm a fool.'

'Most Macedonians are,' Neiron said, but his smile took the sting out. 'Tonight we'll be on the beach at Sinope. That's the end of any surprise we ever had – and the dog among the chickens, too. I'll wager a gold daric against a silver owl that every merchant in the port runs when they see us coming.'

Draco shrugged. 'So?'

Satyrus cut in again. 'Until we land at Sinope, we're fairly secret. Heraklea and Pantecapaeum aren't exactly friends. We don't think Eumeles knows how many ships we have, or their power.' He rolled his hand back and forth. 'Once we touch at Sinope, everyone knows what we have and we have to go for the jugular.'

'Sinope to the entrance to the Bay of Salmon is eight hundred stades,' Neiron said. 'One good day's sail. If the weather holds – we'll land by the Bay of Salmon, rest the night, and eat.'

'And the day after tomorrow, we'll row up towards Pantecapaeum with full bellies,' Satyrus said. His hands shook just saying the words.

Draco looked back and forth between them. 'Two days?' he asked.

'At the soonest,' Satyrus said.

Draco sat down on the helmsman's bench and started to un-buckle his thorax. 'I'll just catch a nap, then,' he said.

The sun was still high in the sky when they raised Sinope. Satyrus watched the sea-marks come up and then he turned to Helios. 'Get the shield,' he said.

Neiron was stretching his right leg. He'd wrestled two falls with Draco and done better than Satyrus had expected, and now the two men were talking while they stretched in the late-afternoon light. 'What do you have in mind, Navarch?' he called.

Satyrus walked to Stesagoras, who had the helm. 'I'm going to order battle formation,' he said.

Stesagoras nodded. 'Philaeus!' he called. 'Look alive! Get your brutes in their harness.'

There was the thunder of bare feet on smooth wood as the oarsmen, who had been enjoying a day of relative peace, sailing calmly along the south coast of the Euxine, were ordered to their stations.

'Signal "Man your benches".' Satyrus waved at Diokles, who had *Black Falcon* just astern.

Helios got up on the stern bench and took the cover off his shield. He flashed it.

Satyrus clambered up next to him. 'Gods, we need work,' he said. 'Send it again.'

Three more repetitions got the benches manned, although Satyrus assumed that most of the pirates had accomplished this by emulating the ships closest to them rather than by reading the signals. In addition, it became clear that some of the pirates were well out of formation.

Panther sent a long signal. The whole signals system was Rhodian, and Satyrus had enough trouble understanding a long signal to pity the captains who'd never seen such a thing.

Helios had no such issues. '"Better than I expected,"' he translated. 'Letter for letter,' he added.

'Signal "Form Bull",' Satyrus said, and Helios flashed the order.

It was just as well that Eumeles' fleet was not waiting in ambush off the coast of Sinope. The sun was well down in the west and it seemed possible that the rowers were going to miss their meals when Satyrus gave up, cancelled the order to form the Bull and sent the ships into the beach. Every merchant ship had long since fled, many of them heading north.

'The dog is among the chickens,' Neiron said when they had a fire lit and food in their bellies. 'The eagles have flown at the pigeons. Chaos is come again.' He laughed. 'That was the worst manoeuvre I've ever seen.'

'Wasn't totally wasted,' Satyrus said.

'How so, lord?' asked Panther, who had come up with his captains.

'None of the pirates chased the merchant ships,' Satyrus said.

Panther looked at him with new respect. 'Navarch, you have a point. What's for tomorrow?'

Satyrus raised his hand to forestall Neiron. 'Along the coast east, under oars,' he said.

Neiron shook his head. 'The weather's perfect,' he said. 'We can be off Pantecapaeum in two days.'

Demostrate was there, too. 'Yes, but should we? I'm with you, lad. Let's row along the coast and get the lard off their backs.'

Satyrus smiled. 'Next one of you who calls me lad will have the privilege of a little pankration, man to man.' He made himself grin. 'That display out there was so pitiful that I have to expect that Eumeles will hear about it in roughly twelve hours and make his adjustments accordingly.' He walked a few steps and turned. 'The playing-off of pirates and Rhodians is over now. You are all my captains, and I expect you to spend the next week learning the signal book and the tactics we'll use when we find Eumeles at sea.'

Demostrate shook his head. 'That's not for my boys, lad—' He stopped.

Satyrus walked over. 'Strip,' he said.

Demostrate narrowed his eyes. 'If I sail away, you have no fleet,' he said.

'I have no fleet anyway,' Satyrus said. 'Your precious pirates proved it just now, when they couldn't form a line of battle. Strip.'

Demostrate shook his head. 'I'll apologize,' he said softly. 'But if you make me fight, you'll have to kill me. *Lord.*'

Satyrus nodded curtly. 'Apologize then.'

Demostrate nodded. 'I apologize, lord,' he said. 'I'll not slip again.'

'Fuck him,' Manes said. 'Fuck him and fuck all this pansy shit. I say we kill the Rhodians and sack Sinope and stop playing at kings.'

Satyrus had been so busy plotting the rise of his kingship that he had all but forgotten Manes.

A foolish mistake. The sort of mistake that could cost you your kingdom.

Time to correct that right now. He took a deep breath, crossed the circle of officers as fast as the ripple of comments spread and stood in front of Manes.

'Get a sword and a shield. We fight. Now. And when you are dead, I claim all your ships and men as mine.' Satyrus was so angry he had no trouble meeting the bestial glare. 'You heard me – or are you the same chicken-shit who ducked fighting me in Byzantium?'

Manes bellowed.

Satyrus turned his back and walked towards Helios – watching his squire for a sign. Helios gave him his aspis and his sword. Satyrus fitted the shield snugly on his arm, gripped the *antilabe* in his left hand and drew his father's long kopis so that the blue blade glittered in the last sunlight. Then he turned.

'Ready?' he asked and began walking across the now silent circle of officers towards Manes.

Manes turned to Ganymede, who handed him his shield. His sword was immense – longer and broader than a Keltoi cavalry sword.

Crax stepped in front of Satyrus, with Carlus at his shoulder. 'Let one of us do this,' he said. 'Carlus could put him down in a heartbeat.'

Satyrus shook his head. 'This is for me, friend. I need the pirates to fight. I need them to drill and cooperate. When I kill him,' he pointed the tip of the kopis at Manes, 'they're mine.'

'And if you die?' Crax asked quietly.

'Then kill him, take the fleet and make Melitta queen of the Bosporus.'

Crax shook his head and stepped back.

Manes stepped out from the circle.

Satyrus lowered his shield and charged him.

Around him, he heard the crowd roar, but then all he heard was his own footsteps on the sand. Manes stood rooted to the spot for too long, clearly unable to believe that a smaller man was charging him.

Satyrus didn't hesitate. He ran right in and slammed his aspis against the face of Manes' shield even as the man bellowed like a bull, hoping to frighten him. Then Satyrus rolled to the right, using the centre of his shield against the rim of Manes' shield. He cut under with the kopis, and the long blade scored immediately on Manes' leg.

Satyrus stepped back, so that Manes' counter-blow swished through the air without even cutting his shield.

Satyrus saw that he'd cut the pirate chief deeply. He wanted to let him bleed and he backed a step. Manes took this for weakness, leaped forward and struck *fast*, landing two more blows on his shield. They were powerful blows that took chunks from the face of Satyrus's shield and hurt his arm, and Satyrus realized with a sudden prickle of fear that his arm couldn't take many more like that. He retreated and Manes advanced, bellowing, striking out again with the great sword like the claw of a giant lobster – *Slam! Slam!* – into the face of his shield, no effort at swordsmanship at all, just simple, overwhelming strength.

Satyrus struggled with his own fear of the man – a fear now reinforced by feeling his physical power.

He had to stop retreating.

Manes stumbled, a reminder that he, too, was hurt – that Satyrus had cut his leg. Satyrus shook his head and the giant blade slammed into the face of his shield again – *Bam! Bam!* – and he felt a scream of pain that shot up his arm and through his body, and he went *forward* into the pain, his arm barely able to support the shield slammed into Manes' chest. Satyrus was a hand's breadth shorter than the pirate, and his shield rush was a puny thing, except that his sword arm shot out in a long overhand cut – past Manes' blade raised in desperate parry – then rolled and *snapped*, so that the blade of the Aegyptian sword cut *back* into the base of Manes' skull. It was a perfect cut, and the unsharpened back edge of the kopis smashed into the heavy muscles at the base of the pirate's neck and his left arm dropped nerveless, his shield falling off his arm.

Manes roared with pain and stumbled back.

Satyrus had moments – only moments – before the tide of pain from his arm killed his ability to fight. He changed feet, lunging forward with his right leg and cutting down, so that his blade severed Manes' right hand at the wrist.

'ArrGGH!' the beast screamed, and suddenly they were down on the sand together, and Manes' blood was everywhere, and the man was kicking, hammering his mangled right arm and his un-injured left at Satyrus – his own wounded arm as loud in his head as the pirate's rage, even as his helmeted head was snapped back by a blow from the blunt end of Manes' maimed limb and his helmet filled with Manes' blood.

Satyrus had not fought pankration for eight years without learning to channel pain – and to grapple, even injured, even covered in blood and badly hurt. He dropped his sword, got his thighs locked on the other man's waist and rose over him, even as that right arm clubbed him again – but his helmet held the blow and he was on Manes like a rider on an unbroken stallion. Even a flailing blow into his arm didn't end his bid – his body was running through the winning moves of a domination hold without him, and he seemed to be watching from a distance as his thighs clamped the bleeding pirate's body, pinning him so that he could do less harm. Then Satyrus's swordless right hand slammed down, breaking his adversary's nose and slamming the broken bone into his head – and *still* Manes fought him, his spasming arms somehow inflicting pain.

Then Satyrus felt Philokles, the Spartan, take control of his hand in the forbidden strikes that the Spartans taught and that were forbidden in the games. His strong right hand reversed and he drove his thumb into Manes' left eye, the soft matter explod-ing outward.

Satyrus never quite lost consciousness. He rose shakily, with no sense of how much time might have passed since Manes' body ceased moving. His shield slipped off his right arm, which was bent at a bad angle, and rang as it hit a stone.

Theron was there. He put a hand on Satyrus's shoulder.

'I killed him three times,' Satyrus breathed.

Theron didn't answer. In a quick motion, he wrenched the arm – putting it back in its socket – and Satyrus was gone.

When he came to, he was on the sand.

'He's still dead,' Theron said, following Satyrus's eyes.

'Zeus Soter,' Satyrus said. 'I'll never fear a man that much again. I killed him three times.'

'Your men were watching,' Theron said. 'That was a fight they will long remember.'

'Get me up,' Satyrus said. 'And – get Manes' head.'

'His head?' Theron asked.

'I'll do it,' Abraham said. 'By all that is holy, sir, that was the most – amazing – fight.' His voice was hoarse.

Sir. Abraham called me sir. Satyrus wanted to laugh, but lacked the ability. 'Get me up,' he said.

He heard the meaty sound as Abraham's sword bit into Manes' neck, and he had to watch – worried, at some animal level, that the man would yet rise up and fight him.

He did not.

Satyrus got to his feet. He picked up his father's sword and cleaned it on Manes' tunic, wiping carefully. Then he took Manes' head from Abraham and held it by the perfumed hair as he raised his eyes and looked around the circle.

'Tomorrow, everyone will drill at sea. Manes' ships are mine. See to it that their crews are dispersed among my squadron. All of his officers who care to swear faith to me may do so. The others may walk home.' He had no trouble keeping his voice steady, although he was talking too fast. He had done it. In his head, he thought, *I wonder if I'll ever be afraid again?*

The circle was silent.

Satyrus bowed to Demostrate. 'I apologize for my poor temper. Tomorrow, as we row, your men will drill.'

Demostrate smiled. 'Very well.'

Behind Satyrus, he heard the sound of dozens of swords and knives slipping back into sheaths.

'Listen!' he shouted. He looked around. The wind – the

precious wind that blew straight for his target, that he was about to misuse – blew hard enough to make torches snap and hiss. He raised his voice. 'Listen! Eumeles has more ships, bigger ships, and he's had a winter to drill them. We have better marines and better captains – better men.'

That got a grumble of appreciation.

'Better men work harder. So we'll row for a few days to harden our muscles, and every officer can take his turn rowing. We'll practise the manoeuvres – we'll make the Bull, we'll form two lines, we'll practise diekplous until we can do it asleep. There won't be a second chance at this!' He wanted to yell at them, tell them what children they were, how they'd squandered their time at Heraklea instead of practising, listening to a fool like Manes when they could have a kingdom, but there was no point. None at all. 'Work now, and you'll find winning the battle *easy*. Easy means fewer dead. Or – squabble among yourselves, and die.'

He caught the eye of Manes' senior captain, standing behind Ganymede, who was weeping. The man flinched.

'Understand?' Satyrus asked. He looked around. He'd shocked them silent, and the silence had quite another quality. Satyrus dropped Manes' head in Ganymede's lap and dusted his hands together, the universal sign of a craftsman satisfied with his work. 'Excellent. We will row away at dawn. Watch for the shield.'

He turned and walked up the beach.

Four days of rowing along the coast and they had begun to resemble a fleet. He rowed all day, regardless of the wind, and the men were too tired to quarrel in the evening. He practised the formations even as they travelled, so that they often made less than thirty stades an hour, sometimes as little as six or seven. They emptied his store ships, one after another, all the way up the coast.

The day of his appointed meeting off Pantecapaeum came and went. There was nothing he could do about it. Until his fleet was ready to fight, there was no point in trying – none at all. At first he felt like blaming his officers for not telling him how bad they all were – but then it came to him that it was his failure. He was in command. They trusted him. The pirates expected to win by numbers and courage and luck. The Rhodians, Satyrus guessed, had never expected to win at all. They were here to see that the pirates didn't survive.

He rowed through a day of south wind and rain, and another that was cold enough to count as winter. Five days saw them off Phasis, where the fleet formed the Bull to his satisfaction in a time that was not too humiliating. The Bull was his favourite formation, because it allowed his elite vessels to form on the flanks where they could actually manoeuvre, while his heavier units and all the pirates formed the loins in the centre, two deep, where their heavier crews and boarding tactics stood the best chance of success.

They sailed north for an hour in the battle formation. That did not go so well.

Satyrus sighed, and they landed for the night. Helios got men together from every ship and went over the signals again. Panther stood and declaimed about diekplous to a circle of pirate captains and Diokles gave prizes to rowers nominated by their captains – prizes of a gold daric each, twenty days' pay.

Satyrus roamed among the fires, eating garlic sausage and listening to the men. Most were quite happy. He shook his head. Into the darkness, to Herakles, or perhaps to the shade of his father, he said, 'I have so much to learn.'

The night was silent.

Another day and they made Dioskurias, where he bought every head of cattle in the market and emptied the grain warehouses to feed his fleet – and laughed to hear that his sister was operating on the Hypanis River with an army. And Eumeles was at sea with his fleet, lying off Olbia.

An Olbian merchant told him that Eumeles had heard that the army of Olbia had marched, and had put all his troops on shipboard to seize the rival city while she was denuded of troops.

'Our Eumenes has marched on Pantecapaeum,' the man said. 'Eumeles is in for a rude awakening.'

'Two days,' Satyrus said. His heart was nearly bursting. His sister was still holding out, and his delays had not ruined them, and Eumeles was off Olbia. 'Two days, and we'll have him.'

But merchants are not always right. The next morning, Satyrus had been less than an hour at sea when his lookouts spotted the lead ships. After he'd heard twenty counted, Satyrus felt his fingers turn cold and his stomach began to flip.

Eumeles wasn't at Olbia. Eumeles and his fleet were right there, waiting at Gorgippia.

20

Melitta had saddle sores because her legs were always wet. Her body ached all day and she slept badly at night, and she wondered if she was really fit to lead the Sakje. None of her riders ever complained.

They rode south and west, across the rising ridges that would eventually be the Caucasus. In the valleys, they visited the farms, riding up in a swirl of horses and angry cattle. Closer in to Tanais, they were seldom the first Sakje party – often they found the farmstead deserted, or found the families on the road, their belongings on their backs.

But soon enough they were the first hint that the farmers had that their world was on fire. Melitta got to know the whole routine, the whole exhausting duty that brought her as close to cynicism as anything she'd encountered. The initial hostility, the slavish courtesy, the hidden anger, the acceptance, the obedience and exaggerated reverence for her person were all stages she saw enacted, day after day, as her party cleared the southern valleys ahead of Upazan's expected invasion.

By the time her saddle sores had festered into angry red weals with disgusting yellow-pus centres, she'd cleared the high ground as far east as her mother's writ had ever run in the south, and she was heading down the Hypanis from the east – a neat reversal of her winter trek the other way. Gaweint, her best outrider, brought her daily news from Ataelus, who was operating one valley farther north.

Melitta had begun to worry that she was costing her farmers a season of sowing and reaping for nothing. What if Upazan didn't come? What a fool she would look! And how her farmers would loathe her.

Being queen of the Assagatje had never been so unappealing. The more so as the old people called her 'Srayanka' to her face, never 'Melitta' or even 'Lady'. Sometimes she could overlook it – an old woman in a highland village near the headwaters of the Hypanis was nearly blind, and she touched Melitta's face and called her fellow-peasants to come and see the Lady Srayanka, back from the dead. But others were not so innocent. They simply wished her to be her mother. The power of their wishes was enough to make her conform, but inside she squirmed.

As she rode west, downstream on the Hypanis, her party began to collect other parties – a war band of Grass Cats, another of Standing Horses, each of whom had completed their sweep south.

The day after they met up with Buirtevaert, a young sub-chief of the Standing Horses who greeted her by her own name and raised her spirits, she found herself at the head of a long column of Sakje as she rode around the last bend in the road to Gardan's farm.

Outriders had warned Gardan, and he was mounted in his own farmyard with his family all on shaggy ponies behind him. He had a heavy wagon pulled by his oxen, and she could see his small forge and his anvil roped to the back of the wagon, right on the back axle. She rode up and he saluted like a Sakje.

'Lady – we are ready to ride.' He bowed and looked at her from under his brows, which were just as bushy as she had remembered. 'So you came back.'

She grinned. There was something about Gardan that was hard not to like. 'I did,' she said.

Buirtevaert rode up and waved his whip. 'You know this dirt man?' he asked in Sakje.

Gardan laughed. His Sakje was better than Melitta's. 'Greetings, sky-rider,' he said. 'I am guest-friends with the lady.'

Buirtevaert was not without courtesy, even after a spring spent herding dirt people. He saluted with his whip. 'And you are a smith – dirt man, I mean no insult. The lady's friends are mine. Is your family ready?'

'As you see us,' Gardan answered. He turned to Melitta. 'Do you remember what I told you? When I guested you?'

'"Be sure,"' Melitta answered. 'I've never forgotten it.'

'Be *fucking* sure,' Gardan said. 'We're going to lose a whole season, lady. People will *starve*.'

'You have your grain store?' Melitta asked.

Gardan shrugged. 'Every grain that I could get in the wagon.'

'And you destroyed the rest?' Melitta asked. She had not picked up the now-familiar smell of dry grain being burned.

Gardan's eyes flicked away. 'Hmm,' he said.

She rode closer, until they were eye to eye. 'Gardan – you ask me to be sure. This is war – I can't be *sure*. But I'm doing my best. And I know that my duty – my first duty – is to protect my farmers. But if you leave a store of grain in the ground for Upazan, you aren't helping me be *sure*. You think he won't find your grain, with dogs and horses and men?'

Gardan's wife, Methene, glared at her husband. 'I told you,' she said.

Gardan shrugged. 'People will starve,' he said. 'Twenty years I built this farm.' He had tears in his eyes. 'I'd rather fight for it than leave it to the wolves,' he said.

Melitta nodded. 'Where's the grain, Gardan?'

He hung his head. Accepting her authority. 'Buried in the old well. Come.'

She shook her head. 'No – go and burn it yourself. Hurry.' She didn't have to order him to hurry. As far as she knew, Upazan was still twenty days' ride to the east. But she had ten more farms to visit, or twenty – more families to send to join the river of refugees heading north and west to Tanais.

They left to the smell she had missed, the smell of burning grain. Gardan bowed his head to hide his tears. The children looked at her as if she was a goddess – inscrutable, good and evil all at once. Protector and oppressor. It was a great deal of meaning to be carried in a child's gaze, but she'd seen it so many times now that she didn't need their hushed, embarrassed words to confirm their stares.

Dawn, and she made herself roll from her blankets and furs. Spring was fully upon them, and the trees had leaves, but mornings were still cold, and the ground was no mattress, no soft couch. Her hips ached, and her back hurt, and her neck had developed its own special torment that lasted all day. She had to exercise her fingers to get them to behave. She sat by the fire her knights had made and drank two cups of hot liquid before she could face the ritual of lancing the sores on her thighs, dressing them with linen that had once been clean and relieving herself – all in private.

'I miss other girls,' she said to the morning. Her fingers were cold right through as she sat on a downed tree, but she stuck to her task, braiding her hair. She'd have liked help, but asking any of her knights was an invitation to mischief. Every one of them was in love with her, the useless bastards. She made a face. The only warrior woman for a hundred stades? The untouchable queen? Of course they loved her. Hence, she had no one to braid her hair.

Mother, how did you deal with the worship and the love and the foolishness? I need a trumpeter – a girl to be my companion. How do I go about finding one? Any girl she got would have lovers and favourites and clan-friends, all of whom would involve her in a new web of obligations. *Better to braid my own hair,* she thought.

She heard the hoof beats far off down the valley, even as her thoughts continued questing for an answer to the companionship problem. She looked north and east. There was the rider – a single figure moving fast.

She got up off her log, already annoyed that one of her bandages was slipping, angry at another day of facing the minor pain in her legs. *I used to love riding,* she thought. 'Scopasis!' she called.

He was standing in the middle of her knights. He had grown in stature so that the tall, handsome man before her, so sure of himself, so *genuinely* sure of himself, didn't even *look* the same as the outlaw boy she'd met four months ago. 'Lady?' he asked.

'Rider coming in,' she said. 'Any more tea?'

He handed her his own cup, full to the brim, and then he turned and looked at the distant stand of trees where their northern vedette sat on his horse. 'Scylax has him,' Scopasis said.

Melitta walked over to the Standing Horses' fire and nodded to Buirtevaert, who smiled. He had a long braid that he wore on the side of his face, wrapped in gold wire and braided with gold bells. The love-lock said that he was married. 'What's her name?' Melitta asked.

'Daen,' he said, his face breaking into a smile that raised her opinion of him still higher. *One day, may a man light up like that at the thought of me.* So far, Buirtevaert was a competent and obedient sub-chief, one of the few men his age not made foolish by her presence.

'I look forward to meeting her,' Melitta said.

'Porridge, lady?' he asked. The Standing Horses had a huge copper cauldron in which they made all their meals. This morning's grain had no doubt been put straight in over last night's deer-meat stew.

When I was in Alexandria I longed for the plains. Now I long for Alexandria. Where is my son? What kind of mother am I?

'You are sad,' Buirtevaert said. 'Do you have a man you miss?' He looked away, as if just asking such a thing was outside the bounds of courtesy. 'I am sorry, lady.'

'Do you know that I have a son?' Melitta asked. 'He'll be eight months old in a few days.' She shook her head. 'My man – is dead.'

Buirtevaert shook his head. 'I had heard that you were widowed,' he said. 'To be young and alone in spring ...' He shrugged. 'It is like all the songs ...' He trailed off, embarrassed. Most of those songs were about randy widows.

She had to smile at his confusion. Her position as lady seemed to have added twenty years to her age. Young people amused her. Perhaps she was becoming her mother.

'Lady!'

Melitta turned to see her knights mounting. Scopasis was pointing at the approaching rider. At this distance, Melitta knew her as Samahe.

'News!' Scopasis called. He trotted up with Melitta's riding horse, and she made herself mount. All her sores cracked open together, and she felt the blood and pus creep into the dirty linen – already cold where the outside air crept under her coat.

Samahe came up and hugged her. She returned the embrace with interest. 'I was just wishing for a girl,' she said. 'And here you are.'

Samahe smiled. 'You need a trumpeter,' she said laughing. 'Maybe a lover.'

'A girl?' Melitta asked. In Alexandria she knew lots of girls who lay with girls. The whole idea made her laugh. She slapped her thigh and cursed at the pain.

Samahe laughed too. But then she was serious. 'A girl in your bed means no talk and no babies,' she said. She shrugged. 'I've never done it myself.' She rolled her eyes, suggesting that perhaps she had. 'Listen – I am not here for bed-talk. Ataelus thinks Urvara's seen Upazan's advance scouts – yesterday, and far from here. North and east and east again.'

'How old is this news?' Melitta said, suddenly all business.

'Three, perhaps four days.' Samahe looked around. 'You have a fair force. Ataelus asks you to come north to him. If you come, you must come now and ride hard.'

Melitta gestured to Scopasis and to Buirtevaert to join her. 'We've cleared the valley to the ferry. Not much else to be done.' She looked at her commanders. 'Can we move back north and find Ataelus?'

'With Samahe to guide us?' Buirtevaert asked. 'Let's be on our way!'

Scopasis nodded. 'I long to put my sword against this Upazan's throat,' he said.

Melitta nodded, feeling the new crusts of the sores on her thighs. 'Me too,' she said.

Five days in the saddle – five nights with a warm companion who braided her hair and talked, sometimes, of things other than how many men she might kill, or how many horses such and such a man took in such and such a raid. Of babies and harmless gossip about who had whom in her blankets.

Samahe's greatest contribution was the salve she had for riding sores, and the discipline she brought to changes of clothes. Samahe travelled with two pairs of trousers and two coats, and every time they crossed a stream, she stopped, stripped and changed, drying the wet pair on the rump of her packhorse. Melitta learned that women *nomades* needed to take special care of themselves to avoid the sort of sores she had, and worse. She learned a great deal from travelling with Samahe, and the best of it was that Samahe taught her without comment or superiority.

They found two more of the war parties before they caught Ataelus, and when they found him, he too had been collecting the outriders, so that together they had a polyglot force from all the people of almost a thousand riders.

Melitta embraced Ataelus for almost as long as Samahe did, and before he could tell her his news, she called a council of all the leaders present, and they stood around a fire on the first warm evening while young men and women sketched their patrols in the soft black earth and bragged of their deeds. Thyrsis told his tale well, as usual, and his hair gleamed in the firelight, and Melitta thought he was the handsomest man among the Sakje. And she saw Tameax, who smiled and frowned when he saw her.

Two girls – Grass Cat girls, bent on mischief – had ridden to within sight of the old fort that Crax had once manned on the great inland sea that some called the Kaspian and others the Hyrkanian. There, on the good grass north of the fort, they had counted four thousand riders – or more.

'Counting so many riders is hard,' the eldest girl admitted. 'Always my father asks me to count the stars. Now I know why.'

A clump of boys came forward. They had seen Upazan and his golden helmet, they said. 'Breyat died,' one said. 'He was my friend. We saw them Sauromatae and they saw us, and we ran, and ran, over the grass, but Breyat's horse stumbled and he died.'

There were dozens of such reports and the more recent were the most detailed.

When the last scout, the last far-riding girl, had told her story, Ataelus rose. 'Upazan is coming into the high ground with his whole strength,' Ataelus said. 'Ten thousand warriors, more or less. Five times that number of horses. The grass is green, the ground is hard and now he comes.' Ataelus grinned. 'He is already too late. All the farmers are in the forts. All the grain is stored or burned.' Ataelus bowed to Melitta. 'You have already done well against him, lady. Without a saddle emptied, he must march into a desert.'

'A desert with green grass,' Melitta said.

Ataelus grinned, and it wasn't a pleasant sight. 'Green grass is good for a night or two, eh? But not if you have to sit in one place more than a day. Then the horses eat all the grass. Then you need grain.'

Buirtevaert nodded. 'And if we had ten days without rain,' he said, 'we could burn the grass.'

'Aye!' a dozen voices shouted.

'Aye!' Ataelus said. 'That would be the end of Upazan's campaign. Eight years ago, he gambled everything on catching us unprepared, and he succeeded. Upazan thinks that the Sakje are soft. He hears that we live in the valleys, that we winter in houses. He caught us sleeping by the fire in the year of the flood, and he thinks to do it again.' Ataelus nodded, as if to himself.

'This time, we have all the people on this side of the Borysthenes, and we are one people,' he said.

'We will have a great battle,' Scopasis said.

Thyrsis punched a fist in the air. He and Scopasis were suddenly friends – an unexpected development.

Melitta looked around. They were all so – male. 'I don't want a great battle,' she said. 'I want to bore Upazan to death. I want to worry him like a pack of wolves with a buck in winter. I want to chew on him like worms on a corpse.'

Ataelus grinned. 'That is your father's way!' he said. He turned to the others. 'Many of you are too young to have been at the Ford of the River God. Kineas and Marthax – they pulled in harness, those two, whatever happened afterwards.'

Melitta knew a good political speech when she heard one. Ataelus was wooing the Standing Horses by catering to their version of events.

'Together, they bled the Greeks, killing every straggler, taking their food, burning the grass. When we fought, their horses were like caribou in the last of winter.' Ataelus looked around, and every leader nodded with him. 'Melitta is right. No battle – or only a battle to finish the buck when the wolves have brought him down.'

Buirtevaert raised a hand, but Graethe, his chief, interrupted. 'Ataelus, none here will doubt you – or the lady. But it is only three hundred stades down the Tanais River to the fort. Not much distance to bleed the buck. Not like the great sea of grass.'

Ataelus scratched his chin. 'You are right. But once he is on the river valley and over the high ground where the last of the sea of grass rolls, every tree will hide one of Temerix's archers. The valley is full of our dirt people, and they have bows.'

Melitta rose to her feet. 'It is true. *If* Upazan comes down the Tanais – and I pray he does – then every stade will pull him deeper into our nets. You see a war of horses, because you are horsemen, but this will soon be a war of farmers, a war where a flight of arrows flies from a stand of trees – and what can the Sauromatae do? Ride in among the trees?'

'Temerix's boys would reap them like wheat!' Gaweint said.

'When do we start?' Scopasis asked.

'Now,' Melitta said, and Ataelus gave her a nod. 'Tonight. We will move tonight while we have the moon, and ambush them as they march in the morning.'

Melitta lay by Gryphon in the wet grass, cold, miserable and as nervous as she'd ever been, and worried that the enemy might actually hear the beating of her heart. And it wasn't her first ambush by a long shot. She remembered lying in a hole of her own scraping near Gaza – remembered waiting for the Sauromatae in the snow, just a few valleys away.

Gryphon's eyes were open, his ears pricked, intent. Off north, a bird circled.

Melitta rolled her head in a slow circle, feeling the pain as her head passed the same point – over and over. Then she flexed her fingers in the dead man's gloves, trying to warm them.

The wet grass had soaked through every layer she was wearing. *How did these people do this, again and again?* She wanted to raise her head, wanted to *do something*. She wondered if her bowstring was wet. She wondered if she looked foolish, lying in long wet grass with her household knights all around her. *I'll bet my mother never worried about looking foolish*, she thought.

She heard them a long way off. Curiously, the first thing she heard was the dogs barking among the wagons, and then she heard the jingle of harnesses – the Sauromatae were great ones for chain-bits and cheekpieces, both of which made noise.

This was Ataelus's battle. She was barely a commander – she'd given permission for it and then he'd done all the rest. It stood to reason – this was his ground, where he'd led his band for five years, where he knew every fold and every hill. And the site was magnificent – a gentle bowl with knife-sharp ridges rising high and clear, the last high grass before the trees started at the great bend of the Tanais. The trees provided them with somewhere to run, and the tiny folds of the hills, each a dozen horse-lengths from the next, allowed Ataelus to hide a thousand riders in ground that appeared to be as empty as a tabletop.

Ataelus's plan depended on enemy arrogance. He assumed that Upazan would have few outriders, and they would mainly be on the trade road – after all, this was ground that the Sakje hadn't contested against the Sauromatae in five years. And Ataelus had ordered that when they attacked, they should kill everything – *everything*. Every animal, every man. This, he said, was not just vengeance. It was the kind of blow they had to deal Upazan to win the war.

As Melitta listened to the sounds approaching, she wondered about Upazan – the man who had killed her father. Her mother had hated him, but never sworn vengeance. She had described him with contempt and yet some admiration. He was a skilled war leader, but a bad, greedy king, who ruled more by fear than by love.

While she had the image of her mother's stories of Upazan in her head, she saw a rider cross her own small ridge. He was no Upazan. He was – *she* was – a mere scout.

Not so arrogant. This one is far from the road and right in among us!

The girl was riding without seeing, letting her horse do the work as the beast picked its way down the slope towards Melitta's knights. Already, the horse was sniffing the air.

Melitta got her bow out of the gorytos by her side and thanked Artemis that she had lain on her right side. Gryphon twitched and the Sauromatae horse pricked its ears.

The girl was lost in a waking dream. *A lover? Can anything else cause you to lose yourself so completely?* She pitied the girl, even as she rose to her knees.

The girl turned, mouth open.

Scopasis's arrow hit her in the side and Melitta's in the open mouth, and she fell with a dull *thump*.

Her horse stood over her. After a long moment, it began to crop grass.

Melitta put another arrow on her string. She wasn't cold any more. She looked right and left. Her household knights were crouched by their horses, bows in their hands. Their damp armour glowed in the orange light.

She turned and looked back up the main ridge, trying to see Ataelus. He had woven himself a hide of grass, where he could sit on sheepskins with a whistle in his mouth. Melitta couldn't see him. She hoped he could see her.

The horse started to move and Scopasis *flowed* forward and caught it before it could climb the little ridge in front of her and alert the enemy. The dead girl's eyes were wide open. She'd fallen with her head against a small rock, and her blue eyes seemed to watch them with the idiot stare of death.

Melitta heard the hooves in front of her and a voice called out. Gryphon twitched again – responding, no doubt, to the Sauromatae voices.

Anything for a few more seconds. Were they close? Far? Had the ambush already failed?

Childhood came to her aid. 'Here I am!' Melitta called in soft Sauromatae. Scopasis flicked her a look – delight in her guile.

A young warrior came over the ridge that covered their front, his horse lunging forward as the boy leaned on his neck, showing off for his girl.

This time all of the household were ready, and he was dead before his horse could pull up. The horse itself took a dozen shafts and fell to its knees, then the animal gave a shrill scream – surprise and agony – and went down.

They froze, as if the horse's death had cast a spell. Again, Melitta tuned her head, looking for Ataelus, listening for his whistle, and there was nothing. Melitta prayed to the Huntress in her head, begging that the slaughter of children be over. Greeks had a horrible myth, where Apollo and his sister slaughtered the children of a woman who had dared to suggest that her children were as beautiful as Leto's. It was on a hundred pots, it was pictured in temples, woven into wall-hangings, engraved on armour – a horrible, horrible story.

Having just killed two children, Melitta loathed it more than ever. *Artemis, free me from this burden. Let my next foe be a man, or a woman grown.*

Somewhere below them, a bit made a metallic sound and a man gave an order.

How close are they? Melitta wondered.

Her heart pounded against her chest. She wondered how she had managed to be nervous earlier, when the enemy had been out of earshot. Now her hands trembled, and Gryphon kept stirring under her hands.

In front, she heard a woman's voice call out 'I can't find them!' in the tones of a mother.

Artemis! she shrieked in her mind. To kill the mother after the children!

A man's voice answered, saying they were 'up the hill' and there was some rough laughter, and then—

Ataelus's whistle.

She had Gryphon on his feet and she was in the saddle – no idea how she'd got there, reins in hand and bow. All the knights were up and they surged in one line to the top of their ridge and *there* was the whole of the Sauromatae host at her feet, a sea of horses on the sea of grass.

A row of wagons moved in front of her, pulled by oxen just like Sakje wagons.

Scopasis gave a shrill yell – *AIAIAIAIAIA!* – and all her knights took it up and they went down the ridge and began killing.

Melitta shot automatically, intent on clearing the wagons as Ataelus had suggested. She shot the drivers and then she rode in close and killed oxen with her long-handled axe. Scopasis kept her knights close, but they left a trail of corpses behind them, and this was *not* battle. The men Melitta shot had no weapons and some of the bodies were very small.

She closed her heart to it. This was life or death for the Sakje. *I am the queen of the Assagatje*, she said to herself, and shot down another young mother by a wagon. *I am Artemis, and you are not my people.*

They ripped through the wagons like a boat cutting through the sea, and to her left and right were the other bands, doing equal execution. Before the sun had risen the width of a finger, the Sauromatae had lost more wealth in people and animals than they could replace in ten years. The Sakje took nothing. They slaughtered. As Ataelus had ordered.

Beyond the chaos of the massacre, she could see the enemy rallying his warriors. They had not been among the wagons, but now they were coming.

Ataelus had ridden in a hundred fights, and his guile was a fathomless ocean compared to most men's. He had prepared ambushes to attack the rescuers, had placed them carefully, and now he released them, so that the first avenging brothers, husbands, sisters, turning to rescue their loved ones, riding blind with hate to the massacre, were caught in the flank and rear, riddled with arrows and driven into the blood-soaked earth to join their families.

Melitta had stopped killing. She allowed Gryphon to pick his way free of all the death, and she leaned from the saddle only to use her axe on a horse that screamed, over and over again, as it dragged its entrails across the ground.

Suddenly Ataelus was at her shoulder. She glared at him, for a moment hating this jolly small Sakje the way she'd never *hated* Upazan or even Eumeles.

He raised an eyebrow. 'Time to withdraw,' he said. That was all.

'We're winning!' she said, disgusted. Disgusted in a dozen different ways. Perfectly aware that Philokles would say that there was no real difference between this and her private war against the Sauromatae in the winter valleys. None at all.

Ataelus shrugged. 'Always leave an ambush while you are winning,' he said.

'I'll write that down, shall I?' she said.

She rode back among her knights, wishing *again* that she had a trumpeter. 'Withdraw!' she yelled, and Scopasis came up by her side.

'Here they come!' Gaweint roared, and shot his bow.

Angered, Melitta glanced at Scopasis. His axe was in his hand, red to his elbow, and with it he tried to parry a lance-point that appeared out of the fog of her anger and slammed into the side of her head, twisting her helmet.

Gryphon reared, punching with his hooves, and another blow rang on her back, and then she lashed out with her whip, the only weapon in her hand, and she felt it connect and then she was down, all the breath torn from her body, mouth full of bloody grass. She rolled over – blue sky – and her head rang with pain.

Above her towered a man in a golden helmet, his lance cocked up overarm, and he rammed it down into her gut. The scale coat held the point, even though the blow made her puke and choke, and she managed to roll on her right elbow and *pushed*, not a thought in her head, *pushed*, and she was on her knees. She had her akinakes in her hand and she plunged it into the horse's guts and entrails blew out over her face and the horse bounded away. She kept the blade in her hand and ripped the animal from girth to cock, and it stumbled two leaping steps and collapsed, its last effort tearing the weapon from her grasp.

The melee was all around her. She wiped her face, the bronze and silver scales of her hauberk ripping the ordure from her cheeks as she wrestled with her helmet. The chin strap was broken and the helmet was on sideways, which had saved her life from the last blow but now limited her vision too much. It came off and her braided hair fell free.

Golden-helmet was on his feet, limping, and he had a sword and an axe.

She threw her helmet at him – a last act of defiance. He was big, middle-aged, scarred under that magnificent helmet.

'Upazan,' she said. He was *much* easier to hate up close.

He hesitated on hearing his name. Then he *smiled*.

Hands grabbed her under her arms, heedless of the scales of her armour coat, and suddenly she was being borne away through the press. Her knights closed in around her, and then she was on Gryphon.

'Oh, my lady, I failed you,' Scopasis cried, and she thought his heart would burst before her, he looked so abject.

'You're an idiot,' she said, and touched his cheek. 'You saved my life. Twice. Ten times.' She looked around – Gaweint was there, and she didn't see anyone missing. 'I'm alive. You're all alive. That was Upazan.'

'Upazan!' Gaweint said, turning in the saddle. 'Uh! I am cursed! Upazan unhorsed, and we missed him?'

'Hush,' Agreint said. 'He cannot be killed by sword or spear. It is prophesied!'

A dozen young men competed to tell each other that they feared no prophecy.

'Well, he can't be killed by a thrown helmet,' Melitta said. 'I tried that.'

An hour later, Upazan tried to rush their retreat with a sudden charge across the last fields of the sea of grass. Instead of turning to fight, Ataelus's rearguard – Buirtevaert's men – made for the forest edge. Then a sudden shower of Sindi arrows fell like deadly hail on Upazan's knights, reaping their unarmoured horses. Ten went down in tumbling heaps and the charge swerved and became a flight.

Ataelus grinned like the very image of death, but he forbade any warrior from a counter-charge.

He turned to Melitta and Scopasis. They were the last three mounted warriors on the road. All around them, Temerix's Sindi were shooting from cover. Melitta could see Upazan in the setting sun, his helmet flaming gold – but he was falling back. He had only a thousand warriors – more joined him every second. He'd hoped to surprise Ataelus with a sudden charge, and instead, he'd been galled.

'We could have had him,' Scopasis spat.

Ataelus smiled and shook his head. 'Upazan is not for you,' he said without looking at the former outlaw. 'Many men, and not a few women, claim the right to kill him.' Ataelus watched the Sauromatae king retire with undisguised glee. He rode out on to the grass, and the last light of the sun turned his armour to fire.

'Hah! Upazan, I feel your hate from here, and I laugh at you!' Ataelus called. 'You fight like a fool! Your women have more sense!'

Arrows began to fall near Ataelus.

Upazan sat alone, out of range, his golden helmet like a beacon, and he said nothing.

'Or are all your women dead?' Ataelus yelled. 'Go home, usurper, or we will water the grass with your blood.'

A man – a man in good armour, well mounted – reacted. He set his horse to a gallop and rode at Ataelus, his voice a scream of rage. He had a long-handled axe over his head, and his face, as he came close, was a mask of grief and rage.

Temerix stepped out of the woods and shot him. It was a long shot, and a man less desperate would have seen the flight of the shaft.

'That makes me happy,' Temerix's grim voice said.

'This is not a war of revenge,' Melitta said.

Temerix looked up at her. 'Yes,' he said. 'Yes it is. Revenge. They burned us, and we will bury them. Anything else is foolishness.'

Ataelus rode his horse back under the trees. He shook his head. 'Not for revenge?' he asked. 'I heard that you swore an oath that made the hills ring. I heard it on the sea of grass. So it must have been quite an oath.'

Melitta hung her head. 'I did. So did my brother.'

'Lady, Upazan hunted us like animals. Our women and our children and our animals have been prey for his lance for many years.' Ataelus's eyes seemed to glow in the last light.

'We killed their *children*,' Melitta said.

'Yes!' Ataelus said. 'And now their hate will be a pure thing – a *blind* thing. Only blind with hate could Upazan be so foolish as to follow us down the Tanais.'

Melitta took time to sleep. And when the images of the day came back again and again, she rose, collected a wineskin and drank it. She was scarcely the only warrior to behave so, and soon enough, she was asleep.

PART IV

─────────────

TANAIS RIVER

21

NORTH EUXINE SEA

Eumeles looked out over the morning waves and spat contemplatively into the dark waters.

'Where did my little nemesis get so many ships?' he asked.

None of the officers on the stern chose to answer him. Idomenes took a deep breath and said what was on his mind.

'I warned you,' he said. *Go ahead and kill me, you Cretan*, Idomenes thought. *I said it. I feel better. I hate him*, Idomenes realized with a start.

'Yes,' Eumeles said, looking at the rows of masts on the horizon. 'Yes, you did. Why is he keeping his ships in column?'

Aulus, his admiral, bowed his head. 'He hides his strength. Until he deploys, we cannot count his ships. We're in formation – he can count ours.'

'Then why are we in formation?' Eumeles asked with the impatient tone of the superior mind who must do *all* the thinking.

Aulus kept his eyes on the deck. 'His rowers must be better trained, lord. I cannot trust mine to deploy so fast. You saw, lord.' The man was aggrieved. 'It took us an hour to form this line.'

Eumeles continued to watch the oncoming fleet. 'I suppose it is fruitless for me to ask where he got these ships with their trained oarsmen. Ptolemy must have given him the whole fleet of Aegypt. I have been used as bait.' He shook his head. 'Never mind. If I survive, I'll work this out. What can we do? Half our ships are inside the Bay of Salmon, covering Nikephoros. *Advise me.*'

The officers all looked at each other.

Idomenes was in the remarkable position of actually having an answer – and yet, in his head, he'd changed sides. *Murdering bastard wants to enslave his own farmers? Too dumb to live*, Idomenes thought, but at the same time, he spoke good advice. Perhaps he was so used to being ignored, he didn't think his advice would be followed. He thought that it was strange how his head could be so divided.

'Run,' Idomenes said.

The naval officers all breathed together – relief, because he had stated what they all feared to say.

Eumeles turned his head slowly, until his mad eyes rested on Idomenes. 'Go on,' he said.

'Run to Nikephoros, combine the fleet and fight with the beach and our new fort at your back. With Nikephoros's men aboard as marines, you'll have an advantage.' Idomenes was shocked at his own temerity, but he kept right on. 'You may lose Pantecapaeum – for a week or a month.'

Eumeles' pursed lips jerked as if he'd been struck. 'Pantecapaeum may already be lost,' he said. 'My not quite namesake and those treacherous curs from Olbia ...'

Idomenes shrugged. 'I doubt that the Olbians can take the city, lord. But I don't doubt that Nemesis can. Either way, when you combine your fleet, you can beat him. And then take it all back.'

It occurred to Idomenes that he *was* giving bad counsel. The people of Pantecapaeum loathed Eumeles. He would never recover the city once it was lost. Even if he won a naval victory, he'd become a species of pirate.

I could kill him, Idomenes thought, but he was not a killer.

'Foolishness,' said old Gaius, one of their Italiot mercenaries. 'Fight now. Once you run, his men will be heartened. Fights like this are all heart, lord. None of it is skill. The harpists lie. Once his men have a taste of our fear, we're done.'

And Idomenes could see that there was truth in that argument, too.

'Even now, my ally Upazan must be in the vale of the Tanais, reaping the peasants like wheat and sowing fear among the barbarians,' Eumeles said. 'We lose nothing by retreat. At the Tanais, I'll have our new fort at my back, beaches packed with our men and Upazan to counter any landing ashore.' He nodded at Idomenes. 'I recognize that I have not always followed your advice. In this I will, and perhaps in future I will be slower to ignore you.'

Idomenes couldn't hide the smile that crossed his face. And in his head, the god said, 'This is irony. And so hubris is punished.'

*

Satyrus watched his enemy's ships flee with something akin to despair.

At first, they'd rowed backwards, attempting to lure him into a bad deployment. But Satyrus had signalled the Bull, and his columns had deployed like the unfolding of a cloak, and that had destroyed any lingering thoughts of resistance. It occurred to Satyrus that he might have trained his men *too well*.

When it was clear that there would be no engagement, both sides raised sails and suddenly his squadron and the Rhodians had all the advantage – their masts stood all the time, and their rigging was up, so their sails went up like a cloud rising from the sea and suddenly the two flanks of his formation were shooting ahead, minus their borrowed Aegyptian ships and recent captures.

Neiron ignored his rantings and continued on his course without raising sail, because the *Golden Lotus* was alone in the centre of the great crescent and if he raised sail he would be alone in her pursuit.

'Don't be a tunny,' Neiron said. 'We've won. Let your boys play.'

Eumeles lost eight ships in an hour – slower triremes, or those that usually beached to raise a mast. The Rhodians and Leon's ships – all the triemioliai – swept in like hawks among pigeons and took what they wanted.

Satyrus wanted to be in the thick of the fighting, but he was not. And when night fell, his fleet beached, with his own squadron fully manned and sleeping on their oars out in the roadstead. Eumeles was an hour's row along the coast.

At Diokles' suggestion, they rose with the morning star, launched in the dark and rowed as if for a prize – but Eumeles had done the same. They caught a store ship, slow off the beach, and Melitta's friend Idomeneus boarded the ship and then swam from it to the *Lotus*. He reported aboard dripping wet.

'Full of wine,' he said cheerfully.

'Sink him,' Neiron said, even as some sailors began to cheer. 'Shut up, you lot.'

Satyrus looked at his helmsman. 'Sink him?'

'Probably poisoned,' Neiron said. 'An old trick. We stop and get drunk ...'

Idomeneus shook his head. 'And people think Cretans are evil?' he said.

They set fire to the wine ship and sailed on.

'He'll make his stand at the Cimmerian Bosporus,' Satyrus predicted.

'He'll run till he finds the rest of his fleet. Where do you think they are?' Diokles asked Panther.

Panther shrugged. 'I have to admit this is going better than I expected,' he said. 'But we're a long way from home, lad. That is, my lord. We need to get this over with.'

Satyrus looked at Diokles. 'Why not make a stand at the Bosporus?' he asked. 'It's so narrow where the sea runs into the Bay of Salmon that his ships will form two lines and still have a reserve.'

'And then we come with bigger, better crews and better marines, plough in bow to bow and eat him alive.' Diokles shook his head. 'We've got him, lord. And we'll get a little better every day. He's running – his rowers are afraid. And they don't try to keep formation as they run, so they're not practising anything but running.' Diokles poured wine on the sand. 'I speak no hubris. Unless the gods take a hand, he is ours.'

Satyrus shook his head. 'How I wish you hadn't said that,' he said.

The next day, Eumeles made no attempt to hold the straits that the Greeks called the Cimmerian Bosporus. And when the *Golden Lotus* appeared, leading the centre column, a swarm of small boats put off from the sandy beaches on either hand, local Maeotae fishermen at the helm.

'Let a few aboard,' Satyrus called out. 'But don't take the way off the ship. We're going on. I don't want to let Eumeles out of my sight!'

He heard the thump as a fishing boat came alongside, but he and Theron were stripped, wrestling falls in the deck area just in front of the helm, a sacrifice for Poseidon and Herakles of their strength and sweat. They were well matched – Theron's shoulders were still a finger broader, and Satyrus was now a touch faster – and every man off duty was gathered to watch, so that the *Lotus* was down a strake by the stern.

They were locked on the deck, grappling, when Satyrus became aware of the silence. And it was clear that they were getting nowhere.

'Break?' Satyrus grunted.

Theron slapped the deck and they both rolled to their feet.

'This is how you keep my flagship?' a familiar voice asked. 'Sporting events at sea?'

And then Satyrus had his uncle Leon locked in an embrace. Behind him, Nihmu looked ten years younger, and Darius had a certain glow of satisfaction. Satyrus embraced each in turn.

Darius wrinkled his nostrils at Satyrus's sweat. 'I've been a slave for a month, my dear,' he said. 'I only want to smell good things.'

Theron laughed. 'You are too fastidious, Persian!'

But Leon stepped in. 'I owe him my life – at least. By all the gods, Darius, I never thought it would be your face I saw! And you should see him with a sword!'

Nihmu nodded. 'Kineas always said he was the best,' she put in.

Satyrus picked up his discarded chiton and laughed. 'Now,' he said. 'Now I feel the favour of the gods.'

In truth, Leon was shockingly thin, and he looked old. His hair was grizzled white and grey, and his sheath of muscle had vanished. His arms were like sticks.

'You look like a young god,' Leon said.

Satyrus bowed at the compliment. 'It is so good to have you back among us, Uncle,' he said.

'I do not look like a young god, do I?' Leon shook his head. 'They didn't feed me for – some time. I wasn't tortured, but suddenly the treatment went from ransom captivity to something worse. Later I found out that Melitta had landed and raised the Sakje, and suddenly I was a liability.' He coughed into his hand.

Darius put a hand on the Numidian's shoulder. 'We got to you as soon as we could organize,' he said.

Satyrus shook his head. 'I feel guilt, Uncle. I left you at the battle, and then I left your rescue to others.'

Leon smiled. 'Lad, you lived, and I lived, and now ...' He

grinned, and some of the wrinkles fell from his face. 'And now, we'll have our revenge.'

The story of the rescue came out over two days – how Darius recruited Persian slaves inside the palace, then insinuated himself among them, armed a dozen, massacred the guards and opened the cells.

'I suspect that some truly bad men are now free,' Darius said. 'I can't really bring myself to care. But I do have half a dozen Persian gentlemen who have come with me, and would expect a reward.'

'Can they ride?' Satyrus asked.

'I did say they were Persians,' Darius said.

'I'll take them,' Diodorus said, coming out of the darkness with a wineskin over his shoulder. 'Leon, you bastard, you made a lot of work for us!'

Satyrus was one of them, but in a way, he was not. He sat with his knees drawn up to his chin, his back against Abraham's back, and he listened to them – Leon and Crax, Diodorus, Nihmu, Darius and all the men who had ridden with Kineas. He listened to them tell stories far into the night.

Abraham laughed. 'Is this what we'll become?'

Satyrus shook his head. 'Only if we're lucky,' he said.

'Listen to them brag!' Abraham shot back. 'They sound like pirates!'

Satyrus reached over and took the wine his friend was hoarding. 'Darius walked into Eumeles' palace and rescued Leon. Leon survived without food for a month. Nihmu found Darius disguised as a slave and then joined him. These people are larger than mere mortals, Abraham. They are like the men of former days, or so they have always seemed to me.'

Abraham grunted. 'Like Philokles, then,' he said.

Satyrus was silent for a while. 'Yes,' he said. 'They are all like Philokles.'

'Makes you wonder what your father was like,' Abraham said.

'Yes,' Satyrus said. 'Yes.'

'I think I have a pretty good idea,' Abraham said. He took a breath and got up. 'Where do you think your father found these demi-gods?'

Satyrus used his friend's hand to get to his feet. 'They find you,' he said.

In the morning, Diodorus asked to land the horses. 'The Exiles can ride from here,' he said. 'Our horses will be fat and happy in three days. But if we sail another day, we'll have nothing but rotting horse meat.'

All the Exiles nodded.

Satyrus shrugged. 'Can you get to Tanais?'

Diodorus scratched his head. 'I think I can puzzle it out,' he said.

Crax laughed aloud.

Diokles cut in. 'If we get under way immediately, we might yet catch him today. Wind's against us, now. Against Eumeles, too. So we row – and our rowers are better.'

'If we don't fight today, we'll raise Tanais tomorrow,' Satyrus said. 'I dislike dividing my forces.'

'Tomorrow, really?' Diodorus asked. He looked at Crax.

'Transports only slow us down,' Diokles observed. 'Leave 'em here and we'll double our chances of catching that bastard.'

'Try the Coracanda,' Leon said.

'That's it!' Satyrus said. 'I need – one of the fishermen. Darius? Are they gone?'

'Stayed for the wine. And the reward.' Darius was chewing bread, uncharacteristically human. 'I'll fetch them.'

The fishermen were delighted to receive a silver mina each for their part in the rescue.

'And the same again if you'll pilot us around the island and through the Coracanda.' He looked at them expectantly. Leon spoke to them in Maeotian, and they shrugged.

Phanagoreia island filled the north end of the strait. The main channel ran north and west, away from Tanais. Satyrus knew from childhood that there was a much narrower channel east around the island, a channel that ran all the way up to the mouth of the Hypanis. The enemy fleet knew these waters, too – or had pilots who would – but they'd taken the safe channel.

'What's the Coracanda?' Diokles asked.

The fishermen all shuffled their feet.

'It's an old channel through sandbanks. It runs east of the island and it'll cut hours off our time.' Satyrus was emphatic.

Diodorus nodded. 'It won't save you that much time,' he said, 'but it'll save us three hundred stades. We'll be at the Hypanis by tonight.' He'd marched and sailed here before.

The lead fisherman scratched his beard. 'She's shallow, lord. Many places no deeper than a man is high, or even a child. And if a ship touches, she never comes off.'

'Can you get us through? *Lotus* has the deepest draught.' Satyrus spoke to the fishermen, but he sent Helios for the Rhodians and the pirates.

The fishermen talked among themselves in their own tongue. By the time the leader spoke, Panther was there, and Demostrate.

Satyrus was amused to see the pirate king and the Rhodian approach together, laughing. And relieved.

He saluted both, and then the fisherman spoke. 'I can but try, lord. I can put a fisher-boat through the gullet in the dark. But these here monsters are another thing. I can't say. I don't think she's ever been done.'

Leon shook his head. 'I've done it,' he said softly, and the other men quieted for him, even Demostrate. Leon was a man who explored, who had walked and sailed everywhere he could go. 'I took a trireme up the gullet – ten years back. And again in the Olympic year.' He nodded to Satyrus. 'We can do it.'

Diokles made a face. 'Is it needful?'

Satyrus nodded. 'I need those horses. One day of bad weather and they'd be dead.'

Diokles looked at the sky and the sun, and was silent.

An hour later, the *Lotus* turned out of her column, heading east up a channel that seemed from a distance to be narrower than the hull of the ship. And behind them, all sixty-five ships sorted themselves into a single column with the horse transports in the lead, each one reinforced with oarsmen from the lighter ships.

Neiron shook his head. 'You put the heaviest draughts in front? They'll ground and plug the channel.'

'Then we push the horses over the side and float them,' Satyrus said. 'Leon is the greatest sailor I have ever known. Let him lead.'

Before the sun was a hand's breadth up in the sky, the line was threading its way through the channel. Satyrus looked back and there were ships as far as his eyes could see – a single line, like dancers at a festival, each ship copying the motions of the *Lotus* in the lead.

'This is – mad,' Neiron complained.

Satyrus felt the wind change on his cheek, a gentle breeze that ruffled his hair and breathed on their sterns.

'I don't believe it,' Neiron said.

The fisherman coughed in his hand and spat over the side for luck.

Helios came up behind his master. 'Why are they so happy?' he asked.

Satyrus grinned. 'The gods send us a wind,' he said, pouring a libation over the side. 'It is against our enemy, who must go north and west. And it is gentle, so that we can use it as we coast east.' He laughed. 'May it blow all day.'

Helios made a sign, and the fleet stood on.

22

Upazan followed them down the Tanais, and every step of his advance was contested, and men died.

Archers shot from woods and from barns. The woods were burned, the barns stormed. And men died.

By the river, in the fields, in the woods and on the high ridges, men fought – a slash of bronze or iron, a flight of arrows with deadly tips. The Sakje used poison, and the farmers never surrendered. There were skirmishes in every open space. Bands of Sakje harried bands of Sauromatae, who harried the refugees, killing the weak. Women died, and children.

Ravens feasted until they were glutted, and corpses lay on the roads and no animal mauled them, because there were so many.

This was not war the way Melitta had seen it in Aegypt. This was the war of all against all. The farmers fought to avoid annihilation, and the Sauromatae fought to exterminate them.

On the evening of the third day, Ataelus sat with Temerix and Melitta on a low hill, watching their exhausted rearguard retreat in a soft rain that favoured the enemy with every drop, rendering the strong bows of the Sakje almost useless.

Ataelus shrugged. 'We kill two or three of Upazan's for every farmer, and ten for every Sakje.'

'And yet we will run out of men first,' Temerix said.

Melitta looked back and forth between them. 'What are you telling me?' she asked.

Ataelus looked away, across the great river, where an eagle rose on an updraught. His face was blank, all the wild energy of the ambush drained from him by four days of heavy fighting and constant losses.

Temerix said, 'The men on the ships are killing us.'

Melitta nodded. She knew that the ships coming up the river to harry the farmers from the water had been an ugly surprise. Nikephoros had returned, just as Coenus had said, and established a fortified camp across the river from her fort on the bluff. Using it as a base, his men sailed up and down the river, disrupting her defences.

'If Upazan's men actually cooperated with the tyrant's soldiers, we would be the ones taking the losses,' Temerix said.

Ataelus sighed. 'It was a good plan,' he said, 'but it isn't working. Upazan is too strong – he must have had fifteen or even twenty thousand riders. And where are the other clans?' He sounded bitter.

'I don't know,' Melitta said.

'We must give up the valley,' Ataelus said. 'Send the farmers into the fort, and the Sakje ride away on to the sea of grass.'

Temerix shook his head. 'No, brother. You will not do that.'

Ataelus raised an eyebrow. In Sakje, he asked, 'Why not?'

Temerix met him, eye to eye. The two had been friends and war companions for twenty years and more. But this was conflict. 'If you ride away, you will not come back. And we will die. And I will not allow that.'

It was the longest speech Melitta had ever heard from Temerix. She met his eye. 'Listen, Temerix. My brother *is* coming. He *has* a fleet. I built that fort to buy time. If we ride away, we *will* come back.'

Temerix shook his head. 'When you undertook this war, you promised the farmers that you would win.' His eyes were accusing. 'We are not your pawns to stand in that fort ringed by enemies, while your precious Sakje ride the plains, free. If we lose this war, we will be dead, or *slaves.*'

Melitta drew herself up. 'Temerix, you are tired. We all are. Do not do this. We are close – we are *so* close.' She looked at the two of them. 'By the gods – we are not beaten. We are fighting a bloody delaying action, and we *knew* that it would be like this.'

Ataelus shook his head. 'Samahe says that there is talk. That some of Marthax's chieftains talk of riding away. When there is talk like that, it is best to move first, so that they feel that their grievances got to your ear – and yet you don't seem to have swayed in the wind but made your own way.' He shrugged. 'It is the Sakje way. Your mother knew it.'

Melitta was tired. She had shot a hundred arrows in four days, and twice she'd been sword to sword with an enemy. Her vision was odd, her bones weary, and when she pissed, there was blood and she didn't know why.

'Gather my chiefs,' Melitta said. 'Temerix, gather your principal men.'

'We will have a council?' Temerix asked.

'No,' Melitta said.

They made a huge fire, consuming an entire old oak tree in a few hours of warmth and light. The nights were warm now, but not so warm that men and women didn't value a fire nearby and a cup of warm cider or mulled wine. And the fire was big enough to burn hot even in the rain.

It was full dark – a time when exhausted fighters rolled in their damp furs and Greek blankets and tried to snatch a few hours of haunted sleep before rising in the first grey day to kill and be killed again. Fighters in total war do not come eagerly to council. Words are no longer the coin of decision, and all a warrior wants is wine to dull the aches and sleep. Oblivion.

Melitta knew this. She walked among them, taking the mood, and it was bad. And then she stood on a stump and called for silence.

There was a buzz as talk died.

'Silence!' she roared. Every head turned to her, and men flinched. She wished that she had had time to change out of her armour, which weighed on her like a skin of lead, or even to rebraid her hair, to appear as a queen instead of as a tousled mouse in scale mail.

She wished she had something heartening to say.

'My brother is coming,' she said. As soon as she said it, she knew that she had said the right thing, so she said it again. 'My brother is coming with fifty ships and three thousand men. Hardened fighters – my father's men. We must hold out until they arrive. If we surrender the valley of the Tanais, then all this was for nothing. Every man, every woman and child who died, sky people and dirt people – all for nothing.'

'We don't have any *arrows* left,' a voice called. One of Buirtevaert's leaders.

'Half my riders have wounds,' called another. Both Standing

350

Horses. Men who had followed Marthax against her mother.

Melitta struggled with anger, disappointment and fear. And won. Anger wouldn't sway them. They could answer anger with anger. But a little derision ... 'I have wounds on half my body,' Melitta answered, her voice strong. 'I piss blood. You, boy? Do you piss blood?'

'I'm no boy!' the young man called, but the other warriors grunted, and a few laughed.

Buirtevaert was close to her. 'I have pissed blood,' he said. 'It passes.' He nodded. 'My clan is hurt, lady. I have taken deaths. I have lost horses.'

Melitta looked at him. 'Hurts heal,' she said. 'Until we take our death blow, we heal.'

'That's what they fear,' Scopasis said behind her. His voice was quiet – advising, not deriding. 'They fear that this is the last stand of the Sakje.'

She raised her voice, and it was firm. 'When we have defeated Upazan, we will grow our strength back. We will not waste the peace that we must buy in blood. But we must complete the job. Another week. Another few days, and my brother will come.'

'What if he does not come?' Buirtevaert asked. He looked apologetic. 'I must ask, lady. All here follow you willingly, but we lead clans and we are the men – and women – who must keep our people alive.'

Temerix pushed forward. He was big, bigger than most Sakje, and his black beard shot with grey shone in the firelight. 'Then we die. All of us die together. Earth people and sky people. If Satyrus does not come, we are dead.'

'Fuck that,' called a voice from the darkness.

'But he will come,' Melitta said.

'If only we knew that,' Ataelus muttered.

'Where are the other clans?' the catcalling voice asked. 'Where are the Grass Cats? Where are the Stalking Crows or the Silent Wolves? Where is the strength of the Cruel Hands? Why are we fighting this war alone?'

Melitta took a deep breath to steady her voice. 'Why don't you come into the firelight and talk?' She looked for the voice. 'It's very safe out there in the dark, I suppose.'

Graethe, the chief of the Standing Horse, came into the fire-light. 'I had a spot I liked, lady. I have no need to hide. I ask the questions every Sakje asks. And I'll add another – why should we die for the dirt people?'

Temerix grunted.

Ataelus put a hand on his shoulder, and Graethe smiled. He turned to the crowd. 'The farmers cannot defend themselves, and we are too few to defend them. It is time to end this foolish war – a war Marthax was too wise to undertake – and ride away, as our fathers did from the Medes and Persians. Why are we fighting this war alone? Is it perhaps because—?' Graethe smiled like a fox, but he was interrupted by a voice from beyond the fire.

'You are not alone,' the voice said. 'Urvara is three days' march away, with Eumenes of Olbia and five thousand men.'

'Who are you?' Graethe asked, but the voice went on.

'You are not alone, because the war fleet of Satyrus has sailed, and Nikephoros is about to be trapped on the beach.' Coenus emerged into the light, and he bowed to Melitta as soon as he entered the firelight. 'I rode as hard as I could, and none too fast, I see.'

Men crowded around him, and he embraced Ataelus and then Temerix, and then Scopasis.

'Your brother sent me. He should be right behind me. When I set off, he was only awaiting the arrival of Diodorus to sail with sixty ships.' He smiled. 'And Eumenes is north of the Bay of Salmon and marching hard. He's gathered the western clans and he has all the infantry of Olbia.'

Melitta could tell that Coenus was unsure, or lying, but only because she'd known him all her life. And all the clan leaders were gathered around him, pressing close, as if his news brought them physical strength.

Ataelus turned to her. 'Now they will fight,' he said. He watched for a while. 'But not for long.'

Melitta shrugged.

Much later, when all of them had shared wine, and many of the Sakje had shared smoke, and they had fallen into their blankets, Melitta pulled a fur over her shoulders, cold even in high summer, and caught Coenus's eye where he lingered by the fire. The two of them walked away from the fire and into the darkness. Scopasis made as if to follow, and she gave him a small sign and he went back to Samahe, where the two of them had been playing a game of polis on a blanket.

'You were lying,' she said, as soon as they were alone.

Coenus shrugged. 'Not lying, exactly.'

'You are Greek. Greeks lie. Coenus, this is life and death for these people.' Melitta shook her head. 'Tell me the whole truth.'

'Your brother is waiting for Diodorus, who is late. Very late. He has troubles with his captains, and trouble with Heraklea. It's not pretty. But when I left, Nihmu and Crax had just ridden in from Diodorus. He should have sailed the day after I rode out – two days at the most.' Coenus shrugged. 'That's not much of a lie.'

'But you didn't see him sail,' Melitta said.

'I *saw* Urvara at the fort, and she said Eumenes was three days away and marching. And that was this morning. And she has three thousand horses and almost as many Sindi and Maeotae in the fort. Damn it, girl! In ten days, we'll *outnumber* everything Eumeles and Nikephoros and Upazan can muster.' Coenus grabbed her shoulders.

Melitta pushed him away. 'Don't you get it? I'm risking people – real people – and they're dying like houseflies at the end of summer. Why didn't Urvara send those riders to me?'

'Urvara is containing Nikephoros. Without her raids, his men would be all over the river, instead of just sending a boat or two to harass the farmers. Even outnumbered two to one, Urvara is keeping him busy.' Coenus put his hands on his hips. 'Keep it together, girl. The tide is turning.'

'I am not *girl*. I am the lady.' She shook her head. 'By all the gods, Coenus, I am staking my people on Eumenes of Olbia and on my brother's fleet. If they are late, we're dead. We don't have ten days. We have two days. In two days, we'll be pushed back right into the fort, and then Upazan and Nikephoros join hands, and exterminate us.'

Coenus rubbed his beard. 'Well, lady – and I concede, you are lady, even to me – then we fight for two days with everything we have. And trust to the gods.'

Melitta laughed. 'That's where I was, just a few hours ago. Now, all I see is the end. Perhaps Satyrus will come and destroy Eumeles after I am dead.' She laughed, and it was a harsh sound. 'Is this all there is, Coenus?'

'I spurned command all my life, lady,' he said, 'because as far as I could see with my friend Kineas, that is all there is – one damned decision after another, and watching friends die, whether you made the right call or not. That's how it has always looked to me.'

'I don't think I want to be queen of the Sakje,' Melitta said.

'Too late now,' Coenus answered.

Melitta left him then, her heart empty, unsure even of how much truth Coenus – her beloved uncle, the father of her first lover – was telling her. She walked away into the darkness, past the horse lines, watching the tail of the moon for a while. She wept a little.

'Lady?' Scopasis asked. He came out of the dark with a blanket. 'You are troubled.'

'Fuck off,' Melitta said savagely.

Scopasis, the former outlaw, stood his ground. 'Take the blanket,' he said.

'I don't need your help,' she said. Mostly to herself.

He held the blanket out mutely.

She found herself inside the blanket, her arms around his chest, weeping, and he held her for a long time as she felt his warmth and comfort.

'When I was outlawed,' he said, 'my anger kept me warm for a while, and then I was cold and alone.'

She couldn't see him, with her cheek pressed against the warm wool of his coat. She waited for him to say more, but he didn't, and they were silent.

Finally he said, 'I told all the people who tried to help me to fuck themselves,' and laughed. Melitta wasn't sure that she'd ever heard Scopasis laugh.

'This makes you want to help people?' she asked.

'It makes me immune to people I love telling me to fuck off,' he said.

*

354

In the morning, Melitta was relacing her armour while Samahe did her hair. Scopasis didn't seem to see her – he moved about, getting horses and preparing the bodyguard for another day of combat. They had thirty riders now, and Coenus joined them in full armour.

Scopasis saluted. 'You are back, lord.'

Coenus nodded. 'As a trooper, Scopasis. You are the captain now. Half these men barely know me, and frankly, if I have to tell Darax one more time how to do up his girth, I'll kill him.' Coenus grinned. 'You're the captain, lad. I'll cover the lady and give her advice. You run the troop.'

Scopasis gave the Greek man a hug. 'You are like my second father.'

Coenus didn't deny it.

After that exchange, Melitta managed to corner Scopasis while he rolled his blankets. 'About last night,' she said, the best opening she could manage after an hour of furious thinking.

He looked at her, puzzled. 'Last night?' he asked.

'I was—' Melitta wanted to be clear about how much she valued the comfort he had offered, but that she was still his queen.

'Darax!' Scopasis called past her. 'Look at the girth on that saddlecloth. You are no use to the lady dangling under your horse! Get your arse over here and see to it. Now!' His level gaze came back to hers. 'I have no memory of last night, lady. Please do not embarrass me.'

She met that gaze. 'I'm surrounded by liars.'

He shrugged. 'Hmm,' he grunted. 'No man likes to be called a liar.'

Coenus appeared at her elbow, making her flush. 'If we lie to you, perhaps it's for good reasons.' He looked at the sky. 'Dry day.'

Ataelus came up, eyeing a new arrow, the fletches just dry. Melitta could smell the fish-glue. 'A day for shooting,' he said.

Their first contact came almost immediately. Upazan's advance guard came down the valley with the sun, flooding the farm fields on either side of the road. Temerix's men had been up for hours, and they stayed on the ridges north of the river, showering the Sauromatae flanking parties with arrows and retreating beyond their reach. Today the Sauromatae seemed content to ignore the galling of their flanks. They pressed straight down the river, and the ground was dark with riders all the way back to the purple hills to the east.

'Where did he get so many riders?' Ataelus asked again.

And then they were fighting.

It was a swirling fight, where a warrior who slowed down to a trot was already dead. Today, the Sakje bowstrings were dry and the gut in the belly of their bows was flexible and hard, and their arrows lashed out from half a stade, pricking armoured men and slaying horses.

Graethe surprised them all by leading the whole of his clan in an attack. The Sauromatae were spread wide, but their advance guard was thin and the main body was ten stades back. Graethe shot three thick volleys of arrows from the high ground on their left and then charged with five hundred warriors, pushing the Sauromatae down into the road.

Ataelus watched him with a disapproving frown. But Coenus slapped his thigh. 'He may be a big blowhard, but he's our blow-hard. Look – he's lost honour, and he's buying it back.' Coenus looked at Melitta. 'If it were me, I'd push right up the road now, and blow their advance guard back on their main body.'

Ataelus shook his head. 'We lose a hundred riders.'

Coenus pulled his horse in. 'Look, I *get it*. These are not professional soldiers and I am not throwing them away. But if we charge now, we can *wreck* Upazan for today. We won't have to fight again until tomorrow. A day gained, and not an inch of ground lost. And then – listen! And then we get up in the dark and ride away, breaking contact, and make him face blank country and a new ambush.'

Melitta raised her whip. 'So we fought for the first three days, Coenus. Upazan ignores the damage and comes forward. He never hesitates. If we crush his advance guard, he'll *attack*.'

Ataelus pursed his lips. 'Do it,' he said. He waved at his own clansmen, and the wolf-tails waved.

'Why?' Melitta asked.

'Because your brother is coming, and we are here to bleed Upazan,' Ataelus said.

They charged down the road and her well-armoured knights led the way. The Sauromatae didn't make a stand until they had to, which was by a burned-out farm where the road pinched down by the riverbank. The crowd of routed Sauromatae couldn't get through the gap, and the Sakje slaughtered them, killing a hundred in a minute.

Melitta shot three arrows. Her knights kept between her and the panicked men, and she was glad.

Upazan's counter-attack was slow in coming, and the attack itself was hesitant. The first wave of riders were well armoured, some even having horse armour, but they weren't immune to the powerful Sakje bows. The wave failed before a single lance made contact, and the attackers were harried again as they retired.

As Upazan prepared his second attack, the Sakje melted away, conceding the ten stades of ground they had just won, and providing him with no target for his carefully assembled main attack. The sun was high as the Sauromatae came forward, big squadrons of heavily armoured men who were immediately galled by arrows from the Sindi, who couldn't miss, shooting into the packed squadrons.

But today they only shot once or twice, and then they ran back into their cover. And Upazan's squadrons seemed unwilling or unable to follow. They were tentative in their approaches, bunching up on the road.

In mid-afternoon, Ataelus led all of his clan forward in a raid, and they rode right across the line of the Sauromatae advance on fresh horses with full quivers, and the Sauromatae died. Not a rider pursued them as they rode by at a gallop, sometimes less than a horse-length from their enemies.

Melitta watched as a flight of Sauromatae arrows landed short, just a single Sakje falling to lie in the untended wheat. There was no way the Sakje could save the body – a horde of vengeful Sauromatae fell on the downed rider and hacked it to bloody ruin.

But the loss of that one rider seemed to take the life out of Ataelus's raid, and they did little damage thereafter, although it became clear that the exhaustion was mutual. The Sauromatae army rolled to a stop well short of the Sakje camp, in a good position with abundant water, and they began to make camp before the sun was well down in the sky.

Then Temerix led the farmers down from the hills, pouring arrows into the camp.

Ataelus returned while the farmers shot their revenge into the invaders. His head was down.

Coenus took his arm. 'You reaped them! By Ares, Ataelus – they can't take another day!'

Ataelus raised his eyes, and they were dull, as if his soul was gone from his body. 'Samahe is dead,' he said.

23

Satyrus cursed every hour that it took them to unload the horses of the Exiles, but he could see the condition of the animals as they were pushed into the sea and swam weakly ashore, and he knew that Diodorus was right.

Leon watched his Numidian mare, fetched all this way by Diodorus, make a splash as she hit the water. Leon already looked better, although Satyrus doubted he would ever carry the weight of muscle he'd had a year before. He stood with Diodorus, wearing only a simple white chiton and a bronze circlet.

'I'm going with the hippeis,' Leon said. He grinned and put his arms around his nephew. 'You're all but through the channels.'

'It's your fleet, Uncle,' Satyrus said. 'I stand on your command deck, and I speak with your voice.'

Leon smiled and shook his head. 'No, lad. This is *your* fleet. This is your hour. Go and finish Eumeles, for all of us. As for me, I want a horse between my knees when I meet Upazan.'

Satyrus remembered then that Leon had sworn something about Upazan's death. So he embraced his uncle. 'May Poseidon of the ships and horses go with you,' he said.

Leon glanced around. 'Be careful of my ships,' he said, and grinned. 'The gods are with you, lad. Go and finish Eumeles!'

'That useless bastard,' Diodorus growled. 'To think that we have to do all this work to put him down in the sand, eh?' He embraced Satyrus. 'We'll be there in two days – maybe three. Don't fight a battle without us. And one piece of advice, eh? You need to be on the south bank of the Tanais. If you fight on the north bank, we won't get across.'

Satyrus nodded. 'As you say, Uncle. But I must tell you – if I get the sea battle I want, there won't be a land battle.'

Several of Satyrus's officers grinned, and Diokles smacked his fist into his palm.

Diodorus shook his head. 'You don't know Upazan, lad. We'll have a fight yet.'

As soon as his ships could get clear of the transports, they stood on. Nonetheless, clearing the mouth of the Hypanis River took two hours, and then he had to negotiate the last of the channels and mudflats north of the mouth of the Hypanis. Twice the *Lotus* touched bottom, knocking men down and making his heart race with fear. Behind them in the long column, *Hyacinth* struck hard on a bank, but Aekes got him off before the column had passed him.

When the *Lotus* cleared the last sandbar and the long bay of the Hypanis opened to the sea, Satyrus could still see the transports riding high and empty down the bay, and the dark masses of the Exiles marching inland.

Satyrus couldn't wait another minute to know where he stood. He stripped his chiton over his head and climbed the mainmast. He hung from the yard while he watched the waters to the north and west, and saw Eumeles' fleet well out, heading east.

'Neck and neck,' he shouted to Diokles after he slid down the mast, recklessly scraping his arms and thighs.

Diokles leaned over the rail of his ship. 'Hope Eumeles doesn't come after us now!'

Satyrus was aware that his whole command was strung out in a long file that went back for ten stades of channels and turns, while Eumeles seemed to have his whole force on the horizon. He was tempted to make a derisive comment, but that would be hubris. 'With the gods!' he shouted back piously.

They landed just one headland north of the stone pillar that marked the bay of the Hypanis. Satyrus posted sentries on every headland and a guard squadron – his recently acquired pirates, all of Manes' former ships – because now he feared surprise more than anything else.

He drank wine with his captains and then sent Diokles to check on the former pirates who were rowing sullenly back and forth across the beach.

'I don't want this ruined by a foolish mutiny,' he said, and every officer on the beach nodded.

Draco caught his arm. 'Send us,' he said.

Amyntas nodded. 'Send us. Diokles can row us out. Those are

our boys out there as marines. Put me on one ship and Draco on another. I *guarantee* no surprises.' He took a knife out from under his armpit and ran his thumb over the edge.

When the two Macedonians were gone, Satyrus drank his wine with more satisfaction.

'Tomorrow,' Panther said.

'I think so,' Satyrus said. 'I don't *think* Eumeles knows how close we are. Or that we've shed the horse transports. So he'll straggle.'

Theron and Demostrate were playing knuckle bones together. Demostrate got up and stretched. 'You have all my money, you black Corinthian thief, and now I need a battle to restore my fortunes. King of the pirates? I'm king of the paupers.' He glanced at the sky. 'Good day tomorrow. Sunny. Light winds.'

'So?' Neiron asked.

'Muster when the morning star rises,' Satyrus said, watching Panther to see if his orders were well received. 'Put to sea at first light and form up by columns off the beach.'

Panther nodded.

Theron lay back on the sand. 'What if Eumeles refuses to play?' he asked. 'I mean, see it through his eyes. He's running for his other squadron, isn't he? So why won't he just keep running?'

Panther looked at Satyrus. Satyrus shook his head. 'Our ships are faster, now that we're rid of the transports,' he said. 'Remember last time? Our fastest laid waste to his slowest, and we were losing light. Tomorrow we'll have a whole day, if we're as close as we think.'

Satyrus nodded. 'And – and he's got to stop rowing when he reaches Tanais. But if we're right up with him, there's not really time for his other squadron to man and launch.'

'Unless they're waiting for us,' Demostrate said quietly.

Satyrus had never been the commander of a force this large. When Leon joined them, it had been as if a great stone had been lifted from his shoulders, and when Leon left, riding away with the old hippeis, the stone had settled back on his neck.

But Satyrus had been around professional soldiers and sailors all his life, and he knew what was required of him, although it made his stomach hurt with anticipation just to think of the morrow and everything he had riding on it. He took Abraham, whom everyone loved, and Diokles, and they left the fire where the commanders drank wine, and the three of them went from fire to fire down the beach. Satyrus shared a sip of wine and a libation at every fire he joined – at some, he was greeted like a demi-god, and at others, usually the fires of the pirate crews, he was feared like a leper. He watched their reactions, and tried not to show his own feelings.

Between two fires of pirate oarsmen, Satyrus made a face, spat in the sand and stopped. 'Some of them hate me,' he said.

'And you want them to love you?' Abraham nodded. 'You make them fight. Not all of them want to. Not all are brave, and very few are good. You expect to be cheered as a hero by your *rowers*? Sufficient that you are prepared to pay them.'

Satyrus looked at his friend. 'When did you become such a sophist?' he asked.

Diokles tugged his beard. 'They won't love you, lord. Best be used to it. The Macedonians probably cursed bloody Alexander, and he was half a god.' He jutted a thumb at Abraham. 'He's got more sense.'

Abraham shrugged. 'I learned a great deal in Byzantium,' he said.

'Your father wanted me to send you home. And yet – he's very proud of you.' Satyrus had meant to say this earlier, but there was never time. That was the greatest lesson of command – there was never either privacy or time.

Diokles gave a little wave and walked away a few steps, granting the two of them the illusion of privacy.

'Really?' Abraham grinned, his teeth glinting in the fire-lit dark. 'You're not just fashioning words to please me?'

'I swear by Herakles,' Satyrus said.

'I'll go home when this is over,' Abraham said. 'Unless I'm dead.'

'Don't even say such a thing,' Satyrus said, making a peasant sign of aversion.

Abraham laughed, and it was a grim laugh. 'Not all of us are born the darling of a god, to restore a kingdom and shine with the light of battle. I was born to count coins and raise my family fortunes.' He looked away. 'If I die tomorrow, I'll curse the pain of it – but by my god, it will have been worthwhile. To be *lord* and to have command – to live at the break of the wave.' He laughed. 'I'm a fool. Or I've tasted too much wine. Listen, Satyrus – I sound like some awful stock character in a play. But I love this life. Every instant, I have to pinch myself to see if I'm awake – walking on the beach with you, waiting for the day of battle, with my own ship, my armour, my sword by my side!' Abraham laughed, and now it was a genuine laugh. 'My jealous old god will probably take my life tomorrow, if only to show me who's boss.' He walked over to Diokles and slapped him on the back. 'You sailors have better manners than most of the merchants I know, but I don't need privacy. To hell with that!' He pulled his wineskin over his shoulder, took a drink and handed it to Diokles.

'Night before a battle, a man should drink,' Diokles said.

Abraham took the skin back and held it expertly, so that a dark stream curved, glinting in the distant firelight, and fell into the open darkness of his mouth. 'Oh, I've learned all kinds of things in my year at sea,' he said.

Diokles shook his head in mock sorrow. 'And never a flute girl around when you need one,' he mourned.

Satyrus shook his head, squeezed their hands and led them on to the next fire. 'We'll win tomorrow,' he said. And he meant it.

They rose with the last watch and the rowers filed aboard before the bronze shield rim of the sun ascended above the edge of the world. And as fast as the ships came off the beach, bow first, dragging their sterns clear of the sand and mud and rowing shallow so that the gentle surf was turned to muddy froth, they formed in columns and turned north, so that they were in formation while the scent of their cooking fires was still wafting over the sea. Wood smoke and sea-wrack.

But Aulus, Eumeles' navarch, was no fool, and he had not served thirty years at sea to be caught in the morning. His men must have risen just as early, whether or not they knew how close Satyrus was. The smoke of their fires still rose to the heavens just twenty stades north of the bay where Satyrus had camped, but the ships were gone.

It was noon by the time they raised the masts and sails of Eumeles' squadron, but the moment the lookout screamed that he could see the top yards of ten sail, the mood of the *Lotus*'s command platform changed.

'Fifteen!' the lookout shouted. 'Dead on the bow!'

Satyrus looked at the sky and at the sun. 'Is it too late?'

Theron ran his hand though his hair. 'Don't mistake me for a sailor, lad. But no. Now we find out if the gods love you, or whether they've lured you to madness.'

Satyrus grinned. They were overhauling the enemy squadrons so quickly that he could already see nicks in the horizon. His eyes met Neiron's. Neiron nodded, and he had a smile like a death's head.

'Now or never,' Neiron said.

'Helios!' Satyrus shouted, and the boy came running, already pulling the cover off his gilt-bronze shield.

'Signal "General chase",' Satyrus called.

Helios flashed the signal – one, two, three, four.

And the rowers roared back from every ship.

Satyrus's heart began to beat so fast that it seemed to interfere with his speech. Carefully, he said, 'Don't push them so hard that we can't fight.'

Neiron shook his head. 'All or nothing now. You made that call. Now let it happen.'

Amidships, Philaeus called the new stroke – the fastest sustainable stroke – and he began to beat the tempo on the deck with his staff.

The rowers growled and the ship sounded like a live thing. Satyrus *felt* the increase in speed in his legs and hips. The thumping of the oar master's staff seemed to be the living heart of the ship, pumping blood like the heart of an Olympic runner.

Satyrus tried not to watch the horizon. Even now, Eumeles' captains would be ordering an increase in speed. It all came down to fitness and training – a long stern chase, rower against rower into a gentle wind so close to bow-on that no one could raise a sail. Man to man.

His carefully ordered columns shredded immediately, as the fastest ships passed the slowest and the whole fleet raced. *Golden Lotus* was in the forefront, neck and neck with Panther's *Rose* and Aekes' *Hyacinth*. Behind them came the pirates, lighter, lower vessels with heavy crews who might be slow to manoeuvre but whose crews lived for this very function – to chase down a fleeing vessel and catch him.

An hour, by the sun, and the coast of the Euxine was racing by to the right, stade after stade, and they didn't seem to gain a finger's breadth on the enemy. Some of his least-trained vessels – the half-squadron provided by Lysimachos, for instance – began to lose ground, and they were left behind, as were two of the Aegyptian ships, *Troy* and *Marathon*. Throughout the fleet, the slowest ships struggled.

Satyrus watched helplessly as his fleet began to disintegrate.

'Keep your wits,' Neiron said.

'Too late to change your mind,' Theron said. 'You went for the hold. Keep your arm at his throat until you black out.'

Satyrus nodded. He knew they were right. But it hurt to watch ships fall out of the columns, their rowers already spent, or just too slow – ill-built or trailing weed.

If Eumeles has his second squadron at Tanais – if they are oared up and ready ...

The second hour of afternoon crawled by. Satyrus took a turn at an oar, as did Theron. Neiron clung to the steering oar. Men were taking turns – sailors, even the most willing of the marines. On the *Lotus*, they had practised this, and even at such a fast pull, a man knew he'd get a break.

Satyrus rowed a full hour by the sand-glass. The men around him smiled at him, and he loved every one of them for their eagerness.

'We'll catch the bastard, right enow!' called his mate across the aisle, as they lulled together. 'Never you moind, sir. Never you moind it.'

He grinned back, his heart raised by this pronouncement by a man who had to know far less about the chances of the day than he did himself, and then he went forward, the fear sweated out.

By now half of his own fleet was gone behind him, lost over the edge of the world.

'Two hours to the Tanais at this rate,' Neiron said. He was nodding, as if he could hear music. The staff still thumped the deck, a fast but steady heartbeat. 'Still six hours of light.'

Satyrus made himself look forward.

Eumeles' fleet was suddenly *close*.

'When did that happen?' he said, and his voice broke.

Neiron grinned, and so did every other man on the command deck. 'We got all the officers to row,' he said. 'Must have made a difference.' Then Neiron pointed. 'We broke their hearts,' he said.

Theron nodded. 'We are the better men,' he said.

It was a race while it had contestants. Now it was just predator and prey.

Panther's *Hyacinth* drew the first blood, smashing his beak into the oar bank of a heavy trireme whose rowers were so tired that they didn't even attempt to turn their ship and fight. Panther crippled the enemy ship expertly and rowed on, barely losing way.

As *Lotus* swept past the cripple, his archers shot down into the helpless crew, and they surrendered, the captain kneeling on his deck and begging for mercy.

Eumeles' ships lost their nerve completely as soon as they saw the loss of the first ship, and they began to scatter. In the rearward ships, more than a dozen raised sail and tried to sail clear, going west across the wind as best they could. A few made it; most were caught, helpless, and smashed. The Rhodians, who could raise sail faster, ate their wind and killed them.

The afternoon was old and the *Lotus*'s mast was casting a long shadow when Eumeles' navarch decided to turn and fight. The Tanais headland was well in sight, with a beacon burning clearly on the height of the bluff. Satyrus didn't know what the signal was or for whom it was meant, but that was the site of his mother's city.

The mouth of the river was only twenty more stades along the coast, hidden by the multiple headlands, but Satyrus knew the sea-marks here as well as any captain. The enemy ships had to fight, or run upriver – and the river was shallow in midsummer.

They turned, and their tired rowers formed a ragged line. Just one ship stood on, racing for the mouth of the Tanais.

Satyrus looked around and realized that, by the irony of the gods, he would face Eumeles outnumbered, because his ships had chased off to the west after the stragglers or stopped to loot the defeated. He had his own ships, and one Rhodian, and the *Glory of Demeter* formed next to him. Daedalus leaned over the rail and waved his fist. Satyrus waved back as Helios put his aspis on his arm.

'Twenty to ten,' Satyrus said.

Neiron wrinkled his lip and spat in the water. 'They're spent,' he said. He pointed his bearded chin at the rowers without taking his eyes off the enemy line. 'Ours are just scenting victory. And *this* is the moment for revenge, Satyrus.'

Satyrus smiled. 'In other words, I should tell them so,' he said.

Neiron nodded.

Satyrus ran forward and leaned over into the oar deck. 'Eumeles has just formed a sloppy-arse line and he's going to fight. His rowers are finished. Are you finished?'

They didn't roar. But they growled, a low sound that made the ship tremble.

'Ten minutes,' Satyrus shouted, his voice rising. 'Ten minutes of your best, and they are ours. Blood in the water and silver in our hands!'

The growl rose. Like a wind rising, the growl came up as the whole oar bank cocked back, the oars at the top of their motion, and as the oars bit, every voice on the *Lotus* spoke and the ship seemed to leap forward with its own spirit.

His ships formed up on him so that they were in a loose arrowhead. Two of the slower ships, scenting a fight, came up from behind, rowing for all they had, close enough now to engage as a second line.

'Not the battle I'd planned,' Satyrus said.

No one said anything.

'But I'll take it,' Satyrus said. He looked at the enemy line, now less than a stade away. 'Diekplous against their admiral,' he said, pointing out the blue-hulled ship in the centre of the line.

Satyrus's ships were moving much faster than their opponents

– indeed, the enemy squadron was oar-tip to oar-tip, in close order, but many of their ships were partly turned or still manoeuvring to close gaps, and they had very little forward motion. The *Golden Lotus* was a whole ship's length ahead of her line, but the *Troy* was now so close behind that she was in line with the *Glory of Demeter* and they were all moving at the speed of a galloping horse, the wind of their passage like a song of speed and madness.

'Are you taking command?' Neiron asked quietly.

'No,' Satyrus said. 'I'll board with the marines.'

Neiron nodded, and Satyrus winked at Helios, suddenly feeling as if he had the stature of the gods. Win or lose, he was done. He'd brought his fleet to Tanais, and now it was down to muscle and spirit.

We are the better men.

Theron handed him his helmet. He pulled it on, fastened the cheekpieces and together they ran forward.

'Oars in!' Neiron roared, and Philaeus echoed in his singer's voice. Even as Satyrus ran, he had to jump to avoid the oar shafts coming across the lower deck.

It was eerie, the silence as they hurtled forward. Satyrus stopped just short of the marines' box in the bow, grabbed the rail and pressed tight. Helios did the same.

'Brace!' yelled the marine captain.

Satyrus caught a glimpse – they were going in bow to bow. *Poseidon, they were going in right on the enemy ram!* It was terrifying in the bow, where the ram was part of you. His sphincter tightened and his whole body convulsed.

Neiron flicked the steering oars and the bow of the *Golden Lotus* seemed to dart to the left the length of a man – just enough to change the angle of their attack. The bow of the *Lotus* slammed into the enemy's upper-deck rowers' box and *pushed* the enemy bow, just a horse-length, but suddenly the enemy ram was pointing east and not south, and their own bow was ripping the strakes off the enemy ship.

As the impact brought them almost to a stop, Satyrus leaned forward to the marine captain. 'Clear the command deck. Ignore the rowers.'

The marine grinned.

'Blood in the water!' Satyrus yelled and leaped up on to the rail, heedless of the weight of his armour. He was on the rail for a fraction of a heartbeat, but for that instant time froze, and he saw the length of the enemy vessel – saw that he would be the first to board – and he felt that he was a god.

Then he was on their deck. One leg slipped from under him and a deck sailor went for him with a spear and died with an arrow in him, then Satyrus was up on his feet, pushing his shield into a man's gut. Hacking under it, over it, he brought the man down and pushed forward, pushed again then dumped his next opponent into the rowers and set his feet on the narrow catwalk. The marines on the command deck rushed him, but they had to come one at a time and the reforged Aegyptian sword sang in his hand. He glanced a heavy overhand cut deliberately off the man's shield, then rotated on his hips, driving forward with his sword foot and cutting *back* with the long kopis. He took the first marine's head clean off at the neck with the power of his blow, and his men let out a cry together.

The next man flinched and died with Helios's spear in his groin, pushed *under* both their shields, and Satyrus was free to push forward again. He could feel the weight of his own men behind him – and then more men were dropping on to the deck.

'Clear the command deck!' Satyrus roared.

The man behind the man he was facing was already turning to run.

Satyrus took a blow on his shield – an immense blow – and his shield split. He cut twice, as fast as he could, and then a third time, and then a fourth, and his opponent fended off every blow, but Satyrus's blows were so fast and so hard that the man couldn't launch an attack, though his shield was being pounded to splinters in turn.

Satyrus cut low, cut high and the man blocked, their swords ringing together like a hammer and anvil, the strokes keening over the wind. Satyrus began the feint for the Harmodius blow and his opponent stepped back to void his attack. He tripped over the body of a sailor behind him and went down. Satyrus stepped over him on to the command deck, leaving his fate to Helios. He had fought well.

He felt Helios's shoulder pressed into his back, and then it was gone as the boy pushed up the catwalk next to him. Then Theron was on his right, and as soon as he had flanks, he advanced, his shield foot forward. The man who faced him across the deck wore elaborate purple plumes in a plain Attic helmet and a long red cloak. Marines stood on either side of him and he cursed them for running, and there was a lull – one of those moments when men stop fighting for no reason, or every reason.

'Eumeles!' Satyrus called.

The man in the purple feather laughed. It was a hollow laugh, but not a coward's. 'Eumeles has run,' the plumes said. 'I'm Aulus, the navarch of Pantecapaeum.'

Satyrus took a deep, shuddering breath, and then another. Disappointment flooded him. 'I want Eumeles,' he said. 'Drop your sword and I'll spare every man on this deck.'

Aulus shook his head. 'When I'm bought, I stay bought,' he said, and slapped the face of his aspis with his blade. 'Come and take me.'

'Herakles!' Satyrus roared, and he went across the deck like a dart from a war machine. His aspis shattered as he rammed it into the enemy navarch's, but his sword was already moving and he ignored the massive pain in his shield arm and cut from high to low. He felt his blade bite into the man's thigh below his shield and the man screamed into his face.

And then the deck was clear, and they were moving on the waves. He looked down from the platform into the rowing decks, and the rowers looked back with slack, exhausted faces, almost uncaring if they lived or died.

He dropped the remnants of his aspis on the deck.

'Theron,' he panted. 'Theron – take command of this ship.'

Theron saluted silently.

Satyrus got over the rail with a hundred times the effort with which he'd come aboard and all but fell into his own ship. But willing hands caught him and put him on his feet, and Philaeus embraced him.

'Look, lord!' he shouted in Satyrus's ear, as if Satyrus might have become deaf.

Neiron was pounding his back.

The sea battle, such as it had been, was already over. And the enemy squadron on the distant beach was still there, bows moving in the gentle seas, sterns still clenched in the mud. One enemy ship was skimming the waves, just going ashore.

'That will be Eumeles,' Satyrus said. 'We're not done yet.'

Neiron pointed at the enemy camp beyond their line of ships. At the landward edge of the camp, an army was formed, and beyond it, men were dying.

'Ares,' Satyrus muttered.

'They started the battle without us,' Neiron said.

Satyrus couldn't make out who was fighting, although he could see Urvara's Grass Cat standard on a far hill.

'But ...' Satyrus shook his head. His sword arm was a dead thing, and he massaged the muscle at the top of his arm. 'To Tartarus with them. We've *won*. We don't *need* a land battle.'

Neiron pointed at a swirling cavalry melee several stades away to the east. 'Try telling them.'

Satyrus took a deep breath, tempted to rail against the gods. A land battle just risked his sister without accomplishing anything. By crushing Eumeles at sea and trapping him here, far from his city, the *war* was over. He breathed again.

'Helios!' he called. 'Signal "All ships rally on me".'

Helios had a bandage on his arm and a blank look on his face.

'Helios!' Satyrus said again.

'Lord?' the boy answered.

'Signal "All ships rally on me"!' Satyrus put a hand on the boy's head. 'You going to live, lad?'

Helios nodded sheepishly.

Satyrus turned to Neiron. 'As soon as Panther comes up, I'm putting him in charge with orders to burn those ships or take them. Then I'm going ashore by boat – to the beacon.' He pointed at the beacon burning in the strong fort on the opposite headland.

But Panther didn't come. Abraham did, and Satyrus gave him the command.

'Don't delay. Go in and drag their ships off the beach, or throw fire into them under cover of your archers.' Satyrus was going to continue, but he could see irritation on Abraham's face.

'I think I can be trusted to burn some ships,' he said. But then he smiled. 'By god, Satyrus – we're doing it!'

'Not done yet,' Satyrus cautioned. Then he dropped into the small boat that they towed under the stern. 'Row!' he said.

24

The day after Samahe died saw the least combat of any day since the start of the campaign.

Both sides were exhausted.

At dawn, Melitta moved her camp, dragging her tired army by force of will to go south and west along the Tanais another thirty stades. They went up the ridge behind the Ford of Apollo's Shrine and camped behind the crest. The weather was clear and the sun high, and as soon as they stopped moving, most warriors were on their backs, sleeping in the sun.

Melitta arranged guards and put every man in the camp that could make an arrow to fletching. She did these things herself, or through her guard, because the level of exhaustion was so high that she could no longer trust that her chiefs would get everything done. So Laen and Agreint stalked the camp, waking men up to ask after fletchers, while the rest of them under Scopasis stripped their armour and became scouts.

Coenus seemed unfazed, despite riding a thousand stades and fighting. He shrugged. 'This was my life,' he said simply.

Ataelus shook his head. 'I for horse – every day for horse. But you? Greek man.'

Coenus nodded. 'You served with Kineas. I had eight years of it.'

Ataelus nodded. 'We need for Kineax.'

Melitta didn't know what to make of that. So she said nothing.

After she had her guards out and when the pile of arrows was growing at a rate that seemed glacial but would have to do, she went to Coenus. 'I need to be in touch with Urvara every day,' she said. 'Will you be my herald?'

Coenus nodded. 'That's good thinking. I'm away. Can I put the seed of an idea in your head?'

Melitta shrugged. 'Of course.'

Coenus pointed at Temerix. 'The farmers could hold that ford all day. Against the whole of Upazan's force.'

Melitta shook her head. 'So? Upazan's on the same side of the river as we are.'

'He is now,' Coenus said. He already had the reins of his horse. 'If you retired across the river, he'd be stuck on the wrong side. Quite a ride north to get to the next ford, or take truly staggering casualties to get through Temerix.'

Melitta rubbed her chin. 'I see it.'

Coenus nodded sharply. 'I'm not saying that it is the right thing to do. But ...'

Melitta looked downstream. 'No enemy boats for two days.'

Coenus nodded. 'Makes you wonder. I'll be back in three hours.' And he was gone. Melitta saw, with the eyes of a commander, that his horse's hooves raised dust today where yesterday the ground had been soft.

Good to know.

She lay down and slept.

Coenus returned while she was drinking beer with Temerix, outlining for him how she'd like him to drive stakes into the ford.

'Well?' she asked.

'Eumenes of Olbia is a day's march away – I saw a girl called Lithra, a spear-maiden of the Cruel Hands, who'd just ridden in with a message.' Coenus said this in a loud voice, and men making arrows looked up, and many of them smiled. The Cruel Hands were the royal tribe, and heaviest in warriors.

'By the Warrior and the Ploughman,' Buirtevaert said. 'I'm sorry I doubted you, Greek.'

Graethe came up. He had a wound on his chest that was suppurating through his wool coat. Melitta embraced him anyway.

'That was a bold charge, Lord of the Standing Horse. It will long be remembered, that we followed your banner to victory.' She took his hands, and he winced as some movement of his arm caused him pain, but his face lit up at the praise.

'If Kairax of the Cruel Hands is two days' ride away,' he said, 'I owed you that charge.' He grinned. 'And I had to strike hard before he comes and steals all the glory!'

Melitta came back to Coenus. 'But you do not look like the bearer of good tidings.'

Coenus squinted in the bright sunlight. 'I don't know if it is good or bad, but you need to hear it. Urvara is taking her Grass Cats and all the farmers in the fort across the river. She's been feeding riders across for two days, raiding Nikephoros's foragers and cutting into his ability to send out parties. Now he has his boats crewed all the time, trying to catch her people, but they swim the river and now they can shoot his rowers from both banks.'

'And that is why we no longer see boats up here!' she said. She clapped her hands. 'No bad news there!'

'No. But in pushing so many of her warriors across the river, Urvara is committed to fight. Today, I saw Nikephoros march his whole force out of their fort and form a square. They marched up-country, seizing food. Urvara's men shot at them but did little damage. Now she's determined to cross in force and hem him in his camp. And of course, with Eumenes right behind her, she can do it.'

Melitta understood. 'Urvara is committing us to a battle.'

Coenus nodded. 'Yes.'

'Just to cover her archers, who she needed to close the river, which she did to keep us alive up here.' Melitta ticked the points off with her fingers.

Coenus nodded again. 'Yes. You are your father's daughter, Melitta. Many grown men with ten campaigns never understand the cause and effect like that.'

'I love your praise, Uncle. You knew of this in the morning, when you recommended that we close the ford.' She wasn't accusing him, just asking.

'I didn't *know*,' he said with a shrug. 'I merely suspected. Urvara means to fight – or close the fort – tomorrow. The Cruel Hands and all of Eumenes' cavalry are riding all day to join her, and the phalanx of Olbia will come when they can. I don't see how we can get them over the river, but we'll do that when we have to.'

'And the farmers?' Melitta asked.

'Swimming with the Sakje horses. Not something most Greeks can do.' He shook his head. 'Any movement from Upazan?'

Melitta looked upstream, where the calm day devoid of dust

showed that her enemy was resting. 'Nothing.' She sat on a stump. 'But if Urvara commits to fight Nikephoros – then what? It is a very unequal fight, all cavalry against all infantry.'

Coenus nodded. 'Just so. It will, in fact, be a race between Eumenes' phalanx and Upazan. Upazan has more cavalry than all of ours combined – twice over, even now. But he has no infantry. If we can destroy Nikephoros before Upazan arrives, he will be helpless. But if Nikephoros holds us until Upazan arrives ...'

Melitta shook her head. 'Urvara has committed us to a mighty risk. What if I call her back?'

Coenus sat down. Men were gathering around – Scopasis and Graethe, Ataelus, his eyes red with weeping, and Buirtevaert with his hand on Ataelus's shoulder, his son Thyrsis behind him and Tameax the baqca watching from under his eyebrows. But they all stood silent and listened. This was not their way of war.

Coenus looked around. 'If you call her back, then we face Upazan on this side of the river, and Nikephoros recovers his wits, puts all his men on ships and comes across.'

'Ahh,' Melitta said. Now she saw it. 'This is not risk. We are, in fact, desperate.'

Coenus put his hands on his knees. 'Unless your brother comes,' he said, 'we have little choice.'

Melitta stood. 'Then let us strike with what we have. Upazan has lost a day. We will march at dawn – across the ford. Temerix, your best two hundred, with ponies, to hold the ford. If Upazan crosses north of us, scouts will inform your men and they can ride to join us. Otherwise, you hold the ford until you die. The rest of your archers follow me. Perhaps we can bury Nikephoros in arrows.'

Ataelus shrugged.

Graethe looked at the men making arrows. 'Only if we have them to shoot,' he said.

Upazan's scouts found them in the dark, but they were ready enough, and Melitta slept through the fight and rose to be given hot wine and a report.

Scopasis pressed the wine into her hand, and she could see blood under the nails of his hands.

'We hit them, but many got away.' He shrugged. 'We killed more than some.' He frowned. 'But they saw the stakes in the ford.'

She kissed him then. He was shocked – he stumbled back. 'Lady?' he mumbled.

She smiled. 'Life is not all war, Scopasis. One day, we will not be wearing armour.'

She caught a glint – the outlaw lived. 'Lady,' he growled.

She felt better than she had in days, and she swallowed the wine in four hot gulps. 'Armour,' she called, and then remembered that she no longer had Samahe to braid her hair. She was surprised – appalled, actually – at how quickly the dead were left behind in her head. They died so fast.

She shook her head to clear it. That way madness lay.

Gaweint came with her armour, and the day was moving.

She got her rearguard across the ford without incident, and she clasped hands with Temerix and a dozen of his archers. Then she turned and rode west along the south bank of the river. It seemed odd – a reversal of the natural order.

Ataelus was closed to her, and she tried to reach him.

'I missed Samahe this morning,' she said bluntly.

'I miss her for every beat of heart,' he said in Greek.

'I—' she began.

'I want her body back,' he said in Sakje. 'I failed to recover her, and she will go mutilated to the after-life, and wail for revenge, and what can I give her?'

Melitta leaned close. 'Upazan's head?' she asked.

Ataelus shook his. 'Upazan will never die by the weapon of a man,' he said. 'It is told. Even Nihmu said it.'

Melitta summoned her Greek learning. 'If Philokles were here,' she said, 'he would tell you that Samahe lived a good life with you and gave you two sons and a daughter, and that what happens to her body after death means nothing, because she is *dead*.'

Ataelus looked at her with a face almost alive, it was so full of grief. 'But you and I know better, eh?' He shook his head.

'We'll find her and build a kurgan,' Melitta promised.

Ataelus said nothing, and they rode west.

*

She sent Coenus to find Urvara, or Eumenes, and bring her a report, and then they rode all day. The sun was low in the west, the rays direct in their faces, so that they could hear the fighting and yet not see it.

Melitta found Thyrsis riding with her baqca, and she smiled at them. 'I need a scout,' she said to Thyrsis.

Tameax frowned. 'Why send him? He wants to fight and he can't count above ten. Send me.'

She frowned. 'I need a good account of what is happening in the sun.'

Thyrsis nodded. 'I'll find a dozen riders, and we'll go together,' he said. She was glad to see how much spirit he had. He was handsome like a Greek, and his armour was clean and neat – mended every day, the mark of a first-rate warrior. He had wounds, and he had killed – he was perhaps the best warrior of his generation. And yet nothing about him moved her in the way Scopasis moved her.

'Keep my surly baqca alive,' she joked, and rode away, leaving Tameax frowning at her back. *How many army commanders have to worry about men competing for their affections?* she asked herself. But in an odd way, she was happy. Today, *she* was in command. Not Coenus, not Ataelus and not Graethe, or even Tameax or Thyrsis. They obeyed.

It was Scopasis who saw the beacon first. He scratched the scar on his face, and she looked at him, but he was looking south and west.

'I think that the beacon is alight,' he said. 'The beacon on the fort.'

'You can see a fire in the eye of the sun?' she asked.

He shrugged.

Tameax galloped out of the falling darkness like a raven, all black wool on a black horse. 'Urvara is on this side of the river,' he said. 'I saw her standard but didn't ride in. She is fighting on foot.'

Melitta felt a chill of fear. 'Spear to spear with a phalanx?'

'She has dismounted all her household,' Thyrsis said. 'They make a shield wall on the Hill of Ravens.'

'The beacon on the fort is alight,' Tameax said.

'Read me this riddle,' Melitta said. 'Why is the beacon alight? Why does Urvara fight?'

The other men were silent. Tameax scratched his beard. 'I think that Eumenes must have come,' he said. 'He came and lit the beacon, so that Urvara knows he is here. Now Urvara fights to protect the lowest crossing, so that Eumenes comes behind her.'

Ataelus spoke up, his voice rough. 'He is a wise man. I think he has this right in his head.'

Melitta gave Tameax a long look. 'If you are right ...' she said.

He nodded. 'I am right,' he said.

Melitta looked around. She had about eight hundred riders left. They had been in action for seven days. 'We must appear on Nikephoros's flank and make him draw off,' she said. 'We may have to fight in the dark. Eumenes of Olbia *must* get across to the south bank and join us.'

Up and down the column of Sakje, every warrior changed horses. The farmers, three hundred strong, had only one pony each. Melitta mounted Gryphon and rode to Temerix's lieutenant, a big, ruddy smith named Maeton.

'Follow at your best speed. When you come, look for my banner. Do you understand? If all else fails, kill as many enemy as you can.' She took his hand, and he bowed his head. Behind him, she could see Gardan. She raised her voice. 'By this time tomorrow, we will be done. Eumenes is here from Olbia. We can win now, and we will never face foreign taxes and raids from Upazan again.'

They gave a cheer, and she waved and rode away.

When she got to the head of her Sakje, she drew her axe. 'Now we ride,' she said.

And they were off.

Ten stades of open fields. Twice they crossed farm walls, following Thyrsis, who had left riders to guide them over, and then, faces to the setting sun, they came over a low ridge and they could see two full taxeis of enemy phalangites facing the last ford, and at the ford, Urvara's knights, all wearing scale armour from throat to ankle, standing with their axes at the top of the riverbank. The ground in front of her household was littered with bodies.

'Follow me!' Melitta shouted. She bent low on Gryphon's neck and kicked her heels, and he went from a canter to the gallop.

Sakje needed no orders to form for battle. They were in a long column, and now they spread wide across the plain, drawing their bows from their gorytoi as they galloped and nocking the first arrows, the faster horses pulling ahead of the slower.

Their hoof beats announced their arrival, and long before they neared Nikephoros, his pikes were changing direction, and they faced a wall of spear-points. Melitta was still a horse-length in advance of Scopasis and her knights. She didn't slow the big horse, but leaned her weight to the right and he turned away from the spear-points and she passed an arm's length from the glittering hedge, She shot her first arrow into the blur of faces and leather armour so close that her shaft was in a man's gut before her galloping horse carried her past.

As she nocked her second arrow, her thumb feeling for the burr on the nock, Scopasis buried his first in a man's shield and cursed.

'Lock your shields!' a phylarch shouted.

She saw him, his mouth open for the next order, but Macedonian shields were small things compared to the great aspis that her brother carried, and she shot him over the rim of his shield – missing the open mark of his mouth, so that her shaft went in over his nose and right out again through his helmet.

The pikemen could do nothing but bend their heads to put the peaks of their tall helmets into the arrow storm and pray to their gods. The Sakje were riding so close that they could choose where to shoot – above the shield or below – and men fell with arrows through their feet. Eight hundred Sakje thundered along the flank of the phalanx, and a hundred pikemen fell, wounded and screaming, or dead before their helmets hit the ground.

Melitta released a third shaft, missed seeing the result, and then she was past the last man and in the open. She kept going until she pulled up by Urvara, who stood with a bloody sword between her banner and her tanist. The iron-haired woman pulled her helmet free and dropped her sword to catch at Melitta's hand.

'I knew you'd come,' she said. 'Between us, we might finish him.'

Melitta held up her quiver. She had eight arrows left. 'That was all bluff,' she said.

Urvara gave half a smile. 'There he goes,' she said. Even as she spoke, they saw a single figure on horseback arrive in the enemy phalanx.

'Messenger from the fort?' Melitta asked. 'Shall we harry them once more?' she asked.

Urvara shook her head. 'They're going to retreat – you can see it in the front-rank men. I've lost a lot of people today – I'm not sure I can help you. Let him go.'

There were dead pikemen and dead Sakje all the way across the plain – three stades of dead.

Nikephoros was less than a stade away. It was somehow odd that Melitta knew the sound of his voice. He was shouting at someone. And then the pikemen began to march, their ranks closing up over the dead, and they formed even closer. The back ranks walked backwards as they withdrew, and the spearheads were still steady.

'Good men,' Coenus said. He was in armour again, and had a fine Attic helmet on his head with a red crest. 'He's going to ride over and ask for a truce.'

'Give me all your arrows,' Melitta called to her household, and in seconds, her quiver was full – forty arrows, all they had.

She turned to Coenus. 'You're with me. The rest of you wait here. Scopasis – here!' More kindly, 'Coenus can protect me. And I want him to see a full quiver.'

Sure enough, Nikephoros was riding towards them, mounted on an ugly bay. He seemed unconcerned to be alone in front of a host of enemies.

'I wish that man was mine,' Melitta said.

Coenus nodded. 'If he lives, make him yours,' he said.

Nikephoros met them in a clear space among the dead. 'I would like a day's truce to collect and bury my dead,' he said. 'I concede that I was bested.'

Melitta shook her head. 'No, I'm sorry, Nikephoros. I like you, but no truce. We will finish you in the morning. Unless you'd like to ask for terms.'

'My master's ally Upazan is coming,' he said. 'You will not finish me in the morning.'

Melitta shrugged. 'I have no need to bluster or bargain. Begone.'

She turned her horse, and as she turned, she saw the shock on Nikephoros's face. Even as she saw it, she saw where his eyes were, and she followed them.

The bay was full of ships.

And closer, at the seaward edge of Nikephoros's camp, there was fire.

'No truce,' she spat. To Coenus, she said, 'Ride!'

They left Nikephoros in a swirl of dust and galloped back across the dead to where her people had dismounted. Most were swilling wine. Tameax spat a mouthful and it was like blood from his mouth – a poor omen, she thought.

'My brother is here,' she shouted.

Coenus pulled up behind her. 'Of course!' he said.

'Satyrus is attacking Nikephoros's camp,' she said. 'We need to harry him every step and slow his retreat, and we may yet have him in the last light of the sun.'

It is a hard thing for a warrior to believe that he is done – that he has lived another day, that he can drink, sit on the ground, enjoy the small pleasures that make life worth living even in the middle of the unbelievable tension of daily war – and then be summoned back to the risk of imminent death. It is a hard thing, and it is only the best who can rise to meet it.

'Now for revenge!' Thyrsis said, leaping to his feet as if he'd never shot his bow or ridden a stade all day.

'One more ride,' Scopasis shouted, and then they were all on their feet. Many changed horses. Many cursed.

Urvara leaned on her sword hilt and drove the point into the grass. 'We're done.'

Melitta was sorry, but she forced a smile. 'I can see Eumenes,' she said, pointing across the river, where a long column of horsemen were splashing into the river. 'Send him to me.'

Then she took her warriors and went back to the pikemen.

Nikephoros had plenty of time to see her coming, and at her orders all the Sakje shot carefully and slowly, riding close to be sure of every shaft, and the pikemen halted and closed even tighter. Melitta rode to Graethe. 'Take your Standing Horses and get arrows from the Grass Cats,' she said. 'Then come back.'

He waved his axe in acknowledgement and rode away.

Her numbers halved, she led her people past the phalanx again. Only fifty or so arrows flew, but men fell.

The phalanx shuffled into motion again.

She cursed the lack of arrows and rode past a third time. This time, pikemen leaped out of the spear wall and killed Sakje, dragging the victims down with charging thrusts of their spears – but every brave pikeman died, spitted or shot by the following riders.

And again the phalanx retreated, opening a gap.

She rode by a fourth time but scarcely a dozen arrows flew, and the phalanx didn't even stop. Nikephoros was on to her. He was going to march away.

But Graethe returned and led his men straight to the attack, and his first run blocked out the first stars with arrow shafts, and fifty more pikemen fell. Again they halted and closed up.

'They may be the best infantry I've ever seen,' Coenus said. 'They won't break. By the gods, they're good.'

Graethe rode back. 'Now what?'

'Give every warrior one arrow,' she said. 'We'll hit both of their flanks together and try to make them fold.'

Graethe agreed, and they rode out to the flanks. On the left, where Melitta rode, she could see horsemen crossing the last ridge. She had no idea who they were, but they were clear in the last light of the sun.

'Rally at the ford if we do not break the Greeks!' she shouted.

There was no answering shout. Her people had no life in them – they rode, and obeyed. That was all. Every face had the lines of exhaustion.

She led them wide to the left and the Greeks began to march, and then she turned inward, just as Graethe's men did the same on the right. This time they would go straight at the Greeks instead of riding along the face of their formation. If men flinched, if the arrow storm took enough lives, a rider might slip into the ranks, and then another behind, and then ...

The Cruel Hands were across the ford. She could see

Parshtaevalt leading his warriors forward – a thousand fresh Sakje with full quivers.

But the sun was gone, and the last light was augmented by the beacon on the fort and the line of fires burning on the beach. They had a few minutes of ruddy light, and then it would be dark.

Nikephoros had halted and was again closing his files.

Melitta put her heels to Gryphon and they went forward.

And the infantry held them. Not a Sakje died, but they were tired. A young warrior who might, in the morning, have risked his life to thread the little gap where the phylarch died with a barb in his throat reined up and turned away instead. And as the very last light died, the Sakje rode away.

It was not for nothing. All along the beach, Eumeles' second squadron lit the night sky with the fires in their hulls. And Nikephoros, driven from his camp without a fight, turned his still unbeaten phalanx from the burning gates and marched away north and east. A rider joined the phalanx, a lone man in a purple cloak. Melitta was watching him as his cloak turned from purple to black in the failing light.

'Eumeles!' a voice by her elbow called. The man turned his head and then rode on, joining the retreat of the phalanx. She turned to see who had shouted.

'To Tartarus with him,' Satyrus said, and threw his arms around his sister.

25

They camped on the field with the dead. Temerix came in an hour after dark with all his men and reported that Upazan had crossed the river to the north and was coming up fast.

Satyrus was bigger than she remembered. He seemed to have swollen to fill the role of king. She let him do it. Men called him *Wanax*, the old title, and *Basileus*, and he was like a demi-god. She felt tired and dirty next to his magnificent armour, his perfect physique and his unscarred face.

Before the night was an hour old, he had set the camp and together, the two of them walked from fire to fire, visiting Sakje and Olbians, farmers and sailors.

'My men are annoyed that they have to put out the fires they started,' Satyrus joked. His ships were still working, transporting the Olbian infantry over the river after disgorging all the Macedonians who had served as marines. 'We could have had all Eumeles' ships. But we didn't know you and Urvara could hold so many men for so long.'

Melitta smiled. 'We did it with our teeth,' she said. 'Don't you sleep?'

'We're going to fight in the morning,' he said. 'I don't want any mistakes. Most of our people fought today, Lita. If we don't put spirit in them—'

'You could start by putting some of that spirit in me, brother,' she said. 'If I thought I could, I'd desert. I'm done.'

He put his arms around her, and she stayed there. 'You are superb,' he said. 'You were going to do it all without me, weren't you?'

'We thought that you were dead, until we landed and heard the news,' she said.

He smiled. 'Listen, honey bee. We've got them. *We've got them.*' He pulled his shoulder blades back sharply and flexed his arms. 'Their fleet is gone. Upazan is nothing – a horse lord with his power base a thousand stades away, deep in our territory.'

She shook her head. 'Spirit is all, Satyrus. If we lose tomorrow, we are the ones who are finished.' She paused. 'I wish Diodorus were here.'

They were between fires. Behind them, Olbians shouted and poured libations. They were fresh men, and their father's friend Memnon, hoary with age and still hard as a rock, led them in the hymn to Ares.

Memnon came and embraced them both. 'Tomorrow, we will put Eumeles in the dust, where he belongs, the cur,' he said.

'May Ares protect you, Memnon,' Melitta said. 'You have grown old in his service – and few of his servants grow old!'

Memnon looked around. 'I had to come,' he said. 'I couldn't miss this. My last fight, I suspect – some kid will put a spear in my throat and I'll curse the dark when it falls.' He thumped his chest. 'I was at Issus with the Great King. This will be my tenth battle in the front rank.'

Satyrus was moved by the old man. He put a gentle hand on Memnon's back. 'May Herakles protect you. You deserve better than a death in battle.'

Memnon laughed and went back to his men. 'Better a spear to the throat in the storm of bronze than dying of the shits in painful old age, lad,' he called.

At the north end of the camp, Ataelus's clan was a silent, mournful knot – those who were awake. As they walked there, Satyrus stopped, looking out over the sea in the moonlight. He could hear the sound of wild beasts rooting in the bodies.

Satyrus set his face. 'About Diodorus – you are right – and right to remind me.' He shook his head. 'I left the horse transports to catch Eumeles at sea. I had to do it – but a thousand professional cavalry would be the balance of this battle.'

Melitta had to smile at her brother. 'People and spirit,' she said. 'With or without Diodorus, what will win tomorrow is spirit. So let us talk to every man and every woman, even if we get no sleep.'

At Ataelus's fire, Ataelus was awake, with his son by his side. The little man embraced Satyrus. 'You look for your father,' he said, enigmatically.

Satyrus nodded. 'I look like him?' he asked.

'For him,' Ataelus said. 'You have looks for him.'

Melitta introduced her brother to Tameax as her baqca, and to Thyrsis, and to all the nomads with whom she had lived in the weeks before she'd made her bid for kingship.

And while they stood on the low hill, Urvara came with Eumenes of Olbia and many of their people, all carrying torches. Nihmu came, and Coenus, and Lykeles and Lycurgus from the Olbians. All the old people, the ones who had gone east with Kineas and Srayanka twenty years before.

They surprised Satyrus by singing. First the Sakje sang, and they clapped while they sang, and Melitta joined them, her low voice merging seamlessly with the tribesmen and women around her. They sang about Srayanka and her horse, and how her eyes were the blue of winter rivers in the sun. And then they sang about Samahe, and how she had nursed infants, and how many men she had killed in battle, and how she had killed a snow leopard in the high mountains north of Sogdiana. And another song about how she and Ataelus had hunted something monstrous in the east, and lived.

Then Coenus and Eumenes rose and sang, and many of Eumenes' young men took parts. Abraham appeared with Panther and Demostrate, Diokles, Neiron – dozens of the sailors and marines from the camp on the beach. They all knew the Greek songs. Satyrus walked from his place by his sister to stand with the new archon of Olbia. They sang a song from the *Iliad*, and another about Penelope, and a third song about Athena, the warrior goddess, that men said was by Hesiod, or perhaps Homer himself. They sang well, for men who didn't sing together, and when they were finished, Ataelus stepped into the firelight.

'Sometimes, a Sakje is lost,' he said. His voice was tired with weeping, and he didn't attempt Greek, so that Eumenes, who had so often interpreted for Ataelus, did the office once again. 'Sometimes, a rider vanishes in the snow, or on a scout, and we never find his body. So my beloved was lost, although she fell in full view of a thousand of the people.'

He walked to Melitta, and then led her to Satyrus. 'Our spirit is back with us,' he said. He pointed at the sword Satyrus wore. 'That is the sword of Kineax, that has returned. The stories of this spring will live for ever. You, every one of you, are in the songs now. You are *in the songs*.' He nodded. 'Samahe was in the songs from her youth. If we lose tomorrow, all these songs will be forgotten. If we win, she will live for ever.'

He let go of the hands of the twins.

And then the Sakje passed wine around, and drank.

'My father does not expect to live through the battle,' Thyrsis said to Melitta.

Satyrus shook his head. 'I hear that too often,' he said.

Satyrus felt as if he had never been to sleep – and he had had a straw bed and two heavy cloaks, and Helios to massage the muscles of his arm.

'Nikephoros has asked for another parley,' Helios reported.

Melitta had insisted on sleeping with Ataelus's people, and Satyrus wasn't sure whether to go to her or send for her – but that was just foolishness, and he pulled a chiton over his head, arranged the folds, clasped his cloak. 'Boots, Helios. I'll probably ride. Panther – will our sailors serve as peltasts?'

Panther was drinking wine at Satyrus's fire. He had a wound – all of them had wounds. But he smiled. 'Satyrus, I have done more fighting in the last ten days than in the last ten years – and you are asking me for another fight. I'll arm them and hold the camp. If we get bold, we might harry a flank. Think of the rowing these men gave you yesterday.'

Satyrus nodded. 'Too true, and I will not offend the gods by asking more. Care to come to the parley?'

Panther nodded. 'Yes. I may tip the scales.'

Together they made their way across the camps in the first light. Satyrus was stiff in both shoulders, but the massage helped. 'Helios? I need a new shield.'

'I'm on it, lord,' Helios answered.

Melitta was up and drinking wine – Satyrus never drank wine so early, and he was worried to see his sister drink down two cups of unwatered wine for her breakfast.

'Parley?' Satyrus asked, and she gathered her war leaders. Eumenes and Memnon joined them, and they all clasped hands and embraced, one by one, with Parshtaevalt and Ataelus, Coenus and even Graethe.

'Like old times,' Graethe said.

'We need Diodorus to be complete,' Eumenes said. He suddenly appeared older, taller, in a white chiton and a purple-edged white cloak. He had a chaplet of gold oak leaves in his hair.

'You're out-dressing me,' Satyrus said, and smiled, because when you are a king, men mistake humour for assault.

Eumenes grinned, suddenly the young man they'd grown up with. 'I knew I'd be in brilliant company,' he said.

They poured a libation from an old cup that Eumenes had.

'This was Kineas's,' he said. 'Every time we fought, we poured wine from this cup, and then we all drank from it. To all the gods,' he said, and one by one they drank.

When it came to Satyrus, he saw that it was a plain clay soldier's cup. But he drained it, and in the bottom he saw his father's name in the old letters, and tears came to his eyes.

He looked around. His hand reached out and he took his sister's hand. 'This is my father's dream,' he said. 'And my mother's. A kingdom on the Tanais, where free men and women can make their lives without fear. Upazan and Eumeles decided to destroy that dream.'

Melitta spoke up, as if they had planned the speech together. 'Today we reverse fifteen years of their evil,' she said. 'Many of you have fought for days already. This will end it. And when we look at the kurgan by the river, we will remember Kineas and Srayanka as the founders, not as the defeated.'

Panther spoke up. 'Is there anything that you would accept from this parley?' he asked. 'I am the closest thing to a neutral party here, as a man of Rhodos.'

Satyrus and Melitta looked at each other.

'Let's hear what they have to say,' Satyrus said. But they shared a different message.

'We would confirm you in your kingdom,' Eumeles said. His voice was reasonable. He had Upazan behind him, and Nikephoros, and his advisor, Idomenes, and a dozen other officers, Sauromatae and Greek. 'You will have restored to you all the kingdom that your mother held, and we will recognize your sister as the lady of the Assagatje on the sea of grass. And my friend Upazan will go back to his land, keeping only the high ground between the Tanais and the Rha.'

Melitta watched Eumeles the way a farmer watches a snake while he repairs a fence. The farmer knows that if he goes too close, the snake will bite, but from a distance, the snake is merely – fascinating. She looked at her brother. He looked back, and they shared a thought as clearly as if it had been spoken aloud.

And he left it to her to speak.

She stepped forward. Eumeles bowed – Eumeles, who had murdered her mother. She let herself look at him, and in her mind, she allowed Smell of Death to take her face from Melitta, so that her face settled into a mask, and the scar was her face to the world.

'No,' she said. She spoke in a calm, low voice, more like a mother soothing a child than the voice of doom. 'No,' she said again, even more quietly, so that Upazan leaned forward to listen.

Eumeles shrugged. 'Tell us what you want,' he said.

'Your head on my spear,' she said, and looked him full in the eyes, so that he could see the hate, feel it come across the gap of air and go down his spine.

And it did.

'No peace, killer of my mother. No peace, killer of my father. You are dead men. Go from here and be *dead*.'

Even Upazan flinched.

'We will have peace when Upazan and Eumeles lie in their blood and rot,' she said, her voice still quiet and calm. 'If the rest of you wish to give them to us, so be it. We will then arrange a peace. Otherwise,' she smiled for the first time, 'let's get down to the thing.'

'You are mad,' Eumeles said. He stepped back. Satyrus's lip twitched.

'Goodbye, Eumeles,' Satyrus said softly.

'You are mad!' Eumeles said again, his voice rising.

Upazan shook his head. 'You are a fool, and I am sorry I have a fool for an ally. But I am strong.' He turned to Melitta. 'You will not find me easy. And if you come under my spear again, it is you who will feed the ravens.' He had shrewd eyes, and he was tall, strong and fearless. 'We could make peace. I killed Kineas with a fair arrow, not a back-stab at a parley.' He looked at Eumeles with contempt. Then he looked at Nikephoros and the Greek commander met his eye.

Melitta's voice did not waver. 'How many times must I say no?' she said.

Upazan drew himself up. 'So,' he said.

Nikephoros spoke for the first time. 'Then we'll fight.'

Eumeles gathered his dignity. 'Expect no mercy,' he said.

And that was the parley.

Satyrus and Melitta arranged their armies in the order they had camped. Eumenes had the left, facing Nikephoros, with all the infantry, including the Macedonian marines. Satyrus was in the centre with Melitta and the best of the Sakje knights all formed together, and opposite them was Eumeles' banner, and the aristocracy of Pantecapaeum and all the Euxine cities he held save only Olbia, flanked by thousands of Upazan's warriors. But Upazan himself faced Urvara and Parshtaevalt and Ataelus on the right by the beach and the remnants of the fortified camp, now full of javelin-armed sailors who had enough spirit to annoy Upazan's horsemen as they attempted to move forward.

Both sides were tired, and neither side formed quickly. Nikephoros's men marched to the right and then back to the left, and the phalanx of Olbia shadowed them, moving east and west along the riverbank.

'Should we worry that our backs are to the river?' Melitta asked her brother.

'Yes,' he said. Then he shot her a grin. 'You scared the *shit* out of Eumeles.'

She nodded. 'I've been to some dark places.' She retied the sash at her waist for the thirtieth time. 'But I'm glad they taught me something useful.'

Satyrus nodded. 'Me, too.' He took her hand again, raised it and called to the men and women around them. 'If I fall,' he said, 'I name Melitta's son Kineas my heir.'

No one cheered, but people nodded. It was good to know that

there was continuity. A man who saw him fall might keep fighting if he thought that Satyrus's death didn't mean defeat.

'We aren't making a speech?' Melitta asked.

'If they take any longer forming up, we'll be fighting tomorrow,' Satyrus said. He looked for Coenus, who was at his shoulder. None of his companions – Helios, Abraham, Neiron, Diokles – were horsemen. But Satyrus was fighting mounted in the middle of the aristocrats of Olbia because that was where the king had to be. Melitta had all of her guard to back them up, and Satyrus had Coenus.

Coenus pushed his big mare forward.

'Should I be making a speech?' Satyrus asked.

Coenus pointed across to where Upazan was trying to get his flank to refuse so that he wouldn't lose more men to the javelins and arrows coming from the sailors. Even as Satyrus watched, he saw the Cretan Idomeneus stand up on the pilings of the camp and shoot one of Upazan's knights out of his saddle at two hundred paces. The whole of the Sauromatae line *moved*.

Satyrus turned to Melitta. 'You, or me?'

Melitta touched Gryphon's side. 'Together. You talk. I'll wave.'

They rode the line from one end to the other. At the eastern end were the farmers – almost three thousand of them, facing Nikephoros's few peltasts and open fields beyond. They were eager. They began to cheer. Satyrus raised his sword and Melitta took off her helmet and shook out her hair so that it streamed behind her, and they rode.

After the farmers were the hoplites of Olbia and the taxeis of Draco's veterans. The Olbians cheered hard enough, and the Macedonians stood their ground – resigned to another day fighting for foreigners. Satyrus reined in to the front of Amyntas.

'Macedonians!' he said. 'If we triumph today, every one of you will be a farmer on the Euxine tomorrow!'

That got a cheer, and they were off again, crossing the centre. There, Satyrus waved. 'Do you remember my father?' he called to the Olbians, and they roared. 'Say *Kineas*!' and they roared it out, and he was away, Melitta at his heels, riding across the front of the Sakje. Satyrus reined up, but it was Melitta who spoke. She reared Gryphon and pointed at her brother.

'I promised Eumenes, and he is here. I promised Satyrus, and he is here. I promised one last battle, and it is here. Avenge my mother! Avenge my father! Avenge your own dead! Today!'

And they cheered – men and women who had been in action for seven days, but they cheered. Some of Ataelus's Sakje had fewer than twenty arrows in their quivers, but they cheered.

'He's got to come or he's done,' Satyrus said, pointing at Upazan's golden helmet. 'The sailors are hurting him. Either he charges or he rides away.' He put his heels to his horse and rode towards the camp, where Abraham was standing on the wall with Demostrate and Panther and Diokles. Satyrus reined in under the wall.

'Anything you can do,' he said. 'Just the archery is helping.'

Panther nodded. 'We'll do what we can,' he said.

Abraham had his armour on and a shield on his arm. 'I have two hundred marines,' he said. 'If I can, we'll come into their flank. Right now, we cover the archers.'

Satyrus snapped a salute and Melitta blew Abraham a kiss. He turned as red as blood over his beard, and men laughed at him.

And then they saw Upazan's line start forward.

'Back where we belong!' Melitta called, and they rode like the wind.

Satyrus got a new horse – his was already blown – but Gryphon was still as strong as an ox, and Melitta stayed with him. She had forty arrows. She loosened her akinakes in her scabbard and watched her brother check his weapons.

'Long time since I fought mounted,' he said.

And then Eumeles raised his arm a stade away, and the whole enemy line came forward.

Satyrus looked at the sky. 'Already late,' he said. He drew his sword – Kineas's sword – and just the sight of it caused men among the Olbians to shout.

'Nike!' he cried.

Eumenes' trumpeter sounded the call, and they went forward.

Satyrus went from the walk to the trot with the front line and let himself obey like a trooper. He saw Melitta's set face – she was aiming for Eumeles.

So was he.

He angled to cover her flank, and saw Scopasis, her guard commander, do the same on the other side.

Ten horse-lengths from the enemy, and they were a wave of riders, their mouths open, the horses as wild-looking as the men. Eumeles was a rank or more back, not in the front.

Both sides shot their arrows, but the Sakje bows were dry and strong, and the Sauromatae arrows reaped half the shades that the Sakje arrows took.

Satyrus felt a blow as an arrow hit his chest and all the breath went out of his body. He tried to get his arm up but something hit his head and he almost lost his seat. As his horse burst through the first line of enemy riders he was struggling to breathe but he managed to get his sword up and parry a cut from a man going by.

Coenus was there, and his arm moved as fast as a striking cat's paw. A Sauromatae knight went down, armour clattering even over the rage of battle, and *that fast* the air was full of dust.

Satyrus finally ripped some air into his lungs and the pain almost made him vomit, then he put his bridle hand to his gut, glanced down—

The arrow was point-deep in the muscle of his stomach. He pulled at it. The barbs ripped his flesh and the leather lining of his thorax – caught. Growing fear and pain powered his arm until he tore the head free and blood coursed out, but he could *breathe* and he was not dead.

He dropped the arrow. The fight was all around him. He put his knees to his mount, sawed the reins and caught a long cut from a Sauromatae knight. He pushed forward and cut the man from the saddle, the sword easily penetrating his leather armour. He was deep in their formation now – no fault of his own – but the men around him seemed uninterested in fighting him. He cut down two more, riding in close and stabbing, and saw Coenus's blue plume. He leaned and his horse obeyed his change of seat, turning sharply. He parried a cut and got his charger in close to Coenus.

And there was Melitta. He watched her shoot a man out of the saddle. She used her bow the way another fighter would use a lance – close in. Even as he watched, she put the point of an arrow almost against a man's chest and released as she rode by, so that he exploded backwards over the tail of his horse.

And then he saw Eumeles. The tall man was fighting with a mace, a long-handled weapon with a head of solid gold. Whatever his failing, he was no coward.

If Satyrus had had a javelin, he could have killed the man easily.

Nothing worth doing is ever easy.

Satyrus pushed his borrowed horse forward and slammed into Eumeles' horse, head to flank, so that the other horse stumbled – a magnificent white charger, probably a Nisaean.

Eumeles turned and swung the mace, catching Satyrus's horse a glancing blow on the head – and then their eyes locked.

'Here's where we settle the battle,' Eumeles said.

Satyrus's horse was hurt – it bucked, rose on its haunches and shook. Satyrus struggled to keep his seat and Eumeles swung at him with the mace, catching his left hand on the reins.

Satyrus rammed his heels into his horse to no effect. He cut at Eumeles, but the taller man had a better horse and managed to stay just out of his reach. He flicked the mace and Satyrus only just avoided losing his sword.

'I kill you, and the rest is easy,' Eumeles said.

Satyrus couldn't control his mount, and Coenus was locked spear to spear with another man. Satyrus's thoughts flashed to Sappho: *Eumeles could say the same of your mother! He killed her because he feared her!*

Satyrus's horse was shuddering. The mace blow had hurt it – there was blood in one ear.

'Kill me, and you will *still* lose this battle.' Satyrus had to shout, but Eumeles heard. '*And* your kingdom. You are a fool, Eumeles.'

Eumeles flushed with anger. Being smarter – cleverer – than other men was the measure of his life. The word 'fool' carried. It struck like a blow.

Satyrus followed it up as if it was part of a combination. Just for a moment, the gods gave him control of his horse. He thumped its sides like a boy on his first horse and it leaped forward, breast to breast with the big Nisaean. Satyrus let go of the reins and got his left hand on Eumeles' elbow as he cocked back his mace for the final strike and pushed – the simplest of pankration moves.

Then he smashed the pommel of his father's sword into the open face of Eumeles' helmet.

Satyrus's horse stumbled but he managed to cut the tyrant across the thigh under his guard, then he caught at Eumeles and dragged him from the saddle as his own horse went down. The tyrant screamed, front teeth gone, and rolled clear. Satyrus grabbed his ankle and got a kick in the head from his free leg. Satyrus was on the ground but he cut overhand with the sword in his right hand and landed a blow on Eumeles' breastplate. It held. Eumeles had his hand on his sword and he drew it and kicked Satyrus again. Satyrus rolled and parried. He locked his legs around the other man's trunk and sat up. His side flared like fire, but he got his sword point in under Eumeles' arm—

An arrow had appeared in Eumeles' throat. Satyrus looked up and Melitta was leaning over, reaching for another arrow.

'We got him!' she shouted. 'Now it's our time!'

Satyrus sat still for long heartbeats, looking into the empty eyes of his enemy. There was, truly, nothing there.

'You need a horse,' Coenus said.

Satyrus forced himself to his feet, his gut throbbing. Coenus had the tyrant's Nisaean. He looked taller than a mountain.

I get to try this once, Satyrus thought. *And then I just won't be able to.*

He got up on an aspis and flung himself – fatigue, hurt gut, arm wound and all – at the saddle. He got his right knee over the horse's back and clung – a pitiful figure of a king, he assumed – for a long moment, and then his knees were locked against the tall horse's sides and he had the reins in his hand. He pulled off his helmet and gulped air. No one was watching except Coenus, who looked concerned, and Satyrus managed a smile.

He looked around. Eumeles' centre was going with his death. The Sauromatae in the middle had had enough, and they broke, and the Olbians and the best of the Sakje knights exploded through them, shredding their formation and then harrying the survivors. Satyrus let them go, pulling up in the dust to check his own wound. He felt weak. But he was *alive.*

The blood from his gut ran all the way down his crotch, but it was slowing. Unless the tip had been poisoned ...

The thought made him feel weak. And it hurt.

Coenus reined in at his side. 'How bad, king?'

Satyrus had to smile. 'You've never called anyone king, old man!'

Coenus pointed behind them. 'Eumeles is dead. You are the king. I ought to get you off the field.'

Satyrus shook his head. 'No king worth following would quit the field until it was won. Upazan's still on the field,' he said, 'and Nikephoros. Find me that trumpeter and rally the Olbians. We need to help somebody. My money is on Ataelus.'

Coenus found the *hyperetes*, and the trumpet calls to rally rang out over the rout of the centre.

Melitta heard the calls and she slowed Gryphon. She was un-wounded, and he was still as strong as he'd been when she mounted in the morning. She patted his neck and looked for Scopasis – right at her elbow.

Behind him, Laen and Agreint and Bareint and all the rest of her knights. No one seemed to be missing.

No brother.

'Where's my brother?' she asked.

Scopasis shook his head. His full-faced Thracian helmet made him look sinister, a monster with a beard of bronze. 'I saw him remount,' he said. 'Coenus put him up on Eumeles' horse.' He shrugged. 'You ride away. I follow you.'

The Sindi waved an axe. 'We broke them!' he shouted.

She wished she had her own trumpeter. The Olbian hyperetes was sounding a recall, but he was a stade behind her and half of the centre was with her, the rest far down the field.

'We should go to the left,' she said.

No one questioned her. So they turned their horses east, ignor-ing the call of the trumpet. Men formed on her household – many of them Sakje, like Parshtaevalt, who came and rode with her as they turned.

'Lady!' he said.

'Parshtaevalt!' she called. 'I need to know what's happening on the left!'

She borrowed his trumpeter and together they rallied much of the centre and faced them to the left. It took time, and she could hear fighting – heavy fighting – in the haze to the east.

Kairax went himself, and came back when they had three hundred knights, all facing east with the setting sun at their backs.

'The Greeks are spear to spear and breast to breast,' Kairax said. 'No one will give a step. The farmers carry all before them, but they will not try the flank of the phalanx. And who can blame them?'

Melitta took a deep breath. With one order, she would expend her last throw of the dice. Could her three hundred break Nikephoros?

They had failed the day before.

She rode out a pace and turned her horse so that she faced the Sakje knights.

'We will go right into the back of the phalanx,' she said. 'There must be no hesitation. No warning. There will be no second time and no arrow rush. Are you ready?'

Most men nodded, tipping the plumes of their helmets so that they seemed to ripple.

'Let's do the thing,' Parshtaevalt said.

Satyrus felt the pain in his gut spreading to his limbs, and he wondered again if there was poison, or if cowardice was spreading to his groin like the pain. While the Olbian cavalry rallied – slowly, because they were not his father's men, for all they claimed the title – he had time to think about his wound, and Coenus's willingness to take him off the field. To lie in a tent and wait for news.

The battle was won. Nothing here to fight for, except reputation.

What if he was poisoned?

Satyrus sat on the horse of his dead enemy, surrounded by corpses. *If I am poisoned*, he thought, *it is in my blood, and these are my last hours.*

His head came up, and he straightened his back. He was a son of Herakles, and Kineas, and he was not going to ride away and die in a tent, of blood poisoning.

When the Olbians were rallied, he put them in a rhomboid – a formation they knew – and they walked their horses west into the setting sun, moving slowly, looking for a new foe.

In a stade, they found one.

Upazan had not routed Ataelus – but he had numbers and he had arrows, and only Ataelus's rage and ten years of bitter resistance sustained Ataelus's outnumbered riders. They fought like demons – like dead men. And when their backs were to the river and they couldn't run, they died.

Satyrus didn't see Ataelus fall. Upazan put him down with an axe, from behind, while the little Sakje commander put an arrow into Upazan's tanist in the swirl of the melee.

Satyrus didn't see Graethe die. The wolf lord went down covered in wounds, and when he fell the men of his household stood over his body and died with him.

Nor did he see Urvara die, almost the last warrior standing as her banner was swamped by enemies determined to ride down the flank and win back the battle. She, too, died on the blade of Upazan's axe, her arms too tired to parry it one last time.

But their warriors didn't break. Some of their horses were up to their hocks in the river, but they fought on, desperate, often out of arrows, sword to sword, axe to axe.

Satyrus heard the shouts of Greeks before he ordered the charge, and he knew that Abraham was leading whatever he could from the camp by the river into Upazan's flank. It had to matter.

Satyrus had put himself at the point of the rhomboid. He smiled, despite the pain in his gut. He heard the fighting, and he knew the shouts were Sauromatae, and he didn't need scouts to find the next fight.

He raised his sword. 'Ready!'

The Olbians shouted his father's name and charged, and then they were into Upazan's men.

Satyrus struck and struck again, neither weak nor godlike, but merely the warrior he'd been trained to be, and his father's sword flashed like fire in the red sunlight and his helmet took a blow here and there, but he fought on, looking for Upazan's golden helmet. That was his goal now.

He had too few men. He could feel it. Just a few hundred more and the Sauromatae would have broken from his impact, but the Olbians were too slow and too few, and although his wedge went deeper and deeper into the horde of Sauromatae, they were not breaking.

He could hear Abraham and Panther now. They were less than a stade away, all but surrounded, and their charge, too, had lost its impetus, so that they were being pressed back to their camp.

Satyrus could see it, as if he was above the battle – could read the sounds, the shouts, the screams. Ataelus's flank had held long enough. Upazan might win here, but he could no longer win the day.

Tired men swung heavily at tired men. The Olbians were better armoured and fresher.

It wasn't quite enough. But for a while, it was better than nothing, and the Olbians were lifted above themselves, possibly just because they were the men of Olbia, who had once been Kineas's men. They pushed forward, even when they should have been stopped.

Satyrus cut a man down – the man had a wolf-tail banner, and Satyrus could only hope it was Upazan's. His sword arm was bloody to the elbow. His shoulder was weak, the muscles burned with the effort of a thousand overhead cuts, and he could barely manage his captured horse.

But he could feel Herakles at his shoulder.

I am going to die well, he thought.

He blocked a blow, catching a heavy axe blade far back in its cut, and his blade slipped down the haft so that the head caught him a weak blow in the left shoulder. Most of it fell on the yoke of his corslet, but the axe blade still sliced his skin. He got his bridle hand up and on the shaft of the axe, and his sword went up and over the haft, only to have his wrist grabbed by the axe-man.

Upazan.

Their eyes came together as they caught each other's attempted death blows – arm to arm, hand to hand.

Upazan rose on his horse's back, trying to use his immense strength to bear Satyrus down.

At a great distance, Satyrus heard Greek singing and wondered what it meant. Then his full attention was on Upazan. He met him, strength for strength, and their horses moved under them, and then Satyrus's arms began to break Upazan's hold. Upazan redoubled his effort, and he gave a great shout as he threw his weight on Satyrus.

Satyrus held him and bore him back.

He lost Upazan's left hand – their horses were pulling apart – and he snapped a short cut with his sword. It went home, cutting deeply into Upazan's left arm just as Upazan rammed a dagger with his own left, so that it cut right into Satyrus's sword arm and he dropped the Aegyptian sword to dangle from its chain around his wrist.

Satyrus's horse stepped back and a blow hit his side, but Coenus was there. He hit Upazan twice – hard blows to the helmet that rocked the big man in his saddle. And then, as if he'd practised the move all his life, Coenus cut back into another Sauromatae, using the bounce off Upazan's helmet to speed his back cut, and he lost his sword in the man's head – it sheered into the helmet and wouldn't come free.

Satyrus stripped the chain off his right wrist and took the sword in his left. He was backing his horse now – the captured Nisaean responded beautifully, turning on its front legs. Satyrus managed a clumsy parry that saved Coenus from a spear in the side.

It was getting dark. He fought on, determined to save Coenus, who had always been there for him and who had done as much to win this kingdom as any other man.

Coenus took the dead man's spear from his limp fingers – the press was now so tight around Upazan and Satyrus that the dead could not fall to the ground, and a man's knees could be broken by the press of horses.

Upazan was recovering. He had his axe in a short grip, one-handed. He landed a weak blow against an Olbian, who fell backwards across the rump of his horse but could not fall to the ground.

He cut at Satyrus, and Satyrus blocked it.

The sound of the melee had changed. The horses were moving and suddenly Upazan was slipping away, but Satyrus, wounded and without the use of his sword arm, followed him, cutting almost blindly at Sauromatae who were as tired and used up as he was.

'UPAZAN!'

Satyrus stopped and let his sword slump to his left side.

'UPAZAN!'

Now the Sauromatae were giving way. Something had happened. And Satyrus knew that voice.

'UPAZAN!' shouted Leon the Numidian as he burst through a ring of Sauromatae, the only man in the fight with a big round oxhide shield, his spearhead glinting in the red sun, his beard white.

'You!' Upazan growled in recognition. He turned his horse to face his nemesis and lengthened his grip on the axe.

'Remember Mosva?' Leon said.

Upazan swung the whole weight of his axe up.

Leon pushed in close and the tip of his spear rammed into Upazan's face and out through the helmet. Blood fountained. 'That's her spear!' Leon shouted, but Upazan was already dead.

And all around them, the Exiles rode through the Sauromatae like a Sindi farmer's scythe goes through ripe wheat in the last days of summer.

Satyrus sat on his horse and watched the last moments, as the Sauromatae broke or died.

He watched as Diodorus threw his arms around Coenus, and he watched as Leon's horse trampled Upazan's broken body into the hard-packed earth.

It all seemed far away.

After a while, he realized that men were cheering. There was Crax, pointing at him, and there was Abraham of all people, holding his sword in the air like Achilles. And Diodorus, turning his horse and rearing.

And Melitta, and she was crying and smiling at the same time.

He was crying too.

But he was not dead. And neither was she.

He straightened his back.

And slowly, with all the will he could muster, he raised his father's sword over his head, so that it caught the light of the

402

setting sun, and then the sound came at him like a final blow – suddenly the cheers were like a song, and the song was for *them*. It was everywhere, on and on.

EPILOGUE

It took days to bury the dead, and days more to feel anything but a vacant mourning – pain and numbness, and then aches and raw grief.

Satyrus had lost half his youth in an afternoon, and Melitta had lost more. Urvara was gone, and Graethe, and Memnon, dead in the phalanx, fighting in the front rank – the oldest of his father's men, and perhaps the best.

And there were thousands more dead. Many he did not know. Some, like Lithra, he knew too well. He had the misfortune to find her body himself – a body he had held in his arms.

Ataelus proved too hard to kill. The axe blow that knocked him flat left him unconscious, but within a few days, he rose again.

Later, Satyrus would say that the days *after* the Battle of Tanais River changed him more than the whole campaign that led to it.

And before he had stopped mourning, while the grief was still a raw thing that could move most of them to tears, he had to be king. Because even while the flies gathered on the dead, so the requests for his attention, his decisions and his judgment began buzzing around his ears.

Four days after the fight, when some of the older veterans had begun to make it a story, and the wound in his belly was still closing without rot, he put on a chiton and rode out of the camp with Melitta. They left all their well-meaning friends behind and rode north along the river to the foot of the kurgan of Kineas.

'Still want to be king?' Melitta asked, and he shook his head.

'I think the price was too high,' he said. 'I feel like – like I used to feel when I spent all my money in the market. On a toy. And then – I wanted to take the toy back.'

Melitta looked up at the kurgan. 'Still going to do it?'

Satyrus nodded. 'You with me?'

'All the way to the top,' Melitta said.

They climbed the kurgan together as the sun set in the west.

Below them, the Sakje and the Greeks moved around, making dinner, and the smoke of their fires rose to the heavens.

Satyrus had to stop three times in climbing the mound, and Melitta swore when her arms failed her. She was still that tired, and she had rested just long enough that every muscle ached.

But they got to the top before the rim of the sun settled in the Bay of Salmon. There was a broad stone at the top, and in the centre was a deep cleft.

Satyrus drew the Aegyptian blade and handed it to Melitta.

She held it high, so that the sun caught the blade and made it a tongue of flame. Then she brought it down into the cleft, so that the blade grated as she thrust it to the hilt in the stone.

They stood together until the sun set, and then they walked back down the kurgan to the camp. And the sword held the light for a long time.

HISTORICAL NOTE

Writing a novel – several novels, I hope – about the wars of the Diadochi, or Successors, is a difficult game for an amateur historian to play. There are many, many players, and many sides, and frankly, none of them are 'good'. From the first, I had to make certain decisions, and most of them had to do with limiting the cast of characters to a size that the reader could assimilate without insulting anyone's intelligence. Antigonus One-Eye and his older son Demetrios deserve novels of their own – as do Cassander, Eumenes, Ptolemy, Seleucus, Olympia and the rest. Every one of them could be portrayed as the 'hero' and the others as villains.

If you feel that you need a scorecard, consider visiting my website at www. hippeis.com where you can at least review the biographies of some of the main players. Wikipedia has full biographies on most of the players in the period, as well.

From a standpoint of purely military history, I've made some decisions that knowledgeable readers may find odd. For example, I no longer believe in the 'linothorax' or linen breastplate, and I've written it out of the novels. Nor do I believe that the Macedonian pike system – the sarissa armed phalanx – was really any 'better' than the old Greek hoplite system. In fact, I suspect it was worse – as the experience of early modern warfare suggests that the longer your pikes are, the less you trust your troops. Macedonian farm boys were not hoplites – they lacked the whole societal and cultural support system that created the hoplite. They were decisive in their day – but as to whether they were 'better' than the earlier system – well, as with much of military change, it was a cultural change, not really a technological one. Or so it seems to me.

Elephants were not tanks, nor were they a magical victory tool. They could be very effective, or utterly ineffective. I've tried to show both situations.

The same can be said of horse-archery. On open ground, with endless remounts and a limitless arrow supply, a horse-archer army must have been a nightmare. But a few hundred horse-archers on the vast expanse of a Successor battlefield might only have been a nuisance.

Ultimately, though, I don't believe in 'military' history. War is about economics, religion, art, society – war is inseparable from culture. You could not – in this period – train an Egyptian peasant to be a horse-archer without changing his way of life and his economy, his social status, perhaps his religion. Questions about military technology – 'Why didn't Alexander create an army of [insert technological wonder here]?' – ignore the constraints imposed by the realities of the day: the culture of Macedon, which carried, it seems to me, the seeds of its own destruction from the first.

And then there is the problem of sources. In as much as we know *anything* about the world of the Diadochi, we owe that knowledge to a few authors, none of whom is actually contemporary. I used Diodorus Siculus throughout the writing of the *Tyrant* books; in most cases I prefer him to Arrian or Polybius, and in many cases he's the sole source. I also admit to using (joyously!) any material that Plutarch could provide, even though I fully realise his moralising ways.

In this book, for instance, I have an entire campaign that receives only a few lines in Diodorus and no mention whatsoever anywhere else. The other day, much to my horror, I read an article suggesting it was all a fabrication. Perhaps. But the Greco-Scythian culture of the Euxine was real, and the Bosporon Kingdom was born and endured for hundreds of years – a good, long run that left an enduring mark on the region. For the novelist, it is sufficient to tell *a* story, perhaps not *the* story, of how that might have come about.

For anyone who wants to get a quick lesson in the difficulties of the sources for the period, I recommend visiting the website www.livius.org. The articles on the sources will, I hope, go a long way to demonstrating how little we know about Alexander and his successors.

Of course, as I'm a novelist and not an historian, sometimes the loopholes in the evidence – or even the vast gaps – are the very space in which my characters operate. Sometimes, a lack of knowledge is what creates the appeal. Either way, I hope that I have created a believable version of the world after Alexander's death. I hope that you enjoy this book, and the two – or three – to follow.

And as usual, I'm always happy to hear your comments – and even your criticisms – at the Online Agora on www.hippeis.com. See you there, I hope!

Christian Cameron
Toronto 2010

AUTHOR'S NOTE

I am an author, not a linguist; a novelist, and not fully an historian. Despite this caveat, I do the best I can to research everything from clothing to phalanx formations as I go – and sometimes I disagree with the accepted wisdom of either academe or the armchair generals who write colorful coffee table books on these subjects.

And ultimately, errors are my fault. If you find a historical error, please let me know!

One thing I have tried to avoid is altering history as we know it to suit a timetable or plotline. The history of the Wars of the Successors is difficult enough without my altering it. In addition, as you write about a period you love (and I have fallen pretty hard for this one) you learn more. Once I learn more, words may change or change their usage. As an example, in *Tyrant* I used Xenophon's *Cavalry Commander* as my guide to almost everything. Xenophon calls the ideal weapon a *machaira*. Subsequent study has revealed that Greeks were pretty lax about their sword nomenclature (actually, everyone is, except martial arts enthusiasts) and so Kineas' Aegyptian *machaira* was probably called a *kopis*. So in the second book, I call it a *kopis* without apology. Other words may change – certainly, my notion of the internal mechanics of the *hoplite phalanx* has changed. The more you learn . . .

A note about history. I'm always amused when a fan (or a non-fan) writes to tell me that I got a campaign or battle 'wrong'. Friends – and I hope we're still friends when I say this – we know less about the wars of Alexander than we do about the surface of Mars, or the historical life of Jesus. I read Greek and I look at the evidence and then I make the call. I've been to most of these places, and I can read a map. While I'm deeply fallible, I am also a pretty good soldier and I'm prepared to make my own decisions in light of the evidence about everything from numbers to the course of a battle. I may well be 'wrong', but unless someone produces a time-machine, there's no proving it. Our only real source on Alexander lived five hundred years later . . . that's like calling me an eye-witness of Agincourt. Be wary of reading a campaign history or an Osprey book and assuming from the confident prose that we *know*. We don't know. We stumble around in the dark and make guesses.

And that said, military historians are, by and large, the poorest historians out there, by virtue of studying the violent reactions of cultures without studying the cultures themselves. War and military matters are cultural artifacts, just like religion and philosophy and fashion, and to try to take them out of context is impossible. *Hoplites* didn't carry the *aspis* because it was the ideal technology for the *phalanx*. I'll bet they carried it because it was the ideal technology for the culture, from the breeding of oxen to the making of the bowl to the way they stacked in wagons. Men only fight a few days a year, if that – but they live and breathe and run and forage and gamble and get dysentery 365 days a year, and their kit has to be good on all those days, too.

Finally, yes, I kill a lot of characters. War kills. Violence and lives of violence have consequences, then as now. And despite the drama of war, childbirth probably killed women of warrior age about twice as fast as it killed active warriors – so when we get right down to who's tough . . .

Enjoy!

ACKNOWLEDGEMENTS

I'm always sorry to finish a historical novel, because writing them is the best job in the world and researching them is more fun than anything I can imagine. I approach every historical era with a basket full of questions – How did they eat? What did they wear? How does that weapon work? This time, my questions have driven me to start recreating the period. The world's Classical re-enactors have been an enormous resource to me while writing, both with details of costume and armour and food, and as a fountain of inspiration. In that regard I'd like to thank Craig Sitch and Cheryl Fuhlbohm of Manning Imperial, who make some of the finest recreations of material culture from Classical antiquity in the world (www.manningimperial.com), as well as Joe Piela of Lonely Mountain Forge for helping recreate equipment on tight schedules. I'd also like to thank Paul McDonnell-Staff, Paul Bardunias, and Giannis Kadoglou for their depth of knowledge and constant willingness to answer questions – as well as the members of various ancient Greek re-enactment societies all over the world, from Spain to Australia. Thanks most of all to the members of my own group, Hoplologia and the Taxeis Plataea, for being the guinea pigs on a great deal of material culture and martial arts experimentation, and to Guy Windsor (who wrote *The Swordsman's Companion* and *The Duelist's Companion* and is an actual master swordsman himself) for advice on martial arts.

Speaking of re-enactors, my friend Steven Sandford draws the maps for these books, and he deserves a special word of thanks; and my friend Rebecca Jordan works tirelessly at the website and the various web spin-offs like the Agora, and deserves a great deal more praise than she receives.

Speaking of friends, I owe a debt of gratitude to Christine Szego, who provides daily criticisms and support from her store, Bakka Phoenix, in Toronto. Thanks, Christine!

Kineas and his world began with my desire to write a book that would allow me to discuss the serious issues of war and politics that are around all of us today. I was returning to school and returning to my first love – Classical history. I am also an unashamed fan of Patrick O'Brian, and I wanted to write a series with depth and length that would allow me to explore the whole period, with the relationships that define men, and women, in war – not just one snippet. The combination – Classical history, the philosophy of war, and the ethics of the world of arête – gave rise to the volume you hold in your hand.

Along the way, I met Professor Wallace and Professor Young, both very learned men with long association to the University of Toronto. Professor Wallace answered any question that I asked him, providing me with sources and sources and sources, introducing me to the labyrinthine wonders of Diodorus Siculus, and finally, to T. Cuyler Young. Cuyler was kind enough to start my education on the Persian Empire of Alexander's day, and to discuss the possibility that Alexander was not infallible, or even close to it. I wish to give my profoundest thanks and gratitude to these two men for their help in re-creating the world of fourth century BC Greece, and the theory of Alexander's campaigns that underpins this series of novels. Any brilliant scholarship is theirs, and any errors of scholarship are certainly mine. I will never forget the pleasure of sitting in Professor Wallace's office, nor in Cuyler's living room, eating chocolate cake and debating the myth of Alexander's invincibility. Both men have passed on now, since this book was written – but none of the Tyrant books would have been the same without them. They were great men, and great academics – the kind of scholars who keep civilization alive.

I'd also like to thank the staff of the University of Toronto's Classics department for their support, and for reviving my dormant interest in Classical Greek, as well as the staffs of the University of Toronto and the Toronto Metro Reference Library for their dedication and interest. Libraries matter!

I'd like to thank my old friends Matt Heppe and Robert Sulentic for their support in reading the novel, commenting on it, and helping me avoid anachronisms. Both men have encyclopedic knowledge of Classical and Hellenistic military history and, again, any errors are mine. I have added several new readers – Aurora Simmons and Jenny Carrier and Kate Boggs; all re-enactors, all well read, and all too capable of telling me when I've got the whole thing wrong.

In addition, I owe eight years of thanks to Tim Waller, the world's finest copy-editor. And a few pints!

I couldn't have approached so many Greek texts without the Perseus Project. This online resource, sponsored by Tufts University, gives online access to almost all classical texts in Greek and in English. Without it I would still be working on the second line of *Medea*, never mind the *Iliad* or the *Hymn to Demeter*.

I owe a debt of thanks to my excellent editor, Bill Massey, at Orion, for giving these books constant attention and a great deal of much needed flattery, for his good humor in the face of authorial dicta, and for his support at every stage. I'd also like to thank Shelley Power, my agent, for her unflagging efforts on my behalf, and for many excellent dinners, the most recent of which, at the world's only Ancient Greek restaurant, Archeon Gefsis in Athens, resulted in some hasty culinary re-writing. Thanks, Shelley!

Finally, I would like to thank the muses of the Luna Café, who serve both coffee and good humor, and without whom there would certainly not have been a book. And all my thanks – a lifetime of them – for my wife, Sarah.

If you have any questions or you wish to see more or participate (want to be a hoplite at Marathon?) please come and visit www.hippeis.com.

Christian Cameron
Toronto, 2010